About

Chris Limb is a writer and designer based in Brighton, UK. After many years hovering on the periphery of the music industry – originally just going to gigs but graduating to selling T-shirts and badges plus operating the lighting rig, running fan clubs and eventually playing in bands – in 2011 Chris published a pop memoir *I Was A Teenage Toyah Fan*, which went down well with its core audience, received good reviews and continues to sell at a steady rate.

A number of Chris's short stories have been published over the past few years – most recently in the anthologies *Suspended in Dusk*, *Kneel Downe's Stolen Indie* and *Beachfront Starter Home, Good Bones and Other Stories*, as well as in *Daily Science Fiction*, *365 Tomorrows* and *Theme of Absence* online magazines. Thirteen of these tales have been gathered in the collection *The Demon Face*.

Comeback

Chris Limb

unbound

This edition first published in 2021

Unbound

6th Floor Mutual House, 70 Conduit Street, London W1S 2GF

www.unbound.com

All rights reserved

© Chris Limb, 2021

This book is a work of fiction and, except in the case of historical fact, any resemblance to actual persons, living or dead, is purely coincidental.

ISBN (eBook): 978-1-78965-090-7
ISBN (Paperback): 978-1-78965-089-1

Cover design by Mecob

Printed and bound in Great Britain by Clays Ltd, Elcograf S.p.A.

1: Through the bottom of a glass

London, late 2007

It was a long way down.

Genie stood trembling on the terrace, hands gripping the balcony railing, braced against the night, staring down into the alleyway below.

She was fucked.

There was a full fucking litre of Absolut vodka in her bloodstream now, but the oblivion she craved remained out of reach. The comforting alcoholic blanket it usually wrapped her brain in was absent; instead the booze had just brought the panic and paranoia forward from the next day's hangover, serving them up to her now. There was nothing she could do about the series of bad decisions that had led her to this moment. What was done was done and couldn't be undone. Her heart raced. She was caged by her past and there was no way out.

She was fucked.

Everyone was going to find out she was a fraud, that she'd always been a fraud. She didn't even write her own songs. She didn't even *like* her own songs. They were shit; whatever glib rationales Malcolm might have come up with, Genie knew that Wendi would have hated all this commercial rubbish. This shit.

She was fucked.

She didn't belong in this world, and people were going to find out. She'd never really been into music in the first place; when she'd finally discovered what she'd liked it was a bloody *revelation*, a revelation she was betraying with this commercial pop star life. What was someone with her background doing playing at being street? Bloody hell, she was a Roedean girl, a rich fucker. Posh totty. Sooner or later, they were going to find out, and they wouldn't like it. A dark mass of raw anxiety bloomed in her brain and the alcohol-tainted blood roared in her ears.

All the car alarms below only fuelled the panic attack, and Genie imagined stepping out and falling, spread-eagled in the air, down into the bins behind the Wan Chai Garden restaurant.

So easy to do it.

After all, what did she even have to live for? Ollie was dead. He'd been dead for six months now and she still felt no better.

Wendi had been dead for four years, of course. The only thing worse than that was the fact that she sometimes forgot. She didn't deserve to feel any better.

The two people she'd got the closest to had died.

There was a low rumble as an airliner crawled down from the dark orange sky, close enough for her to see the tiny row of yellow pinprick windows in the fuselage. She wished she was up there. But that would just be further to fall. No matter what she did she couldn't change the basic facts of her life. Oliver Fox was dead. Wendi was still gone, and now Ollie was dead too.

It wasn't that she found herself unable to live without him. She knew that what some of the press had said was true, that he'd been a bit of a trophy boyfriend really. But so what? She'd been enjoying herself. Having a laugh with Ollie had taken

Genie's mind off the fact her career was being forced into a shape that... made her so bloody miserable. There was no one to have a laugh with any more.

But his absence wasn't the worst thing.

His presence at her side had helped her cope with the demands made on her, and as far as the press were concerned, having him in tow had transformed her from simply That Tall Attractive Girl Who'd Won The BRIT into perfect tabloid fodder. Not only had Ollie been tall and pretty too, but there was a risqué aura that still lingered about him from that infamous billboard campaign for boxer shorts. That had given the headline writers plenty to work with.

He had been a bit dim, sure, but he'd treated her differently from everyone else in the industry. He was *interested* in her. Fascinated by her creativity, the very thing that was being crushed by bloody Malcolm, Thomas and the whole fucking label. She felt bad that she hadn't been able to muster much more than a physical interest in him. He was hot. And nice.

But the fact that she hadn't really loved him wasn't the worst thing either.

There'd been a huge furore about his death in the papers, of course, but by and large the public had now forgotten. The press were no longer interested either: her grief wasn't hysterical enough for them. The record company meanwhile weren't exactly giving her much real support – they'd even suggested she try exploiting it, make a grief-stricken album inspired by his death. What was it Malcolm had said? Guaranteed unit-shifter? Fuck's sake. For once she'd stood up to him, said no.

They'd created her in this image she'd come to despise. And now the image wasn't doing what it was told, they could just as easily dispose of it. If she threw herself off the balcony *right now*, they'd just make another one, wouldn't they?

Genie leaned over the railing, breathing in the petrol fumes and the aroma of beef noodle soup. She thought of her parents. She hadn't seen them for months. Of course Father had been right. She should never have dropped out of university, this kind of life wasn't for the likes of her. But could she go crawling back to them? It wasn't even the 'told you so' that she feared, it was the emotional void in that house, a place where she could never have a conversation that scratched deeper than the surface of things.

Still, her current life had been just as lousy recently. She tried to think of the last time she had talked to someone sympathetic, but came up blank. People were avoiding her, unsure how to react to her bereavement. The kind of company she'd been keeping recently preferred partying and didn't know the first thing about coping with someone else's distress. They stayed away.

But the loneliness wasn't the worst thing either.

Closing her eyes, Genie leaned even further forward and steeled herself for the drop.

It had become clear just how much in the descendant her star was when she'd been called into the Mallard offices earlier that afternoon.

Monika had shown her into one of the lounge areas and left her alone there for ten minutes. Where was Malcolm? Usually he showed up within seconds of her arrival, head full of schemes and mouth full of spin, charting the next levels of the Genie-machine's journey through stardom. His absence made her nervous. And whenever she got nervous her fears grew even more solid, clambering over the seats to sit next to her in the darkened auditorium of her head and whisper all the things she'd never admit to in public.

She was a fraud. She'd only got where she was now on her looks and connections. Any talent Wendi had seen in her had been filed off with the sandpaper of marketing to ensure she fitted the nice, safe middle-of-the-road niche she was temporarily occupying. She needed to stand up for herself, take control...

Oh god. There was always music playing in the background at the Mallard offices, and today Monika had chosen to put on Nick Cave's *The Lyre of Orpheus* of all things. Wendi had introduced Genie to Nick Cave's music and this... this had been the first of his albums released after Wendi's death, the first Genie had listened to by herself.

This was real music, music that meant something. Not the shite she'd ended up peddling. This was music with intelligence behind it. The classical allusions here were nothing to be ashamed of knowing. Not something that should be hidden, like her unfinished classics degree.

Of course she could never go back and finish it, no matter how much she might want to. No one would take her seriously. She remembered the kind of music her fellow students had been into; fuck, that was how she'd ended up meeting Wendi in the first place.

No, she couldn't go forward and she couldn't go back. The only option left for her was to fucking disappear off the face of the earth altogether.

Or under the face of the earth. If only it *was* like the ancient Greeks had believed, a nether realm where... people you'd lost were waiting for you. Somewhere she could sing for Death to get back what she'd lost. Yeah, right.

She looked up as the door opened, but it was only that fool Thomas. The hippy-dippy-trippy idiot who managed – what? – one faux-crusty boy band and that annoying girl with a guitar who'd just signed to Mallard. Grey hair chopped in a style far too young for him, he peered at her through his half-moons with a matching half-smile before dropping down next to her on the grey leather sofa. The cushions hissed their irritation at the extra weight.

'Genie...' He took her hand. 'How are we coping?' The glasses were an affectation. From this close Genie could see that they didn't contain actual lenses.

'Where's Malcolm?' She pulled her hand from his clammy grip and slid away from him. The cushions sighed.

'He's busy, I'm afraid.' Thomas made himself more comfortable and put his arm along the sofa back. 'Which is why they've sent me to look after you.' His belly wobbled beneath the orange striped T-shirt he was wearing under his jacket.

'What do you mean?'

'Well, love, you see...' He reached for her hand again so she stood up, flounced over to the armchair opposite, sat down and crossed her legs. Even now, she still felt guilty about being so rude, but if anyone deserved it Thomas did. There was something about him that made the hairs on the back of her neck stand up. She shuddered.

'You see, Genie...' Thomas was unperturbed by the snub, 'we felt that you might benefit from a lighter schedule at this difficult time, and seeing as Malcolm's such a busy man, I'm going to be looking after you for a bit. If you need anything, just let me know.'

Him? The shock dispelled any guilt she'd been feeling. This dullard was hardly going to help. But perhaps, her doubts whispered, this was all she deserved? Because of what she was. A sell-out. What would Wendi have said about the direction she'd been steered in by Malcolm after... after Wendi? Fuck it, she knew very well what Wendi would have said. The gnawing anxiety started up within her skull again. She needed something to take her mind off it.

'Have you got any toot? Malcolm always used to get me some.'

Thomas looked taken aback, but only for a second. He reached into his jacket pocket and pulled out a plastic bag full of unpleasant-looking grass. He held this out to Genie with an attempt at a sympathetic expression on his face.

'No!' Genie stood up and walked over to him. 'Not weed. *Toot*. Cocaine!' She rolled her eyes and then glared at him for a second before snatching the baggie anyway and sticking it in her jacket pocket.

'I'll just go and ask Monika.' Thomas stood up and backed out of the room. Genie flung her jacket down on the chair in fury and then sat on it.

She couldn't believe it. She simply could not fucking believe it. They were sidelining her, putting her on the back burner. Thomas was the useless manager as far as she was concerned, hanging around in the corridors of Mallard doing fuck all. Certainly his acts seemed to have bugger all going for them; Genie had always suspected they were kept on as padding to make the Mallard roster look full on the company's website. And now they expected her to join them.

Just because for once she'd had the guts to say no. She had a BRIT, for fuck's sake. Maybe she hadn't really earned it, but she was the winning hand the label had used to get it on their mantelpiece. Couldn't they show patience, compassion? Did everything have to be exploited, even Ollie's death? She should walk out, leave, go elsewhere.

But who else would have her? She still felt like a fake, an imposter. She always had; it was all very well putting on an act in front of other people, but when it came down to it she couldn't fool herself, not really. Since becoming a star in her own right, when had she ever done any serious work, actually sat down and even *tried* to write a song, let alone one that meant something? She'd never have got anywhere near this world if it hadn't been for Wendi. Wendi had encouraged her. But Wendi was long gone, and the most Genie could hope for now was a slot on *Celebrity Big Brother* in two years' time...

Thomas came back in with another baggie, this one containing a number of small paper wraps. That was more like it. Genie held out her hand.

'I realise it's a very sad time for you.' Thomas lowered himself back onto the sofa. 'You must miss him terribly.'

'Who? Malcolm?' Genie knew very well what Thomas had meant but was keen to steer the conversation away from there. She tucked the new baggie into her bra for safekeeping. 'Not really.'

'No, love. Ollie. I expect it's difficult to talk about, hmm?' Thomas was doing his best to be supportive and sympathetic – there was probably a chapter about it in the Mallard handbook. Genie would almost have felt sorry for him if he hadn't been such an unholy arse. As it was, she took out her frustration and despair on him with a torrent of abuse. The last thing she wanted was to end up crying on his shoulder.

'What do you fucking think? My boyfriend's fucking dead, and he seems to have taken my fucking career with him. Prick.' This wasn't the official line being fed to the media, and it wasn't what Genie really felt either. She knew that even as she said it. It was an emotional shield, a furious carapace that she donned whenever she had to deal with people inside her career. It was a way of hiding from the truth of what had happened, a way of stemming the torrents of tears that tore at the back of her eyeballs demanding to be let out.

Thomas sat there nodding with a solicitous expression on his face.

'You know, Genie,' he said, leaving a respectful pause after the conclusion of her rant, 'it's OK to feel like that. That's how we deal with grief. But Ollie's in a much better place now, and...'

'Hardly fair, is it?' Genie stood up, stomped over to the window and stared out at the damp King's Road shoppers, trying to keep the fires of her fury stoked. Anger would get her to the end of the day in one piece. 'He's in a better place? It's all right for some. I wish *I* was in a fucking *better place*.'

'I hope you're not having any... er... self-destructive thoughts...'

'Yeah, sure. Like you lot think I'm so devastated by his death, I might throw myself off a cliff. As long as I record a bestselling album about it first, right? Maybe I'll just toddle off the mortal coil, find him in the afterlife, and sing a song so fucking sad, so fucking *unit-shifter*, Death lets him come home with me. And then I'd bloody well dump him for leaving me here, the dick.'

Thomas looked uncomfortable, sat there in impotence, unused to dealing with Genie's scattergun approach to anger. She didn't hear a peep from him as she stormed out.

When she strode back in for her jacket five seconds later, he was still sitting there.

'Was that it?' she demanded.

'Oh, well,' Thomas looked really scared now, 'the BBC called to cancel your appearance on *Buzzcocks* next week...'

On the way back to the Soho flat she asked the driver to stop outside an off-licence. Donning a pair of shades, she ran in and bought a litre bottle of Absolut vodka on the company credit card.

'Spare some change?' Genie glanced down at the figure huddled in a blanket down at knee level, all dirty wool and beard. She hadn't even noticed him on her way in, wedged as he was between the window and a *Time Out* shop board advertising *Orpheus and Eurydice* at the English National Opera. Yeah, fucking typical. Of course it was. On a whim she reached into her jacket pocket and dropped the baggie of grass into his outstretched hand.

'Knock yourself out.'

By midnight Genie was shit-faced. She lifted the glass to her lips only to find it was empty again. Bollocks. Reaching for the bottle, her fingers missed, instead knocked it off the glass coffee table, spilling the last few drops of vodka over the rug. Fucking bollocks. She rolled off the sofa, cursing, crawled across to the drinks cabinet and pulled herself up to look inside.

Bugger. Out of vodka. All that was left in there was a couple of bottles of tonic water and a six-pack of that Red Stripe Ollie had drunk but which had always given her a headache.

Thirty seconds later she was standing at the sliding door to the terrace, forehead against the glass, struggling with the ring pull on one of the Red Stripes. She peered unsteadily out at the rooftops of London.

Whatever you said about Ollie, at least he'd always done what he was told. What's more, he'd cherished her. He hadn't deserved *this*.

Genie had been hoping the alcohol would take her mind off it all; when she was alone it was harder. There was no hiding behind an egotistical veneer with no one else around to lash out at, and there was only so long she could hide from herself.

Everything you touch turns to shit.

The can finally opened, overflowing with foul-smelling foam, which oozed across her fingers and onto the floor. That was the last straw. She yanked open the door and, oblivious to the cold air, ran onto the roof terrace and flung the can out over London as hard as she could. It disappeared off in the general direction of Neal Street, trailing a spiral arm of lager behind it as it spun.

'Bastard!' she shrieked. There was a moment's silence and then the distant sound of glass breaking, followed immediately by the whooping of a car alarm. After a few seconds some more car alarms joined in.

Everyone close to you dies.

It had happened on a pleasant spring evening earlier in the year. Genie and Ollie had spent the last couple of days at the penthouse and were due at the UK premiere of *Pirates of the Caribbean 3* in half an hour. Malcolm had told her that if they played their cards right they could get snapped next to Johnny Depp, which would send her career into the stratosphere, he said, if it caught the attention of the American media.

In the walk-in wardrobe, Genie was examining a ridiculous dress Mallard had hired for the occasion – she was struggling to work out how to put it on without her underwear showing. They should have hired her a dresser with it, she thought. She tugged at the solitary shoulder strap. Hmm. That looked as if it might be right. She straightened up and regarded her reflection in the full-length mirror. Difficult to tell – she'd have to do her make-up first.

She walked out into the lounge. The bathroom door was shut which meant Ollie was in there. Bugger. He probably hadn't locked it, knowing him, but Genie decided to give it a miss.

Across the room, she caught sight of her reflection in the mirror next to the front door. It looked… well to be honest, it still looked ludicrous. Still, it might get her onto the front page of tomorrow's tabloids, which was all Malcolm seemed to care about at the moment. She sighed. When were they going to let her just get started on the new album, for fuck's sake? She knew Mallard's secret songsmith with the actual talent and the airtight NDA had already written most of it.

She closed her eyes and just for a second imagined she could see Wendi laughing at her. It was a laugh of scorn.

Back in the wardrobe, she returned the dress to its hanger and started going through alternatives. Would Malcolm be very cross with her if she didn't wear it? She suspected he would; it had almost certainly cost a lot to hire. But she'd be far more comfortable in something simple, elegant and black.

'Gene? Have you seen my straighteners?'

Having finished in the bathroom, Ollie was demonstrating his unerring ability to miss what was right in front of his eyes, the hair straighteners sitting in full view on the glass coffee table. Genie had seen them not half a minute before. She opened her mouth to deliver a sarcastic put-down and then closed it again.

There was no point. He might be stupid and, not to put too fine a point on it, lazy as fuck, but he was a good person at heart. If she had a go at him he wouldn't understand and would give her that kicked puppy look. Oh this was ridiculous. There *was* a time when the thought of him wandering around the living room in his underpants would have driven her into a frenzy of lust, but now all she felt was irritation. She was tired of having to think for both of them. Why couldn't he be a bit more like Wendi? Just a bit.

'They're on the table.' She pulled one of her other dresses off the clothes rack and examined it. It was the one with all the straps across the back. That would do the trick, but she couldn't remember now whether she'd been seen wearing it recently. Shouldn't she have someone to take care of all this stuff? With a jolt she remembered that she did, and that he'd already told her to wear the hired dress.

Fuck it. It was only for one evening.

'Which table, Gene?'

Oh Jesus...

'On the coffee table, *darling.*' She was unable to keep the sarcasm out of her voice this time. The only other table in the penthouse was the dining table, pushed up against the wall in one corner with chairs stacked on top of it. (It had been a while since they had last entertained.)

Genie could now tell from the quality of the silence that, yes, he was wearing that bloody kicked puppy dog expression on his face. The expression that made her feel like an utter dick. The expression that reminded her just how easy she found it to be mean these days. Great.

Being reminded of her darker side was all she needed. It was one thing being unkind to the management and industry hangers-on; they didn't take her seriously, viewed her only as a commodity. Any little digs she made slid past them almost unnoticed. She wasn't a real person after all, just The Talent. The Product made flesh. And if the flesh answered back occasionally, they ignored it. Ollie was different. He listened to what she had to say, expressed genuine curiosity about her interests and concerns, and as far as she could tell still adored her.

It was a pity she didn't still feel the same about him. She kept hoping he'd get bored and run off with someone; that way they'd both be happy. But no chance. He'd never even looked at another woman, didn't seem to get jealous either – despite the attention she got sometimes. On paper he was the perfect boyfriend. But he just bored her now – fuck, at times he downright irritated her. Every time she snapped at him she felt bad, and when she felt bad she got irritable and snapped at him. Without even noticing it, she'd become trapped in a particularly vicious circle.

She wriggled back into the hired dress. It would probably be OK; she was overthinking things. Despite Malcolm's enthusiasm she doubted she'd get within ten feet of Johnny Depp, so it was academic. She might get her picture taken. She might not.

The sound of the power shower switching on snapped her from her thoughts. Ollie had no doubt already forgotten about her snapping at him. By the time he stepped out of the shower, he'd be as cheerful as ever. And just as unthinking. If only he could learn to dry himself off a bit in the shower rather than stomping out into the bathroom, covering the floor with dirty water. Which she always ended up slipping in. And would it kill him to pick up the towel after he'd used it, maybe hang it on the heated rail rather than kicking the sodden mess into the corner behind the bidet?

Oh god, what was she going to do? If he wasn't going to leave her, fuck knows, it would be simpler if he just... just *died* or something.

There was an odd cracking noise, then the thud of something heavy hitting the floor. Now what had he done?

'Ollie?' Sighing, Genie stepped from the wardrobe. Something smelled odd. She poked her head around the bathroom door that Ollie hadn't even bothered to shut this time.

She'd forgotten why she was sitting in a little room with Malcolm. In her confusion and distress, Genie kept imagining that she was on trial, awaiting the ordeal of questioning in a witness box. If only she could remember what she was supposed to have done. Then the posters reminded her that she was in a small waiting room in the Accident and Emergency Department of University College Hospital. And she remembered why.

In her bewilderment and shock, the first thing she was aware of having done back at the flat, after discovering Ollie, was calling Malcolm, although she had no idea now what she'd told him. To his credit, he'd been very composed and taken it all in his stride, advising her what to do and how best to remain calm.

She wasn't sure if the latter had done any good. She must have wandered back into the walk-in wardrobe at one point, because when the doorbell rang she was kneeling down in front of one of the racks of clothing, staring at the boots she'd first worn when shooting the video for 'Suspended Animania' and wondering if she'd be allowed to wear them again when she went out, because if they'd been seen in a video, did that count as her having worn them already, or would her wearing them make people excited?

What had she done?

She stood ten feet away from the bathroom door looking through at the paramedics examining Ollie. They looked very bright, dressed to fluoresce like traffic police or the people you saw digging up Leicester Square. She wondered if this helped.

The hair straighteners lay on the floor beside him.

At one point Malcolm took her arm, pulled her aside and began asking questions but even though she heard all the words, their meaning slipped past her. She shook her head, ran out onto the balcony and stood, arms braced on the railings, taking deep breaths and staring down into the alleyways below. The air smelled of Chinese food as usual. They were so near to Leicester Square that they could have walked to the premiere, but it wasn't the done thing to arrive other than by limousine. The plan had been for it to pick them up in the basement car park. She wondered where Johnny Depp was staying.

Is this some kind of curse?

Malcolm was by her side guiding her back into the flat and the paramedics had Ollie strapped to some kind of stretcher and then without having been aware of the intervening period she was sitting next to Ollie as he lay in an ambulance which whooped and shook from side to side for the duration of a short journey that seemed to consist of sharp corners and little else. Malcolm wasn't there but when the ambulance doors opened again and she climbed out – almost shocked to find that they were somewhere else – he was walking along next to her. She stared down at the concrete forecourt of the hospital as she walked across it and realised that she had forgotten to put any shoes on and that she was still wearing the expensive hired dress.

Is everyone I love going to die? Even someone I don't fucking love?

They'd sat in a large waiting room at first, Malcolm dealing with all the talking at reception, but then there had been some sort of commotion, a flash and a smell. She'd looked up to see a young man in a South Park T-shirt taking a picture of her with his camera phone; sitting behind him in a raincoat, an angular woman with red hair was staring intently at her.

They were in the small room now and she had forgotten why again. The clock above the door said ten past nine but she had no idea whether that was morning or evening. She looked across at the poster, which was very red and had a picture of an insect and a drop of blood on it.

MALARIA: It Only Takes One Bite.

She didn't think that could possibly be what had happened to Ollie. It was the wrong poster. They'd put her in a room with the wrong poster. If only she could find the room with the right poster then perhaps Ollie would be OK. She stood up.

She felt Malcolm's hand on her arm, but before he could say anything or she could pull free the door opened and a man wearing a white coat entered the room. She assumed he was a doctor, although it didn't necessarily follow, did it? Her dentist wore a white coat, as had the make-up artist when she was being made up for the video for 'Suspended Animania'. She should have worn those boots, shouldn't she? She looked down at her feet, then up at the man in the white coat. From the expression on his face, she could tell that it was bad news, he didn't have to speak. She hoped he wouldn't speak and then she could remain here in this part of her life where she still didn't know that...

It should have been you.

The doctor put it differently, but the effect was the same. Like electricity and water. Such a difference a few words made to the universe.

When they left the hospital there were photographers outside. And so it turned out that in the end she did appear on the front page of the tabloids wearing that dress.

Genie opened her eyes again and straightened up, still gripping the balcony railing, braced against the night, staring down into the alleyway below. She waited for the rage and despair to abate. As one by one the car alarms stopped, she calmed down by degrees, till by the time the ambience had returned to the baseline traffic roar, she was OK again. Relatively OK. The panic attack was over. She wasn't going to follow the beer can into oblivion. Not now. The outburst had done her some good. The omnipresent hollow at her core still tore at her, but not quite as much, and she knew what it was that she needed.

She pulled the deluxe edition of Graves' *Greek Myths* off the shelf and held it open so that the wraps of cocaine dropped out of their hiding place in the spine and into her palm. She slipped the book back on the shelf. She hadn't read it since university. As ever she felt a stab of guilt at having abandoned her adolescent enthusiasms merely to replace them with... this. At first her extended sabbatical had been exciting; touring with Wendi and her band felt like it *meant* something, Beam's music had moved her and she'd been thrilled to be a part of it. When Wendi had played her favourites for Genie and they'd listened to My Bloody Valentine, Cocteau Twins and Lush, finally Genie had understood music as a passion.

After Wendi's death she should have gone back and finished her degree, but instead she'd allowed herself to be sucked into the conveyor belt of this self-indulgent money machine, part of something that both her parents and Wendi would have despised. The way Malcolm and his cronies had taken superficial elements of the electronica in Beam's shoegaze sound and beefed up the beats, giving her 'crossover appeal' for the dance crowd, had stripped the music of passion. Her true self was far closer to the shy classics student than the hedonistic celebrity. These books were more than just the recommended texts; they were a link to her past she was still unwilling to altogether abandon.

But was it too late? Perhaps her past had already abandoned her.

Sitting cross-legged on the floor in front of the coffee table she began chopping out a couple of fat lines while mulling her situation over. What was she going to do? How could she make herself feel better? She was tired of having to project these false selves into the world, just wanted *someone* to talk to about her real feelings. She couldn't think of a single person. Since the accident, all the so-called mates she used to hang out with had evaporated, and there wasn't anyone left in her life from before. She hadn't spoken to Tabby for nearly two years – Malcolm didn't want her hanging out with an old Roedean chum. Too off-message.

She was isolated.

As the cocaine kicked in she began to think about things in what she hoped was a more rational manner, although given the amount of booze she'd already chucked back it was a confused brand of rationality. But she was at least able to step away from the all-consuming despair and examine it in a dispassionate manner while it was out cold. Ten minutes later she was sitting bolt upright on the rug flicking through the channels on the TV in a methodical manner as her brained churned over the available information.

Why couldn't she fix it? Who said? She was Genie DC. It wasn't that long since everyone had loved her. She remembered being able to make the front page of all the papers simply by falling over outside a nightclub (deliberately on more than one occasion, just to see what would happen). She could do *anything* if she put her mind to it. Positive thinking, right?

All this misery was just the crippling remorse she still felt about Ollie, wasn't it? And rationally, that was just nonsense. Just because someone died immediately after you wished them dead, didn't mean you'd somehow done it. So really...

She was lying to herself. Deep down she knew it was more than that. She knew perfectly well what this was all about.

Dead girl's shoes.

But she wasn't going to think about that. No, positive thinking, right? Instead she focused on what mattered. What had happened to Ollie *wasn't her fault*. And yet every morning she awoke to the sound of her despair and hopelessness sniffing under the door and scratching at the windows. *It should have been you.* Even now it had begun to stir on its slab as the tranquilliser dart of the cocaine she'd taken began to wear off.

She was in the wrong universe now, the wrong world. Back when Ollie was still alive her problems had been so simple, so mundane – she'd begun to find him frustrating and annoying. And so what? The solution was simple: they could have just split up. Back then it had seemed impossible though – the press would totally cast her in the role of villain if she initiated the split, and no doubt some tabloid rag would have made Ollie an offer he couldn't refuse in return for the inside scoop on life with Genie DC.

And so what?

It would have been a small price to pay. Compared to what she was going through now, it would have been nothing. Ultimately, the papers would have found Ollie and his kiss-and-tell disposable.

Like her career. She snorted at the thought.

And so what? If she could return to that previous world in which Ollie wasn't dead, fuck, what she wouldn't give for the chance to sort things out for herself. She could even give up this life, go back to university. But that world was now as unreachable as the moon, on the other side of an unbridgeable chasm of causality.

On the muted TV screen in front of her, a fleet of starships flung themselves through space in the blink of an eye.

Genie chopped and straightened another line of coke and hoovered it up. The moon was unreachable and time travel was impossible. Ollie was dead. She glanced up at her copy of Graves on the shelf, remembering the board outside the newsagents. The music playing at the office. As if you could simply go and fetch someone from the afterlife. Fuck Orpheus. The death of a loved one was something you *couldn't* fix.

She'd known that for four years.

On the TV screen in front of her a woman was piloting a tiny spacecraft down into a whirlpool of cloud, a dark hole, down, down, down. Like the void at the centre of her own gut. Her own dead soul. Yeah, inside she was already as dead as Ollie. And as Wendi. Fuck...

Genie's brain began to spin like the whirlpool on screen; she closed her eyes, but without the anchor of her vision the world just spun even faster.

The coke had been a bad idea, thrown the drunkenness into sharp relief. The vodka had denied her oblivion but perhaps she still had something else that would just knock her the fuck out? Put her out of her misery...

Of course. Her bottle of Valium – the tranquillisers Malcolm had 'prescribed' her that time she'd had difficulty sleeping. She lurched to her feet, stumbled over to the bathroom and started rummaging in the cabinet. If she took enough of them...

This is a bad idea, her rational self murmured, but she was no longer listening. She didn't care, she was too far gone already, what harm would a few Valium do on top of everything?

If she ended up dead, then so what? So fucking what?

It should have been her all along. Her instead of Ollie – she'd been dead inside since Wendi's death. Her instead of Wendi who would never have let herself be manipulated like Genie had. She was nobody, she was nothing.

She struggled with the bottle of pills. Her fingers weren't doing what she was telling them and she was starting to feel sick. The cap came loose and she tipped some pills out into her hand, before dropping both bottle and cap into the pocket of her white towelling dressing gown (nicked from Chateau Marmont). She threw the pills into her mouth and bent to the sink, banging her teeth on the tap as she drank straight from it to wash them down.

What's the point of me?

It was the only way to stop them using her like this. She was a commodity to them. They didn't want her having anything else, doing anything else in case she stopped being useful.

She was already in hell. At least this would stop it. She should have done this a long time ago. It should have been her instead of Ollie. It should have been her instead of…

She grabbed the frame of the bathroom door, pulled herself out into the main flat. She swayed for a few seconds before padding unsteadily towards the next gap in the wall, fingers trailing along the top of the radiator.

She screwed up her eyes against the lamp in front of her. Her eyelashes were wet, tears shattering the light into jagged rainbows, flaring even as dark clouds rolled in from the edge of her vision. She could hardly see, she could hardly think.

The darkness formed a whirlpool inside her head towards which her thoughts spun, repeating themselves over and over.

What's the point of me? It should have been me.

She staggered, reached out for support, felt her hands grabbing door frame. Bloody extra door. Where the fuck was she? This wasn't her bedroom. The walk-in wardrobe? She'd done it again. She was always doing it. Always, always, always, fucking always. She stepped forward. A wave of giddiness swept up her spine and into her brain, and she stumbled. She took another step forward, her feet tangled with each other and she pitched headlong into the darkness.

2: Down the rabbit hole

Clunk-clunk-clunk-clunk... Squeeeeeeeeeeeee...

Genie opened her eyes and found herself staring at some grubby tiles from a distance of about two inches. There was a grey blob of chewing gum stuck to one of them. OK. That was a bit odd.

Clunk-clunk-clunk-clunk... Squeeeeeeeeeeeee...

What was that bloody noise? Where was she? How had she got here? Her last memories were blurred ones; she'd been on her own, back in the flat, fucked up on vodka and coke. This was not the flat. A cold, liquid fear flooded through her as she realised what must have happened.

Blackout.

Her consciousness had walked out on her and she'd left the flat. What had she been up to? Had someone done something to her? Who else was involved? She was lying face down on the ground. Had she fallen or was she pushed? Were they still around here somewhere?

Clunk-clunk-clunk-clunk... Squeeeeeeeeeeeee...

She climbed to her feet, wincing at the sooty grime all over her hands and the front of her dressing gown. The dressing gown. *Fuck!* She hadn't even got dressed.

How long had she been lying there? Hours? Her head was much clearer than it had been back in the flat. Where was the hangover? Where was the headache, the nausea? She looked about.

She was in a dimly lit hallway decorated with purple-and-cream ceramic tiles, the air warm and stale, filled with the smell of burnt dust and urine. *Shit.* This had to be a tube station. Closed for the night of course. How had she got in? How was she going to get out?

She hated blackouts.

At one end of the hall, a dark archway was sealed by a filthy brass scissor-gate. She crept towards it, careful not to step in the occasional puddles which she had a nasty suspicion were the source of the worst part of the general odour.

Blackouts were the worst.

Beyond was a grimy, unlit passage that ran at right angles to the door, disappearing off into dusty darkness to both left and right, torn posters peeling from the wall opposite her so grimed in dirt as to be unreadable. The gate was held closed by a large padlock. She pulled at it. It barely moved; she wasn't getting out this way.

She probably couldn't have got in this way either.

She spun about. At the other end of the chamber, she could see that it turned a sharp right angle.

Clunk-clunk-clunk-clunk... Squeeeeeeeeeeeeee...

So that was where the bloody noise was coming from. Squaring her shoulders, she strode forwards and around the corner.

The ceiling fell away upwards to at least twice its previous height, and the area was better lit. In front of her, a tunnel led away downwards at a sharp angle containing the source of the noise – two old-fashioned wooden escalators. Both going down.

Above the escalator shaft a large, chipped enamel sign was mounted, displaying blocky white capital letters on a navy-blue background. Definitely a tube station.

TenarO

The name was familiar, but she couldn't have said what line it was on. She preferred taking taxis. It sounded like the name of one of those swanky new stations on the Jubilee line, but the decor was definitely Northern line squalid.

She stepped forward and eyed the shiny metal teeth between which the battered slats of the steps squeezed out. She felt nervous and vulnerable, her heart beating fast – though not fast enough for a fully blown panic attack, thank fuck. Blackouts always gave her the fear, and this time she had no fucking clue where she was.

There was something wrong about going barefoot on an escalator, but it was the only way forward, the only way out. Before she could change her mind, she ran onto the left-hand one and was swept along the short horizontal stretch and down onto the steep incline.

There were no posters on the walls, just more of the purple-and-cream tiles. The flat area between the two escalators contained ornate art deco uplighters every couple of metres that cast blobs of jaundiced light on the curved ceiling overhead. And ahead of her...

Down.

The escalators stretched to infinity, with perfect perspective. Her head spun and she closed her eyes, gripping the black rubber handrail.

Fuck it. Where else was she going to find a way out?

3: Nominee

London, early 2007

'You're on your way now, sweetheart!' Malcolm said, leaning across the table and taking Genie's hands in his for a second. Genie shook her head and pulled back, picking up her glass.

'Don't count your chickens.' she said. 'There are six nominees...' That sentence had been a bit difficult to say, she thought. Bit of a tongue twister. Especially the word 'nominees'. She'd stayed sober for the first two hours of the BRIT nominations ceremony – she'd been due to sing and didn't want to mess that up – but now that her performance was over, she was making up for lost time. Malcolm shook his head, dismissive.

'One of that lot? No chance, sweetheart. The decision *has* already been made...' He leaned closer and lowered his voice, regarding her over the tops of his horn-rimmed glasses. 'You don't think it's a coincidence that they asked you to sing here and then you just *happened* to be nominated for two awards? These things are planned way in advance, with military precision. But' – and here he raised a finger to his lips – 'not a word to anyone, eh? Don't want to spoil the surprise!'

Genie tossed a lopsided grin at him. She had to admit that the song had gone down well. Despite the imperious facade she'd been trained to display in public, in the privacy of her head she knew she didn't deserve all the attention. But this evening it had all gone perfectly. She was beginning to understand why the journalists said those things about her. Sometimes her voice *was* magnificent, even if that was the limit of her contribution to Malcolm's carefully manufactured 'artiste' story. She could be proud of herself.

She stared down at the interior of her glass. It was empty again. She reached for the bottle in the ice bucket at the centre of the table before remembering that was empty too. How much had she had? True, Malcolm had been drinking it as well, but it didn't seem to have affected him at all – he was still smartly dressed and in control, as if he'd just stepped out of a board meeting.

Genie stood up, which seemed to take longer than it should have. 'I'm just…' she said, one long finger extended in the direction of the toilets. 'Back in a minute.' She wove her way between the tables towards the Roundhouse main hall's circumference. It was huge. So many people. And this was just the nominations ceremony – what would the awards themselves be like next month? Could Malcolm be right – had she in fact already won? It didn't feel real. Despite the high she was on after her performance, even now she was half expecting to discover that it had all been a mistake and that she had to go home.

She staggered and grabbed hold of one of the iron pillars for support. Bloody heels. Bloody dress. Bloody bloody. Still holding onto the pillar, she reached out and swiped a glass from a tray being carried by a passing waitress and downed it in a couple of seconds. Better. Now where was that toilet again? Twirling the empty glass's stem between finger and thumb, she stalked along the curve of the hall's outer rim and—

Genie became aware that she was being talked at by that

annoying bloke from... one of those comedy quiz shows on TV. He looked much smaller in real life. She had absolutely no idea how she'd got there. Fuck. She looked around. It was a bar. OK, right. That was a start.

The TV guy cracked a joke. She smiled, but wasn't really listening; the terror of time unaccounted for was rising in the pit of her stomach. *What was his name again?* Sipping her drink, she suppressed a shudder – neat vodka.

What might she have done? She spotted the Roundhouse logo at the top of a wine list lying on the bar. Good, so she was still at the nominations then.

What might have been done to her? A cold panic exploded in her brain, cascading down her spinal column and into her nerve endings. The last thing she remembered was trying to find the way to the ladies... although, hang on, there was something else. A brief snapshot.

She'd been standing at a wide glass sliding door that led to an outside terrace – obviously a back entrance to the venue – planning to nip out for a cigarette. She'd spotted a group of people though, loitering by some gates in the middle distance, and had worried in case one of them was that bloody geeky fan of hers, she couldn't cope with him right now...

TV Guy – was it a Rich or an Alan or a Frank? – was boasting about something now and had his hand on her hip. Normally she'd have done something but she was still too frightened to object. She felt sure that something else had happened; it was lurking there just below the threshold of memory. She looked over at the clock above the bar. 1:05 a.m. There was about an hour and a half unaccounted for. Hopefully that was all that was missing. Excusing herself, she walked over to the bar, set her bag down and rummaged through it.

What was this? She pulled out a couple of business cards. *Alan Evener. BAM. Big Air Management.* An email address and a website. She flipped it over and saw a mobile phone number scribbled on the back in biro. Another snapshot.

A loud man had been talking to her. Talking a lot. He was quite enthusiastic about something and then it had clicked for her that she was being headhunted... He'd pressed the card into her hand and patted her on the bum as he left.

She tossed it onto the floor. The other business card was more cryptic. An oddly familiar-looking, intricate red logo incorporating a broken heart icon and the initials *DUDA*. It was classy, printed on expensive textured card, but aside from the four letters there was no other information. No email. No website. Was she supposed to remember whose it was? Had there been anyone else? A scent and the half-memory of an older woman in a red dress flickered at the verge of recall before dissolving in the naked panic and horror that was now threatening to overwhelm her.

She dropped the card back into her handbag and picked up her phone. There'd been a missed call from Malcolm about an hour ago. Oh god.

TV Guy – perhaps a Sean or a Mark or a Ben? – had joined her at the bar and was ordering more drinks. Without even looking at him, she walked back across the room and plonked herself down into one of the semicircle of low leather armchairs in one corner. She fiddled with her phone, nervous. Should she call Malcolm? She was feeling sick and had the beginnings of a monstrous headache.

TV Guy was soon back, alighting on the arm of her chair and droning on about himself – occasionally touching her cheek, her hair, her arm. Her irritation started to get the better of her confusion, and the next time he tried it, she swatted at his hand, but before she could say anything she spotted Malcolm on the other side of the room, talking to Jonathan Ross. He turned to look at her with an impassive stare before smiling briefly and approaching with Jonathan in tow.

She stood up and shook hands but before they could say very much, TV Guy had leaped up and was rabbiting away to Jonathan, nineteen to the dozen.

'I'll let you know, OK?' Malcolm said, tapping Jonathan on the shoulder, escorting Genie away towards the exit and—

She was in the back of a black cab now, staring out at the street lights and their reflections on the wet pavements; the rain drummed on the cab's roof and the wheels hissed against the tarmac. She felt a bit better, and this time the gap in her memory didn't bother her: she didn't remember leaving the Roundhouse, but she'd been with Malcolm, and there he still was, sitting in the other corner murmuring into his mobile phone. The cab swung around onto Euston Road and then onto Gower Street, and Genie slid awkwardly about in the back seat for a couple of seconds. She squinted at the meter but her vision was still a bit too blurred to make out the fare.

'Where are we going?' Malcolm looked up at her and held up a finger – he'd only be a minute.

'OK. See you then. Ciao.' He flipped his phone shut and tossed a thin smile at Genie. 'Where would you like to go? We could go on to Storm, although if you're tired perhaps we should take you back to the flat?'

The penthouse flat – one of a couple of Mallard Music-owned properties that they used for housing the Talent when in London – sounded much more tempting at this point. But then Malcolm reached into his jacket and held out a small paper wrap and she wasn't so sure.

The following Friday afternoon Genie was in another cab – this time a private hire – with Malcolm. It was ferrying them from Chelsea to White City. Genie wasn't sure how Malcolm had swung it, but she was going to sing on *Friday Night with Jonathan Ross*. Of course if Malcolm was right about the impending BRIT it could only be good for the show too, but nevertheless Genie was getting spasms of butterflies, the feeling that she was out of her depth. The worry that she'd be revealed as a fraud. Suppose she was asked about her family? Her musical background, her time as Wendi's backing singer? Her influences?

She stared out of the window at the January streets. It was raining again, the clouds an oppressive low ceiling. She had another headache coming on. Since the BRIT nominations she'd been well behaved and had only been out after midnight twice – at Malcolm's insistence! – but she was still feeling run down and she'd become prone to sudden migraines. What she wanted was a holiday. Somewhere hot, but with interesting things to look at.

And she wanted a partner. According to Malcolm that was also what she *needed*. As far as the tabloids were concerned, she'd been spotted out and about with some of the right people on several occasions, which had certainly set tongues wagging, but in reality nothing had happened. True, there'd been that journalist from that muso magazine the previous year, but that had only lasted for a week. At least it had got her a good write-up. But now apparently she needed someone cute to be *seen* with, a human ornament who would put a fresh spin on the Genie DC press-machine.

She *needed* someone who would behave himself. She *wanted* someone genuine, a friend as well as a lover. Someone who was interested in the real *her*. She missed Wendi.

'We – or rather *you* – just need some good-looking guy,' Malcolm had said, 'someone compliant who's already in the public eye. Doesn't matter if they're dim, as long as they're pretty. Could even be a girl, if you're that way inclined – would certainly help appeal to the gay fan base. But whatever. Your choice.'

Genie wondered how much he knew about what had happened between her and Wendi. She opened her bag and popped a couple of painkillers. Malcolm, on the phone again, glanced over. He was always right about everything, of course, and he knew it. Which had started to get on her wick. At first she'd just been grateful that there was *someone* around who knew what they were doing, so she'd blindly gone along with his every suggestion, but recently... They kept telling her that she was wonderful, that she was amazing, that she was *the Talent* – but shouldn't this mean that *she* got to say what she did sometimes?

Still, at least he was a reliable source of Colombian marching powder. That was what Wendi always used to say. But Wendi always stood up for herself and the band. She'd never have let him talk her into anything she didn't want to do.

The taxi decelerated and swung right into the checkpoint behind which BBC Television Centre sprawled.

Once they were out of the spacious metal-and-glass foyer it was far less glamorous. The corridor curved away to the left, a door every few metres, the grubby red carpet deadening the sound. Genie felt as if the curvature was speeding her up, giving their journey a false sense of urgency.

Malcolm stopped, and Genie overshot him and had to backtrack a few steps. He stood outside a door marked *Genie DC*.

Inside, a couple of swivel chairs stood in front of a Formica dressing table that took up the whole length of the mirror-covered wall. A clothes rail ran along the opposite side of the room, upon which Genie recognised that annoying silver dress. Those bloody shoes were probably somewhere as well.

There was a distinct odour of Febreze.

'All your stuff's here.' Malcolm dropped a laminated pass onto the dressing table. 'I'll let you get on with it and send someone from make-up along in twenty minutes or so, OK? After that I'll come back and take you along to the meet and greet before the sound check.' Without waiting for a reply, he slipped out. Genie listened to his retreating footfalls before dropping herself into a swivel chair and giving it a spin, pulling faces at herself in the mirror on each rotation.

She stood up and, feeling dizzy, walked over to a narrow door at the back of the room that revealed a grimy en-suite shower and toilet, tiled in Victoria line grey. The showerhead dripped, and had obviously been doing so for a long time: the beginnings of a baby stalagmite were visible next to the plughole.

A quarter of an hour later, having showered, changed and treated herself to a quick top-up, Genie was feeling a lot better. Scrutinising her reflection, she could see the appeal of the silver dress now – its gaudiness diverted attention from her height, which deep down she was still uncomfortable with.

She still hated the bloody shoes with their bloody heels.

There was a knock.

'Are you decent?' A male voice. South African.

'Mm-hh...' Genie sat down at the dressing table, deciding to leave the shoes until the last minute.

A short, whip-thin man with bright-red hair slid around the door. He was dressed in a tight black vest and skinny jeans.

'I'm Art.'

Genie was confused.

'Er... I'm music?' she hazarded.

The man snorted.

'No, silly... Art. Artie. I'm make-up. And *you* must be Genie.' He reached out for the second swivel chair and mounted it backwards, sliding over to Genie and peering at her face.

'Right. So what have I got to work with here?' Close up, Genie could see that he was older than his hair and style of dress indicated, his intense eyes peering out at her from a nest of deep wrinkles. There was a trace of stale coffee on his breath.

'My, you are pretty, aren't you?'

Genie was won over.

Genie followed Malcolm down another stretch of curved corridor. She was beginning to wonder whether they'd come full circle yet. There weren't any windows, but rather than making her feel claustrophobic Genie felt that this gave the whole place a comforting womb-like atmosphere. Her headache was gone too. A shame her feet were killing her now.

'You're looking great, sweetheart.' Malcolm stopped outside a door, turned and put his hand on her shoulder for a second. 'Good luck.' He opened the door and stood back to allow her through into Hospitality. 'See you later!'

Genie froze as the door clicked shut behind her, leaving her alone in a room with half a dozen assorted men and one other woman, all strangers. They turned to look at her, and then the man in the purple suit strode over to say hello.

Genie was starting to relax and enjoy herself. The bad news was that another of the guests had turned out not to be a stranger, but TV Guy from the Roundhouse. He'd latched onto her again and was trying to ply her with the free wine.

'No thanks. I've got to sing, remember?' She scanned the room and caught the eye of a tall, striking man who grinned and rolled his eyes. Had they met before? He looked familiar. Good hair. Smart suit. Nice bum.

Wait, that was it! He was a model – the pants guy from that ad campaign with the sausages and the frying pan. She remembered admiring him on the Euston Road billboards on more than one occasion. Despite her nerves she was feeling uncharacteristically bold. What was the worst that could happen?

Abandoning TV Guy, she ambled over to Pants Man.

'Hi. I almost didn't recognise you with your clothes on,' she grinned, arching her eyebrows.

Pants Man blushed and looked uncomfortable. Now *that* was more like it.

After the sound check and camera rehearsal, Genie made sure that she bagged a seat next to Pants Man – who she'd discovered was called Ollie Fox – on one of the sofas in the Green Room just before transmission. Aside from her, Ollie and TV Guy, the guests included Rob Brydon and a dark-haired American actress who, like the Green Room, appeared much smaller in real life. The latter two were deep in conversation, leaving TV Guy on his own in the middle while Genie continued chatting up Ollie.

'I expect you meet a lot of sexy women in your job,' she said, giving him the ideal opening to compliment her. She could tell he fancied her from the way his eyes wandered over her torso and legs when he thought she wasn't looking.

'Well...' he said. Silence. Genie tried again.

'What about all those supermodels? Haven't you ever done a shoot with any of them?'

Ollie grimaced. 'Not my type…'

'What, too tall? Too blonde?' Genie ran her fingers through her short peroxide crop and wondered when the idiot was going to take the bait.

'Not that. Just that half of them…' He lowered his voice and leaned towards her; Genie reciprocated and dropped her left hand onto his leg. 'Half of them have got dicks.'

'What!'

Everyone looked around at Genie's yelp. She grinned and rolled her eyes at the room before turning back to Ollie.

'What do you mean? They're transvestites?'

'Nah. It's…'

Before Ollie could explain, a loudspeaker hissed into life. 'OK, ladies and gentlemen, we're ready to start in five, four, three…'

The plasma screen that linked to the studio went black for a couple of seconds before the familiar theme tune burst forth. Genie squeezed Ollie's arm. There was no going back now.

'Go on… just tell him… It'll be a laugh.'

'OK,' replied Genie in a whisper. 'Watch this.'

The show had gone well. Her performance had been at the end but she'd managed to snatch some screen time before that in the Green Room, their host turning how close to Ollie she was sitting into something of a running gag. Now it was over, they were back out in Hospitality, getting stuck into the complimentary alcohol.

Genie sashayed over to TV Guy, looking over her shoulder for a second to wink back at Rob Brydon. TV Guy was fiddling with some cheese on a cocktail stick, but turned as she approached. His face lit up.

'Oh, er, hi… Loved the song.'

'Thanks,.' Genie rested her forearm on his shoulder. 'You were good too.' Actually he hadn't been. He hadn't had anything interesting to say and didn't seem to have anything to plug either. Genie had rather got the impression that he was a last-minute replacement for someone much more interesting.

'Oh, er, thanks.' He looked up at her. Genie thought he looked bemused. Now that he'd finally got the attention he'd so obviously been after from her, he didn't seem to know what to do with it. She wondered if she was being mean, but went ahead with it anyway. What harm could it do?

'Oh yes. I don't know if you noticed,' she went on, leaning in a bit too close and brushing his upper arm with her bust. 'Your flies were undone the whole time.'

Genie could actually see the blush climbing his neck and breaking over his face. He looked down, fumbled at his crotch, glanced around the room in panic and then fled.

Genie gave a thumbs up to the explosion of laughter across the room before flopping down on a sofa next to Ollie, who was engrossed in his Nintendo DS.

'So what was it you were going to tell me about penises?'

'What?' Ollie looked alarmed.

'You know,' she said, butting him with her shoulder, 'the models. You were saying they had dicks. Which is why you didn't fancy them...'

'Oh yeah.' Ollie looked relieved. He slipped the DS in the pocket of his Armani jacket and turned to face Genie. She wondered if he'd been getting training in the right body language, or whether he was one of those lucky people for whom poise came naturally.

'I was doing a shoot – a while ago, before the underpants – working with Hayley P. Sawyer. I went for a piss and she was in there at the urinal! Thought it was some shewee thing at first, but then Ben explained.'

'Ben?'

'My manager. Ben said that a lot of them are haematites, which is why they're so tall and skinny. Like stretched boys. Perfect for modelling women's clothes.'

'None of them ever tried it on with you, did they?' Genie assumed he'd meant hermaphrodites but decided not to correct him. In her experience most men didn't like that. She was fascinated, but more by Ollie himself than what he was saying. He pulled a face.

'Nah. Not my idea of cute. They're a bit strange – with all these weirdos hanging round them...'

Definitely into girls then, thought Genie. She was trying to work out how to steer the conversation around to whether he was single or not. She was also trying to work out how soon she could slip off for a little nasal top-up without losing her momentum. She was becoming torn.

'How's it going?'

Genie looked up to see the make-up man Art standing in front of them. She gave him a weak smile, hoping he'd get the message and move on.

'Oh don't worry, I'm not going to steal this handsome young man away from you. I just wondered if your pretty face needed a touch-up?' He tapped the side of his nose and waggled his eyebrows. Genie took a second or so to catch on. Art must have been a mind reader.

'Yeah, you're right.' She stood up and turned round, looking down at Ollie. 'Don't go away! I'll be back. I just need...' She gestured at the door and started after Art who was already halfway through it.

'I could tell,' he began, once they were in the corridor and making their way around the curve, 'that you'd been *up to something* earlier.'

'Really?' Genie had to struggle to keep up with him – small

as he was, he was moving along at a fair clip. 'What gave me away?' She was feeling daring. Malcolm had always advised her to keep some of her habits private, but she was in the mood for rebellion. What did Malcolm know, really? She'd never even seen him take any himself.

'Darling, when you're working with people's faces all day you can see the signs.' He opened the door of her dressing room with a theatrical gesture. 'Besides, it takes one to know one!'

The silence in the dressing room was almost unnatural after the party atmosphere in Hospitality. Art leaped astride the swivel chair again and scooted over to the dressing table, pulling something out of a waistcoat pocket. Genie sat down beside him. He held up a small silver straw.

'This,' he said in a reverent tone of voice, 'was given to me by Amy Winehouse.' He placed it on the surface and looked at Genie with a half-smile that disappeared after a few seconds. The penny dropped.

'Oh sorry!' Genie scrabbled around in the holdall under the table and handed the wrap to Art, who began chopping out a couple of fat ones with professional aptitude.

'You seem to have taken quite a shine to This Year's Model,' he remarked without looking up. Genie tried to sound nonchalant.

'Well, you know...' she said.

'I would,' Art sighed, handing Genie the straw. 'Why do the pretty ones always think they're straight?'

'I worked out he was straight.' Genie handed the straw back to Art once she was finished. 'I just can't work out whether he's single.'

'Oh he's single all right, my darling.' Art rolled his eyes and hunched over the tabletop. 'I did his face too – flirted with him a bit. Even though he didn't like it, he didn't do that thing most straight guys always do, dropping a random reference to their girlfriend or wife into the conversation at the first opportunity. He just looked a bit scared.'

'You sure? Oh, good.' Genie sat back in her chair with a smile.

'You're welcome. I do a favour for you, you do a favour for me.' Art tapped the side of his nose again. 'And should you find yourself working in the Concrete Doughnut again, do ask for me by name. Always happy to help.' He stood up and offered Genie an elbow. 'Shall we get back to the party?'

The first thing Genie saw on arrival back in Hospitality was Malcolm. Her heart sank. Playtime was over. He was talking to a short woman, also dressed in a business suit. Two of a kind, thought Genie, I wonder if they're flirting with each other? She looked around. Where was Ollie? Art peeled off and headed for the drinks table, waving at her over his shoulder without looking round.

TV Guy was back in the room – Jonathan Ross seemed to have taken pity on him and was listening to whatever it was he had to say. Still no sign of Ollie. She reached into her bag for a pen. Perhaps when he reappeared she should give him her mobile number?

Malcolm looked up. He clapped the short woman on the shoulder and then strode across to Genie.

'You ready then? Shall I send the driver to the dressing room for your things?' He pulled his phone out and held it to his ear.

'Well I was wondering...' began Genie. She'd found a biro, but the only paper she could find in her handbag was the swanky business card with the red heart logo. Still, that would do.

Ollie walked back in. He caught her eyes and smiled. The short woman moved quickly across and straightened his lapels for him.

'OK, Oliver,' she said. 'Time we were off.' She turned and offered Malcolm what almost looked like a salute. Malcolm waved back.

'Bernice Street,' he explained to Genie. 'Used to work with her at NBG Management before I came to Mallard. She mostly handles models now. Useful contact – getting you a couple of decent photo shoots at this point would be very handy.'

Genie wasn't listening. Ollie smiled at her and shrugged helplessly before disappearing.

Bollocks, she thought. Her headache was back.

4: *Stand facing the direction of travel*

Underworld, no time

Clunk-clunk-clunk-clunk... Squeeeeeeeeeeeeee...

As the narrow wooden step bore her ever further away from the stairhead, Genie noticed that the *clunk-squees* seemed to be getting quieter – they must have been caused by something in the top of the mechanism. Right now though, that was the least of her concerns.

The infinite perspective ahead of her was bewildering and did unexpected things to her sense of balance. Surely it wasn't possible for an escalator to be this long. She'd have heard of it.

Some kind of optical illusion? A trompe l'oeil relying on distortion and point of view? The lines converged on a point, but there was something about the light and clarity of the air down there that gave the impression she was seeing much further than possible. The self-similarity of the shaft played tricks too: sometimes it seemed as if it were the walls moving up past her while she remained stationary; and then, with a lurch, her perception would shift again, and she'd resume her forward and downward motion, perhaps a little faster than before. Or maybe that was her imagination.

If it was all a trick, then what was its purpose? Who would build such a folly and then allow it to fall into disuse?

Clunk-clunk-clunk-clunk... Squeeeeeeeeeeeee...

If this was some kind of tourist attraction, a haunted house or London Dungeon type experience, then Genie couldn't see the appeal. No matter how convincing the illusion.

No, of course she wasn't dreaming. No matter how real dreams felt at the time, their reality proved flimsy on awakening, their logic flawed. How she'd got here might be eluding Genie for the moment, but this experience had the stamp of authenticity. All her senses were on red alert; she was aware of everything happening around her even though she'd no idea where she was or why.

Clunk-clunk-clunk-clunk... Squeeeeeeeeeeeee...

Yes, it was definitely getting quieter. She could now hear the deeper sounds of the mechanism, a low-pitched *thud thud thud thud* that she felt in her eyeballs and her teeth. She held a finger to the blood vessels at her throat and realised that the thudding was in perfect step with her heartbeat. This uncanny environment was remixing her.

There was also a mechanical whispering from beneath the steps, a fluttering sound almost beyond the range of hearing, persistent but irregular.

The shaft dragged at her viewpoint again and she felt as if the angle of descent was starting to steepen. She screwed her eyes shut tight in an attempt to stop this impression before it could take hold. A gust of warm air caressed her face and she opened her eyes again.

Thud thud thud thud.

She turned around and looked back up the way she'd come.

Whisper.

The top of the escalator was still visible but it was beginning to become indistinct. She could tell that there was *something* different up there, a knot of irregularity in this world of vanishing points, but... it no longer looked like the way out.

45

Way out. What had she committed herself to when she stepped onto this escalator?

Thud thud thud thud.

She had no idea where it led. Aside from downwards. Impossibly, endlessly downwards.

Whisper.

She was running back up two steps at a time before she'd had the chance to fully articulate the thought of attempting to outpace the mechanism. It might take a little time, but she was sure she was making headway as the uplighters crept slowly back downwards. After five minutes of this though, she noticed that far from appearing nearer, the top of the shaft had disappeared altogether, its perspective now mirroring that visible below. She howled and stopped. Fuck fuck fuck fuck.

Thud thud thud thud.

She'd been getting out of breath anyway. Even if she *had* been able to reach the top again, what then? The gate up there had been locked. She turned back to face the shaft below. Wherever it led, that was where she was going, and there was fuck all she could do about it.

This was all wrong. But she couldn't afford to lose her grip and have a panic attack. Not here, not now. What was it her doctor had said she should do? She closed her eyes and focused on her breathing.

It's going to be all right. It's going to be all right.

Without opening her eyes, she started tapping her fingers on the rubber handrail in time to the thud of the machinery and the beat of her heart and began crooning a wordless song under her breath.

She moved her knees in a subliminal dance as she succumbed to the rhythm of the staircase.

5: *Also sprach USA*

Los Angeles, early 2007

Genie dozed. The unrelenting roar was preventing her getting any deep sleep, but she'd been here for over ten hours and had spent the first half of the flight drinking champagne. The alcohol had gone to her head far quicker than normal.

It had been a chaotic time. As Malcolm had assured her, she'd won the BRIT; that had only been the start of the insanity. The album, *New Mania*, had been selling very well indeed, according to Malcolm. Jonathan Ross and about twenty thousand other people had started following her on Twitter despite the fact she hardly ever used it. Mallard Music had now engaged that creepy fan with the website in a semi-professional capacity, promising him any number of exclusives provided he stayed on message. She was in demand every minute of the day and every day of the week. She'd lost count of when she'd said what, let alone to whom. Or where. The journalists passed through the plush offices of Mallard Music on Malcolm's conveyor belt schedule, and Genie had been kept so busy appearing in all the right places at all the right moments and on all the right channels that she'd barely had time to sulk about Ollie slipping through her fingers at the BBC. Not that she'd have had a free evening to spend with him anyway. She'd seen him pop up on a couple more TV shows, but never the ones she was on; their paths hadn't crossed again. She could of course have asked Malcolm to arrange a meeting, but she felt inexplicably shy about broaching the subject. She continued to be plagued by headaches and self-doubt, neither of which she mentioned to Malcolm.

Genie shifted in her seat and pulled the mask down further over her eyes. They'd be arriving in Los Angeles in a couple of hours, and tomorrow would embark on getting her seen in all the right places on *this* side of the planet. A BRIT was impressive, but it was only a BRIT; if she was to have any staying power, Malcolm had said, they'd have to get the US music business on side too.

The plane shook in an alarming manner and Genie sat up, peering out from under her mask, more irritated than afraid. Malcolm was nowhere to be seen; the occupants of all the other reclining seats were still unconscious. The window blinds were pulled down but every now and then a shaft of bright sunlight would thrust its way through a chink.

This was insane, thought Genie. Her body clock told her it was approaching midnight. The sun shouldn't be shining. She stood up and stretched, letting the airline blanket fall unheeded to the floor. They'd got on the plane at Heathrow in the late afternoon. She'd had a couple of meals but nothing substantial. She was starving. And now, hungover.

There weren't any cabin crew around. She padded over to the curtain and pulled it aside, peering into economy class.

The smell. Farts and feet. Passengers squeezed in nine abreast and stretched back as far as the eye could see. Ungainly bodies sprawled in awkward postures as comfortable as the tiny space would allow. Heads thrown back, mouths open, snoring. Babies grizzled. Genie hurried back into the perfumed comfort of business class.

'Can I help you, ma'am?'

Genie turned. A heavily made-up woman in a cabin crew uniform had just descended the spiral staircase from the lounge on the upper deck and was looking up at Genie with an expression of vapid helpfulness.

'I'm kind of hungry. Can I have something to eat?'

The woman beamed.

'Of course! If you sit down, I'll bring you the refreshments trolley.'

Genie threw herself back down in her seat and pulled the blanket about her shoulders as the hostess disappeared. The air conditioning was making her cold, her throat was sore and the sinuses in her forehead throbbed.

She was half walking, half sliding down a hill – or was it an escalator? There were street lamps, and there was something hot pressed to her face. Someone touched her arm and she jumped.

'Sorry ma'am, but we're landing now. Would you mind fastening your seat belt and moving your seat to the upright position?' It was the hostess.

Genie blinked. She'd been asleep. Probably for a couple of hours, as the jet was now tilted at an angle and shuddering as it descended. The window blinds were all raised and the Californian evening sun was shining on her face.

She raised her seat, buckled herself in and slipped her shoes back on. Across the way Malcolm now sat, as immaculate as ever, reading the *Economist*.

There was a complex thud and the aircraft turned, beams of sunlight panning slowly through its interior. On the other side of the porthole, Genie caught a glimpse of yellow sky, orange hills, blue ocean before the evening sun swung in again and blinded her.

Touchdown. Genie felt a tiny thrill of pleasure spiral though her stomach as she realised she'd arrived in the USA.

The crimson sky was darkening by the minute as the car hurtled along the freeway from LAX. The landscape was far more horizontal than she'd expected, thought Genie, silhouettes of palm trees and electric pylons the only protrusion above the horizon to either side. At one point the car dived into a bewildering tangle of flyovers five deep from which it eventually emerged one level up, heading north.

Now there was something glittering on the horizon. Green gantries flicked by overhead, some bearing exciting names familiar from film and TV – *Culver City, Santa Monica* – others surprising in their prosaicness – *Manchester Ave, Florence Ave.* Ahead, the glittering thing revealed itself to be a nest of skyscrapers, beyond which a dark ridge rose like a thunderhead.

Malcolm leaned forward and murmured into the driver's ear. The driver nodded, but nothing changed; their trajectory along this infinite slab of tarmac continued unchecked. Genie closed her eyes.

Someone was telling her that anything was possible; Genie had the distinct impression she should have known what to say in reply but kept forgetting. She was walking alone around and around, afraid she'd fall in the water. She flew over the water. There was a distant explosion.

She sat up. The car had stopped in a residential street. After the alien landscape of the freeway this felt almost like home. Where was Malcolm? The driver was standing outside, leaning on the bonnet – or rather the *hood* she reminded herself – and smoking a cigarette. The car interior clicked and ticked as it cooled. Genie lowered the window.

Warm air laden with the scent of petrol and unfamiliar flowers rolled into the car's air-conditioned interior. And the noise... it lent the whole situation an unreal atmosphere. Surely crickets didn't really sound like that? She unbuckled her seat belt and craned out of the window. As she peered up the street, the exotic breeze tousled her hair. It was now fully night.

'Sorry about that, sweetheart!' The car shook and Genie slithered back through the window to find Malcolm back in the seat next to her. 'Had a bit of business to take care of; all done now. Straight to the Marmont now, I reckon. How are you bearing up?'

'Still tired. I fell asleep.'

'Not surprising. It's coming up for five in the morning back home. Not that that usually stops you...'

Malcolm was uncharacteristically cheerful. Still, at least he'd given her an opening. There was something that she needed to ask.

'Yeah, but I normally have a little help from the White Lady, don't I?' The car pulled away and headed back towards the main drag. Usually she was too embarrassed to directly ask Malcolm for drugs, it was an admission of weakness. She preferred it when he handed them over to her unbidden. But the urge was becoming strong. Which was, she realised, probably a problem in itself. But one she could sort out another time.

'Good news on that front.' Malcolm reached into his jacket. 'It turns out she'll be joining us this evening after all.' He handed a small plastic packet to Genie. 'Do be patient though, there's a good girl. Wait until you're actually inside the suite, hmm?'

Now that it was fully dark, it felt as though they were careering through a particle accelerator of sodium and neon, the buildings of the city rearing about them.

'There'll be a meet and greet in the terrace bar when you're ready,' Malcolm went on. 'Just a few record company types. The photographers. That kind of thing. They have these little dos every couple of months or so.' The car decelerated and lurched up a scruffy little slip road and then they were on a palm-lined main street.

'Not far now,' said Malcolm. 'This is Sunset.'

A thrill went through her. *Sunset Boulevard.* It was almost as if he'd told her she was in Narnia.

'Doesn't look that exciting,' she remarked after half a minute peering through the window.

'You're thinking of Hollywood Boulevard,' Malcolm told her. The car passed a top-heavy, round, mirrored building. 'But *that's* the Director's Guild of America.'

Genie pointed across the street. 'What's that?' she asked.

'A petrol station.'

The landscape started to rise a little to their right, foliage like a giant's hedge looming out of nowhere. Above this rose the towers and turrets of a building that looked far more old-fashioned than anything else they'd passed. The driver took a sharp right into a narrow lane that continued curving to the right as it rose. After the brightness of Sunset, Genie felt blinded for a moment.

An excited calm settled over her as the car turned again and groaned to a halt. Malcolm leaped out and walked around to open the door for her; she stepped down onto the pavement beside a Gothic arched entrance.

Once more, the film soundtrack crickets assaulted her, this time competing with the background roar of Sunset. She followed Malcolm through the archway and was swallowed up.

As far as Genie was concerned, the Chateau's choice of

furniture was tasteful, low key and convincingly old-fashioned. Despite being described as *Junior* her suite was bigger than a medium-sized studio flat. Not only did it have an en-suite kitchen and bathroom, there was even a separate dressing room, which Genie put to work straight away. There was an urgent matter that needed attending to even before she had a shower.

American drugs – this was almost as exciting as the suite. She held a hundred dollar bill up between thumb and forefinger. That'd do nicely.

It wasn't that much different from British cocaine, if she was honest. Maybe a bit smoother? Probably cut with something else.

Ten minutes later she stood under the shower. Even the water was smoother now. She shook herself off and sauntered back into the dressing room. She was in luck; whoever had packed had done a good job and there was a lot of choice. In the end she settled for the black long-sleeve top and black jeans – the look one journalist had described as a 'yard of Guinness'. She didn't like Guinness, but Malcolm had reassured her that it had been a compliment as the journalist was originally from Dublin.

There was a knock at the door. 'Are you decent?' Genie, who had been kneeling on the sofa and staring out the window at the shimmering skyline, turned round with her standard response.

'Far from it!'

Malcolm entered the suite with an indulgent smile. 'Feeling a little better now, are we?' Genie sprang upright and gave him a twirl. He nodded.

'Ah. A drop o' the old *Black Stuff*. That'll go down well. And...' He strode forward and peered at her eyeballs. 'Good.

You haven't overdone it. Not too jetlagged, not too wired. Don't want you pulling a Britney at this stage.'

Genie didn't like the comparison. Malcolm might be on about how 'Suspended Animania' was getting remixed like crazy in the dance clubs, but that journalist saying she sounded like a Madonna crossed with Aphex Twin was bad enough. Fucking *Britney*? She was too happy to object though. The tiredness had gone and for once she didn't have a headache. She sat down on the end of the bed and looked up at Malcolm with a smile.

'What shoes were you planning to wear?'

Genie stared at her feet and shrugged. 'Don't know, is it important?' Malcolm appeared to give this some serious consideration.

'Maybe. Play it safe. There'll be some big egos up there, so it might not be a good idea to have you towering over too many people. Best to wear flats.'

The lift was an ancient wood and brass affair that shuddered as it took them up to the roof terrace. Outside, the air was warm and dry, and even from up here the crickets were audible. Spread out below them, an oceanic grid of electricity and light stretched to the horizon, city as landscape.

The foreground was full of suits. But they were far more relaxed than the suits Genie was used to, more crumpled, and none of them was wearing a tie. She glanced sideways at Malcolm. As usual, he seemed to know what she was thinking.

'Ah, but you see, I'm English,' he murmured. 'They like the way I'm a bit different, a bit straight-laced. Stuffy, even. My wearing a tie conforms to the stereotype and confirms their sense of superiority.'

'What should I do?' Genie glanced around. No one knew her here, she had to rely on her wits, and she could feel a tingle of anxiety supplanting her good mood. What if she said the wrong thing and was exposed as a fraud? Malcolm chuckled under his breath.

'Just be yourself, sweetheart, be yourself.'

'Matthew! Good to see you!' One of the more rotund crumpled suits was making a beeline for them, his orange face creased with multiple horizontal lines, one of which opened to reveal teeth.

'Vee Double-You.' Malcolm held out his right hand, seemingly oblivious to the fact that the suit had got his name wrong. The suit shook it. Malcolm turned to Genie.

'My dear,' he began. Genie wondered if he'd gone insane. My *dear*? She then realised he was playing up his Englishness. 'My dear, this is Victor Walton Beadle the Third, head of the US division of our parent company.'

'Which kinda makes me head of the company, period. Call me Vee Dubya, sweetheart.' Vee Dubya grabbed Genie's hand and kissed it.

Genie smiled, but made no move to reciprocate; in fact she was unsure what the correct reciprocation would have been. It was just as well she'd worn flats; as it was, the top of Beadle's artificial-looking hair barely reached her nose. She wondered if this was one of the big egos Malcolm had been talking about, and if so, whether that meant she should sit down. She wouldn't want to tower inappropriately. A giggle slipped out. Luckily Vee Dubya seemed to like this and beamed.

'Matthew here tells me you've got quite a voice on you!' he bellowed, seemingly addressing her breasts. She stepped back. Surely as head of the parent company he would have listened to her already?

'What do you think?' she asked.

Vee Dubya roared with laughter and several of the nearer suits looked round.

'I think we're gonna get on just fine. The great American public are gonna love you!' With that he was off.

'Well done,' muttered Malcolm. 'You made him uncomfortable, he'll remember you.'

'I'm sorry,' said Genie, 'I wasn't really sure what he...'

'I'm not being sarcastic. That really was perfect.'

'Malcolm!'

Another loud voice. Genie began to wonder just how many people here he knew. In one smooth movement she snatched up a glass of something yellow and fizzy from the tray of a passing flunkey, downed it and deposited the empty on the table beside her.

The new voice, like Malcolm, was a suit with a tie. What's more, even though he was somewhat crumpled, he was talking in an English accent. He'd launched straight into a monologue the moment Malcolm had acknowledged him, not waiting for any introductions. He acted unaware that Genie was there, much more interested in filling Malcolm in on the details of something which, judging by the tone of his voice, was very important.

'Yes, hemp underwear. *Organic* hemp underwear. Ticks all the boxes. It's green, no sweatshops anyone can find out about, and most importantly the hemp gives it a cachet of illegitimacy. The kids'll be trying to smoke the things!' He snorted at his own joke and then noticed Genie for the first time. He gestured at her with a finger.

'She your latest find?' This addressed to Malcolm. Genie frowned and stepped forward. There was nothing wrong, she decided, in a bit of towering in this case. In the past she would have shrunk back from such rudeness, but not any more. Appearing to sense her growing hostility, Malcolm put a hand on the man's shoulder and turned to Genie.

'Sweetheart, this is Brian. He's a creative, one of the co-directors of Ministry of Outrage. Brian, this is Genie, the jewel in Mallard's crown.'

They shook hands. Ministry of Outrage, she'd heard of them. They were the ad agency that made headlines by shocking the public, selling an awful lot of their clients' products into the bargain. The one with the baby and the AK-47. Osama bin Laden on the tube. Oh, and... hadn't Ollie's pants ad been one of theirs?

Malcolm excused himself, leaving her alone with Brian. She doubted he even remembered her name.

'That's the thing these days: green sells. Fuck the credit crunch; people will buy anything if they think it'll reduce their carbon footprint. That's where the money is.' It was a one-track monologue.

Genie grunted, looked around and caught something out of the corner of her eye.

'Fair Trade as well, they can't get enough of it. You know,' the volume of his voice dropped and he leaned in, conspiratorial, 'we've got guys trying to work out how to market Fair Trade cocaine. Tricky one, no billboards or TV, obviously, but could be huge.'

What *was* that? In the distance just peeping over the brow of the ridge of hills behind the hotel... a tiny floodlit shape that, despite the odd angle at which she was viewing it, was powerfully familiar.

HOLLYWOOD

Her head buzzed. How could that possibly be real? She laughed out loud with pleasure.

'No, it's true!' Brian was delighted. 'These companies are falling over themselves trying to get Outrage on board. When it comes to greenwashing we're the best.'

'Is that like stonewashing?' Genie was bored rigid, and pretending to be a dumb blonde was one of her favourite games. 'For jeans?'

Brian rolled his eyes.

'No, no, no darling, it's…'

'I'm going for a piss,' Genie announced, and headed inside. She was feeling good again and didn't want the mood spoiled for a second time.

When she re-emerged, Brian was nowhere to be seen. She strode out onto the terrace, swooping down on another waiter with a tray of drinks. Ah. Malcolm ahoy! There he was in the far corner talking to… talking to… oh my god, it was That Woman. Bernice Street. And if she was here, then surely it meant that Ollie wasn't far away.

Her heart started beating faster, her sinuses tingled and a warm glow spread through her guts. She looked round. There was Brian, there went Vee Dubya. Suits crossed and recrossed her field of vision. One tall suit looked familiar, and far less crumpled. Yes, *there he was*, looking over the balustrade at the city below, beer bottle in hand.

He wasn't going to get away this time.

'I said I'd be back,' she whispered in his ear. Ollie jumped and dropped his bottle over the railing. There was a distant smash.

Ollie snored, but for now Genie didn't mind. She lay on the bed in the darkness, her heartbeat returning to normal. She had absolutely no idea what time it was. The jetlag, the drink, the drugs and the sex had all conspired to rob her of her body clock and she didn't care one bit. She hadn't felt like this since… since… well to be honest she couldn't remember the last time she'd felt like this. Before Wendi had died, certainly.

'My cup runneth over,' she muttered to the night and closed

her eyes. Ollie's snoring and the whisper of the air con blurred together, a soporific soundtrack to eight hours and five thousand miles catching up with her and dropping on her head like a ton of feathers.

She was walking along a street, downhill. One of the paving stones tipped up beneath her feet and she fell back onto the bed – and blinked her eyes open. Ollie was snoring and the air con was whispering, it seemed, and – *She walked downhill and the paving stone tipped up* – and a police siren from some movie sounded somewhere in the distance now, and a helicopter prowled, the low rhythm of its blades droning – *and she was walking along a street, downhill, sure she'd just been in the middle of talking to Ollie. He was standing in front of her, but as she walked towards him, the paving stone tipped beneath her feet and* – she was back beside him in the bed and – *walking downhill. This time Ollie was in the distance, far ahead, at the bottom. A paving stone tipped up beneath her feet, and she slid down into blackness, insensible.*

6: *Please stand on the right*

Underworld, no time

Genie sat on an escalator step, eyes closed. Despite the obvious discomfort, there was something almost soothing about the regular rocking movement, and the *thud thud thud* noise had now been going on so long that she'd exhausted its musical possibilities and could no longer really hear it. She was almost dropping off. Every time her head drooped though, it brushed against the stationary wooden panelled sides and she jerked awake with a start.

She couldn't let herself fall asleep. She had to be alert, work out what was going on. Suppose something changed? She needed to be ready to take advantage of it.

Still, that was one thing confirmed: this couldn't be a dream. This proved it. You couldn't fall asleep in dreams. You could wake up in them, but not fall asleep.

So what the fuck was it if it wasn't a dream? What if... no, best not to think about that.

It's going to be all right. It's going to be all right.

She'd been here for ages. How far must she have travelled?

Thud thud thud thud.

Or was she actually stationary while the repetitive scenery scrolled past her?

Whisper.

Tenaro. The name was familiar to her from somewhere. But where? Was she remembering it from the blackout that had preceded this endless fugue, from her arrival at this place, or was it a name she'd been aware of for much longer? Tenaro.

Thud thud thud thud.

Genie pressed her fingers to her neck to feel for the pulse. It was still there, still pulsing in time with the mechanism. Since the first time she'd noticed it, a thought had been stalking her, crazy and terrifying.

Was she dead?

She shuddered. A flush of terror passed through her body, simultaneously hot and cold. What she'd been up to back at the flat could easily have killed her. It would have been a fitting end in some ways; her posh past would have come out, of course, but at least her debauched death would have been at odds with it…

But if she was dead, how could she still be conscious? She'd ranted at Thomas about going to the underworld after Ollie, but that was just a bitter joke. The afterlife was bollocks.

If she was dead, how come her heart was still beating? Why did she still feel so warm? Why was anxiety still swirling around in her mind?

What if the afterlife was just this *forever*?

It was too terrifying. She tried to focus on something smaller that she could get a handle on. Her state of apparel, for instance. How would it look being discovered dead in a dressing gown? Could she make that work? If anyone could, she could. Perhaps it could be a minimalist fashion statement. Something along the lines of her natural beauty and style speaking for itself without the need to be dressed to the nines.

Yes, that might do it. The drugs would just add to that myth. Maybe she'd end up a legend...

When did you become so fluent in bullshit? she asked herself.

Whisper.

7: *Dead girl's shoes*

London, early 2003

After the service at Kensal Green, the convoy of luxury vehicles had crawled through the damp West London streets, depositing the mourners back at Mallard Music's expensive offices in the King's Road.

Clots of people in grey and black drifted from room to room; mixed in with these were members of the Talent, their bright plumage contrasting sharply with the sombre expressions on their faces. After a while, the murmur of conversation started to increase in volume as the alcohol took effect, music business methodology kicking back in. Someone switched on a stereo playing duly respectful anodyne imitation trip-hop. Someone laughed.

Genie was dressed in black, wearing the same jacket she'd worn for her university interview; when getting dressed she'd discovered a crumpled-up map of the campus in one of the pockets. The skirt was new; she'd been worried that it was a little too short for the occasion, but no one had said anything. Then again, she hardly knew anyone. There was Businessman Malcolm of course and Monika the receptionist, but the only member of the old band she spotted was drummer Nigel, and she'd never really spoken to him much anyway since Wendi had warned him off that time. Now she simply had no idea what to say or where to start saying it. Any confidence that had rubbed off on her while hanging out with Wendi had washed away, and her mind was running around in small circles within her skull. She felt sick.

Claudia was nowhere to be seen; that was a relief. She hadn't even been at the cemetery.

Lowering herself onto the arm of one of the grey leather sofas, Genie wondered how long she'd have to stay before being allowed to leave. At this point home was only a small bedsit in Kentish Town, but at least she had it to herself. She wanted to be alone to mourn Wendi in her own way without having to hang around mouthing platitudes along with the rest of the organisation. There was nothing she could contribute to this charade and nothing it could do for her; the shock of Wendi's death had opened her eyes to just how superficial this world really was.

There was a rise in the noise from one of the other rooms. People gasping, exclamations of surprise and awe. It felt inappropriate but in the end Genie's curiosity got the better of her, and she followed her ears to where a small crowd gathered around a large TV.

It was live footage from Brighton; the derelict West Pier was on fire. Genie felt the force of coincidence like a slap to the face; Wendi was dead and now this inanimate witness to the beginning of Genie's relationship with her was disappearing as they all watched. The past being erased.

'Hello, sweetheart.'

Genie looked round. It was Businessman Malcolm. That was odd, he'd never called her 'sweetheart' before, preferring 'ENTS Girl', a reference to their first meeting and her induction into Wendiworld all that time ago. There was also an expression on his face she hadn't seen before. It didn't look comfortable there.

'Hi.'

'I was wondering if we could have a little chat? Now's as good a time as ever; best to get it over before everyone gets too drunk.'

'Sure.' Genie couldn't recall *ever* having seen him drunk. He never gave anything away, although up until now she had been worried that he disapproved of her, of the attention Wendi had given her. She followed him down the corridor and into his office. He closed the door.

Here it comes, thought Genie. She'd been half expecting it. With Wendi dead, Mallard would have no further use for her backing singers. Claudia had probably seen it coming, which would explain her absence. Typical Claudia.

It wasn't as if Genie wanted to hang around anyway, but they could at least have waited until Wendi was cold. Genie was sure that there was an expression for this kind of behaviour but was too numb to remember. It was just beyond the tip of her tongue, hiding behind her brain. *Surplus to requirements?* No, that wasn't it.

Malcolm perched on the edge of his desk, letting Genie lower herself into one of the grey leather easy chairs. *Difficult* chairs more like, she thought, trying to work out what to do with her legs. A relaxed sprawl would have felt wrong; she ended up with her knees almost in front of her face.

Whistling past the graveyard? No, that wasn't it either.

From this angle she could see right up Malcolm's nose.

The incongruous expression had gone from his face, replaced by the default one. Professional.

'I wondered if it was too early for this, but there's no time like the present.' Malcolm smiled.

Snow hasn't fallen that deep? No.

Genie was having difficulty rounding up the words in her head. He really had no morals. Couldn't wait to get rid of her. Didn't want her breathing the company's valuable air for a minute longer than necessary. An angry shout started forming in the pit of her stomach. Had Wendi meant nothing to him other than an entry on a balance sheet?

'I wondered if you'd given any thought to your future with us? You may not be working with Herself any more but you've got potential.'

The shout lost its momentum. Genie's head spun. The certainty and energy her fury had given her disappeared and she worried she was about to start crying again.

'You mean you...'

'No need to go into any of it now. Just wanted to sound you out. Make sure you were amenable with the idea of staying with us. You are, right?'

'Yeah, sure, I mean...' Her head had stopped spinning but now there was something fizzy dissolving in the muscles of her legs.

'Great. Thanks, sweetheart. That's all I need to know for now.'

Genie managed to stand up. She was starting to feel afraid, although if asked couldn't have articulated why.

'I'll arrange a proper meeting for us next week,' Malcolm went on. 'We can set up a session and record some demos. But I guess you can rejoin the party now.'

What party? Then Genie realised he meant Wendi's wake. She turned to the door.

'Oh, one thing...' Genie looked back. Malcolm was rummaging in a large padded envelope he'd picked up from the desk. 'I'm sure Madame would have wanted you to have this.'

He still couldn't bring himself to use Wendi's name, thought Genie. Then again, when had he ever? It had always been *Herself* and *Madame* to other people and *Sweetheart* to her face. She caught the small plastic baggie he tossed her.

Inside were a dozen or so wraps of cocaine. They were made from the pages of manga comics, Wendi's trademark. But hang on...

Wendi had always acted as if she was hiding her drug use from Malcolm. The secret had been one of the many little bonds she'd shared with Genie. Those faces she'd pulled behind his back. Had he known all along? Had he in fact...

It was just what she needed, Genie decided as with a tight little smile at Malcolm she rushed off to the toilet. She still couldn't grasp the expression she'd been searching for and was seized with the odd conviction that if only she could, things would be all right again.

Ten minutes later it didn't matter.

She walked down the King's Road heading for Sloane Square tube. It was raining and her friend was dead. And she was high. It was different this time. Her grief was still there, and it was still one of the worst feelings she'd ever had to cope with, but she was flying above it, soaring over its murky ocean. There was a dark beauty about Wendi's death – the moment she thought this Genie felt bad, but then felt good about the fact that she'd felt bad, as it meant that she wasn't such a wicked person after all, then she felt bad about having felt good, then...

Her mind chose this moment to offer up the phrase *Dead girl's shoes*.

But she didn't want to remember thinking that.

8: Studio time

The problem with being back at the Mallard offices was it reminded Genie of how much she'd lost. Her lover. Her friend. Her confidante.

Wendi's chemical bequest had helped get her through the past week. She still had some left: there hadn't been anyone to share it with. She realised she hardly knew anyone in London; with the loss of their focus, Wendi's crowd had evaporated, no doubt seeking out a new source of glory in whose reflection to bask.

There hadn't been any of them at the funeral.

Stuck in the easy chair again, Genie balanced a rattling cup of tea on her knees. It was like having tea with Grandpa.

'It's going to be a tricky one, but there's no reason we can't get away with it.'

Genie hadn't a clue what Malcolm was on about, so nodded. It was the safest thing to do. She had no choice but to go forward and accept whatever he suggested. It was either that or limp back to university with her tail between her legs. If they'd even have her back. When Wendi had first offered her the position, they'd allowed her a sabbatical year, but she'd more than used that up by now.

It was as if she'd thrown her life away by accident. Remaining in this artificial world was the only option open to her. If she gave up now, Father would be furious. He'd only agreed to her taking time out from her studies on the understanding that it was going to make her lots of money. She was just going to have to make sure that it did.

'Why tricky?' She drained her teacup and set it down on the floor at her feet.

'These days the punters are more fickle, and the business is spread a lot thinner than it used to be.' Malcolm walked over to the window and stared out at the buildings opposite. 'For Mallard to invest in you, you'll need more staying power than the latest *Pop Idol* winner. What we need is something that builds on what we already have but with a broader appeal. We could jump on the post-punk revival thing, but how long's that going to last? We need to get a feel for the next big thing, anticipate that. If we just present them with yet another pretty girl singing someone else's songs they'll lose interest after a single or two, and we need them to invest in you long term...'

Genie didn't like being referred to as *just another pretty girl*. She didn't like the sound of *a broader appeal* either. It was exactly the language Wendi would have hated. It smacked of compromise. However, she kept her mouth shut. Right now she was worthy of Malcolm's precious time – but she'd seen what happened to other people when this was no longer the case.

'A wider audience. That's what it's all about. We've got a massive advantage already, all of Madame's fans already know your face' – even though she was gone Malcolm still didn't seem to be able to use Wendi's name, Genie thought – 'but there just aren't enough of them to risk going exclusively down that road. We've got to spread the net.'

Duck West was a studio in a converted workshop somewhere on a West London industrial estate near a lot of railway bridges. Recording there was like having a day job. The car picked her up from Kentish Town by ten, and once she'd arrived she spent the day drinking tea, reading, eating and going to the toilet, punctuated by the occasional bout of work: an hour or so standing in a booth singing the lyrics they'd given her to whatever it was they were pumping through her headphones. She wanted to get more involved, but the men who worked there wouldn't let her. Very early on, she started to get a feel for the music and tried to make suggestions but was pointedly ignored.

There was something not right about the way the music sounded. There were still recognisable elements of Beam's sound, the electronic atmospheres and ambiences from some of the slower numbers, but it was too... watered down. And it was too busy, threaded through with relentless beats that didn't give the music time to catch its breath. Genie was sure this wasn't what Wendi would have wanted. Why hadn't they brought some of the old band on board?

'Ah well, it's a juggling act, sweetheart,' Malcolm said when she'd asked him this. 'It's not as if we're just carrying on without Herself. That would be in poor taste, a recognisable cash-in. We want to build on it, creating something new that the fan base can get into as well as everyone else. I trust my instincts. The next big thing is going to be more dance, more pop than what you're used to. If we can segue into that organically and still bring as much of the old audience with us as we can, then all the better. I know what I'm doing.'

It was a politician's answer, Genie thought. The old band probably hadn't wanted to be involved. Malcolm probably hadn't asked them; they'd have known that Wendi would never have gone along with this.

But no one cared about Wendi's opinion any more. It was unfair. Genie thought about the weekend she'd spent in Wendi's flat – the time they'd written that song. It was one of her best memories.

It was the first time she'd stayed the night at the spacious converted stable that Wendi had moved into a year before her death, tucked away in a mews in Kentish Town five minutes' walk from the bedsit Genie had been installed in by the record company. Waking at two in the morning, Genie had opened her eyes to pitch blackness and felt a microsecond of panic before remembering where she was. It was chilly and the other half of the bed was empty. It wasn't unusual for Wendi to get up in the middle of the night, but Genie was uneasy in the unfamiliar surroundings. She climbed out of the bed, pulling the duvet around her as an impromptu shawl before creeping in the direction of the door, one hand held out in front of her.

The living room was deserted, but Wendi's big computer was switched on, the screensaver illuminating the empty swivel chair in front of it with shifting patterns of red, green and yellow. Genie tiptoed to the desk and sat down in the huge chair, pulling her feet under her. She reached out a hand and jiggled the mouse.

The screen was filled with long coloured blocks, piled up one upon the other like geological strata. This was Logic Pro, she deduced, something computery to do with music that she'd heard Wendi mention a couple of times. It was complex, unfathomable; Genie was in the presence of magic, an arcane code that she was sure she'd never be able to decipher.

A cold arm slid around her neck and a small chin came to rest on her shoulder.

'Hi, babe...' Wendi murmured.

They spent the rest of the night making music. Retiring to the sofa, Wendi had fetched an acoustic guitar and strummed quiet patterns and shapes to accompany Genie's initially shy singing.

It was very different from singing backing vocals live; there was nowhere to hide, no thick instrumentation to mask her voice. At first Genie felt as vulnerable as if she was running down the street naked, but something about the way Wendi was looking at her inspired confidence. It was an image that stuck fast in her mind, the strength and serenity of Wendi's gaze a stark contrast to how small and fragile she looked behind the bulky instrument, the paleness of her slim arms and legs standing out against the rich brown wood of the guitar body. Over the next few hours, Genie was surprised to find within herself a talent for the rhythm of words, an instinctive sense of how they fit to the melodies Wendi was pulling out of nowhere. This was where the real magic lay.

'You've got a beautiful voice,' Wendi said at one point, making Genie blush. It was good though.

By the morning they had a complete track, and moved back over to the computer to record it over the course of the next day. It was quieter than Wendi's usual style, thoughtful and raw, just a guitar and a voice. Genie shivered with the excitement of creation. It was hers, hers and Wendi's. They'd made it. Before last night it hadn't existed, but now there was a new song in the world. Wendi seemed pleased with it too, saying it was 'very Patti Smithy'. She burned it onto CD for Genie to take home. Genie played it several times a day for months.

It was the last song Wendi had ever written.

And now sometimes Genie wondered if it was going to be the last song she would ever write too. No one had suggested she write anything at all. Certainly none of the men who worked at Duck West had any time for her thoughts or opinions.

A lot of them were called Mike. Chief Mike was the producer – a skeletal man with a long grey ponytail and beard. Genie had never seen him wearing anything other than grubby jeans and a faded T-shirt – usually with either Dire Straits or Iron Maiden on the front. He didn't like talking to her at all and always passed on his suggestions through one of the other Mikes or the session musicians.

The session men were usually called Phil, Dave or Andy. They were more of the tame Talent that Mallard had on tap. Most of them had long hair, although unlike Chief Mike's it was always brown. They didn't seem much like musicians to Genie – there was none of the enthusiasm she remembered from Wendi or her co-writer Peter, none of the passion. They were very good at their job and knew what they were doing, but weren't anyone's band; they were more like the handyman teams of painters and decorators she remembered Father occasionally employing when corners of the house started to get run down.

The best songs always seemed to come when keyboard player Dave was involved. He listened to what she had to say and incorporated some of her suggestions into the music. This gave her the confidence to attempt her own lyrics and use them rather than the generic hack words Mallard had been supplying. Here was somebody with whom she felt a ghost of the spark she'd had with Wendi that night, someone who believed in what she could contribute, someone who believed in *her*. When he said how impressed he was with her singing, she knew he was sincere. The others treated her with less respect than they did their stupid guitars.

She began to wonder if perhaps Dave would become her

friend, but he always rushed off at the end of the day, muttering about 'the little woman'.

And she had no idea whose decision it was, but the takes with her own lyrics were never used.

Christmas came; Genie spent two weeks in Berkshire. Father disappeared on business after the first week, so she was left rattling around the house with Mother. Her friend Tabby's parents had treated her to a fortnight in the Bahamas, so Genie couldn't even go and see her and catch up. It came as something of a relief when the car arrived during the first week of January and whisked her off back into the slowly turning wheels of the music mechanism.

Keyboard Dave wasn't around any more, and there were one or two new musicians in the studio. One of them, a guitarist called Neil, paid her somewhat more attention than the others. Pity he was such a creep though. He was always talking about what he was going to do next, and how much money he was going to make. He was really into the idea of tribute acts. The punters couldn't get enough of them apparently.

'You see, Genie' – he overused her name somewhat in what she suspected was an attempt to appear friendly – 'the punters are never gonna get to see Abba now, but the music's just gonna get more and more popular. That's where the money is.'

His hand brushed against her shoulder. They were sitting on one of the sofas in the lounge. Thankfully these ones weren't as squashy as the ones in Mallard's offices and Genie was able to move away slightly without unexpectedly ending up on the floor.

This didn't put him off. He merely used the space to turn even more towards her, pulling one of his legs up on the sofa, nudging her thigh as if by accident.

'Or Blondie. Debbie Harry's getting on a bit now, Genie, but you just bet people are gonna pay through the nose to see her songs. I'm putting a Blondie one together now.'

'Really?' Genie stood up; there was nowhere else on the sofa to go. 'I'm going for a piss.'

She still felt a little bad when she used that trick, but it always worked. It was something she'd picked up from Wendi, although she'd never dared to be quite as rude as Wendi sometimes had.

When she came back from the toilet, Neil was in conference with Chief Mike. She'd probably managed to avoid being roped into his little scheme for another couple of days then.

And then it was all over. Her stint at Duck West had produced enough material to satisfy Malcolm.

They were in one of the lounge areas in the King's Road offices, her songs playing over the stereo. Genie was perched on the edge of one of the too-soft sofas but Malcolm was pacing up and down, unable to relax. He nodded, he smiled, he grimaced. When the last song was over, he turned to face her.

'We need to make you more interesting. You can sing, you've got a sweet face and you've got a good body, but we need more. We need our customers, your fans, to believe you're far more than just another manufactured pop star.'

Genie was taken aback. At the very least she'd been expecting a *well done*. Spending all that time locked up with the Mikes and the Session Men, she had earned the right to challenge this.

'I'm not just another manufactured pop star!' she protested. 'I'm creative. I can write my own songs. They just didn't want to use them.'

'So far you've only written *some* of the *words* to *two* of your songs,' corrected Malcolm, 'and if they didn't want to use them, then I trust their judgement. But you're right, that's a good angle. Let's spin you as a musician as well as a singer. All your stuff's done in the studio anyway, so all we need to do is get you to publicly knock around some ideas with a couple of serious-looking session boys and hey presto, you're writing songs. We could probably do some photo shoots of you playing the guitar or sitting at the piano or something. Minimal make-up, casual in-the-studio kind of thing. Black and white, serious artist vibe.'

He'd gone on so much in response that Genie had forgotten she was annoyed. She watched him pacing up and down, up and down. Today he was dressed in one of the dark grey suits that always made him look as if he was on his way to work in a bank, his hair as usual short and immaculate.

'That will help,' he went on, 'but we'll need to spread the net a bit to maximise your potential. Tap into the power of the pink pound. Give you a bit of a makeover – maybe even shorter hair, more extreme peroxide, get a bit of an androgynous look going, perhaps record an unexpected Donna Summer cover version...'

'You just said I was supposed to be writing my own songs, not doing cover versions.'

'Yes, but it's not as straightforward as that.' Malcolm raised an eyebrow. 'Cover versions can be quite effective if used properly. Especially if we have a fiddle with your image first. But before we go for the gay thing, we'll have to ensure the indie kids stay on board if we can. I'm certain most of Herself's old fans are still on side, but it's a good idea if you're seen at the right gigs, dress down a bit, get a tattoo and some piercings, maybe be seen having a drink with Pete Doherty or something. Then when you do the cover song, some people think it's ironic. Other people think it's a gay scene thing.'

'Piercings? Pete Doherty?' Genie was starting to become a little alarmed. 'Tattoos?'

'Why not? You can get rid of it later, no problem. I'll have a word with marketing, see if they have any ideas for good designs. Original, but with the right resonances.'

Half the time, Genie was out of her depth, hadn't the faintest idea what he was on about, but she'd been told that Malcolm got results. For all her rebellious attitude, even Wendi had appeared to respect him.

What was more, when Genie was dealing with him, at least she didn't have to worry about all that *other* stuff. She'd already had to deflect the unwanted attentions of unsavoury industry males during her brief career. But even though Malcolm was clearly aware of her image and what it could do to some people if correctly handled, he obviously wasn't remotely interested in her in *that way*.

To Genie's surprise, within a couple of months they'd already done the fake indie thing. Malcolm had pulled in favours and got her slots supporting this month's darlings of the scene at The Barfly and The Falcon.

It was very different from her time as a backing singer; then the venues had been bigger and she'd been able to hide behind Wendi and the band. Here the audience were inches in front of her nose and all she had to hide behind was a microphone stand. She sang along to pre-recorded tracks on DAT, although for effect there was a giant reel-to-reel tape recorder running at the back of the stage. Malcolm had told her that it used to belong to Depeche Mode.

She only sang for twenty minutes. Malcolm had picked four of the less obviously commercial numbers she'd recorded and had advised she dress all in black, with heavy eye make-up.

The audience had loved it. Genie looked down – there was no stage to speak of, but she was wearing rather high heels – at a sea of adoring adolescent faces. Mostly boys.

It did the trick. She was rewarded with a feature in the *NME*.

Genie had found this very hard work. Malcolm hadn't been allowed to sit in, but he'd carefully primed her with all the correct names to drop and references to make. Normally she didn't have to worry about all that stuff, but in the interests of appearing genuine, she had her work cut out for her. She'd spent the two days before the interview boning up on what her influences were supposed to be and which were the right bands to mention – not just the bands Wendi had introduced her to, but some ambient dance stuff like μ-Ziq and Aphex Twin. Her own sound was only superficially like Beam, and her own childhood tastes were clearly inappropriate topics. She was reminded of revising for her GCSEs, and just like then it had all turned out very well in the end. She'd apparently known her stuff and had flirted with the journalist just the right amount to get a glowing testimonial.

'You see?' Malcolm said. 'We've made you the right kind of cool.' He flung a copy of the *NME* down on the coffee table in front of her. A ferocious-looking version of herself glowered back at her from the glossy cover.

Genie picked up the magazine and began to leaf through it. She was relieved that the right kind of cool hadn't involved too much body modification, although it had to be admitted she was now becoming rather fond of her new tribal butterfly tattoo. In the event, Pete Doherty had been unavailable, although she had spent an evening at a club with a guy who said he used to be in Underworld or Leftfield or something like that. By pure luck she'd also happened to stand next to Thom Yorke in a bar when there had been a photographer from *Q* in the room.

'We need to get something released though,' Malcolm went on. 'Just a one-off indie-friendly thing, then we can move forward with the real money spinners. Must be catchy. Track two of the set will do.'

They remixed and remastered 'Suspended Animania' over one weekend, returning to Duck West to do so. Genie wondered whether she actually needed to be there; for some reason the mixing itself hadn't required much input from her and she'd spent most of the day sitting around in the lounge area eating Pringles and watching MTV. However, at the end of the day both Malcolm and Chief Mike were quite pleased. Chief Mike even acknowledged her existence with a half-smile. The master tapes were duly whisked away somewhere to be fiddled with.

A fortnight later, Genie was sitting at Mallard listening to her new single. She wasn't that keen on it, to be honest – it wasn't really her cup of tea – although by this point, what with one thing and another, she was increasingly confused as to what her cup of tea actually was. As a little kid, she'd adored Kylie and Bros, and when her enthusiasm for them had waned, it hadn't really been replaced by anything else for long. When she'd been at school there had been a lot of music around, but also a lot of bullying based on who you liked or who you *said* you liked. She still cringed at the thought of that time Emily Courtenay had come across her singing along to Pulp's 'Common People' on the radio. Didn't she realise, Emily had sneered, that song was written about a woman just like them by some lout with a chip on his shoulder? On one level it had just been another stick for Emily to beat her with but there was an element of truth there. Bands hated people like her. Their music wasn't meant for the likes of Genie.

But then she encountered Beam. Wendi's passion had swept

her along and engaged her. That had been music that meant something.

But this – it didn't really sound anything like Beam even though it was clearly supposed to. Beam's sound had been hypnotic, sometimes a wall of noise and sometimes a huge empty space, but always pregnant with meaning and emotion. But this... it didn't mean anything. It didn't make her feel anything. It was all surface. It didn't sound enough like 'Genie' either, and when listening to it, she certainly didn't feel anything like the thrill she'd had when she and Wendi had written that song.

'Suspended Animania' came with a number of different remixes ('One for each potential market' as Malcolm put it) and Genie had to assume that the right words were being whispered in all the right ears, as the radio edit made its way onto XFM's main play list some months before its eventual release and was heavily rotated.

'It'll make them all the more hungry for it,' explained Malcolm, 'and gives us a bit of time to work out a strategy for when it finally comes out – by then it's all over bar the shouting.'

They did the tasteful monochrome photo shoot where Genie was pretending to write songs at a North London house with a short, hairy young man who was apparently quite the tunesmith. Unfortunately his personal hygiene didn't match the alleged level of his genius. Genie wondered when he'd last taken a shower and whether he'd ever heard of deodorant. She kept having to make excuses to wander out into the garden simply so she could breathe, and then wondered if he'd ever heard of gardening, either.

In the end, the Genie publicity machine managed to retrieve a couple of hundred arty photographs and about half a song from this session. It did the trick, one of the pictures ending up on the news page of the *NME*.

They shot a video. All Genie had to do was dress provocatively, spend an hour in make-up and then mime to a recording of the song a few times in front of a green screen. It took an afternoon, and given how simple it had all been, Genie hadn't been expecting that much. This made the end result all the more astonishing – a frightening amazon version of herself who spent her time gyrating in underpasses and hurtling across midnight cityscapes. What was more, it seemed to star her legs; her face was merely given second billing although her mouth did enjoy special guest star status.

It was impressive; she had to admit that. More persuasive words were murmured into more influential ears and the video started appearing on MTV's *Biggest! Hottest! Loudest!* two or three times a day. After a couple of dozen views Genie began to realise that perhaps the song wasn't entirely terrible. One morning she even caught herself humming it in the shower. Wendi would have been appalled.

And all this without selling a single CD.

9: Footsteps

Underworld, no time

It was definitely getting a lot warmer. She opened her eyes. There was something different. Another sound. Something apart from the regular rumbling of the machinery. Something other than the thuds and whispers. A clumsy, haphazard clumping, stumbling noise.

Footsteps.

They were coming from behind her.

She leaned back and looked upwards. Nothing there. From a seated viewpoint, there was even less to see than there had been when she was standing up, just an interminable succession of empty wooden steps disappearing into the distance. Certainly nothing that could be causing the lurching thumps which were now quite distinct.

Alarmed, she stood up.

Of course. The *other* escalator. There was a human shape walking awkwardly down her escalator's twin. It was a man. A skinny man dressed in a duffel coat with a small satchel over one shoulder. After a bit she could see he had scruffy ginger hair that was badly in need of a trim. His skin was pale, almost white. As he drew level, he glanced across and stopped just a bit higher than her, staring. His jaw dropped.

'G-Genie?' he called.

Oh. My. God. It was Nathan Clay, webmaster of *Hermania: The Unofficial Genie DC Fan Site.* Genie closed her eyes.

Nathan walked down a couple of steps until he was just below Genie, turning to keep her in his field of vision.

'What are you doing here?'

What the fuck? thought Genie.

10: Fans

London, 2004

With the MTV coverage, the fan letters started to arrive at Mallard. Genie suspected that Malcolm was disposing of some of the more frightening specimens, but even so, what arrived was disturbing enough.

It was surprising how similar they all were. Many of them said they'd never written to a celebrity before but now they felt they just had to. A lot of them couldn't stop thinking about her. On the whole, every single one of them was her biggest fan.

They were chiefly boys.

Dear Genie

I never written to a pop star before, but when I saw your clip on MTV I new I had to. I recorded it on BHL and watch it every day. I hope your CD is coming out soon. I wish I could meat you. May be if you do some concerts you can come to Buckley then we can have a drink as I can't stop thinking about you. I am you're number one fan. Please can you send me a singed photo?

Love

Nigel
xxxxxx

Malcolm had ordered a batch of two thousand monochrome Walkerprints which Genie had spent a tedious afternoon signing. Still, it could have been worse. She had expected to have to write back to these strange young men individually, or at least personalise the autographs, but Malcolm assured her it wasn't necessary.

'They'll soon wear them out and come back for more,' he remarked. 'Next time we can get them to pay for it. Nice limited edition. Autographed. Arty. Make them think it's a press-only thing; we can set up a false eBay account, make it seem illicit.'

Dearest Genie

Ever since I saw your video I find I can't stop thinking about you; I dream about you every night. I am in love with you. I realise this will seem odd coming from someone you've never met; don't worry I am not some mad stalker.

I hope one day we can meet. Where do you live?

All my love
Nazim
x

PS: Please can you send me a signed photograph?

'Shouldn't we have a website or something? Myspace?' Genie felt quite proud of herself; it was unlike Malcolm to have slipped up on such an important detail. She was sure he'd have mentioned if she already did have a website.

'Good point, sweetheart,' Malcolm smiled, 'but don't worry, I've thought about that.' He picked up one of the letters and regarded it. 'I think an absence from Myspace at this point can only add to your appeal. Make people eager to find out more. Or even to do it for you.'

Dear Sir or Madam

Please can you send me a signed photo of Genie DC? I enclose a stamped addressed envelope.

The order I would do Genie is: vaginal, anal, oral, then finish off with anal.

Yours sincerely

Noah

'Oops, sorry.' Malcolm snatched up the offending letter and crumpled it into a ball one-handed. 'Thought Monika'd removed all the sex cases. Never mind, I won't let any of them get near you.'

Well it was nice to have her suspicion confirmed, she thought, but '*all the sex cases*'? How many were there for god's sake?

'And we'll be hiring some kind of security when we do the mini-tour.'

'What's that?' Genie felt alarmed by the loss of control she felt when Malcolm left her out of the loop, but she supposed it was mainly because he didn't want her worrying. 'What tour?'

'Not a real tour. A PA tour.' Malcolm tossed the ball of

crumpled paper across the room into the bin. 'A handful of dates around the country the week before the single's released; maximise sales. No need for a band; you'll just be singing along to backing tracks like we did in London. Twenty-minute set.'

'That's next week, isn't it?'

'The week after next; the release date's undergoing a controlled postponement. We figured one final week of anticipation would give us that extra sales boost. And would give us time for some more pre-release press.' Malcolm looked at his watch. 'Talking of which, you've got a two o'clock. Provincial hack from Halifax. Shouldn't take longer than half an hour. Hasn't mentioned a photographer so we can palm him off with a couple of the press shots.'

'Oh...' Genie had been hoping to slip out for something to eat.

'We'll do it in the meeting room. Less comfortable, less chance of him hanging around. We don't have to schmooze local press. We're doing him a favour. Last person he interviewed was probably Bernie Clifton for the Christmas panto.'

'What's his name?'

'Who cares?' Malcolm shrugged.

Ten minutes later, having freshened up and retouched her make-up, Genie was sitting behind the table in the meeting room staring out of the window at the tops of the double-decker buses as they crawled past. She looked round as the door opened.

'He's waiting at reception,' Malcolm poked his head into the room, 'Monika'll keep him there until I come and fetch him. I'll let you get ready in peace.' He disappeared again and the door clicked shut behind him.

Genie took this as her cue for a top-up. Even though Malcolm was now her regular supplier – and he never seemed to want any money – they still played this little game whereby he never watched her indulging. She supposed it was some kind of plausible deniability; if asked he could say with all honesty that he'd never seen her taking drugs, thus maintaining his professional image.

It was unusual for him not to have briefed her on what to say to the journalist, but by now she knew what not to mention. Her background for one; in this world, academic prowess was frowned upon almost as much as rich parents or a posh school. There were some things best not talked about. Some things she didn't even want to think about.

Dead girl's shoes.

There was a tap at the door. 'Are you decent?' Malcolm asked. Genie swept the evidence off the table and into her handbag before calling out in the affirmative.

Malcolm walked back through the door, a clumsy silhouette behind him.

'Genie, this is Nathan.' Malcolm slid around the table, took the seat next to Genie and started flipping through his Filofax. Genie half stood and offered a hand. The pale, skinny figure shook it listlessly with a cold hand and stood regarding her through small lashless eyes.

'Nice to meet you,' Genie lied, giving Nathan a big smile. His eyes flickered across her torso before coming to rest on the tabletop.

'Do sit down.' Genie dropped back into her seat, leaned across and hissed in Malcolm's ear.

'Don't leave me alone with this freak!'

The freak was busy scrabbling around inside a large satchel, which it didn't seem to occur to him to remove from his shoulder. Out came a bottle of water and a Dictaphone held together with sellotape. Nathan's hair was a dirty ginger, badly cut. As he rummaged further, Genie could see flecks of dandruff detaching themselves and drifting down into the satchel.

A sheaf of handwritten notes joined the Dictaphone on the table. Nathan pressed one of the buttons, secured it down with more sellotape and coughed with a passion.

'So, er, Genie... What do you think you'd, er, be doing if you weren't a pop star?'

'Recognise this?' Malcolm tossed a sheaf of laser-printed web pages onto the coffee table. The mini-tour was over and they were back at Mallard, waiting for details of the new Top 40. Malcolm had been confident of a decent placing: 'Shame *Pops* isn't primetime any more, you'd be guaranteed a slot and that would have sent you stratospheric. Still, it'll get the right tongues wagging.'

Genie picked up the printout and started to read. It took her a while before she realised that it was Nathan's interview; on paper he was intelligent and articulate, witty, almost likeable. She glanced up at the top of the sheet. Hang on.

Hermania! The Unofficial Genie DC Fan Site

'I thought he was working at a local paper?'

'So he lied.' Malcolm shrugged.

'Well can't we... he shouldn't... we...' Genie unfolded herself from the sofa, walked over to the desk and, still standing up, started hammering at the iMac keyboard *www dot hermania dot co dot uk.*

News. Gallery. Features. She had to admit it looked well designed. Professional, despite the 'unofficial' epithet, which somehow contrived to give the impression it was being worn as a badge of honour. *Unofficial? Well it's got the word 'official' in it so surely that's the next best thing? No, of course I'm not claiming that, but even so you have to admit...*

'Is there anything we can do?' Genie glared at Malcolm, who smiled.

'Send him some more photos?'

'What? You don't think we should... oh I don't know, sue him or something?'

'Why?' Malcolm sat down at the desk, pulled the keyboard over and flicked through the site. 'Could end up saving us a hell of a lot of money in the long run. Why should we pay a load of Shoreditch web-monkeys fifty grand for a half-baked generic product when this idiot's going to do a much better job for a handful of signed photos and promo CDs? It's sound business sense.'

'Do you think you can trust him?' Genie collapsed back into the sofa. This was another of Malcolm's 'curve balls', she decided. Doing the opposite of what people were expecting for reasons only he understood.

'I'm sure we can. As long as he remains on message and uncritical, he gets a steady stream of goodies. Plus occasional access to you, of course.'

'Must we?' Genie pulled a face.

However, Genie decided to give Nathan another chance. She was a good-hearted person, and after all, perhaps he'd just been shy and awkward at the interview because he'd been in awe of her. Under different circumstances he might be as clever and easy-going as his writing. She got Malcolm to arrange an evening out for them at a local wine bar and, given the distance Nathan would have to travel, a cheap room for him in a B&B in Camden.

It was a disaster. If awe was the problem then Nathan still had it bad. He was incapable of talking to her about anything other than the minutiae of her brief career and wasn't forthcoming about his own background. He was also unable to take his drink and after a couple of hours Genie called Malcolm and got him to come over and bundle the almost unconscious Nathan into a cab bound for the B&B.

'Never again!' Genie yelled the next day. 'He's too weird for me!'

Malcolm didn't appear that bothered; if anything he was quite pleased.

Over the next year or so Genie noticed that Nathan had an almost supernatural ability to divine her itinerary and be there at the stage door, oversized camera around his neck, satchel bulging with who knew what.

Malcolm eventually admitted that he was tipping him off.

'I know what I'm doing, sweetheart.'

And despite the 'unofficial' tag, Nathan's website came to be considered *the* source of knowledge and wisdom for all things Genie-related, much to the chagrin of some of the marketing people at Mallard. Malcolm relented a little and let them add a Genie page to their artists' roster, but even that had a link to Nathan's site on it. Genie imagined the creep was probably very pleased at the recognition, but as she made a concerted effort to minimise any time she had to spend in his company, it was very difficult to tell. Even after a couple of years, he came across as shy and awkward in her presence; he was very hard work. Genie decided she didn't like that kind of hard work. It tired her out too much.

It was Malcolm's idea to get him involved, she reasoned, let Malcolm do the work.

11: Styx Embankment

Genie had eventually worked out a way to recline on the escalator without being driven insane by discomfort and now lay across several steps awkwardly, eyes closed.

To her relief, after an awkward half-shouted exchange between escalators, Nathan had volunteered to scout ahead – rather pointless given the unvarying nature of their surroundings, but at least it had given her a break from his inane questions and the ubiquitous miasma of cheese-and-onion crisps that she imagined she could smell even across the gap and that he seemed to have retained, even after... after... ending up wherever they were now.

That was still bothering her. It was still too real to be a dream. So wherever she was, it was somewhere Nathan could be as well. Something bothered her about Nathan – something more than usual.

She'd reached across to take his hand for a second; relieved to see someone else, anyone else, even him. It had been icy cold, despite how warm it was getting down here now. And he'd always been pale, but not *that* pale. There was something not quite right about him.

On top of that, Nathan had been cagey about how he'd

come to be there. Even more than normal. He'd claimed that the last thing he could remember was coming out of a West End show and having an altercation with a homeless guy.

Perhaps this... tube station was in the West End? Tenaro. There was something else nagging at her too.

She shuddered. She'd got the distinct impression that Nathan was... dead.

Her earlier musings about the afterlife gnawed at her. It was ridiculous, but was it any more ridiculous than running into him in a mysterious closed-off station on an escalator that went down seemingly forever? She stared down into the depths of this impossible, empty place. He might well be dead and he might well be the last person she'd have wanted to see, but right now... he was all she had. If he ever came back, that was.

She'd lost all track of time. After a while, she'd stopped worrying about whether she should stay awake; she'd discovered it was impossible to fall asleep anyway. She *had* managed to drift off a little into... thoughts, memories, but she was aware throughout of the feel of the wooden treads under her body, the perpetual waft of warm air, the acrid smell and the sound of the machinery as it bore her ever onwards and downwards. She focused on it, the rhythm oddly calming.

Thud thud thud thud.

What if he was dead and she wasn't? She touched her neck again, reassured by her own constant pulse, the warmth of her skin. Physically she was fine; there was no denying the reality of her own living flesh. Mentally was another matter. Was there a part of her that just didn't care that much if she was on her way to... wherever?

Whisper.

Lying down like this, the fluttering whispers were a little easier to make out. She was sure they were voices. Some of it was even in English; words flitted into earshot before disappearing again, the voice of an unintelligible hypnotist.

...Stygian realm... look behind... the jaws of Taenarus...

Familiar words, but from where? What were they trying to tell her? She concentrated further but got the impression that some of the words' meaning was coming from her, her mind seeking patterns in the noise of the chaotic machinery.

Thud thud thud thud.

She hummed a new little song to herself. It was odd, she thought, but she'd lost the capacity for boredom. Normally, without stimulation or the oblivion of unconsciousness, such a long stretch of time would have driven her round the bend, but she was... OK. On one level, her mind was actually counting the thuds made by the mechanism. On another she was even drawing a sort of pleasure from this mindless activity. How very odd.

Whisper.

So Nathan was dead, and she was alive, but they were both in the afterlife. Why? The absurdity of the conclusion she was approaching wasn't lost on her. By all rights, she knew, her thoughts should be spiralling out of control. But the monotonous calm held her in its embrace.

Clunk-clunk-clunk-clunk... Squeeeeeeeeeeee...

She felt around inside her dressing gown pocket, discovering the pill bottle and its lid. She replaced the lid automatically. Wouldn't do to have the pills spilling around everywhere. She was down here for a reason.

Clunk-clunk-clunk-clunk... Squeeeeeeeeeeeee...

She could do with something to read. Some classics texts from university would have been nice. Graves' *Greek Myths* for example. Which reminded her. Her fingers located a couple of wraps in her pocket as well. It had to be an obvious reason.

Clunk-clunk-clunk-clunk... Squeeeeeeeeeeeee...

Her phone was in there as well. She pulled it out. No signal.

Well what had she expected? She was underground. Even if this wasn't a tube station, she'd been travelling down for so long she had to be in the underworld by now.

Clunk-clunk-clunk-clunk... Squeeeeeeeeeeeeeee...

Genie's eyes snapped open. She guessed that the return of the *clunk-squees* could only mean one thing – she was nearing the escalator's lower terminus.

Fighting off the hypnotic stupor, Genie sat up and grabbed onto the handrail, pulling herself upright. She'd guessed right. Not far below she could see the regular procession of wooden steps flattening out and disappearing beneath wide metal teeth. And beyond that lay a filthy yellow-tiled floor.

Genie ran down the remaining steps and leaped over the teeth, stumbling a little as she landed in the space beyond; her knees were stiff after the inactivity. Like the one at the top, this chamber was decorated with a geometrical – and rather dull – pattern of purple-and-cream tiles. Unlike its counterpart above, this was much wider, and – more significantly – had one arched side open to the elements. A rectangle of chipped blue enamel hung from the ceiling in front of this exit, the faded words 'WAY OUT' just visible at its centre.

Why hadn't Nathan come back to tell her about this...? Oh. Still, he could have waited.

Genie looked back at the escalators. Just like at the top, another sign was fixed above them.

CAPE TENARO

It was on the tip of her tongue. It made sense, it was all to do with what she'd just been thinking, why she was here in the underground, the underworld, she wasn't dead...

Genie walked over to the archway in search of fresh air to clear her head.

Outside was very dark, the yellow light from the chamber only illuminating the ground a few feet in front of the exit.

No fresh air was available; instead a hot breeze ruffled her short hair. It was like standing in front of a giant hairdryer. In addition to its unusual heat, there was something damp and unpleasant about the air. She was put in mind of sewers. Taking a few steps further forward across warm flagstones, she looked back at the building containing the escalator. From the outside it was completely unremarkable – just a low, grey single-storey building with a simple sign 'No exit' fixed to the wall beside the archway she'd just come through.

What had happened to Nathan? Where had he wandered off to?

Hang on. She looked back at the building again. There wasn't anywhere for the escalators to have come from. Surely there should have been a diagonal shaft poking out from the building's roof and heading off into the sky?

The sky. Goose pimples prickled Genie's scalp and upper arms as she stared up at it. It was dark as an overcast, moonless midnight and yet possessed a sense of infinite distance. There were no stars up there, but as her eyes adjusted to the darkness she could make out huge indistinct forms and variations in the blackness, terrifying shapes that made no sense; a slow, inexorable movement. She tore her eyes away and stared at the ground, waiting for her heart to stop racing.

Cape Tenaro. Oh fuck. She remembered. And it made a crazy kind of sense.

It was in Greece. She'd been there with her parents on that Mediterranean cruise. She'd insisted they visit, because... because *she wanted to see where Orpheus had entered the underworld in search of Eurydice.*

If she was alive, no one else down here was. That meant she had a mission.

Oh for fuck's sake.

Earlier on, when she'd been ranting all that bollocks at Thomas about singing for Death to get Ollie back and dump him...

'It was a JOKE!' she screamed out loud. The muggy air instantly swallowed her shriek of anger as if it had never happened. But seriously – of all the times for the universe to have been listening to her, of all the times for it to have decided to take off its mask and reveal that the weird shit beneath was real... Fucking OLLIE?

Did they not have sarcasm in the hereafter?

She started to laugh. So the mythological world she'd been so obsessed with as a child turned out to be real, but populated by idiots? Who had decided that of all the times she'd needed supernatural help, *now* was the one that mattered...

She straightened up and wiped the tears of mirth from her eyes. She hadn't laughed like that for a long time. Nearly five years in fact.

Ok, fair enough. Why the fuck not? She could play at being Orpheus if they wanted. It was not as if there was anything else to do. It was absurd, but then so was this place.

Some fifty feet away from the building, there was a whitish globe of light on a pole – a street lamp, just one of a row, she could see as she walked towards it, stretching off into the distance to both her left and right. The lamps stood just in front of a waist-high stone wall, blocking her progress in that direction. Leaning her elbows on it, she peered over.

The sluggish undulation of a pitch-black body of water reflected fragments of the street lamps' illumination back to her, tiny ripples slapping feebly against the wall with the sound of lazy kisses. It was far too still to be a sea, but peering out into the gloom, Genie could see no indication of the other side, as she would have expected of a river or lake. She squinted into the distance to her right and to her left – but there was no sign of anything to indicate a way across.

A hand tapped her on the arm and she shrieked, leaping sideways and knocking painfully against one of the street lamps.

'Oh! I'm… I'm really sorry!' Nathan blushed and stared down at his shoes.

'You twat,' growled Genie.

Nathan glanced at her and then away again. He looked as if he was about to cry. Genie felt guilty.

'Look, sorry I snapped,' she said. 'You just gave me a shock, that's all. Where were you anyway?'

Nathan frowned and glanced up and down the embankment, gesturing weakly.

'I thought,' he said, 'I thought I was walking *that* way. I came out of the building here and started walking *that* way. Away from the building. *That* way. In a straight line. Everything looked the same; just these. And just when I finally thought I'd found *another* building, I saw you coming out of it. So it's got to be the same one. I don't get it.'

'Are you sure you didn't get turned around?'

'Er… n-no…' Nathan clearly wasn't comfortable contradicting Genie. 'The water was on the same side all the way and the path's straight.' He paused. 'Why not try it yourself? Walk *that* way. I'll wait here. See what happens.'

Genie didn't like admitting it, even to herself, but she wasn't about to get left on her own again, even if the only company was Nathan. She felt in the pockets of her dressing gown. The wraps of cocaine. Her iPhone. The bottle of Valium tablets. Her Ray-Bans. A bottle opener. Nothing useful.

'You haven't got any… any… string in that bag of yours, have you?'

Nathan looked dubious, but dutifully removed his satchel and unzipped it, rummaging around inside with graceless haste. After a few seconds, he looked up at Genie and shook his head. From his expression, Genie could tell that he wanted to ask why, but was too afraid of her. She grinned.

'I was just thinking… if we had some string we could tie it to one of these lamp posts and then test your theory. See if we ended up in the same place.'

Nathan rummaged in his bag again, extracting a piece of paper.

'Will these do?'

It was a sheet of stickers, each of which bore the legend '*Genie DC unofficial fan site: www.hermania.co.uk*'.

Ten minutes later Genie was striding along the embankment, Nathan trailing in her wake. Once they'd got past the building, the exit, she'd been able to see that it was set against a twenty-foot-high, black brick barrier. Nothing was visible across this except for the sky, and Genie was still avoiding looking at that. It was the kind of thing that no human being should ever see and she had the uncomfortable impression that it was *aware* of her.

And there was now her stupid quest to think about. She thought back over what she could remember of her mythology. Was this body of water the Styx or the Lethe? She'd just arrived. It had to be the Styx.

She still hadn't entirely discounted the possibility that this was a dream – if nothing else these stories were a big part of her childhood, so it wouldn't be surprising if she dreamed about them – but fuck, it was all so *real*…

Nothing changed. Every few seconds they passed another identical lamp post, underfoot the warm flagstones were indistinguishable, and across the wall the water's listless movement made the same small, wet noises.

'Hang on.'

Genie glanced over her shoulder to see Nathan struggling with his satchel again. After a few seconds, he brandished an expensive-looking digital camera, a sheepish grin on his face. He turned away and fiddled with it. There was an electronic whine and a flash; Nathan peered at its screen intently before looking up, disappointed.

'Not enough light.' He carried on tinkering with the settings as they resumed their journey.

12: Charon Cabs

After twenty more minutes, something was different. Up ahead, Genie could just make out a source of light in addition to that from the lamp posts, and she quickened her step. It soon became obvious that it was a building, exactly like the one they'd left behind. As she approached, Genie heard the faint *clunk–squee* of the escalators within. She walked up to what she guessed was the equivalent lamp post, the lamp post to which they had affixed the sticker.

'*Genie DC un__ficial fan _ite: www.__mania.co.uk*' it read. Even in the dim light, Genie could tell that it had yellowed with age, the laser-printed ink faded and patchy, the glue failing as it curled away from the metal of the post. She stood back.

'We're back where we started, but... we were only gone half an hour. This thing looks like it's been here for months.' As she tugged at a corner of the sticker the glue gave way and it fluttered to the ground.

Nathan shrugged.

Genie pulled a face, wandered back into the building and stared up at the escalators. No sign of anyone else. She had nowhere to go and was stuck with Nathan. Still, it was better than being alone.

'Er, Genie…' She looked over to see Nathan standing in the archway. 'Something's out there…'

A frisson of dread swept across her scalp and down the back of her neck as she considered this. Something? What kind of something? She walked over to the arch and peered back out.

'Where?'

After a few seconds she could hear it; a guttural, unhealthy-sounding, mechanical purr coming from somewhere out on the water. She loped across to the wall and squinted out into the dark. There was something moving there; a darker shape against the black, crowned with a blur of faint orange light. The noise grew irregular, dying off and then surging upwards again. The smell of exhaust fumes reached her. It was a motor boat.

As it approached it veered off to one side, billowing smoke, and manoeuvred itself towards a wooden jetty that definitely hadn't been there earlier. It drew up alongside and sat there, bobbing up and down, engine idling.

'What do we do?' asked Nathan. Before she could answer, Genie felt a faint vibration against her left hip. She was puzzled until a couple of seconds later the ringtone version of one of her songs rang out. Fishing her iPhone out, she touched the answer icon and held it to her ear without thinking (only a few of the Great and the Good had her number).

'Hello?'

'Taxi,' grunted a guttural voice before hanging up. She looked across at the boat. Taxi?

Charon.

Dropping the iPhone back into her dressing gown pocket, Genie walked along the embankment towards the jetty. She wasn't altogether surprised to see that there was now a gap in the wall allowing access to it. At the bottom, the boat bobbed, black and metallic, totally enclosed. Through the window, she could just make out a dark figure at the driver's seat. The orange light on the roof blinked off and a door in the side swung open. Genie turned to Nathan.

'Coming?' she asked. Stepping onto the jetty with care, she walked down towards the open door, feeling the planking start to shake slightly as Nathan followed. She stepped off the end of the jetty and into the boat's interior.

Inside, a wide bench seat with threadbare upholstery faced a scratched Perspex screen beyond which the driver sat, his head an impassive silhouette. Genie sat down and Nathan slid awkwardly in beside her. The door swung shut and a red LED display flashed into action on the side of a meter beside the driver's head. Genie blinked; somehow she couldn't quite make the numerals out. It was as if they were in a foreign alphabet or as if she'd forgotten how to read. She looked away and out of the window across the surface of the water.

With a roar, the engine engaged and the boat leaped forward, swinging sharply round and heading away from the shore, rocking from side to side as water splashed against the windows. Genie felt queasy. She shuffled round in her seat – noticing that Nathan appeared to have his eyes squeezed tight shut – and peered out of the back window. Behind them, the dimly lit building and infinite line of street lamps receded. As she watched, Genie saw the lights blinking out one by one from both directions, and when these disappearances converged on the escalator building its light too was extinguished.

Genie faced forwards again. The illumination from the red LEDs – now their sole source of light – gave the interior of the boat a peculiar, organic feel, and revealed almost nothing about the silent boatman as he guided their vehicle onwards.

Glancing at Nathan, Genie noticed that he still had his eyes shut. She leaned across.

'Are you OK?'

He shook his head.

'No. Yes. I suppose so.' His whisper was almost inaudible. 'I just don't like boats. Never have. I don't get seasick, I just... I just don't like it.'

Genie reached over, took his hand and squeezed it to reassure him. How odd that in the middle of these unearthly circumstances it was something as mundane as taking a boat trip that seemed to be the first thing to really freak Nathan out. It was also the first time she'd ever seen him display any genuine emotion.

His hand was still like ice.

'I'm sure it won't be long now.' Genie released his hand and peered out of the window again. Despite the reassurance she'd just given Nathan, there was no sign of anything out there. The dark water glinted and splashed in the faint red light from the LEDs, blood-like.

Leaning forward in her seat, Genie knocked on the glass partition separating them from the driver.

'Excuse me?' She tried to summon up the air of confidence she normally displayed when dealing with strangers these days. 'Is it possible to tell me how much longer this is going to take?'

After a second there was a faint hiss as the passenger compartment speaker switched on.

'Yes,' rumbled the driver's voice. Genie waited, but nothing more seemed to be forthcoming. She tapped on the glass again.

'Yes, very good,' a note of sarcasm had crept into her voice, 'but how long is this *actually* going to take?'

The engine revved in response and the boat rolled and pitched, flinging Genie back into her seat. Through the windows she could now make out two pale yellow globes atop a couple more lamp posts, these illuminating a short wooden pier that poked out from a shallow gravel beach. With a series of awkward manoeuvres in response to the driver's efficient grappling with the controls, the boat brought itself up alongside this as the engine coughed and died.

The driver reached up and tapped the side of the meter. The incomprehensible display changed, and he turned in his seat. There was still no detail visible within the silhouette of his head. Genie offered him a weak grin as she dug in the pockets of her dressing gown in a perfunctory manner. She turned to Nathan. He was still sitting there, rigid, eyes tightly shut.

'Hey, hey, it's OK,' Genie placed her hand on his shoulder to soothe him, 'we're here. We can get out.'

Nathan's eyes opened and he peered at her. She offered him her most winning smile, and he seemed to relax a little.

'Oh...' She pretended she'd just remembered something. 'Nathan, you don't happen to have a credit card on you, do you? I'll pay you back.' Nathan picked his satchel up from the floor and groped around inside, looking at her with an eager nod. She was ashamed to be exploiting him in such a blatant manner, but what could she do? He was wrapped round her little finger as it was.

'Yes, it's in here somewhere...' He extracted his Visa Debit card and proffered it to the driver through the small gap at the bottom of the glass screen.

He jerked forward as his entire forearm was pulled through the gap. The shape of the driver shifted with efficient movement. Nathan gasped a couple of times and then cried out before slumping back on the seat. His debit card was still held in a hand that was now bleeding from two pinprick puncture marks at the wrist. Instinctively, he raised this to his mouth and began to suck the wound. Genie sat there, mouth open.

'Sorry...'

There was a click and the door swung open, revealing the end of the pier within easy reach. Genie unfolded herself from her seat and climbed out, reaching a hand back in to help Nathan, who stumbled a little, wrist still in mouth. Even before they'd adjusted to standing on solid ground again, the boat's engine spluttered into life as it swung around and disappeared, sending a small wave washing onto the end of the pier and over their feet.

The beach sloped up to a tarmac-covered area like a small car park, illuminated by more of the spherical lamps. Beyond that loomed an indistinct, dark mass of trees. Overhead, the sky was almost imperceptibly lighter, although still containing the same disturbing half-glimpsed impossibilities in slow movement. Genie dropped her gaze back to Nathan.

He was still sucking at the wound on his wrist. Genie stepped towards him.

'Let's have a look at that...' Grabbing his forearm, she turned it wrist upwards and examined it in the yellow lamplight. The puncture wounds were tiny and there was no sign that they'd ever actually been bleeding.

Nathan was still trembling. Genie realised that it was very probably because of her touch rather than anything else and released his arm. It dropped to his side, limp.

'You'll be OK. Have you got any plasters in that bag of yours?' She reached for the satchel where it lay at his feet, but before she could touch it, he'd snatched it up and was delving around inside.

'D-don't know... I might do...' Eventually he gave up, zipped the satchel shut and hefted it over his shoulder. He looked again at his wrist.

'P-probably won't need one now.' He held his wrist towards her for approval. Genie leaned forward and looked at it, careful not to touch him this time. It was true; the wounds had virtually disappeared, well on the way to healing – they probably wouldn't even leave scars.

Genie turned back towards the shore and walked off the jetty and into the 'car park'. The only sounds were the faint whispers of ripples breaking on the gravel behind her and Nathan's footsteps as he followed her at a reverential distance. The tarmac was warm, smooth and totally clean. She could see now that there were more of the lamps among the trees ahead, illuminating a narrow ribbon of tarmac that sprouted from the edge of the car park and twisted off through the forest.

'Don't stray from the path...' muttered Genie under her breath.

'Pardon?' Nathan was close behind her now. She rolled her eyes before setting her features in a more friendly expression and turning back to him.

'Oh, nothing. Shall we be off then? Unless you want a rest or something?' Nathan shrugged and bobbed his head, which Genie took as a sign of agreement. She walked forward into the trees.

Had it not been for the unpleasant warmth of the air, the forest would have given the impression of the depths of winter – skeletal branches crowding around the path displaying not a hint of leaf. Only a few feet away on either side, the darkness swallowed up the lamps' illumination far quicker than it should, making Genie's eyes play tricks on her. Out of the corner of her eye, the mass of grey boughs shimmered and twitched, taking on other forms. And yet as soon as she looked directly at them, they were just branches again.

As they headed onward into the forest, Nathan began to walk a little closer to Genie than he had been earlier. Perhaps he was as unnerved by the silence as she was. She turned and gave him a quick smile, grateful for the company.

The path continued its gentle undulation, now leading them

downhill. Something about this bothered her. It was wrong. Why was that? After a minute or so it hit her: the water, the river, or whatever it had been – they'd started off at whatever passed for sea level in this place and were now considerably below that. Almost involuntarily Genie looked back, half expecting to see a wall of water cascading down towards them.

The flickering of the trees in the periphery of her vision started getting more pronounced. If she didn't look directly, it was almost as if there were people crouched among the branches or draped up against the trunks. Here a head, there an arm, now and then a mournful face peering at her. But no matter how quickly she turned her head they were only ever trees when she stared straight at them.

'Can you see...' she began, turning to Nathan. He nodded.

'I th-think my eyes are playing tricks. I keep seeing people.'

'Me too.' Genie grimaced. 'Must be the light. Let's keep going.'

She glanced back at the trees and out of the corner of her eye became aware that the figure of Nathan at her side was becoming a little tree-like. She glanced sharply at him. Nothing.

Without speaking a word to each other Genie and Nathan linked hands and picked up the pace. The less time she had to spend in here the better. When she was walking faster the hallucinations didn't have time to form.

After ten minutes of this, she began to feel out of breath and stopped, dropping Nathan's cold hand and bending over with her hands on her knees. Nathan continued walking.

'Wait a sec!' Genie called ahead. Nathan stumbled to a halt and walked back up to her. The downward slope was now quite pronounced. She lowered herself onto the tarmac at the edge of the path and sat down, her back against a tree. Nathan dithered for a few seconds before sitting down himself.

'Won't be a moment,' she said. 'It was just getting a bit much for a moment there. I'm not normally this unfit.' In fact she was starting to feel rather dizzy, but wasn't going to admit that. She leaned her head back against the tree trunk and stared up into the branches, not really focusing on anything.

After a few seconds, she realised that it was happening again – only this time right in front of her eyes. Up in the branches, a small figure crouched, staring at her upside down from behind a massive pair of sunglasses. A half-smile formed on its pale face.

'Genie? Babe, is that you?' came a barely audible whisper. Genie leaped up from the ground and was on the other side of the path before the figure swung itself down from the branches and stood half behind the tree, holding onto the trunk with both arms. It was a small woman with spiky purple hair, dressed in a leather jacket.

Good god, it was Wendi.

13: Wendi

Brighton, spring 2000

Thinking back, Genie knew that most of her success was thanks to Wendi. Not directly of course, but there was a very clear line of cause and effect, and if the two of them had never met, Genie's life would have been very different.

It had been the beginning of the new century, and Genie was in her first year at university, but she'd been a very different person back then, introverted and quiet. She'd worn her nondescript brown hair long and, embarrassed by her height, had stood with a stoop which meant that a lot of the time her face was hidden. Among groups of people, she tended to stand at the back, made an effort always to avoid drawing attention to herself. Introversion was just in her nature, she knew. And then there was... what had happened the previous summer. That bastard Cosmo. She still avoided thinking about it, let alone *telling* anyone. She'd hardly spoken to anyone for months.

By the spring term of that first year though, Genie realised that if she was going to make the most of her university years, she was really going to have to do something about this chronic shyness. That... unpleasant encounter at the Reading Festival was in the *past*, she kept telling herself. She wasn't a sixth-former any more; it was about time a new Genie rose from the ashes of the subservient schoolgirl, the bullied teenager. With this in mind, she joined the Student Union ENTS committee.

Not a lot changed. She was still standing at the back. But her new responsibilities meant that she was moving in wider and more extrovert circles than before. She hoped that perhaps something of this would rub off on her.

At the beginning of the summer term everyone was talking about Beam. They'd been booked to play the university some months ago, but since then had had a couple of minor chart hits, and were now very much the top choice of the student indie-kid scene. For the first time in ages, ENTS had something big on their hands.

Genie didn't know much about them other than that they were the band with that rather scary-looking woman singer Duncan in her corridor had a picture of on his study-bedroom door. At first she used to think it was their music he was always playing, but that time a bunch of students had piled into his room one evening after coming back from the bar she realised that his walls were covered with posters of bands she'd never heard of, exotic names like *Stereolab, Mojave 3, Chapterhouse* and *Sonic Youth*...

She'd eventually caught Beam on *Top of the Pops* a few weeks ago; as she'd suspected from the sounds emanating from Duncan's room, they weren't the kind of thing she associated with *Top of the Pops* at all. They were far stranger than the pop she'd been into as a child and free from the judgemental attitude of those bands that had been around when she was at school who had made her think their music wasn't for her. Once unmuffled by the walls of Duncan's room it was clear that this music was... different, refreshing, exciting. Thoughtful.

She kind of liked it.

During the afternoon of the gig Genie and her fellow ENTS members bustled about, getting everything ready for their VIP guests. A large seminar room on the top floor of the building that also held the concert hall had been set aside, its brown plastic chairs lined up against the wall or removed to the corridor outside and desks pushed together and covered with paper tablecloths. The caterers were due to deliver the more perishable items at the beginning of the evening, but there was still plenty to do. Genie spent the best part of an hour walking back and forth across campus fetching the drinks – a couple of crates of beer, a case of wine, five litre bottles of vodka, a number of cartons of fresh orange juice and two bottles of sparkling mineral water. She wondered how many of them there were in the band and just how drunk they were intending to get.

A couple of vans had been parked outside all afternoon, and earlier on a small squad of indistinguishable hairy men dressed in black had been carrying a series of equally indistinguishable large matt black boxes through the building's service entrance.

Josh, head of ENTS, asked Genie to stand guard outside the seminar room (which had been rechristened 'Large Dressing Room' with a sheet of A4, a magic marker and some sellotape) and let the caterers in.

She could hear distant thumps, bangs and fragments of loud music down in the hall, but the floor she was on remained deserted. She sat down on one of the plastic chairs and closed her eyes.

The fragments of music got longer and more coherent. Songs started and restarted, the details blurred by distance and the intervening walls. It was loud.

After about half an hour, silence fell again. After a while Genie began to wonder whether she'd been forgotten.

Round a corner at the end of the corridor, a bell rang and the rumble of lift doors opening announced someone's arrival. Genie stood up and did her best to look attentive and helpful. A tall, slim businessman in an immaculate suit stalked into view and looked about before spotting Genie and making a beeline for her.

'Malcolm Hooke, Mallard Music,' he said, grabbing Genie's hand with a clammy one of his own and squeezing it briefly. 'I take it you're ENTS?'

Genie nodded and gestured at the dressing room door.

'Excellent,' said the Businessman, reaching for the handle and walking quickly through, Genie at his heels. He looked around the room critically, and then glanced at Genie.

'Food not here yet?'

'I'm just waiting for it,' said Genie. The Businessman nodded as if to himself.

'Ah well, the drink's here anyway, which is all they're really interested in now they've finished the sound check. Can you keep an eye on this' – he placed his briefcase on one of the chairs – 'while I go and fetch them?' Without waiting for an answer he hurried off, leaving Genie alone again.

The catering staff chose this moment to knock on the door and Genie spent a few panicked minutes supervising the unloading of a cargo of triangular sandwiches, plates of fruit and a number of large bowls of nibbles, while all the time keeping half an eye on the briefcase. As she ushered the caterers and their empty trolleys out, she spotted the Businessman at the end of the corridor talking to Josh. She backed into the room again and shut the door.

Thirty seconds later it opened again and the Businessman came in, followed by three young men who almost immediately descended upon the food and drink. They were all dressed in a similar manner, black jeans, DMs and dark T-shirts emblazoned with various brightly coloured, incomprehensible slogans. Josh entered in their wake and walked over to Genie, grinning in a manner that suggested he thought of the two of them as conspirators. It was odd, thought Genie, because normally he didn't have time for her. The Businessman left the room again.

She assumed that the three young men were the band, but where was the scary woman? Even though she'd never even heard of her until a couple of weeks previously when Duncan had insisted on watching *Top of the Pops* in the common room, Genie was starting to be nervous of her. She wasn't at all sure why. The strange music had lodged in her head, but it was more than just that. There was an inexplicable sense of anticipation in the air. Josh wandered over to the band and seemed to be trying to interest them in something, although from the looks on their faces Genie could tell he wasn't having much luck.

The Businessman came back, deep in conversation with one of the Indistinguishable Hairy Men from downstairs.

'We'll send the girl,' he said, indicating Genie with a hand gesture without even looking at her. The hairy man nodded and walked over to Genie smiling.

'Hi there,' he said. 'Do you think you could do us a favour?' Genie was surprised at how cultured his voice sounded. Behind the hair, beard and *Saxon* T-shirt he was almost avuncular. Genie flashed a small smile at him.

'I'm Jake, by the way,' he said, reaching out with a weather-beaten hand. 'I'm the sound man.' Genie shook the hand, which was warm and dry.

'Genie,' she said. 'Er... how can I help?'

'Just wondered if you could take some stuff through to

Wendi?' he said, indicating a tray on which someone had placed one of the vodka bottles, an orange-juice carton and, almost as an afterthought, one apple and a couple of triangular sandwiches. 'She's in the room next door – likes to get ready on her own sometimes.'

The 'Small Dressing Room' was the next door along the corridor – normally an office where tutors prepared their seminars. Balancing the tray on her right arm, Genie knocked twice. A muffled voice from within indicated that she should come in.

The scary-looking woman sat in a leather swivel chair in front of the desk, swinging it from side to side as she regarded Genie over the tops of her oversized sunglasses. She was far smaller than Genie had been expecting; on TV she'd seemed a huge, wild spitfire who filled the screen whereas here she barely filled the chair, her feet – clad in oversized motorcycle boots – not quite touching the ground. The leather jacket and dark top she was wearing almost made her body disappear against the leather of the chair which gave the unnerving impression of her head being suspended from a bright-purple mess of short, spiky hair. She leaned forward and pulled her feet up to sit cross-legged on the chair.

'Hi. You can put that over here.' Her voice was quiet; quite a contrast to the confident, angry singing Genie had witnessed on *Top of the Pops*. As instructed, Genie placed the tray on the desk and began to back out of the room.

'No, don't go yet! Sit down!' The woman grinned. With a flick of her wrist she sent her swivel chair into a brief spin before bringing it to an abrupt halt by grabbing the edge of the desk. The vodka bottle wobbled a little on its tray. Ever obedient, Genie sat down on a flimsy orange plastic chair and tried not to stare at this odd woman who was now holding her hand out to be shaken.

'I'm Wendi. What's your name?'

Genie told her.

Without waiting for the handshake, Wendi swung the chair around to face the desk and pulled a couple of empty plastic pint glasses towards her while one-handedly unscrewing the top of the vodka bottle. 'Do you want a drink?'

Genie nodded, noticing that the mirror that had been propped up against the back of the desk had slipped down and now lay flat, reflecting part of a strip light with the remains of Christmas streamers sellotaped to one end of it.

With rapt concentration, Wendi half filled one of the pint glasses with vodka, topping it up with orange juice before pushing the spare glass, the bottle and the carton across to Genie.

'Have as much as you like.'

Genie, still wide-eyed at Wendi's apparent appetite for alcohol, gave a meek nod and poured a sensible centimetre into the bottom of the glass before drowning it in orange.

'Cheers,' said Wendi, and knocked back half the contents of her pint glass in one go. Genie's mouth dropped open. Wendi regarded her over the tops of her shades, amused.

'I'll be fine,' she said, and coughed. 'Vodka always wakes me up. Better than coffee really. What did you say your name was?'

'Genie,' said Genie. 'Actually Eugenie, but no one calls me that.'

'No one calls me by my real name either,' said Wendi, 'but that's mostly 'cause I don't tell anyone what it is. This is my joke name.'

Genie looked blank.

'Wendi House, geddit?'

'Er...' began Genie.

'My surname's House.' Wendi leaned forward. 'I tried to get

Pete to change his surname to Pan but he wasn't having any of it.' Genie's confusion must have showed on her face, because Wendi continued, 'Pete's the guitar player. And resident genius. Or so he says. Tell you what, shall we have some of this?'

Wendi reached into her leather jacket and pulled out a silver box the size of a cigarette packet. Placing it on the horizontal mirror she extracted a short straw, a credit card and a tiny paper packet, which, once she had unwrapped it, was full of what looked like sherbet. Genie had absolutely no idea what was going on, but once Wendi had ladled a small amount of powder onto the mirror's surface and began pushing it into short lines with the credit card, it came to her and she went cold with fear. Drugs.

'I bet I'm coming across a bit posh what with all the Peter Pan stuff...' Wendi went on, but Genie couldn't focus on what was being said. It was happening right in front of her – something she'd heard of but hadn't imagined she'd actually come across. Drugs. There'd been a song about it, hadn't there... 'White Lines – Don't Do It'. She'd never known exactly what that had meant until now, and was overwhelmed by an irrational fear that she was somehow going to drop dead before leaving the room. It had been drummed into her at home and at school. Drugs equals Bad. It was a simple equation, similar to the childhood rule Don't Take Sweets From Strangers. She still remembered the fear that had overwhelmed her when, aged four, an old woman had offered her an orange. She'd been convinced that something awful had been going to happen as a result...

But nothing had happened in the end, had it? Perhaps she was overreacting now as well? She watched with a horrified fascination as Wendi leaned over the mirror and hoovered up a line of powder into each nostril. On a deeply buried mischievous level, Genie was finding this rather exciting.

Wendi looked up and offered her the straw with a wide grin. There was a short battle between Genie's fear and her excited curiosity, but the balance was tipped by her natural inclination to do as she was told. She took the straw and moved to lean over the mirror.

'Hang on, let me…' said Wendi.

Genie felt small, cold hands gathering her long hair into an impromptu ponytail and realised that it wouldn't get in the way now. Her reflection in the mirror was bizarre from this angle. She looked up and over her shoulder at Wendi, still grinning, her oversized shades slipping down her nose to reveal heavily made-up eyes.

'Block up your other nostril, see?' Wendi reached forward with the hand that wasn't holding Genie's hair back and pressed Genie's left nostril shut. Genie manoeuvred the straw above the line and sniffed, unconsciously copying what she'd seen Wendi do earlier.

Instantly, the inside of her nose was burning with a cold, caustic rasp that made her want to sneeze. She jerked her head up, blinking.

'Now the other side,' came Wendi's voice. Genie blocked the abused nostril with her own finger this time as she subjected its twin to the same punishment. This time the cold fire wasn't as bad. Or was it simply that she now knew what to expect? She sat up straight and Wendi released her hair.

'Not so bad after all, eh?'

Genie nodded. It wasn't that bad, although she still felt as if she was going to sneeze, and if anything, a little as if she'd started coming down with a cold. Not exactly exciting, but not frightening either. Was she meant to be feeling something else? She shivered.

'People always make such a big deal out of it,' Wendi went on, 'but it's just fun.'

Genie shifted uncomfortably in her chair, glancing around. She should be doing something. 'Maybe I should be...?'

'No, stay a while!' said Wendi. 'I hate this bit, nice to have someone to talk to. The boys are always too busy taking the piss out of each other and Malcolm's just busy.' There was a knock on the door.

'Later!' shouted Wendi without taking her eyes off Genie. 'That was probably him,' she continued. 'He's our tour manager. Always *fussing* around over me, but he's all right I suppose. Could be worse, like that last guy we had. Gave me the creeps, he did. Looked like someone's uncle.'

Genie coughed – she could feel something sliding down the back of her throat and her teeth felt funny. A bit like having an injection at the dentist. She clicked her jaws together a couple of times in an experimental manner.

'A creepy uncle,' said Wendi, taking off her shades. 'The kind of perv your parents don't ask to babysit.' She twirled her shades around in one hand while rubbing at her eyes with the other. Without any warning she froze.

'Fuckit! Shit! I keep doing that!' She leaned over the mirror and peered down at her eye make-up, absently dabbing at the flecks of white powder with her index finger and licking it. 'No, looks OK. Lucky I remembered in time.' She bounced up out of her chair and was standing right in front of Genie, too close, shades once more in place.

'Can you show me where the toilet is, please?' Ironic little-girl voice.

'OK.' Genie stood up. 'Probably at the end of the corridor over the bridge thing.'

'Let's go!' Wendi opened the door and peered through the crack. 'Coast's clear!' Genie followed her out into the corridor and in what she hoped was the direction of the toilets. As they walked Wendi barely reached Genie's shoulder, but was so alive and powerful that it didn't show. In a peculiar way she was somehow far more *real* than the everyday people Genie was used to.

'I've never been allowed up on this level before,' said Genie. 'Not until today when we were setting things up.'

'Hallowed halls, eh?' said Wendi. They went through a double door and onto the 'bridge', a section of corridor that crossed the upper reaches of the concert hall with a spectacular view of the stage. Jake and a couple of the other Indistinguishable Hairy Men were tinkering with some complex-looking equipment in prime position.

'Jake-O,' Wendi murmured, grabbing Genie's hand and hurrying them past. Jake smiled.

The corridor re-entered the main part of the building again and up ahead Genie was relieved to see the toilets.

The door to the gents opened as they approached, and one of the young men from the Large Dressing Room emerged, raising his eyebrows at Wendi. 'Toilet!' Wendi screeched at him, smiling. 'That's Pete,' she explained after he'd passed.

They entered the ladies (labelled 'female' in keeping with the rather right-on reputation of the university) and Wendi jumped into a cubicle.

'Won't be long,' she said. 'You don't mind waiting for me, do you?'

Genie didn't mind. She didn't feel as if she had a cold any more and her numb teeth had ceased to bother her. In fact, she was oddly excited, a feeling of tingling anticipation building in her spine and, catching sight of herself in the mirror, she saw that she was now grinning. It was an unfamiliar sight – she usually avoided looking in mirrors and couldn't quite recall if she'd ever seen herself smiling before. She bounced up and down on the balls of her feet, humming under her breath. Her reflection did the same, although it no longer looked like her. It looked like the person that deep down she'd always wanted to be – confident and extrovert. A superhero version of herself.

The sound of the toilet flush brought her back to reality, and she turned as Wendi emerged and bounded over to the sink to wash her hands. Moments later they were in the corridor again and heading back. Jake was nowhere to be seen as they passed his equipment on the bridge, but as they approached the door to the Small Dressing Room, Businessman Malcolm appeared.

'All right, sweetheart?' he asked Wendi. 'Do you need anything? Are they looking after you?'

'I'm fine,' said Wendi, grabbing Genie by the hand and pulling her towards the door.

'I just want you to remember,' Businessman went on, increasing the volume of his voice slightly, 'that we've got those interviews tomorrow morning. There's BBC Radio at eleven and then those people from *Indie Cator* magazine are coming to the hotel at midday. They're doing a photo shoot on the beach, so try not to overdo it too much tonight, yeah?'

'Yeah, yeah...' Wendi muttered under her breath as she dragged Genie inside the dressing room and closed the door. 'See what I mean? He's always *fussing...*'

Five minutes later Genie was astonished to find herself deep in conversation. She'd never felt this talkative before in her life, and was asking Wendi what it was like doing interviews and how she worked out what to say.

'Oh no, I don't bother to plan anything.' Wendi shook her head. 'I just say the first thing that comes into my head. It doesn't really make much difference what I say most of the time; a lot of these journos are so obsessed with their own cleverness that they've usually written half the interview before they even turn up.'

'They don't write bad things about you though, do they?'

'Not often,' Wendi grinned, 'but I'm sure they'll start soon. Build 'em up, knock 'em down and all that stuff.' She reached for the vodka bottle and poured herself another half pint before handing it to Genie who, bolder now, poured herself two centimetres before topping it up with orange juice. Wendi picked up one of the limp sandwiches and examined it closely before flinging it across the room and into the bin. At precisely that moment there was a colossal drunken cheer from the Large Dressing Room next door, and the two of them dissolved into hysterics.

There was another knock on the door and after a few seconds Josh poked his head in.

'Everything all right here?' he asked with a polite smile. Genie blushed and started worrying that he might think she was skiving. As if she'd picked up on this Wendi grabbed Genie's hand.

'Absolutely fine.' She squeezed, stroking Genie's palm with a finger. 'Genie's doing a great job looking after me.'

'Brill, cheers,' said Josh. 'Just to let you know we're opening the doors now. The support's only doing half an hour, so you should be on at nine.'

Genie widened her eyes, and once Josh had left, looked at her watch. It was already after seven.

'Time flies,' said Wendi. 'What say we have a little top-up?' She reached into her jacket for the drugs while a low, repetitive thumping started up in the distance as the DJ went to work.

14: Live

Brighton, spring 2000

An hour later, after Wendi excused herself to get ready, Genie made her way to watch the show from the bridge next to the sound desk as Wendi had suggested. Walking along the corridor, Genie felt extraordinary. Surely *this* was what life was really like – standing tall and proud rather than stooping in corners hiding? She pushed open the door to the bridge and was assaulted by the noise, the smell, the darkness shot through with unexpected flashes of vivid colour. The DJ was back, playing something rhythmical, something half familiar, but louder even than that was the noise of the crowd down below. Leaning her elbows on the parapet, she looked down at the assembled throng pulsing and flowing like microbes under a microscope. Tendrils of cigarette smoke reached up to her, adding an abrasive texture to the stench of spilled beer and sweat filling the hall. Even from this height, Genie could feel the overpowering heat radiating off the mob and the sweat starting to bead and trickle on her back.

She looked to one side at the huge black installation of the sound desk at the centre of which sat Jake. A hundred tiny coloured lights illuminated his face with shifting patterns: he was a wizard. Genie knew he was aware of her but was concentrating too hard on what he was doing to offer any acknowledgement.

Genie looked back down at the stage, bathed in red light, and as she did so, the solid mass of bodies down there all began pressing eagerly forward towards it – they could tell something was about to happen.

The DJ's music faded, the light dimmed further and melodic thunder filled the hall. Out of the corner of her eye Genie could see the precise movements of Jake the Wizard as he went to work. Three figures strode out onto the stage below as the crowd shrieked their approval. These were the three young men she'd met earlier in the Large Dressing Room; now they moved with significant purpose, technician-priests of a new religion. Strapping on instruments as if donning armour, they joined in with the thunder which picked up pace and became urgent and percussive. The guitars made noises Genie hadn't thought were possible, howls and shimmering roars rather than the riffs and rhythms. The sounds were familiar from what she'd heard through Duncan's walls, but a thousand times louder, a million times more moving.

A woman ran out and stood motionless at the centre of the stage, head bowed despite the renewed hysteria of the audience. Then she looked up and started singing. The howls and roars fell into formation behind the clear sound of her voice and surged forward.

Genie had never heard or seen anything like it. She'd been too young to go and see any of the pop bands she'd liked as a kid, and her Reading Festival trip the previous year had been… cut short, so her experience of *live* music was limited to the jazz bands that had played at lunchtime at the pub in the village where she'd grown up.

This on the other hand, *this* was perhaps what Live Aid had been like, an event she had hazy memories of seeing on

TV when a child. The music added power to the euphoria already peaking in her head and took her to a whole new level. Without a conscious decision, she started dancing in place.

The song ended, supplanted by another, slower number, menace and power building behind a melodic facade. The heat in the room continued to rise as the crowd boiled; Genie pulled off her T-shirt and continued dancing in her bra, barely aware of the sideways glance and raised eyebrows from Jake up in his technological nest of light and sound. As she gyrated, the sweat and the moisture in the air conspired to turn her hair into sodden ropes, tentacles that slapped her back and flicked water into her eyes.

A gnarled hand clutching a plastic bottle appeared in front of her face. Jake had come down from his tower and was offering her a drink of water. She accepted it from him with a grin and drank it down in large, greedy swigs. The icy coldness trickling down her throat gave her a new lease of life, and when the next song started her dancing became even more frenetic.

It was the one she knew! The one she'd seen on *Top of the Pops*. But hearing and seeing it played here it was... so much bigger, the wry sarcasm of the vocals now full-on scorn, the sound of the guitars now unrestrained by the cage of television. And yet the familiarity added a dimension too; Genie could anticipate that little melody as it went into the chorus, brace herself for it. As Wendi sang down below, Genie joined in with what she remembered of the words. When the song ended, it was time for a short rest – singing as well as dancing had taken it out of her a little. She turned and sat on the floor, back against the balustrade, legs stretched out in front. She pushed sodden hair out of her face, slicking it back from her forehead.

There was a figure standing a few feet away, watching her.

She had no idea how long he'd been there. It was Businessman, the tour manager. She caught his eye as he strolled over to her, his suit still immaculate despite the atmosphere.

'Enjoying the show?' He bent forward, hands on knees. As luck would have it, Genie had no trouble hearing him; the band were now playing a slow, ethereal number, vocals murmured over a tide of melancholy, minor-key waves that rose and fell. She nodded.

'Good,' he said, straightening up and gazing over the parapet at his current protégée. Unsure what was expected of her, Genie continued sitting down for a minute or so before standing up again and watching the band. Another louder song followed the quiet, slow one, more upbeat, and Genie once more felt the urge to dance. As she began to move, Businessman looked her up and down and smiled before walking off towards the door to the corridor. But he slipped from her mind as she once more succumbed to the music.

15: Aftershow

Brighton, spring 2000

The show was over. Genie couldn't have said how long it had actually lasted; all she knew was that it hadn't been long enough. The band had departed the stage and the main lights had come up, revealing the venue as the dull glass chamber of academia in which a large number of engineering students would be sitting their finals in a few weeks. An omniscient goddess, Genie looked down on the departing crowd as they stumbled out through the main doors, a few intoxicated boys emphasising their shouts with wild and unsteady gesticulation in an attempt to impress some of the women there. The indistinguishable hairy men had re-emerged and were closing in on the equipment abandoned on stage, their efforts directed by Jake who had disappeared from his post at the sound desk and reappeared down below without crossing the intervening space.

Genie still felt powerful and happy, but this mood was tinged with sadness – this experience would be ending soon.

'Hey, ENTS girl!' Genie turned to see Businessman poking his head out onto the bridge from the corridor door and looking directly at her. 'Wendi was wondering if you were going to join us for a drink.' Genie nodded and picked up her sopping wet T-shirt, shivering as she slipped it over her head, the cold dampness of it against her skin bringing her out in goosebumps. She followed Businessman down the corridor towards the Large Dressing Room, and entered it behind him.

The room was much more crowded than earlier. There was a whole new contingent present who were nothing to do with the university but apparently knew the band and entourage well. Businessman made a beeline for a couple of affluent types and Genie got the impression that he was carrying on where he had left off. A couple of the lads from the band had women sitting on their laps. It was a party, but the fluorescent light in the room gave the whole thing an unreal aura.

'All right?' A small voice at Genie's elbow. She looked down to see Wendi, her shades pushed back on her head as an impromptu hairband and eyes now clean of war paint. 'Did you enjoy the show?'

Genie nodded – she wasn't quite sure what one said in these situations. Of course she'd enjoyed it, it had been incredible, but what was the right thing to... She frowned as she realised that her default state of anxiety and uncertainty was reasserting itself.

'It was amazing,' she said. Wendi reached up and touched Genie's T-shirt.

'You're soaked!' she said. 'D'you wanna get changed or something? We've got plenty of spare T-shirts.'

'Yes, that'd be nice.' Genie realised that she must have looked a fright.

Wendi grabbed Genie by the wrist, pulling her towards the door. As they crossed the room Genie saw that half the people in the room had an eye on them, some surreptitiously, others more obvious.

They were out in the corridor for only a second before slipping into the Small Dressing Room next door.

'You're a lifesaver, I needed a break from that lot.' Wendi rummaged around in a large black holdall.

'Who *were* that lot?'

'Mostly record company, management.' Wendi pulled a black T-shirt out of the bag. 'A couple of journos, you know the sort...' She held the T-shirt out to Genie, looking up at her. Without the make-up, she looked considerably younger than she had earlier. Genie was struck by just how thin she was.

'Thanks.' Genie held the T-shirt up for inspection; it was mostly black but had a small red logo on the front which consisted of the word *Beam* on the left breast with a red line slashing across towards the right.

'It's supposed to be a laser,' said Wendi. 'Hope it fits.'

Genie peeled off her old drenched garment, dropping it on the floor as she slipped the new T-shirt over her head. It smelled artificial, a somehow comforting scent of ink and plastic. It covered her fine although it was a little snug. Wendi was bent over the mirror again preparing them some more drugs, and a strange conflict stirred in Genie. Inside, part of her was salivating at the prospect of more of this stuff, but a small voice of dissent now wondered if perhaps she'd had enough. She ignored the latter and joined Wendi at the mirror.

Two minutes later, they rejoined the party in the Large Dressing Room, and a short while after that, Genie was perched uncomfortably on the edge of a plastic-covered table, sipping weak beer from a bottle as some bloke whose name she couldn't remember held forth at great length about how casinos were the next big thing. Not listening, she watched Wendi make her way around the room, talking to the right people and making the right noises – and of course making the wrong noises at the right moments to everyone's obvious delight. She was in great demand. At one point, Businessman escorted a young Japanese couple into the room who posed for photographs with Wendi before being escorted out again in a polite but firm manner.

Casino Guy had disappeared, but before Genie could make any plans he reappeared at her side with a freshly opened beer bottle for her. She thanked him and took a swig as he resumed his monologue.

At around midnight, the party started faltering and a large proportion of the supernumerary bodies vanished – including Casino Guy. Businessman was trying to wind things down, despite the stubborn attempts of the band to carry on drinking.

'Come on, lads,' he said. 'There's plenty more of that back at the hotel.'

Genie stood up, figuring it was about time she made an exit. As she did so, Wendi caught her eye and hurried over.

'You off then? Well thanks for everything. It was good to meet you.'

'It was good to meet you too,' said Genie.

'Tell you what, why don't you give me your address? I'll write to you.'

'Sure.' Genie looked around for a pen and paper, a little puzzled by this continued attention. Perhaps it was just a gesture, like the exchange of addresses at the end of a week's holiday.

As she wrote down her details on the back of a flyer Genie's head spun and her vision blurred for a moment. The evening was starting to catch up with her. She was worried she was going to be sick. The best way to avoid embarrassment was to remove herself from the situation as quickly as possible. Businessman was observing their transaction, a faint smile on his face.

'OK, I'd better go then…'

Wendi looked awkward and then reached out and touched Genie's arm for a second.

'See you around, yeah? I'll write to you.'

Genie half ran down the stairs thinking how odd that promise was – they'd only just met. Why had... She had to get out, she didn't want to throw up in here. The jolt of her footsteps threw bolts of pain up into the base of her skull and the fluorescent lighting assaulted her eyeballs. Finally she reached the fire door and burst through out into the balmy night air of the deserted campus. She collapsed to the grass and lay down, closing her eyes and taking deep breaths as the nausea subsided. In the distance a gaggle of seagulls were squabbling. She opened her eyes. She'd left her original T-shirt behind, but wasn't going to go back for it now. Standing up, she started walking towards the halls of residence.

Fifteen minutes later, she was lying in bed with the lights out and curtains closed, having avoided talking to anyone on the way back to her room. Her mind was trembling and the beginnings of a massive and yet strangely numb headache rolled over her brain. Tiny vignettes from her memories of the evening started flashing up on the internal screen of her mind's eye, far brighter and more vivid than she was used to.

Wendi holding her hair for her. Jake offering her the water bottle. Businessman leaning down to talk to her. Wendi spinning in the swivel chair. Dancing on the bridge. Cold hands. Hey, ENTS girl. A creepy uncle. BBC Radio at eleven. Singing along. Wendi holding her hair. Water bottle. Businessman. Mallard Music. Swivel chair. Shaking hands with Jake. Time flies. We'll send the girl. Triangular sandwiches. Swivel chair. Hair. Spinning. Creepy uncle. Time flies. Water. Time. Wendi. Uncle. Spinning. Swivel...

She turned over on her side in an attempt to block the cascade of imagery that was overwhelming her and felt a change within her. Something was rising.

16: Sorted

Brighton, summer 2000

A month after their first meeting at the student concert, Wendi had indeed written to Genie as she'd promised. A large Jiffy bag turned up in the pigeonhole downstairs at the residences, inside which was her old T-shirt, freshly laundered, and a note handwritten in large, childlike letters on a postcard of the Üetliberg Tower. Genie had been worried that she was losing the confidence that night had given her and was delighted to find that receipt of this parcel brought it roaring back.

hi genie

i am writing this by a lake in switzerland which is where we are having lunch today. the tour is going well; tonight we are playing in a tiny club in Zurich. i washed your t-shirt for you. i hope to see you when we get back. i will let you know when the next gig near you is, or perhaps you could come up to london?

love wendi (beam) x

Genie let it be known that the singer from Beam – who

had since appeared on *Top of the Pops* a second time – had written her a personal letter. She was loath to actually show it to anyone, although she did relent and let Duncan read it – he was so excited and jealous that it would have been cruel not to. Genie got the distinct impression that he wanted to sleep with her, and toyed with the idea of encouraging him. Up until now, she hadn't had much luck with boys and hadn't really wanted to. Her terrifying experience with Cosmo the previous summer had frightened her off – did she really *want* her luck to change if they were all like *him*?

She wasn't sure if a dalliance with one of her fellow students was what she was after anyway – they were so childish. Eventually she decided that it might be useful to *imply* to Duncan that she could be interested at some point, so if in the meantime he felt like doing things for her...

She knew this was a bit mean, but Duncan enjoyed giving her the attention. In fact he always looked more miserable when he *wasn't* doing something for her.

It wasn't just Duncan either. Her experience with Wendi had given Genie a certain amount of cool by association and she started to find herself the centre of attention in the Student Union bar. After a while, this itself had as much of an effect on her confidence as the brief time she'd spent with Wendi – she was standing up straighter, dressing up more and wearing more elaborate make-up. She even had her hair cut shorter.

One night, when some rugby club oaf had been buying her drinks all evening, she caught sight of Duncan's expression in the mirror behind the bar. He looked upset. Very upset. In fact she could have sworn he was close to tears. Genie realised that it was because of her – because she was talking to the oaf. Was she being cruel? She couldn't live her life only doing what would make some boy happy. Besides, the power she had over Duncan was almost... magical.

It was because of her.

There was a warm glow in the pit of her stomach. She turned away from the oaf and smiled warmly at Duncan. It was amazing to watch his expression change. It was like using a remote control. Duncan said something, but she couldn't make it out over the noise, so she leaned in close to him. 'What was that?'

Duncan was momentarily confused. 'Er... well...'

Genie placed one hand on his shoulder to steady herself and he dropped his pint. The plastic glass bounced on impact with the floor, lager flying out and drenching the bottom of Genie's jeans.

'You idiot!' she snapped. From the look on his face he was probably in danger of crying again, so she swiped playfully at his arm, grinning, 'What are you like?' Behind her, the oaf forced out a raucous laugh. Genie decided that the best way to respond to that was to ignore him.

'Come on,' she continued, taking a firm hold of Duncan's upper arm in one hand and steering him towards the exit, 'I need to get changed. You can look after this for me.' She shoved the half-finished bottle of Becks into his hand.

It was a relief to be outside after spending so long in the smelly confines of the bar, and Genie took a deep breath of the cool air before striding across the darkened campus, Duncan trailing in her wake still holding her beer.

Within a couple of minutes, she was bounding up the steps to their block in the halls of residence. She waited for Duncan to catch up before entering the door code, and together they went inside.

It was very quiet as they walked along their corridor – half the students were still out, and the other, more studious half probably in bed. Up until recently, Genie would probably have been among the latter. They passed Duncan's door, from which that picture of Wendi's face still scowled. Inside her head, Genie said hello.

'Tell you what,' she said as they reached her door. 'Why don't you go and make me a cup of tea?'

'Sure!' Duncan nodded and scampered off towards the kitchen as Genie unlocked her room and entered. Kicking off her sandals, she rifled through the chest of drawers for some replacement jeans. Nothing suitable. Instead she pulled out a skirt and flung it on the bed. She was enjoying the effect she was having on Duncan; it was why she'd brought him back with her instead of leaving him in the bar. Was that bad of her? No, she decided, he was far happier coming with her. Just as she removed her jeans, there was a knock at the door.

'I've got your tea...'

'Come in!' Genie trilled. Duncan entered the room, a mug in one hand, her beer still clutched in the other. Genie watched the blush spread over his pale face as he caught sight of her bare legs and then, in an attempt to be gentlemanly, averted his eyes.

'Oh thank you, you're brilliant,' she said, walking over to him and taking the mug. She turned and took a sip from it before placing it on the desk. 'Have a seat, I won't be a minute!' Duncan flopped down into the easy chair and buried his face in a copy of the student magazine, *Pulse*. Genie stood there regarding him for a few seconds. She was sure that he wasn't taking any of it in; it was only a pity he hadn't picked it up upside down. He was spoiling her fun by being too polite to sneak another look at her, so she donned the skirt, put her sandals back on and took another gulp of tea.

'Come on! Chop-chop!' she said. Duncan looked up from the magazine to find her standing over him.

'Oh, OK...' He retrieved her beer from where he'd placed it on the floor beside the chair and handed it up to her. She took it and extended a hand to help him up from the chair. His hand was clammy, and he was trembling a little. Genie downed the rest of the bottle in one and dropped the empty straight into her wastepaper basket.

'You can buy me another one,' she grinned and held the door open for him.

Outside, the moon was now visible over the crest of the hill, outshining the inadequate lighting and changing the whole mood of the campus. Genie was about to burst with irrational excitement – as if something was about to happen – and smiled as she skipped down the steps of the residence with Duncan in tow. As they approached the road, a large car pulled up, from which a small figure emerged and began walking towards them.

'Hiya!' said Wendi. 'I was in town!' Genie's mouth dropped open, but before she could say anything she caught a glimpse of movement out of the corner of her eye and turned just in time to see Duncan bursting into tears.

Genie sat back as the car accelerated off campus, leaving the tearful Duncan on the steps of the halls of residence. Wendi was kneeling up on the seat next to her, craning over the back to rummage in a large carrier bag. The slim legs clad in oversized motorcycle boots seemed far too small to belong to someone so famous.

Being confronted with the real Wendi again was overwhelming. Ever since those hours with her back at the gig, Genie had been surrounded by fellow students who wanted to be – or simply wanted – Wendi. Now she was being granted something Duncan would have gnawed his own arm off for.

She didn't quite know what to do with it but, rather than letting this worry her, the new improved Genie was enjoying the ride.

The car swept around the slip road onto the dual carriageway leading into town, and Wendi fell awkwardly across Genie's lap, her shades falling off into the footwell. The shock of this sudden physical contact hammered home the situation. What was she getting herself into?

'Are you OK?' Genie reached down and felt around on the floor. Wendi just flung a weird grin at her, widening her black-rimmed eyes, and lay there for a second before pulling herself upright and settling back into the seat next to Genie.

'Yeah. Got them!' In one hand she brandished a cigarette packet that she dropped into Genie's lap.

'S'OK, I don't smoke,' said Genie, handing Wendi the shades. Wendi pulled a faux shocked face as she stuffed them into her jacket pocket.

'We're doing some more interviews in town tomorrow. Malcolm thought it would be cool to shoot some film for the next video on the beach.' Wendi opened the cigarette packet – which Genie could now see didn't contain any cigarettes – felt around inside, and pulled out a small plastic bag containing a few white pills. 'How about Es? Do you do them?'

'I don't... I've never...' began Genie, a tendril of fear and exhilaration curling up from the pit of her stomach. Wendi licked her lips.

'Perfect! The first one's always the best.' She leaned in and held a pill up to Genie's mouth. Genie stuck out her tongue and took it quickly, swallowing before she had a chance to change her mind.

'I thought we'd go to a club.' Wendi tipped two tablets into her own palm and tossed them back before turning to Genie again. Her breath smelled of vodka and cigarettes. Genie found this exotic. It was certainly better than the stale beer and armpits of the union bar she'd been enduring – what, less than twenty minutes ago? How was it possible for an evening to change so radically? All she'd had to look forward to earlier was toying with Duncan some more, and now... she had no idea what lay ahead.

Wendi kneeled up on the seat again and leaned forward, chin on the driver's headrest.

'Skip? You know The Underground, don't you?' The driver nodded and said something about the boys already being there.

The street lamps flew past as if they were rushing through hyperspace; ahead every traffic signal turned green as they approached. Genie wondered how long it would take before the E affected her and what it would feel like. Despite the speed of their passage, Wendi was impatient, bouncing up and down in her seat like an impatient child, staring out of the window and reaching back again to rummage in the carrier bag.

The car slowed as they reached the seafront and pulled up in front of a building right in the heart of town. Wendi exploded from the car and stood on the pavement as Genie emerged.

It was like stepping from a spacecraft onto the surface of an alien world. After the quiet enclave of the campus, the street was bright and noisy. It was much warmer; the combined smell of car fumes, frying onions and the sea reminded Genie of holidays in Barbados with her parents. Clots of raucous young people shrieking at each other pushed past them. Somewhere nearby, a bottle smashed and people cheered.

'I've only got a couple of quid on me...' said Genie as the car pulled away. Wendi donned her shades and grabbed Genie's wrist, pulling her in the direction of a wide-fronted pub, a building hiding its age with a coat of thick white paint.

'Don't worry about it. My treat.'

Instead of heading up the steps to the entrance, Wendi

ducked to one side and slipped through a gap in the railings in front of the pub basement. Genie followed her down a set of narrow stone stairs to a doorway almost hidden from the street. A man with pink hair dressed in a black rubber top was perched on a stool behind a narrow counter reading a fat Stephen King paperback. He looked up and his expression changed.

'Oh! It's... hi...'

'Two, please.' Wendi held up a twenty-pound note.

Pink Hair raised his hands as if in surrender. 'No, don't be silly! On the house! Good to have you here, hope you have a good one!' he babbled, waving them through. As she followed Wendi past, Genie could see him turning and trying to attract the attention of someone further back in the darkness.

They passed through a second door and into the interior.

'Twat,' said Wendi, obviously hoping Pink Hair would overhear.

Inside, the air was hot and moist, the ceiling low and the sound of Blur's 'Girls and Boys' made it impossible to speak. Through an archway a mass of bodies were squeezed together, young people jerking spasmodically to the music. Wendi grabbed Genie by the hand again and towed her towards the crowded bar. She barged in between other people who looked down in annoyance, realised who she was and then shrank back in shock at the knowledge of who they'd just been jostled by. As a result, they arrived at the bar itself in seconds. Wendi stepped up onto the brass rail running along the front six inches above the floor, but even so Genie, standing behind her, was still able to see over the top of her purple head.

The bar staff noticed their new customer, and all three of them dropped whatever they were doing in the race to serve her.

'Two triple vodka and oranges,' Wendi told the winner, a blonde girl in a white vest, dropping the twenty-pound note into the pool of beer on the bar. That sounded nice, thought Genie, not at all put out that she hadn't been consulted about the choice of drink. She just felt good. Glowy. The odour of hairspray, alcohol and cigarettes filling her nostrils now was like the most glamorous perfume she could have imagined. She realised she'd started leaning forward, pressing herself against Wendi, and pulled herself back with a start. What was she thinking?

'It's OK, I'll bring it through to you.' The blonde girl scooped up the note. 'Where are you sitting?'

'In there,' Wendi gestured over her shoulder with a thumb. She jumped rearward down off the rail and grabbed a handful of Genie's skirt, dragging her in the direction of a closed door.

It was a bit quieter on the other side; battered sofas around the walls, upturned beer crates serving as tables in between. A group of young men stood around a pool table; Wendi walked towards them then threw herself backwards into the nearest sofa. Genie lowered herself more gingerly. Despite its revolting appearance, Genie found the sofa exceptionally comfortable. Probably the best sofa she'd ever sat on.

A couple of the young men looked round and raised hands; Genie recognised them as the rest of the band. Wendi pulled her feet, boots and all, up onto the sofa, and kneeled, hand on Genie's forearm, peering back towards the door.

'Where are those drinks?'

As if summoned by her words, the door banged open and the blonde barmaid shouldered her way through, two tall glasses balanced on a battered Foster's tray. She tottered over to them and placed the tray on the beer crates in front of them. Wendi's change rattled about in an ashtray, which had obviously just been wiped down and pressed into service for the occasion.

As the barmaid left, a couple of young men slipped through the door and stood in a corner, whispering to each other and staring at Wendi. This seemed somehow *right* to Genie, everything was perfect and just as it should be. A wide smile settled across her lips and her head was filled with an endorphin roar.

'Good, eh?' Wendi was examining Genie's face rather than simply looking at her. 'Let me know if you want any more. Back in a minute.' She stood up and wandered over to the pool table and started chatting to the young men. Back on the sofa, Genie started stroking her own arm. Her skin was so soft, and her fingers left trails of tingling sensation where they'd passed. It was wonderful. She leaned back, resting her right cheek against the sofa back, looking over at the pool table in a lazy fashion. Wendi was now playing pool with the boys, whacking the balls around the table with abandon and shrieking '*Cunt!*' every time she missed.

It began to look like a little show put on for her benefit, the tiny figures of Wendi and her band oddly lit by the light hanging down over the green baize, chiaroscuro. She felt as if she could reach out and pick up the table in one hand, limbs distorted like Alice. She looked down the slope of her legs at her sandal-clad feet.

'*Alice's Right Foot Esq*,' she murmured to herself, the words rising from her childhood memories like bubbles in lager. '*Oh dear, what nonsense I'm talking!*' She started giggling at this but then spotted her drink still sitting on the tray in front of her. It looked delicious, a tall glass filled with orange liquid, drops of condensation running down the outside. She started giving some thought as to how she would pick it up while her back brain fizzed, and crowbarred a wide smile back onto her lips. She regarded the back of her hand and was surprised at how long her fingers looked. Perhaps she could use them to pick up her drink?

'Here, let me.' There was someone standing right by her, blocking the view of the pool table and holding the glass of vodka and orange out to her. She grabbed it and downed it in one gulp. Divine.

The figure dropped onto the sofa beside her. She blinked and gradually saw that it was Wendi's drummer – she didn't recall his name – who'd obviously got bored with pool.

"Ow's it going? You having a good time?'

Genie supposed she was and nodded, not wanting to disturb the Cheshire Cat rictus that was still in control of her mouth.

"Ope you enjoyed the gig last time. You coming to the next one?'

'Probably,' Genie managed to squeeze out. He looked funny, like a soft-toy version of a rock star. She wondered if he had a label on the back of his neck and almost had to restrain herself from looking for it. *All new material, 30% cotton...*

'Beat it.' A low, dangerous growl. There was another figure standing there blocking out the light from the pool table, and Genie realised from the purple halo that it was Wendi. For some reason she was glowering at the Drumming Bear with fury in her kohl-ringed eyes.

He disappeared without even standing up; Wendi was back, once more kneeling up on the sofa, elbow on Genie's shoulder, murmuring in her ear.

'Shall we dance?'

Genie felt as if she were on wheels as Wendi towed her through the crowds towards the archway through which the bodies continued their rhythmic spasm. It was still hot and airless but this was now pleasant. As she stepped beneath the archway, Genie imagined she was lowering herself into a warm bath made of people. Everything was making her smile; it was an effort to stop doing so – the moment she relaxed her face, it sprang back into shape. *Coathanger smiles*, her mind whispered to her. She had no idea what this meant.

People started giving her a bit more space, keen to stare at Wendi bouncing up and down in front of her. A strobe light flicked on in front of Genie's eyes as a battered tin nozzle spewed dry ice into her face. Everything vanished except the music and, after a few seconds, Wendi's hand, which came swimming out of the fog and fastened itself onto Genie's left wrist. Genie giggled as she spun around as if on hinges and slammed straight into a large, warm sweaty back.

'Sorry, mate!' the boy bellowed at her before disappearing back into the clouds.

Madonna's 'Ray of Light' must have been playing for at least half an hour, the throbbing synth notes causing goose pimples to stand out on Genie's arms despite the heat, a further detonation of effervescence mounting her spinal column and exploding up into her brain.

They were back on the sofa in the pool room. Genie wriggled her shoulders against the filthy, cosy cushions. The music had decelerated to walking pace and the voice of Eminem was waffling hyperactive gibberish over the top of it in a squeaky voice.

There was another tall orange glass on the beer crate in front of her. She reached out her hand and the glass translated itself into her grasp. Downed it in one and fell back into the sofa, which jolted and started rocking like a Ferris wheel cage when Wendi jumped onto it beside her.

She was on the dance floor again, bending down and offering Wendi her ear to bellow in. She couldn't quite work out what Wendi was *saying*, but nodded anyway. She kept thinking Wendi was a boy. She knew she wasn't.

They were outside again, and a sense of reality dropped over Genie like a cage. The street lamps, the traffic and the cooling air. She followed Wendi up the steps and onto the pavement. Further up the street, knots of screaming teenagers argued with bouncers, police cars hovering in anticipation.

Wendi grabbed Genie's wrist and struck off in the other direction – across the road and down into the urine-soaked subway that led out onto the beach. Genie wondered why even the smell of piss wasn't as bad as usual. No sooner had she thought that than she discovered that it was.

The sea was flat and motionless, disappearing off into mist, the odd ripple flicking at the pebbles. The lights of the piers were reflected in the surface, almost perfect inversions: to the left the brightly lit Palace Pier; to the right the dim red light of the deserted West.

Wendi ran down to the shoreline, pausing for a moment to drop her jacket and peel off her T-shirt, jeans and boots before continuing into the water shrieking.

Genie didn't know if she wanted to follow her or not. Everything was still pleasant, but there was… a bite to reality now, and she could tell that the still-dropping temperature would start to become uncomfortable if she got wet. Wendi's screeches stopped, and the sound of her splashing grew fainter.

I'm coming back, Genie thought, sitting down on pebbles that creaked under her buttocks, *that was a sensible thought I just had*. Somewhere behind her in the city centre, a man bellowed '*Oi OI!*' and continued to repeat himself every ten seconds or so, getting ever fainter. A police siren emerged from Kemptown and pursued the shouter inland.

Genie looked to her right and a little way off could see another figure standing on the stones, silently contemplating the edge of England, and a further figure beyond that. Although this situation was making her feel alone and special, it was probably doing the same for all these others.

I thought you were MY special friend, she muttered to the night.

A splashing, gasping noise grew louder in front of her, as Wendi rose from the sea, pale limbs almost fluorescent against the darkness. She scooped up her garments and yelped in pain as she ran up to where Genie sat.

'What's the matter?' Genie asked as Wendi dropped her clothes then dropped to her knees, shivering in black sodden underwear.

'Stones!' Wendi rolled over and brushed at the soles of her feet before picking up a huge pebble and lobbing it into the water. She put a hand like ice on Genie's arm to steady herself, before rolling back and pulling her jeans back onto wet legs. She donned her boots without bothering with socks, which she stuffed into a pocket, and stood up to finish getting dressed.

'Come on.' Wendi strode off in the direction of the town without looking back to see if Genie was following. Genie was momentarily disoriented as she stepped off the pebbles and back onto tarmac; but walking was much more straightforward again now and she caught up with Wendi easily.

As they continued along the promenade, Wendi lost confidence somewhat and started to shiver; her hair was slicked back with seawater and was dripping onto the back of her leather jacket. She slowed and grabbed hold of Genie's arm with both of hers. Her teeth started chattering – Genie hadn't ever seen that happen to anyone in reality.

The hulk of the dead pier loomed ahead, square red illuminated letters beaming their pointless message WEST PIER back at the shore. Genie started feeling a little unwell; the warm agreeability of everything she'd been feeling had evaporated, and the sheer amount of alcohol she'd had to drink was advancing on her head and gut.

They were about to walk under the dead pier when Wendi

dragged the two of them off in the direction of a tunnel in the promenade wall.

'Here,' she said in a small voice.

This time the smell of urine made Genie gag and she was glad when they emerged from a sloping passageway, now on the inland side of the seafront road. She looked out at WEST PIER again.

As if in response to her attention, the illuminated letters vanished; the dead pier was now only visible as absence, a patch of deeper darkness against the late-night sea. Genie began to feel frightened. And sick.

Still holding onto Genie's arm tight, Wendi dragged the two of them up into a seafront square past a succession of rundown Regency buildings.

'They all look the same to me.' Wendi let go of Genie's arm and ran up and down a couple of times, peering at front doors. She turned around and looked across the square. 'Fuck, I could have *sworn*...'

She started to laugh, but Genie couldn't see what was so funny. Quite apart from anything else, a group of loud young men had just turned into the square from the seafront and were lurching remorselessly up towards them. And she was going to throw up.

'Come on!' Wendi had got her energy back and sprinted across the centre of the square to the far side. She didn't stop when she reached it, but instead ran straight up to the front door of a building and opened it before turning back and beckoning.

As Genie followed, a few drops of rain hit her on the cheek, on the head, on the eye. The night kissing her goodbye. Drawing nearer to the building, she could make out a sign, '*pelirocco*'. She followed Wendi inside and found herself in a narrow foyer, deserted. Wendi was already clattering away up the stairs, unbothered at the possibility of waking up the other guests. Genie followed more slowly, not wanting to startle her stomach with any sudden moves.

It was like being in someone's house. The only hotels Genie had ever experienced were purpose built and boring, whereas this was much more... interesting. She kept worrying that a grown-up was going to open one of the doors and tell them to keep the noise down; it was unbelievable that no one was in charge.

She was going to be sick and needed to lie down as soon as possible.

The room was bright yellow. *Liar, liar, liar.* Genie staggered and fell backwards onto the bed, kicking off her sandals and burying her face in the bright-blue duvet. *Fuck forever.*

Being horizontal had calmed her gut a little.

The lights dimmed and she crawled under the duvet, slipping off her skirt. She closed her eyes and the whole room began whirling as if trying to catch up with her brain. If only she could get them in step, she might start feeling better.

She felt rather than saw that it had got even darker; opening one eye a crack she could see that the only illumination now came from the window, against which the raindrops were flinging themselves, regular and persistent. Something crawled into the bed next to her, something cold, damp and painfully thin. The nausea had passed and this mysterious alien body was a physical manifestation of the migraine sidling into her brain. It clung to her in the dark.

Sometimes it seemed like she'd been lying here forever. The rain on the window, the pain in her eye sockets and the disconcerting sound of someone else's breathing.

It rained all night. At some point Genie fell asleep.

17: Take your time

Brighton, summer 2000

Something was different. Something was better. Genie was still nauseous but... the pain behind her eyes was *gone*.

The noise of the rain had stopped as well, and a warm light licked at her eyelids. She opened half an eye and instantly shut it again. So much *yellow*. There was nothing wrong with yellow; it made it feel as if the room were suffused with sunlight. She opened her eyes again, now more cautious.

It was as if she'd woken up inside a record cover. Vivid yellow walls with stylish stencilled designs in blue, pictures and the words *Liar, Liar, Liar*. Blue curtains, green sofa, red window frame. It clashed perfectly.

She could feel a small, cold body curled up next to her under the duvet. Wendi. Genie lifted a corner (blue cover decorated with the slogan *Fuck Forever*) and peered at her. The purple mop of hair matched the rest of the room perfectly. Not surprising; to Genie this room was like a representation of the inside of Wendi's head.

Wendi whimpered, so Genie lowered the duvet again. She needed to pee.

They hadn't... *done anything*, had they? No, she didn't think so. It didn't feel as if she'd had much sleep, but that had been to do with her headache and Wendi's snoring. Genie got out of bed and tiptoed over to the window.

It was early, but it already looked as if it was going to be another hot day. A Sunday. She had no idea what was going to happen next. She looked back at the bed. Would it have bothered her if they *had* done anything? She couldn't be sure but didn't think so. Girls had done that kind of thing all the time at school.

It was quite exciting. She wondered if her absence from the hall of residence had been noticed.

Two hours later it was no longer so exciting. Wendi refused to wake up, and after all this time the entertainment value of the hotel brochure on the bedside table had begun to pall. Genie couldn't go out as she had no idea how she'd get back in again. She supposed she could always just jump on a bus back to campus, but that wouldn't be right. She wanted to say goodbye. There was a TV, but she didn't want to disturb Wendi. She began to feel a monumental boredom and frustration. Not to mention hunger. She could smell cooking.

She walked over to the net curtains (*no future*), pulled them aside and opened one of the windows. The fresh air made her even hungrier. She wondered if there was a mini bar somewhere, and if so, whether there was any chocolate in it.

A series of strident bleeps emerged from the dark shape sprawled in the middle of the floor, Wendi's leather jacket. There was a moan, and Wendi rolled out of the bed and crawled across to it, rooting around the inside pocket for her phone.

She held it to her ear and grunted a couple of times, before flinging it down again. She seemed disinclined to move again and just stayed there frozen on all fours, head hanging almost directly downwards. Genie wondered if she'd fallen asleep again.

'Are you OK?' she asked.

Wendi's head snapped back and she yelped, jumping backwards onto the bed, panda eyes wide with shock. She then seemed to realise what she was staring at and managed a smile.

'No, I feel like shit.' She patted the bed and Genie walked back over and sat down next to her. Wendi closed her eyes and slumped against Genie's arm for a second before leaping up and disappearing into the bathroom.

Genie switched the TV on to mask the embarrassing and unpleasant sounds that were all that emerged from the bathroom for the next ten minutes. Eventually they were replaced by the sound of a shower, and shortly after that Wendi emerged, pale and damp, wrapped in a bright-yellow dressing gown.

'I've got to go out in a bit,' she said, 'there's a journo coming. Then we've got to film on the beach.'

Genie nodded, not sure what to say.

'There's a journo coming soon,' said Wendi. 'Can I have your mobile number?'

'I don't have one yet,' said Genie, 'I'm getting one for my birthday.'

'What about email?' Wendi picked up her leather jacket and began rooting through the pockets. She found a pen and tested it on her arm, before looking over at Genie.

Genie told her the university email address. She didn't use it much, but supposed it would be nice to get a message that wasn't from her parents or her tutors. Or from Duncan.

Wendi copied it down onto her arm then leaped forward and hugged Genie. She was surprisingly strong for someone so slight.

'I'll see you soon, yeah?' Genie turned to go and felt her

buttock being pinched. She looked back to see an expression of faux innocence on Wendi's face as it disappeared behind the closing yellow door. Moving as quietly as possible she made her way downstairs and outside into the street.

It was nearly a year before Wendi emailed her.

18: The elephant in the room

Genie and Wendi sat opposite each other on the grass at the edge of the path while Nathan sat cross-legged on the tarmac, playing with his iPod Touch. The warm wind was gusting from further down the path, blowing the occasional few grains of gritty sand into Genie's eyes. She was beginning to wish she'd brought her eye drops with her. Even a cheap Superdrug eye bath would have been better than nothing.

Once Wendi had been coaxed out from behind her tree, they'd started chatting about old times as if they'd just run into each other in Camden High Street, rather than in the middle of a mythological underworld wood. Wendi's voice was regaining some of her customary confidence and increasing in volume as she talked; Genie got the impression she hadn't talked to anyone for a very long time. However, she was still a very long way from the Wendi of old that Genie had loved, a shadow of her former self.

And of course there was a very large elephant in the room that it was becoming more and more difficult to ignore. Sooner or later Genie was going to have to ask her about it.

19: Mallard

Brighton, spring 2001

Over the next year at university Genie's popularity continued to build. She moved off campus into a maisonette on Portland Road which she shared with three girls and Duncan, who, even though she'd tired of teasing him, was still content to follow her around and do everything she asked him to.

His loyalty was astonishing. He hadn't even been put off by her indulgence in a number of short-term relationships with tall, attractive third-year boys (and on a particularly memorable occasion one of the tutors). He even provided her with a sympathetic ear when she was on her way in or out of one of these liaisons. They never lasted long. Despite the fact that this had helped her get over some of the trauma experienced back at Reading, none of these boys were able to offer Genie what she wanted.

She couldn't blame them. She'd have been unable to articulate what she really wanted herself.

At Easter she decided to stay in town rather than returning home to Berkshire. She could tell that Duncan would have liked to hang around too, but his mother had already bought him a train ticket.

For the first time, she had the flat to herself. It was liberating.

She no longer had to maintain the overconfident persona she'd built up over the past year, which was a relief, although she was interested to find that on some levels she missed it. But why not? She'd managed to become a big fish in a remarkably short amount of time, although she was fully aware of how small the pond was.

Genie had now been on her own for four days. It was 6 a.m. and the sun had wedged a beam through her window and woken her up. She slipped out of bed and went to the toilet.

On the way back, she wandered into Duncan's room. She wondered if he would like the idea of her standing there in only a T-shirt. She hadn't been in there much before; usually they seemed to spend time together in the living room or in Genie's room (which was bigger).

It was tidy, but smelled stale. She reached over his desk and opened the window. A gust of sea air blew a couple of sheets of paper onto the floor and rattled the enormous My Bloody Valentine poster that he had Blu-Tacked up over the bed.

There was a picture of Wendi regarding her from the wall next to the desk, a moody shot from some glossy music magazine. Perhaps it was from the interview that had been due to take place later in the day the last time Genie had seen her.

Genie didn't know how she felt about Wendi. On the one hand, it was a relief not to have heard from her; it was like being let off the hook. Any strange, dangerous or awkward decisions that Wendi might have asked her to make were moot. There was no way Genie could have contacted Wendi, so the ball was quite clearly in the singer's court, and if she chose to ignore it, then...

But Genie was sad. There had been that feeling of infinite possibilities when she'd been with Wendi, as if her life was opening up into new and unexpected shapes, shapes she couldn't have even dreamed of before. And the attention

Wendi had paid her when they were together... Wendi had been interested in her, but without the stink of needy desperation exuded by Duncan.

Genie backed out of the bedroom, loped downstairs and flung herself onto the spongy sofa, the living room thick with the aroma of chemicals from the dry-cleaners downstairs. She wished Wendi was there. She hardly knew her, but wanted the opportunity to get to do so. Somehow, despite the lengthy separation, the fascination had become mutual.

Genie sat on the bus on the way into university to use one of the student PC labs. Despite his promises, Father had yet to buy her a computer to use in the flat. It wouldn't have been that much use as they didn't have an internet connection, but it would be nice to be able to write in peace without the prospect of an interminable bus journey between the end of work and relaxation.

The main reason Genie was travelling onto campus was to check her email. She'd kind of given up hope of hearing from Wendi, but you never knew... besides, Duncan would be sure to have sent her something.

Not that Wendi had been *totally* incommunicado since that time last year at the Pelirocco. In late November Genie had discovered a grubby postcard from San Francisco with a picture of a tram on the front in her pigeonhole in the undergraduate common room; Wendi had written to her at her first-year address in halls, and since its arrival there, the missive had obviously taken more than twice as long to cross campus as it had to cross the planet.

hi genie
i'm thinking of you are you thinking of me? we've only been on

this american tour for a week and already i feel tired and perpetually hung over. peter accidentally hit himself on the head on stage last night ha ha!

love wendi xxx

Since then there had been nothing, although according to the music papers Duncan always bought and left on the coffee table, it would seem that the tour had ended in late January.

As ever, the campus was at the centre of its own private weather system; back in town, it had been a pleasant late spring day, up here it was grey and wet. Genie jumped off the bus and sprinted for the library.

There was an email from an address she didn't recognise in her inbox, but the subject line dispelled any doubt there could have been about its source: *FROM WENDI.* Her heart started beating faster as she clicked on it.

A week later, Genie was on a train up to London. Wendi's email had been cryptic and confusing, but had mentioned a date, a time and something about a meeting. Genie had let her know she'd be there, but since this exchange, there'd been no contact. She pulled her new mobile out of a coat pocket. No messages, despite having sent the number to Wendi in her email. Wendi had promised to meet her at Victoria, but what would she do if no one turned up?

The train crawled across Grosvenor Bridge, out of the daylight and into the artificial lights of the station interior, sliding to a standstill alongside a vacant platform.

Genie walked towards the gates. No sign of anyone; the train had been empty for most of the journey and the platform was deserted. She showed her ticket to the inspector and then slowed, looking around for Wendi, for anyone. What was she going to do?

Her mobile bleeped at her. There was a text message from an unfamiliar number.

I can see you. Can you see me? Wx

She looked around again. No sign of Wendi.

'Boo!' said the diminutive figure in the woolly hat, shades and long coat that had been walking towards her for the past thirty seconds. Beneath this disguise, Genie abruptly recognised Wendi's crazy smirk. 'How are you, babe?'

Genie muttered something. Her heart was racing again. She hadn't felt like this last time. What had changed? They hadn't seen each other for the best part of a year. Why was she getting so excited?

In fact she'd *never* felt like this before, about anyone.

'There's a car.' Wendi took hold of one of Genie's hands and began towing her off towards a passage. 'Come on.' Wendi's hands were browner than Genie remembered but were just as cold.

The passage led out onto Buckingham Palace Road, where an illegally parked people carrier with tinted windows was sitting, hazard lights flashing. Wendi opened the door and pushed Genie inside.

'We'll go to the meeting and then back to mine.' Wendi sat back in the seat without bothering with a seat belt, pulled off the woolly hat and flung it onto the floor. Her hair was freshly coloured, its purple by far the brightest thing in the car.

'What are we meeting about?' Genie fastened her seat belt, not feeling quite as bold as her friend seemed.

'Didn't I say? We've got a tour starting in July.' Wendi kneeled up on her seat. 'You can sing, can't you?'

'Well, I don't know, not really...'

'Bollocks. Course you can!' Wendi put a hand on Genie's

shoulder. 'Malcolm said you were singing and dancing when you watched the college gig when we met. Said you were great.'

'Well…'

'And we're thinking of using extra singers this time; it'll go well with some of the new material. Two of you.'

'Two of *me*?' Genie was confused.

'Don't be silly. No. Well, yes. Well, sort of. You and Claudia. You'll meet her at the offices. We're nearly there.' Wendi reached into her pocket, pulled out a small brown bottle and tipped two white capsules out of it into her palm.

'Arses up!' she shrieked before flinging them into her mouth and swallowing.

The car pulled over in the middle of a busy shopping street. Wendi opened the door and was outside in moments. Genie took a little longer to extricate herself from the seat belt and unfold herself from the car's interior. She shut the door behind her, and it pulled out again into the slow-moving traffic.

Outside, it was hot, uncomfortable and smelled of plastic and petrol.

'King's Road's not what it was,' said Wendi, walking towards a narrow grey door in between two shoe shops. She pushed a buzzer, and the speaker grill responded with an interrogative screech.

'Who d'you fucking think?' bawled Wendi, attacking the door with her shoulder just as it buzzed to allow them entry and as a result catapulting herself into the narrow hallway.

The space was only wide enough for a single flight of stairs that were doubling as a temporary storage area for cardboard boxes full of flyers and promo CDs. These didn't give Wendi any trouble, but Genie picked her way upwards carefully. She didn't want to misstep and end up buried under an avalanche of marketing.

Once above shop level, the space widened out a bit, and Genie turned a corner into a dingy hallway, lit only by an old-fashioned sash window overlooking a narrow, unhealthy garden. Wendi was at the darkened end of the hall, leaning through an open doorway and conducting a conversation with someone inside.

'So where are they?' Wendi stood on one leg as someone inside the room replied, but before Genie could catch up she'd moved on around a corner. As she passed the open doorway Genie caught a glimpse of a glamorous woman dressed in expensive clothes sitting behind a desk upon which sat an odd-looking computer and several telephones. The woman didn't look up.

Around the corner, Wendi was waiting in the darkness just outside a large door. She reached up and held a finger to Genie's mouth.

'Let's surprise them,' she whispered. At that point, someone inside the room emitted a bark of humourless laughter. Wendi flung the door open and jumped inside.

'Boo!'

At first glance, Genie could hardly see a thing. Daylight poured through large Victorian floor-to-ceiling windows, the room's inhabitants appearing as silhouettes.

'Hello, sweetheart.'

Genie recognised Businessman. He was the only one standing. As her eyes grew accustomed to the light, she saw that Wendi had flung herself down on a grey leather sofa, and was looking at her, patting the space to her right.

On Wendi's left sat a tall girl with short dark hair and small, heavily made-up eyes at the upper corners of a face shaped like a heraldic shield, a pair of over-filled lips, rampant, in the lower segment.

Genie sat down, trying to ignore the filthy look the girl was directing at her.

'My angel and my demon! But which is which?' Wendi bounced up and down in her seat. 'This is Genie. This is Claudia.'

'Hi Claudia.' Genie held out a hand. Claudia ignored it, nodded and looked the other way.

'I, Claudius,' said Wendi, 'I, Genius.'

'Perhaps we could make a start now?' An older man, enthroned in a large leather armchair over by the window. Businessman glanced down at him and nodded.

'What we'd like to cover...' he began, turning back to the rest of the room.

'I, Elf,' said Wendi. Businessman frowned at her and tapped his nose.

'We'd like to welcome a new friend. You've all met Claudia before, but finally we have her counterpart. This is Genie.'

The door opened and the glamorous woman from the office outside staggered in with a coffee pot and several cups on a tray.

'I, Nicodemus,' said Wendi. The woman offered her a weak smile and put down the tray.

'Monika, I wonder if you could...' Businessman's voice tailed off and he completed his sentence with a complicated sequence of hand gestures and facial expressions. The Glamorous Woman nodded and held out a hand. Wendi took it, stood up and then followed the woman out of the room, quiet and acquiescent.

'We've got some contracts drawn up, but I thought it might be best to have a practice session before anyone signs anything.' Businessman picked up a sheet of paper but carried on speaking without glancing at its contents. 'There's a small studio upstairs

160

– perhaps you girls could spend the afternoon up there, give us an idea of your range and how you work together.'

Genie looked over at Claudia and smiled. It was no good; somehow Claudia managed to ignore her even more intensely.

It was going to be a long afternoon.

20: *What are you thinking?*

London, summer 2001

Genie was getting a sore throat. Both she and Claudia had been
singing along to a pre-recorded backing track for what felt like
days and it was beginning to take its toll on her voice.

About halfway through, Wendi had turned up, calmer. She
didn't say much, but spent her time watching them from
behind glass on the sofa in the tiny control booth, cryptic
exchanges occasionally passing between her and Jake, who'd
been at the mixing desk throughout.

Jake's presence made a difference. What with the strange
new situation and Claudia's determined sullenness, the
presence of a familiar face – even one Genie hardly knew –
helped calm her a little. What was more, that night at the
university when she'd first met Wendi had started to take on
mythical status in Genie's head, and so the presence of another
figure from that time transformed her nerves and panic into
excitement. She was sure that something marvellous was going
to happen.

'OK, I think we can call it a day.' Jake was talking to her over
the speakers, Wendi standing behind him. Claudia stalked out
without a glance at Genie and reappeared in the control booth
seconds later. She tried to grab Wendi in a possessive hug, but

the smaller woman stepped neatly away, continuing to stare at Genie through the glass. The silent movie continued as Claudia collapsed onto the sofa and put her head in her hands. Jake disappeared.

It was like watching a TV show on mute. Wendi sat down next to the distraught Claudia and, reaching up and around her neck, pulled the taller girl's ear towards her mouth and whispered something. Claudia looked up, stared into space for a few seconds and gave a slow nod. Wendi said something. Claudia nodded again, a smile on her face, and stood up, leaving the room. Wendi turned back to stare at Genie through the glass for far too long.

Genie dropped her eyes. When she looked up again, the booth was empty.

'Come on then.' Wendi was now standing at her elbow. 'Let's get something to drink!'

Outside, twilight had fallen, but it was still hot. Wendi had hold of Genie's hand again and dragged her off down the pavement in the direction of the nearby light and noise. Genie's heart raced. She just knew that the unknown marvellous thing was about to happen again, and she hadn't even taken any drugs.

Yet.

Soon enough the two of them were sitting towards the rear of a low-ceilinged bar where young men and women kept them supplied with constant drinks. Wendi talked constantly – about the tour, the places she'd been, and the things she'd seen. After a while Genie's reserve fell away, and she found herself talking about her own life.

It was very different from any time she'd spent with anyone before. With Duncan back at university, she felt powerful yet guilty and, despite his attentions, didn't get anything out of their friendship. And she didn't even want to think about the last person before Duncan to have lavished attention on her. Cosmo. Even now the mere thought of his face made her afraid he was lurking in the shadows somewhere. She steered her mind away from that subject, from what he'd done to her, from what he *might* have done to her. She didn't want to remember.

This was different. Wendi gave her just as much attention as Duncan but had so much of herself to bring to the table as well. But perhaps it was simply that Genie found Wendi far more fascinating than Duncan could ever have hoped to be.

There was something frightening about Wendi – but frightening in a *good* way, not like Cosmo. Would it be too much to hope that he'd died since she'd last seen him? And did it make her a bad person for even thinking that?

She nearly told Wendi about him. As they talked Genie came to realise that this was someone she could trust, someone who would understand… she even lined it up in her head as the next thing to say, but even as she opened her mouth, her heart hammering in her chest as she prepared to confront this, the words withered away and died. Was she still afraid of what had happened? Afraid of Wendi's reaction? Perhaps she was afraid it would spoil the mood. This was special, she didn't want what had happened with him to taint this. *Forget him. Think of the marvellous thing.*

It was even closer now.

They were out on the street. Genie didn't remember leaving the bar. This worried her for a minute, but then she realised it didn't matter. She was high and happy. Wendi was holding her hand again, leading her who knew where. Astray. They turned off the main street into a residential road.

Despite the traffic not fifty yards away, it was suddenly a lot quieter, the crack of their footsteps the only thing disturbing the stillness.

Another corner took them into a mews, Wendi letting go of Genie's hand as she reached into her pocket.

Then they were passing down a narrow corridor with a low ceiling and emerged into the warm interior of a relaxed living space; a studio, kitchen to one side, bathroom to another, ladder leading up to a door near the skylights which were the only windows. Wendi flung herself onto a pile of beanbags, pulling Genie down with her. Genie closed her eyes and the room started spinning. Opening them again, she saw that Wendi had discarded her jacket and boots and was fetching them drinks from the kitchen area.

The room started to spin and rock again, but in a more comforting manner, as if Genie was now in the gondola of an airship crossing a calm void of sky. The lights were low.

Wendi was leaning her head on Genie's shoulder and in an unhurried manner slipped her hand inside the front of Genie's knickers.

Genie flinched, she couldn't help it. The last time someone had touched her like that... But this was Wendi. This was different. She could trust her. She could have trusted her earlier too when she'd wanted to talk about... him. But that might have complicated things, and maybe this wouldn't have happened. She could trust Wendi. That was enough.

'You all right with this?' Wendi whispered in her ear. Genie thought about it. She was.

'Yes. Yes, I am.'

'What are you thinking?'

'That I'm very much all right with this.'

21: Suicide note

Underworld, no time

They'd been talking for a little while now. Overhead, the darkness was unchanging. A gust of warm air tousled Genie's hair but had no effect on Wendi. Genie was finding it more and more difficult to keep a lid on what she was thinking; she'd had quite enough of the elephant. The next time her conversation with Wendi reached a natural pause, she went for it.

'Why did you do it?'

Wendi looked across at her over the top of her sunglasses, in a pale echo of their first meeting all that time ago, before withdrawing into herself and staring down at the ground. Genie reached across and took her hand. It was stone cold.

'It was the only thing I could do, babe,' Wendi whispered eventually. 'My life turned into a long chain of events that were nothing to do with the real me. They didn't make me happy, I was just like a... a thing other people needed. Everything was controlled by someone else for their benefit. I'd lost my freedom forever, you know? I wish we hadn't broken up the band. It was my fault. When you ask *What's in it for me?* about your own life you know something's gone wrong.'

'What about me? You should have talked to me!' Genie

knew it was too late, but was unable to let go of what might have been. Then again, she'd kept secrets too, hadn't she?

'Maybe I should've, babe,' whispered Wendi. 'I know you didn't get on, but you and Claudia were the only thing I had going for me. Funny thing was you weren't quite real; you were my angel-girl and my devil-girl, my toys. Dragging you into the feelings in my head would have ruined you for me – you were the only good part of my life. And even that wasn't enough in the end. Remember how I started spending a lot of time on my own?

'After a while the only thing I looked forward to was being asleep. I still had good dreams sometimes. But do you know what the worst thing was?' Wendi pushed her sunglasses up onto her forehead and looked into Genie's eyes.

'The worst thing was when I went out in the evening, when I breathed it in deeply and forgot. The smell of the night air reminded me of... how I used to feel when things were exciting and better. That cold sodium light, dead leaves and petrol fumes. When I was young and my life was gonna be one big version of having the whole Friday night ahead of you as you come out of the tube on your way somewhere good, watching your breath in front of your face, you know?

'But that smell was taunting me, you know? Reminding me of what I could never have again. I was trapped in a cell that was shrinking every day. The cell had a window that opened onto that cool orange night sky, but it was too small to crawl through and just let that smell in to mock me. Every day the cell got smaller, and the window got smaller, until I was squashed into a ball, cushioned by vodka, by cigarettes and by drugs, the window a tiny aperture over my nostrils, feeding me the smell of the unobtainable until... I just couldn't bear it any more.

'Then I stopped sleeping. I was denied even that. It didn't

matter how many pills I took, I'd end up spending most nights lying there in the dark with my mind skittering about on the frozen surface of my miserable life. Then the voice started. It was like there was this rational little voice at the back of my mind. She was giving me advice, we discussed ways and means. She was so measured and calm, her advice always logical and reasonable. When I saw a high building, I started speculating about jumping off it, considering the logistics. I thought about the mechanics of attaching a noose to my skylight. I wondered how difficult it would be to get hold of a gun.'

Wendi stood up, and after a few seconds Genie joined her. The warm wind had picked up and the trees around them were swaying, the susurration of the leaves like a distant crowd roaring approval. Wendi pushed her sunglasses down over her eyes again.

'In the end I made do with what I had to hand. I just did it. It didn't hurt. I went home and listened to some music, took some pills and washed them down with vodka. It seemed to take a while – I definitely remember the CD finishing and having to crawl across the carpet to the stereo to put another one on... I think I knocked something over.

'I wasn't scared. I kept thinking *they* were going to come for me. If ever there was a time I needed them this was it. But they didn't show up. They abandoned me.' The trees howled quietly in unison as the wind gusted once more. Wendi started walking backwards towards her tree.

'Then I was here. It's not so bad. I'm left in peace and I can't smell the past any more,' she said, reaching for Genie, who stepped forward and took her cold hands. 'I can get some rest and I'm not feeling wretched. There's no joy here, but there's no pain. This place is like Prozac. It just rolls on and on.'

Genie stood still, gripping Wendi's hands. Surely there was

something she could do? After all, why had she come down here in the first place?

'Come with me!' she said to Wendi. 'You can start again. Look – if you come with me I'm sure we can...'

'How would *that* work, babe?' Wendi smiled.

'I don't know, but that has to be what I'm here for. I can bring *you* back.' This was a chance, surely. A chance to make this right, this thing that really deserved to be made right.

Wendi didn't respond, as if she hadn't heard. She was now indistinct. The noise of the trees around them had risen and was disorienting, a deafening whisper; cold hands squeezed hers and she felt an impression of Wendi standing on tiptoe to give her a cold kiss on the cheek.

'It was good to see you again... good luck...'

And now there was only another tree that from some angles seemed to Genie as if it might have a small human figure sitting in its branches, or perhaps just a large crow...

Once again, she'd missed her chance to open up to Wendi.

The other trees became silent and Genie looked around. What had happened to Nathan?

She was alone in the Wood of the Suicides.

Part Two

22: The Riddle of the Sphinx

Underworld, no time

'Nathan?' Genie looked around and ran a few yards further down the path. 'Are you there?'

Her words disappeared into the blanket of silence that had fallen over the wood. Genie appraised her surroundings; downhill the trees were thinning out at last so she started walking in that direction. Perhaps he'd gone on ahead again? He hadn't said anything, but perhaps he hadn't wanted to interrupt. If she could get out of the wood, she might be able to catch up with him. Then they could get a clearer view of what was in store. Overhead the sky-ceiling was a little lighter, as if dawn was coming. The warm wind in her face grew stronger.

Without having been aware of approaching it, Genie found herself at the tree line. Taking a few steps forward, she screwed up her eyes as the sky flipped into a bright false daylight. She staggered back a few steps and twilight fell again. It was like pushing her way forward and then back through a thick curtain. Behind her the wood lay in night. Ahead lay a broken, rocky landscape. She walked forward even more slowly this time, but it didn't help – there was no gradual transition. She squinted as she reached into her pocket for her Ray-Bans and donned them before peering around at the dazzling desert.

She'd been hoping for some trace of Nathan, but there was nothing, not even a set of footprints. She walked to the summit of a long, low outcrop, the bare rock hot against the soles of her feet. Ahead more rocks, more outcrops, more sand blurring off towards the horizon. No Nathan.

'What a TWAT!' she shouted.

Her angry shout was muffled by the calm stillness of the place. She looked upwards. It was intolerable to look at for long even with her sunglasses – it wasn't the brightness, there was something utterly wrong with the firmament which her mind wasn't able to accept.

There was no single source of light, just an intense white glow. The sense of infinite depth and huge, terrible movement remained from last time, only now it was inverted, as if she was looking at a photographic negative of the sky she'd seen on arrival. It was as disturbing as before, if not more so, and she cast her gaze back down.

Where could Nathan have gone? She hadn't noticed him slip away, and it wasn't like she'd been talking to Wendi for that long anyway. Even if he was a half a mile away by now, she should be able to spot him. She narrowed her eyes.

There *was* something there on the horizon. Most of it was just a barely perceptible line where the ground fused with the sky, but straight ahead, directly away from the wood, there was a dark patch. It looked vaguely geometrical. A city? A large building? A destination, certainly, Genie decided. Perhaps that was where Nathan had headed.

She jumped forward off the flat rock and slid down the side of a small dune before coming to a rest at its base. It was so quiet she could hear the whisper of the sand she'd dislodged as it slid down like the contents of an egg timer.

The path ahead towards the structure consisted of an irregular line of rocks like the one she'd already jumped off, half buried in fine white sand. She set off, deciding that she'd work out what to do on the way. This wasn't like any desert she'd come across in reality – she wasn't in California or Lanzarote. For a start there was no shade, there were no shadows; the distant ceiling shone down, bathing everything in merciless, indiscriminate light. At least she wasn't thirsty yet.

The sand murmured and sighed beneath her feet as she walked on. Every hundred yards or so she'd emerge from the sand and continue up to the summit of one of the flat rocks before slithering down the sand dune on the other side and repeating the process. She couldn't imagine Nathan was more agile than her – if anything, surely she'd catch him up if he'd come this way?

After an hour or so, the tops of the flat rocks were getting higher and higher, and sliding down the sand dunes from the summit was getting more and more difficult. Genie looked back at the last one she'd made her way down. From this angle it was quite a frightening drop. Perhaps she should try and find a way around? Instead of making her way forward up the slope of the next rock, Genie turned to one side and started walking along the centre of the smooth valley between the outcrops. There probably *was* a way around. She wondered if she was tired yet and realised that the fact she was even asking that question meant that she wasn't. How long had she been here, anyway? How long since the escalator? The change in light made it feel as if it had been days ago although surely it was only a few hours...

She reached the end of the rocks and stepped out into the open desert. About a mile away, she could just about make out another chain of outcrops very similar to the one from which she'd just emerged. She turned to face her destination and walked alongside the rocks. They were quite regular and similar in shape. After she'd passed a few more of them she realised that there was something familiar about them, but it was only when she reached their end and saw the shape of the final rock – far bigger than the others and a different shape altogether – that it all fell into place.

It was a skeleton. She'd been walking up the spine and had now reached the skull. But the skeleton of *what*? Each vertebra had been the size of a small building; the skull was big enough to have housed a concert.

The hair on the back of her neck stood up and she felt a cold fear boiling in her gut. Skeletons terrified her. The copy of Edgar Allan Poe's *Tales of Mystery and Imagination* with the skull on its spine that Grandfather had given her; it had never been enough to slip the book on her shelf with its spine to the wall or even to stick paper over the offending image; it was frightening enough just knowing it was there in her room. If she woke in the night its presence was always the first thing she remembered...

This wasn't the same. It was the wrong scale for a start and didn't look like it had been remotely human. These two facts alone served to defuse her terror. It was only human bones that scared her.

She felt very small as she approached the wall of the skull, aware of herself as a tiny human shape in the middle of nowhere next to something that had no right to be as big as it was. Even half buried it was like walking around the O2 Arena in Greenwich. She reached some teeth, huge canines the length of street lamps. It was so impressive that before she knew what she was doing she'd taken a picture of it on her iPhone.

Still no signal and the battery was at less than 50%. She didn't know what she was saving it for, but switched it off anyway to conserve power. You never knew.

Hanging around a giant skeleton wasn't going to get her anywhere either. Unless Nathan was hiding inside one of the skull's sinal cavities, her time would be best spent getting to the building on the horizon where he was more likely to be.

Twenty minutes walking didn't bring it any closer. Genie flopped down in the sand, and looked back the way she'd come.

There was no sign of her footprints; the grains making up the dunes were far too dry and fine for that. But she was now far enough away from the skull to be able to identify it. It was a dog. An enormous dog. What was more she could now see that the skull had two identical siblings, each half buried about a mile from the skull she'd encountered. Her studies in classics pushed a name into her mouth.

'Cerberus.' She had no idea that he'd be so big. Or so dead. Or, not to put too fine a point on it, so *real*. A kernel of panic started unfurling at the base of her spine as the reality of this unreal situation began to get to her. She was on her own, with not even Nathan to keep her company. She…

Before this sense of dread had time to develop into a fully fledged panic attack, Genie was distracted by a noise behind her. She staggered back to her feet, almost slipping over in her haste, and turned her back on the ridiculous bones.

There was nothing there. Her destination sat on the horizon.

There it was again. It was coming from only a couple of metres in front of her but there was nothing visible. It was industrial, a grunt of metal on metal being driven by petrol-powered brute force. It was the initial moments of a large sheet of glass shattering into a million pieces. It was the laughter of granite.

Something started coming into focus in front of her. Something whirling. It wasn't anything she'd seen before, and yet at the same time it reminded her of something from deep in her childhood. Something she used to play with in the garden, pieces of pink-veined marble left over from the construction of a rockery. And yet the thing in front of her defied description. It was halfway between a visual and an auditory stimulus, a synaesthesia that broke down halfway through the process...

It was there. It was big. It was visible. It was a pale limestone statue of a woman's head and shoulders emerging from the sand, at least four metres high. The sheer size and unfamiliar angle meant that it took Genie at least half a minute before she realised it was a statue of *her*.

'Jesus H. Fuckwit!' One of Wendi's favourite expletives that Genie had adopted. She stepped a little closer. Who had made it? It was old, and yet captured her current appearance perfectly. Without thinking, she pulled out her phone again. It was only while hopping impatiently from foot to foot waiting for it to boot up that she realised what she was doing.

This was insane. Her first thought was to take a picture of this colossal stone portrait? Who had made it? Someone must have known she was coming, must have known all about her. Had they been watching her since she'd arrived? Something like this had been done for her benefit, she was sure. Or for her detriment.

She still took a couple of photos anyway.

It was only once she'd slipped the phone back into her pocket that she noticed that great stone head had moved, and was looking straight at her with the kind of expression she usually reserved for people like TV Guy. She yelped and leaped backwards.

Go away.

It hadn't moved, but had definitely spoken to her. In her own voice. Her *real* voice. Not the false one she heard whenever she listened back to radio interviews or watched herself on TV. The *real* voice she heard when she was speaking to someone. And the voice in her head.

Still, no one spoke to her like that. Not even herself.

'No.' She took a step back towards the statue. They glared at each other with identical expressions. The statue's chin was higher than the top of her head. Genie wasn't used to having to look up at faces.

You can't go on. Go home.

'Why?' The statue's apparent lack of movement had stopped unnerving Genie and was now contributing to her growing irritation. She didn't like being told what to do. Not any more.

It is not your time. Go back. You have no business here.

'Fuck off!' Being told what to do by a giant stone copy of herself was beginning to annoy her.

Fuck off yourself.

Despite herself, Genie giggled. A statue had just told her to fuck off. A statue that was now smiling as well.

Yes, very funny, but you still can't come past.

'Why not?'

You are alive. The only time the living come down here is to rescue their loved ones. And you don't look the type.

Genie ignored the insult. This meant that there was still a chance to salvage what she'd just fucked up again. 'Yes! Yes, that's why I'm here. I'm here for Wendi. I just saw her, she was back there! How do I get her out?'

You can't. If you've already passed her then she's not why you're here.

'Can't I just go back and—'

No. If it was meant to be it would already be. Your being there would have released her. Either you are here for someone else – someone you haven't reached yet – or you shouldn't be here at all.

'But I can try again, I can go back and—'

No. It's more than my job's worth.

'Come on!' Genie put her hands on her hips and stared up at

the two-metre-wide face. 'You're me! We don't obey the rules. We don't just do what we're told.'

Really? The statue now had one eyebrow raised. *That's not been my observation. Yes, Malcolm. Whatever you say, Malcolm. Besides,* it went on before Genie could protest, *I may look like you, but I'm not you. I am the Sphinx.*

'Bully for you.'

You are not supposed to be here and shall pass no further.

'Bollocks.' Genie turned to one side and sprinted as fast as she could, feet throwing up clouds of sand in her wake. She curved back around to resume her previous trajectory, smacked straight into something hard and fell over backwards.

'Ow. OW! Fuck it!' Her skull had taken the brunt of the impact. Eyes still screwed shut, she prodded at her face with cautious fingers. There didn't seem to be any blood but she suspected that it wouldn't be long before she was wearing a psychedelic bruise right in the centre of her forehead.

Bollocks to you too.

Genie's eyes snapped open to discover that the giant limestone likeness of herself had somehow moved and was still blocking her way. It looked down its nose at her, a supercilious expression on its face. Genie wondered if this was how she looked sometimes and made a mental note to be nicer to people in future. Unless they were really annoying of course.

'How did you do that?' Genie stood up and took a couple of paces back from the Sphinx. Its eyes followed her without moving which was most disconcerting.

Well, duh. This is the afterlife. Normal rules don't apply. Get used to it.

Genie wished she'd thought to bring some painkillers along with her; the impact had given her a monstrous headache. Still, if this thing was serious about sending her back it would already have done so. Maybe normal rules didn't apply, but there was nothing to say that abnormal ones didn't. She just had to find out what they were. Shouldn't there be something about a riddle?

'How come you look like me anyway?' She peered up the Sphinx's nostrils.

Don't ask me. Ask yourself. It's probably symbolic. Besides, it's much better than what I really look like.

'Er… thank you, that's sweet I guess.' Genie was unsure how to react to the compliment. 'But don't put yourself down, I'm sure you…'

I'm not going to win any beauty contests. My dad's a two-headed dog and he's also my brother.

'Eh?' Genie gaped. This was worse than *Desperate Housewives.*

My mum fucked her son. I was the result. Given that he was a bi-cranial dog and she was a snake nymph, I think I turned out pretty well. They're both dead now anyway. Can we change the subject please?

Genie was embarrassed now and dealt with this in her usual manner by going on the offensive. 'So, what about the riddle then? The answer's "*a man*" OK, can I go now?'

I don't do that one any more. Everyone knows the answer. If you really want to risk it, I'll ask you my new one.

'Risk?'

If you get it right, I let you pass. If you get it wrong, I get to devour you. Are you sure you want to go ahead? I'd turn back if I were you.

'Yeah, but as you pointed out, you're not me. You're on. Go for it.'

Almost immediately Genie regretted her bravado. What would being devoured entail down here? As Cerberus's skeleton and the Sphinx's talk of its family had shown, you *could* die in this underworld, although it was unclear where you went after that.

Very well. Here is the riddle.

'Er... aren't you going to ask me if I'm *really* sure I want to go ahead?' Genie said.

No. I only ask once. That goes for the riddle too, so pay attention. My mother had seventeen cats...

'As well as the two-headed dog?'

Fuck you. My mother, Echidna, had seventeen cats. In a box. One day, for reasons known only to herself, she decided to give them to the Furies. She promised half of them to Alecto, a third to Megaera and a ninth to Tisiphone. They weren't allowed to share any cats or cut them in half...

'Oh I think I know this one!' Genie laughed with relief. 'Doesn't someone else come along...'

Shut up. I haven't finished. Echidna gave the box of cats to the Furies who immediately started arguing over them. Echidna had told them that if they couldn't divide them as she'd instructed, she'd take them back when she returned. The Furies were particularly fond of cats, so agreed. However, as soon as Echidna had vanished they started arguing over who should get what.

As it happened, an hour or so later Metis passed by while taking her cat for a walk. Once they'd stopped shrieking at each other the Furies explained their dilemma.

'Oh that's easy,' said Metis and dropped her cat into the box so that there were now eighteen.

'Right,' she said, 'Alecto, take nine of the cats. That's half of them. Megaera, you take six, that's a third. A ninth is two, so they belong to you, Tisiphone. That leaves the one I put in, so I can take it back, is that all right?'

The Furies couldn't find fault with this logic and so thanked Metis who went on her way. Each of them felt that somehow they'd been cheated and none of them could understand why Echidna had been so unfair with the cat allocation in the first place. Nevertheless, they sat down and waited for her to return.

So here is the riddle: explain that. How could that be? And what happened when Echidna returned?

'How long have I got?' Genie was very worried now. She'd known the *solution* to the dilemma having heard something like that before, but couldn't explain it, which was what was now required of her. It just seemed like magic, sleight of number. A trick of the brain.

Take as long as you like. But remember this. If you give up, I devour you. If you get it wrong, I devour you.

The Sphinx was now staring into the middle distance with a serene expression on its face. Genie sat down in the sand cross-legged, and pulled out her iPhone. There was still no signal, so she couldn't google it, but there was of course the calculator app...

23: Woodenworld

Genie didn't look back. She was afraid that the Sphinx would change its mind, disqualify and devour her, so as far as she was concerned the more distance she put between herself and it the better.

In the end it had all come down to eighteen. A half of eighteen was nine, a third was six and a ninth was two. However, the Sphinx's mother had only offered the Furies *seventeen* cats. So the numbers they'd ended up with once Metis's cat had been added and subtracted were wrong.

And when Echidna came back, the Sphinx had asked, *what happened then?*

'Well,' Genie felt she was on shakier ground here; there wasn't an app for the behaviour of snake nymphs. 'I suppose she wasn't satisfied and took back the cats. After all none of the Furies had the right amount of cats. One of them had *nine* which is more than half of the total.'

I suppose I'll just have to let you pass then.

'Why, because I got it *right*?' Genie was sarcastic in victory.

No need to be like that. I could always change my mind, you know...

184

'Sorry.'

S'OK. At least you're not expecting me to immolate myself or something. I hate that. Or explode. I hate that too. I hope you find what it is you're looking for.

'So do I. Thanks.' Genie had started walking. Not too fast, but not too slowly either.

It's been fun wearing your face by the way – the Sphinx had begun to sink into the sand – *I might hang onto it for a while.* Within half a minute, there was no sign anything had ever been there.

That had been half an hour ago. As she walked forward now, Genie was struck by a horrified thought. Perhaps the Sphinx had devoured Nathan. She'd been so alarmed by the whole encounter that she'd forgotten to ask it if anyone else had been by. Perhaps not, though. It had claimed to be challenging her because she didn't belong, because she was still alive. Even though he had been vague about how he'd ended up down here, Genie suspected that Nathan was dead, that he belonged.

But she didn't belong. Did they really expect her to go through all this shit just to rescue fucking *Ollie*? After they'd thrown Wendi in her path just to snatch her away again? Genie considered turning around anyway, trying to walk back to the wood, but the horizon in that direction was now featureless. How could she be sure she'd be heading the right way? She'd have to keep going forward, see where that took her.

Fucking *Ollie* though.

The temperature was dropping. Rapidly. Overhead the intense brightness was leaching out of the sky, turning it a dull, uniform grey – still difficult to look at but now because of the way that it sucked at the eyes rather than dazzled them. She pocketed her shades, pulled her dressing gown tighter about her and hurried forward, the structure ahead now revealing a little more detail, although she still had no idea what it was.

The previous silence of the desert was disrupted by an increase in the strength of the wind. The sound of grains of sand rubbing together began to add up, and Genie looked over her shoulder. Back towards the horizon the three shapes of what remained of Cerberus's heads were becoming hazy as if viewed through a fine mist, although the air still tasted as dry as bone. Of the Sphinx there was no sign.

The sand itself was now chilly beneath her feet, and Genie worried that it would soon get too cold to move. In front, her destination was also becoming indistinct. She coughed as she breathed in – the dry air was now gritty. She rubbed at her eyes and squinted. She had sand in them. How had that happened? It came to her.

Sandstorm.

Genie put her sunglasses back on. This dimmed the grim appearance of her surroundings even further, but at least her eyes would be protected. She began muttering to herself.

'Bastard, bastard, bastard, bastard…'

After a while she settled into a brisk march in time to the words, punctuating every fifteenth 'bastard' with a strident 'shit'.

Bastard, bastard, bastard, bastard
Bastard, bastard, bastard, bastard
Bastard, bastard, bastard, bastard
Bastard, bastard, bastard, shit!

Not one of her most inspired creations, she thought. It was all very well surfing the wave of yes-men as she had been for the past couple of years, but when it came down to it, she'd always been afraid that someone would find her out and ask for their money back. And before she knew it her public would begin to realise that Empress Genie had no clothes, that Genie DC had feet of clay...

Right now though she was beginning to feel as if she had feet of ice. The sandstorm had become a blizzard, the individual grains now more like ice crystals than fragments of rock. Despair began to take hold of her. Fucking *Ollie?* Genie hunched her shoulders and stamped forward, staring at the ground and singing The Bastard Song.

Without warning, the ground changed underfoot and Genie staggered to a halt, thrown off-kilter. Instead of the shifting sands she'd become used to, she was now on a firm, flat surface, still scattered with sand but far more stable. She kneeled down and brushed at it. It was wooden. Glancing up, she realised that she was now almost upon the mysterious construction she'd been heading for. It was a vast ramshackle building made entirely of wood in various unexpected forms – floorboard, old doors, sections of decking, what looked like railway sleepers and even complete garden sheds, all nailed together in a haphazard manner, stretching as far as she could see to either side and at least fifty feet into the air. The surface on which she was walking was of a similar patchwork construction. She slowed down and started proceeding with a little more caution lest some old hatchway or pub cellar door open beneath her...

Genie reached the peculiar building's outer wall. The wind speed had dropped considerably, so she removed her shades and looked around. Behind her the sand blizzard raged on, but here it was as calm and quiet as the eye of a storm.

Most of the doors she could see were unlikely candidates for entrances, situated as they were halfway up the wall, sideways on or even upside down. On a whim, Genie turned right and walked, scouring the facade for something more obvious. She passed a section of toilet seats all nailed together overlapping like scales, then a section of flooring from a 1930s tube train, complete with a couple of six-inch square inspection hatches. The interior of the hatches proved a disappointment, as she discovered merely another layer of wood, this time what looked like a section of distressed pine table.

Eventually she came across a door that was the right way up and only six inches above ground level. It was made of a dark varnished wood, with a smooth metal doorknob and a polished brass plate reading '*Wentworth Bilious MD*'. This gave her a moment's pause, but her impatience got the better of her and she turned the handle and went inside.

The door shut behind her with a satisfying clunk. There was no sign of Dr Bilious and the hallway in which Genie now stood was no taller or wider than the door through which she'd entered – the walls, floors and ceiling alike consisting of dark wooden panels listing a series of names by year:

1875: Hodgeson H., Cholmondely R.
1876: Mallinson W., Smith X.
1877: Maynard F., King-Cline S.

Genie didn't give a fuck what this meant and slid down the wall into a sitting position. She massaged some feeling back into her frozen feet and looked along the hallway. Lit by a couple of gas lamps in the wall, it ended after only three metres in another door.

It could wait.

Genie lay down flat and closed her eyes. In theory she should be exhausted. She'd been travelling for... well it was difficult to say. But it was at least twenty-four hours – surely? No that was ridiculous. Was it nearer four? Her arms were heavy as if they were glued to the floor. Her eyelids drooped. She had no idea what would happen if she fell asleep. Or if she even could.

After only a minute she opened her eyes again. Apparently she couldn't. Now that her body had got some physical rest she was fine again. She rolled over onto her front and pushed herself upright. Her hair brushed the wooden ceiling as she stretched to her full height. It was just as well she rarely suffered from claustrophobia these days.

She opened the other door a crack and peered around it. The space beyond was bigger. A short flight of stairs – perhaps a set of library steps – led down into another wood-panelled room. In this one, however, there was at least some concession to decent architectural tradition – the ceiling and floor were quite clear about their roles, the former sporting a rosette from which dangled another gas lamp and the latter covered with a small Persian rug. At one side of the room a leather upholstered chair stood in front of a dark wooden bureau. A further door led from the far end of the room. No windows.

Genie stepped into the room and dropped into the chair. OK, so she wasn't tired, but she could still do with sorting herself out. Cleaning herself up.

She pushed up the bureau's lid and emptied the contents of her pockets onto the green leatherette surface. No make-up. Nothing to freshen herself up with. She spat on the end of her dressing gown cord and rubbed at her face with it. Hopefully that would get rid of the worst of the grime. She glanced around. Shame there weren't any mirrors in here.

Perhaps it was just as well. Now that the physical discomfort had passed, she was left with the mental anguish. She wouldn't have been able to look herself in the face. She should have tried harder to bring Wendi along. It was the kind of second chance no one usually got. And she'd blown it, of course.

But it would do no good sitting here feeling sorry for herself.

She opened one of the coke wraps, pinched up a small amount between finger and thumb and snorted it. Perhaps this would give her a different perspective? Massaging her nostrils she stood up again, repacked her pockets and walked across to the far door.

'How many of these are there?' she wondered aloud.

This third chamber was even bigger, quite a respectably sized living room this. Still no windows though and still entirely panelled in wood. This room also contained a desk and chair but in addition a sofa, a chest of drawers and, most importantly, a large gilt-framed mirror at one end.

Genie scurried across to it and regarded her reflection. It wasn't as bad as she'd feared; she was still halfway presentable, and could easily pass the dirty smears on her left cheek off as a deliberate attempt at grunge chic. Ideally she needed a boiler suit to pull that off though. Her dressing gown *was* already quite grubby, but it didn't fit and...

Oh for fuck's sake! What was she thinking? Did it matter what she looked like? She was stuck down here – and she was no longer sure where here was – as a result of... another absurd attempt to be a bit more like Wendi. But look where it had got her. She was seized with the sudden impression that none of this was actually here, that the surfaces of the room around her were no more than paper-thin brightly coloured representations of reality behind which lay deep layers of dark, cerebral space.

Genie felt her heart flutter as the beginnings of a panic attack seized her. It was unlikely that she'd be able to avoid it this time. Fuck. She didn't have a paper bag to breathe into.

Closing her eyes she took long, slow breaths, and thrust her hands into her pockets. Her fingers closed on the bottle of Valium. They were a lot stronger than beta blockers; that would do the trick.

She opened her eyes, feeling calmer. The knowledge that she had chemical therapy to hand made actually taking it unnecessary. Once she was sure she'd calmed down, she made her way across to the far door and walked through.

Another chamber, this time with something austere about it, something depressing. As previously, the walls were panelled but they were far cheaper, probably chipboard. Along one side of the room someone had placed a row of second-hand furniture, wooden, but painted with thick white emulsion. There were a couple of chairs, a cabinet and a small table upon which rested a plastic jug half full of water, an empty tumbler and a bunch of grapes on a willow-patterned saucer.

Maybe the coke had started working, and maybe it hadn't – as far as Genie was concerned the jury was still out on that. But what would happen if she availed herself of these refreshments? How long had they been down here anyway? She peered into the jug – not a speck of dust on the surface. It couldn't have been in there for very long.

'*Eat me,*' she said aloud. '*Drink me.*'

The refreshments were unmoved by her allusion. With a fatalistic urge, Genie picked up the jug and poured herself a glass of water, plucking a handful of grapes with the other.

Keep moving, keep going forward. She had to stop thinking about what she *could* or *should* have done back there. She *hadn't.* That had always been her problem; always too timid when it came down to it. Willing to go along the path of least resistance. Going along with what others decided.

Just as she opened her mouth to take one of the grapes, she noticed something. The surface of the water in the jug was vibrating, interference patterns of tiny waves crossing and recrossing the meniscus.

A low rumble became audible. Puzzled, Genie put down the glass and froze, hand full of grapes halfway to her mouth.

The noise grew loud very quickly and the room shook to an explosive blast, flinging her to the ground.

Someone in the adjacent room screamed deafeningly.

A wisp of smoke curled under one of the doors, which opened with a click. Genie stood up, made her way over to it and peered through.

The room next door was different again. Unvarnished wooden planking made up all six faces of a long rectangular space with a floor two feet below the level of the door she was looking through. A single old-fashioned high-energy light bulb dangled from a frayed electrical cord, dousing the interior in unsubtle illumination. Roughly fitted steel doors sat at the centre of the other three walls.

In the centre was a man on all fours. A man dressed in drab, ragged greys and browns, the remains of some kind of harness draped over his torso, straps that still smouldered, the source of the acrid smoke. He coughed and looked up.

'Fuck, are you OK?' Genie jumped down into the room, realising as she did so that she was still clutching half a bunch of grapes in one hand. The man stood up without her aid and regarded her with dark eyes set in an unshaven face beneath a badly cut, thick black fringe. His serious and sullen expression abruptly split in a grin. He shrugged off the still-smoking harness and walked up to her. Without warning he pulled her dressing gown wide open.

An expensive reproduction Motörhead T-shirt with rhinestone umlauts and a pair of Agent Provocateur knickers were all that now stood between her assets and this presumptuous creep. Without thinking she punched him square in the face with the hand that wasn't full of grapes and he fell over backwards, cursing. She pulled her dressing gown closed and turned to climb back out of the chamber. An interrogative explosion of unintelligible speech made her turn back to the man who was now looking confused and upset.

'I don't understand you. Piss off.'

'You are… American?'

'No!' Despite herself, Genie was starting to get curious. Who was this and what was he doing here?

'You are… virgin?' A hopeful note crept into the man's voice.

'What? No! Fuck off! Who are you?'

The man stared at the floor.

'Mahmoud,' he muttered by way of introduction. Genie decided to give him a second chance.

'Pleased to meet you, Mahmoud. I'm Genie,' she said, holding out her hand to be shaken. He stared at it for a second before sneaking a glance at her face and then casting his eyes downwards again.

'Fancy a grape?' Genie persisted, holding out her other hand. The man ignored it.

'You are an Ifrit? Why are you here and not in Hell? As a martyr, I should be in Paradise. Where is the Prophet and where are his companions?'

'I wouldn't call this Paradise.' Genie was starting to get an idea of how Mahmoud had ended up there. 'It's not really Hell either.'

'But the first drop of blood shed by a martyr during jihad washes away his sins!' Mahmoud blinked back tears. 'Allah bought my life in exchange for Paradise – and who fulfils his pledge better than Allah? Filthy Ifrit!'

Maybe giving him a second chance had been a mistake.

'I've been here a little while now and haven't seen anyone in charge,' Genie was starting to get angry again. 'No Allah, no Jesus and no bloody virgins either.'

'You lie!' Mahmoud turned, pulled open the steel door

behind him and disappeared through it with a howl, slamming it shut behind him. The single light bulb swung in the unexpected breeze, flickering a couple of times. Mahmoud's wailing punctuated by his footsteps, the thud of further doors and the crash of him tripping over and sending himself sprawling became ever quieter as he vanished deeper into the corridors of the Wooden Labyrinth.

'We get a lot of those chaps in here these days.'

Genie yelped and dropped the grapes. She spun round to face the new voice. A thin young man in an old-fashioned suit was standing just inside a door that led out of the chamber to the left, regarding her with a smirk over the top of his half-moon spectacles.

'Although I must say, this is the first time I've come across such a fascinating creature as yourself.'

'Who are you calling a creature?' Genie recognised another creep when she saw one, no matter how he was dressed, and she pulled her dressing gown even tighter around herself. The man ran one hand through his lank hair while proffering the other in greeting.

'Do pardon me. Aston William Webb at your service.'

Genie stepped forward and glared at him, deliberately ignoring the hand. As she'd hoped, he took a step backwards.

'My apologies young lady... I seem to have got off on the wrong foot. *A fronte praecipitium a tergo lupi* as they say...'

'*Dente lupus, cornu taurus petit,*' replied Genie, beginning to relax despite herself. Latin had been one of her favourite subjects at school. Aston looked surprised.

'Oh, I say! I do beg your pardon; from your appearance I had taken you for some savage hoyden, but quite clearly you're a young woman of some education.'

'Roedean.' As usual Genie felt embarrassed at the admission.

'Of course,' Aston beamed. 'It was either that or Cheltenham Ladies' College. Do forgive me. And your people?'

'The Drummond-Calthorpes.' Genie stared at the floor.

'Drummond-Calthorpe...' Aston removed his spectacles and polished them with his tatty silk cravat for a moment before putting them back on. 'It seems to me I know the name. Berkshire? I've been a bit out of touch down here of course. And naturally how you dress is your own business. Your robe may well be the height of fashion in the twentieth century...'

'Twenty-first.'

Aston looked a little surprised. 'Really? I must be losing track of time, my dear... Come, follow me. All will become clear.'

Genie still didn't trust him, but followed him through the nearest door anyway. After passing through a couple more wooden chambers, they arrived in one larger than she had yet seen, crowded with furnishings and reeking of mothballs and furniture polish. Aston held out a hand, indicating a faded, red velvet chaise longue.

'Do take a seat. I'm afraid I have nothing to offer you except my company, but I suspect I may be able to shed some light on your predicament. You, my dear' – he paused, enjoying the moment of drama – 'You, my dear, are dead, I'm afraid.'

'Bollocks,' said Genie, sitting down. Aston blushed and sat down in a high-backed armchair opposite.

'It's true, I fear. This is the hereafter.'

'Oh, I know *that*,' said Genie, enjoying his discomfort. 'But I'm here under special circumstances.' She was starting to feel playful. She wondered if the coke was kicking in at last.

'Oh really?' Aston raised his eyebrows. Genie got the impression he was annoyed she'd stolen his thunder. 'So how did you reach the Labyrinth then?'

'I walked. Most of the way, anyway. There was a boat earlier on, but...'

'You mean Charon's ferry?' Aston's annoyance vanished and he appeared genuinely astonished. 'I have heard of that but didn't think anyone had arrived in that manner in a very long time! I assumed he'd retired. But even so... how did you get *into* the Labyrinth?'

'Through the door.'

'The *door*?'

'Yeah, it's not far.' Genie stood up. 'Come on.'

She walked back the way they'd come and started retracing her steps, Aston scurrying close behind her. Climbing back through the high door in Mahmoud's arrival chamber, it wasn't long until they were back in the narrow vestibule in which Genie had rested on her arrival.

'It's a bit stormy,' Genie said, reaching for the handle, 'but it *is* outside...' She flung the door open.

On the other side was a wood-panelled room that hadn't been there before. Genie stepped forward.

'No, hang on... I definitely... I can't have...' She looked back at Aston who was leaning against the wall just inside the narrow chamber, arms folded, a smug expression on his face.

'I try not to venture too far from my domain,' he remarked. 'It *is* a labyrinth, after all...'

'You don't understand. I came through this door. From a desert.'

'Perhaps we should return to my accommodation?' Aston stood up and led the way back. Genie followed, head spinning. She was certain that had been the right door. Still, as she'd already discovered, normal rules didn't seem to apply down here.

'I've no doubt that you *believe* what you're telling me,' Aston remarked over his shoulder, 'but when one arrives here, one is understandably in something of a fever. Depending upon what led one here of course. Our noisy friend just now knew he was going to die so was more sure of himself, even if what awaited him beyond the veil confounded his expectations.'

'I'm not confused,' said Genie. 'I know exactly how I got here.'

Genie remained standing when they reached Aston's makeshift quarters again while he sank down into his armchair, steepling his fingers.

'As I say, I've no doubt you believe it yourself, but—'

'No!' Genie stamped her foot. 'You're not listening. Yes, this is the afterlife. You're right. But I'm not dead. I don't think so. Somehow I got here like… like Orpheus.'

'I see. Orpheus eh? Well far be it from me to call you a, should I say, *lyre*…' Aston snorted at his own joke. 'Do tell. Take a seat.'

24: The Misadventurers

Underworld, no time

Genie sat down on the chaise longue and gave Aston a summary of her journey so far, as well as a potted history of the career of Genie DC. He couldn't quite seem to get to grips with the latter.

'Music Hall, is it?'

'No, not Music Hall.' Genie was beginning to tire of Aston's misunderstandings, half of which she suspected were an affectation aiming to make him appear eccentric and endearing. If that was the case, it wasn't working. Surely he'd been down here long enough and met enough contemporary dead people to be up to speed on modern events even if he wasn't sure what century it was? How long had he been down here anyway?

'Ah now, therein lies a tale!' Aston looked pleased to have been given the opportunity to fill Genie in on his background. 'Like all of the folk down here I was, shall we say, a victim of *misadventure...*'

'What do you mean? About the misadventure?'

'It seems to be what we have in common. Not *you* of course,' Aston held up his hands, anxious not to annoy Genie again, 'but everyone else I've come across in the Labyrinth seems to have died in a certain manner. There appears to be no one in charge to confirm this – and if this is a Circle of Hell it seems a rather mild one – but I think it would be fair to say that we have all died as a result of accidental and yet somehow self-inflicted misfortune. Some of us have been indulging a death wish. Others have died fighting for unjust causes; there are a lot of soldiers here. Although soldiers from both sides of the same wars, which rather makes one wonder...'

'You're a soldier?'

'Alas no. I cannot claim that distinction. I was a gentleman investor, a businessman. Never that successful really, which is why I decided to try my luck in the New World. I'd heard tell that a lot of money was to be made in San Francisco. It was there that I discovered opium.'

'Ah. Right,' Genie nodded, 'overdose, was it?'

'No.' Aston looked at the ground. 'True, I *had* been to an opium den in Chinatown that evening, which would explain why I was perhaps a little unsteady on my feet. However, the cause of death was somewhat more mundane. I tripped and slid almost all the way down Nob Hill before being hit by a streetcar.'

Genie clapped a hand over her mouth to suppress a snigger before apologising.

'No need for remorse, dear lady,' Aston was magnanimous, 'it probably did look rather comical.'

Genie decided not to mention the fact that she'd been laughing at the name *Nob Hill*.

'I woke up here instantly. At first I took it for some kind of hospital. However, the lack of medical staff began to erode that belief after a few days. As did the fact that I didn't need to eat or drink.'

Genie was pleased to have one of her questions answered; she'd been wondering whether the necessities of life still lived up to their name in the hereafter. The *un*-necessities she was still unsure about. If the coke had worked at all then it was probably wearing off by now. She was sure it wouldn't be long before she was forced to excuse herself and find somewhere for a little top-up.

'After a while, having had the opportunity to question other new arrivals, it became obvious that this was the afterlife. Not Heaven or Hell. If anything, I suppose it's a rather dull Purgatory. I was as surprised as anyone to end up here; up until my death I was a confirmed atheist. Although as I mentioned, the lack of any evident authority here does make me wonder whether perhaps Nietzsche was right. Do we now inhabit an atheist afterlife? The only authorities here are the walls. Relentless and implacable...'

'I have been outside, you know,' Genie reminded him. Aston nodded.

'So you say. But now you're inside, I am very much afraid that is where you must remain. Still, *nil desperandum*, perhaps you may yet locate your lost beau. From what you say the manner of his death has something of the misadventure about it. While there's... *mind* there's hope.'

It was true. Perhaps far from standing in the way of her goal, the Labyrinth was her final destination. But even if she found Ollie, then what? How would they get out again? And what had happened to Nathan? Was he now wandering around somewhere in here as well?

'So no one's ever got out then? As far as you know?'

'I cannot claim to have met all the inhabitants of this warren world,' said Aston, 'who must number in their milliards. I have never heard of anyone getting out of here. Not that people haven't tried of course...'

'Who? Who's tried?' Genie sat up straight, fingering the wrap of coke in her dressing gown pocket.

'The Army of God.' Aston rolled his eyes towards the wooden ceiling. 'They're always on the lookout for new recruits and yet as fast as people sign up, others get bored and drift away. They once set fire to a whole section of the maze. It burned for days and stank for months. It did absolutely no good whatsoever.'

'It didn't reach the outside then?'

'It had no discernible effect on the structure. It was most peculiar. You'd think this lot,' and here Aston rapped on the wooden panelling behind his head, 'would make perfect firewood, but despite the flames and the smoke, once the blaze had been extinguished you wouldn't know it had ever happened aside from, as I mentioned, the smell. I have a theory about that though.'

'And that is?'

'I'm glad you asked, I'm glad you asked.' Aston started looking pleased with himself. 'You'll have noticed the *singular* nature of this place's decor? And you'll recall I mentioned that all the inhabitants are the victims of misadventure? I suspect that the very fabric of the Labyrinth itself is formed of material destroyed by fire. Inanimate misadventure. You know once I could swear I came across a corner of The Crystal Palace…'

'Right, so even if it burned down here, it still ended up here afterwards.' Genie was starting to get the impression she was about to reach the limits of any useful information Aston might be able to offer. '*Where else was it going to go, Detroit?*'

'You see?' Aston nodded, looking a little confused by Genie's last non sequitur. 'So here it remains and likewise we do. It's not a bad afterlife, there's plenty to read if you know where to look.'

Genie looked at Aston's bookcase, packed with the ghosts of tomes that had fallen in charity-shop fires and book burnings alike over the past century. *Jaws. Quotations from Chairman Mao*

Zedong. *The Da Vinci Code. Marx's Communist Manifesto. Han Solo at Stars' End.*

'You get used to the lack of a need for food and drink and the associated pleasure of their consumption.' Aston looked at Genie. 'But the intellectual pursuits can't be an adequate substitute for every vice I may have enjoyed in life. I miss it you know.'

'Now look!' Genie stood up. Typical man. When it came down to it, only after one thing… 'If you think I'm going to…'

'Oh my dear!' Aston held up a hand and laughed. 'I was in no way implying that you and I join giblets. Good lord, no, what do you take me for? I was referring to my beloved opium. Despite a century's abstinence, I still crave its smoky oblivion.'

'I might be able to help you there,' Genie remained standing, toying with the bottle of Valium tablets in her dressing gown pocket, 'if you help me.'

'How so?' Aston looked cautious but excited.

'How do I find the Army of God?'

'I'd advise against it, but I dare say they'll find *you* soon enough if you stay on the move. I wouldn't be at all surprised to discover that the Mahometan you encountered just before you met me had already joined their ranks.'

'Any particular route?' Genie wandered in the direction of the door furthest away from the direction she *felt* she'd come. She might not be able to get back into the desert, but at least by moving away from it she was making progress.

'None better than any other.' Aston shrugged, looking at her with an expression that implied he felt he'd kept his side of the bargain. 'If I see your beau, I'll tell him which way you went.'

'You do that.' Genie opened the door then tossed the bottle of Valium over to Aston who caught it. 'Knock yourself out.'

25: Labyrinthine

Underworld, no time

It was difficult to keep going in a straight line, as not all the chambers she passed through had doors in all of their walls. However, Genie made sure that she countered every right turn with a left turn as soon as she could – and vice versa.

So Aston had arrived in situ. So had Wendi apparently, and Mahmoud had done it almost before her eyes. Where did Charon come into all this then? And if Genie had found her way in via the traditional entrance – perhaps due to her expectations, her obsessions – how did that explain Nathan?

Very little of the Labyrinth was as well furnished as Aston's nest, but it was still predominantly wooden. The light mainly came from electrical bulbs although this uniformity was broken up by the occasional gas lamp or candle. Genie passed though corridors, attics and basements, once or twice having to clamber through windows or hatches rather than the more usual doors. It was while doing so – into the interior of a garden shed – that she got a splinter in the bottom of her foot.

'Fuck!' She tumbled forward and sprawled onto the shed floor, knocking over a spade and a rake and banging her head on the corner of a paint-spattered table. 'Fuck it to buggery!'

Genie hauled herself upright and bent to pull the splinter out of her foot. As she reached out one hand to the table to steady herself, a sudden noise froze her in a half-crouch.

Thump! Thud, thud, thud, thud...

It was unmistakably the sound of someone else jumping down into a nearby room and making their way forward at speed. As the thuds faded into the distance, she started breathing again. Was she being followed? Perhaps it had been Nathan. Aston had implied that it wouldn't be long before the Army of God found *her*, but Genie decided she'd prefer her first encounter with them to be on her terms. She finished standing up, picked up a rusty hoe from the pile of tools in the corner and pulled open the shed door.

The door led onto the platform of the lower deck of a Routemaster bus with boarded-up windows. There was no clear way out towards the front, so she started climbing the tiny claustrophobic staircase, which smelled of stale cigarette smoke.

'Oh for fuck's sake...' Genie banged her head against a rather unexpected low wooden ceiling that the stairs had ended in rather than the upper deck she was expecting. She put down the hoe, steadied herself with one hand against the handrail and reached up with the other. Her fingers found a heavy bolt that slid aside with ease. She pushed upwards and peered over the edge of the trapdoor.

It was pitch black up there. She pushed the trapdoor harder and it flipped over, falling flat against the floor of this new chamber with a resounding crack. It was big up here. Capacious.

Genie climbed all the way through the hatch and looked around at the darkness. The feeble light leaking though the trapdoor from below was swallowed up within a few metres. She knew she wasn't outside again, that would have felt different, but it was certainly the biggest room she'd come across in the Labyrinth.

And the darkest.

'Hello?'

There was no echo, Genie's voice being swallowed by distance. How far to the wall? Where was the next door? If she stood any hope of keeping to her preferred route, she'd have to head that way, but once she was travelling through emptiness, who was to say she wouldn't start walking in circles?

She kneeled down by the hatch and reached down to pull the hoe up to her. Shame she couldn't set fire to it or something, make herself a torch. Perhaps if she closed the trapdoor again her eyes would become accustomed to the darkness.

She felt unhappy about shutting off her only source of illumination and was relieved to find an iron handle attached to the trapdoor, so at least she wouldn't get stranded up here.

She sat there cross-legged for ten minutes, one hand on the iron handle, the other clutching the hoe, which she'd placed across her lap. The darkness around her remained impenetrable and her eyes weren't adapting themselves. What had she got herself into? She'd had enough of this... this *insanity*. This dream. She pinched her arm.

'Wake up, you stupid cow!'

The silence devoured her angry shout. Perhaps she should go back and find Aston? Get that Valium back off him; maybe if she took enough of them she'd wake up back in the flat in London. She pulled at the iron handle.

The trapdoor was immobile, re-bolted from below.

Genie lost her temper, leaped up and started hammering at the trapdoor with the hoe.

'Open the door, you fuckers!' Tiny sparks leaped from the impact when the hoe's blade met the iron handle. With a howl she flung the hoe over-arm into the darkness where it bounced a couple of times before clattering to a halt. She sank to her knees and started weeping.

Genie had never been particularly good at crying. If there was anyone else around embarrassment was always quick to override upset as the dominant emotion and sometimes it managed to sneak up on her even when she was alone. However, on this occasion it didn't get the opportunity to do so – a series of alarming noises stopped her sobs in their tracks and had her straining into the darkness for their source.

Thud, thud, thud, thud, thud... crash.

This somewhere beneath the wooden floor she was kneeling on. She felt about for the handle of the hoe before remembering that she'd hurled it off into the distance somewhere.

Thud, thud, thud, thud.

A bit further away now, heading in the direction she'd been intending to go, but one storey below.

'Fuck it. Fuck it.' Genie stood up and looked in the direction she'd thrown her weapon. Useless. She couldn't see a thing. She stuck her hands in her pockets and her fingers brushed against her iPhone. Of course!

The battery was low, but hopefully there'd be enough power in it for a couple of flash photos? Shame she'd never got around to downloading that flashlight app Ollie had got so excited about.

Flash. There it was, a few metres away lying askew on the decking. Fixing it in her mind's eye, she scuttled over to where it had appeared to be in a half-crouch, slowing down when she felt she might be in danger of tripping over it.

Got it. She stood up, starting to feel a little better about her situation. The flash had also suggested the notion of dark walls not far distant; could she risk another photo?

She turned in what she hoped was still the correct direction, one hand brandishing the hoe while the other held her iPhone at arm's length.

Flash. She got the impression of a large hall with a high ceiling; detail on the walls too intricate for her to be able to work out in the split second of illumination she had available to her. She carried on walking in a straight line before another thought stopped her in her tracks.

'Dumb blonde!' She slapped herself across the forehead, and laughed. The flash was only a side effect of another of the iPhone's functions. Its *camera.*

She noticed that the battery was now at less than 20%. This worried her. She opened up the photo album and thumbed through the camera roll to the most recent shot.

A bit blurred. Nevertheless of some use. If the photo was to be believed, there was a wall consisting of a lattice of white wooden beams only twenty metres ahead of her, with what could possibly be doors between some of the upright spars. The design was familiar to her; perhaps an architectural style she'd seen elsewhere at some point.

Genie jogged forward faster now, swinging the hoe in front of her. Even if she didn't get to hit anyone with it, at least it would stop her crashing into anything.

Without warning there was a click, a hum and a burst of bright redness. The chamber was illuminated. Genie peered out between her fingers. Even if her eyes hadn't adapted to the darkness, they now found the sudden brightness uncomfortable.

The light came from a single source up high on the wall ahead of her; an illuminated sign spelling out a short message in large, square red lettering.

WEST PIER.

She was in the West Pier. The force of this hit her with a sudden inexplicable guilt and her head spun. Yes, it had burned down, so it was no surprise that it had ended up down here, but to come across it when it had such significance to her seemed almost...

Normal rules didn't seem to apply. Of *course* she'd come across it. It would have been odd if she hadn't; this was her journey. Others would have come across something else.

WEST PIER.

Hang on. This didn't make sense. The letters had been on the *outside* of the pavilion at the end of the pier, and yet she was inside. However, a closer examination of the walls and ceiling revealed them to indeed be the exterior of the building she remembered from her time at university. Somehow inverted, turned inside out.

If the outside was in here, what was out there? The windows lining the walls revealed nothing, their blackness mirroring the interior where a solitary figure in a grubby white dressing gown clutching a hoe stood alone at the centre of a wooden field.

Genie walked over to the nearest windows, cautious, but even close up all she could see was her own reflection, a frightening figure in the crimson glow. Propping the hoe against the window frame, she leaned forward, curling her hands to shield her eyes from the reflection of the interior.

It was very dark out there, but at least she could make out the ground in the windows' faint gleam. More wooden boards, stretching to black infinity as the light surrendered to the distance. The window creaked as she leaned on it; she could probably get it open.

But did she really want to go wandering off into the emptiness? Was it actually outside the Labyrinth or just another even more incomprehensible part of it?

Thud, thud, thud, thud.

She spun round away from the window. That had been very

close, almost directly beneath her feet. She grabbed the hoe and started running sideways towards the end of the chamber, her back to the windows, until she was overwhelmed by the idea of something looking in at her and spun back to face the glass. At least this way she could see the reflection of the rest of the interior as she sidled at speed towards what she hoped was the exit. There were some doors at the foot of the wall directly below the illuminated sign.

What was that? In the distance 'outside' she could have sworn she'd just seen a flash of white, something running through the darkness.

Thud, thud, thud, thud.

Now the sound was coming from near the doors she was heading to. She couldn't help turning to look directly at them, and as she did she saw the white thing again out of the corner of her eye. Something running. Two somethings? A closer look and they'd gone.

Thud.

As she approached the doors, the hum coming from the electricity running through the lettering was louder, and she could hear that it had started to waver. The lights flickered.

Thud thud.

'Fuck!' She turned from the window and started sprinting towards the doors. They couldn't be more than twenty metres away now. The lights flickered again and went out. Genie continued her mad gallop, now whirling the hoe in front of her, her voice rising in a siren howl.

The thuds came thick and fast now, combining with her howling and footfalls to produce a maddening cacophony. The hairs on the back of her neck and arms stood up as, despite the noise, she could now quite clearly hear a large crowd of people whispering about her mere centimetres from her ears.

The hoe was ripped from her grip as she smashed into

the end of the chamber, went sprawling through a door that opened at her impact and ended up in a pile against the wall of a thankfully illuminated corridor. The door swung back and closed with a metallic snick.

The silence was only broken by the sound of her breathing. She was too winded even to swear. Genie sat up and looked down the corridor, which was narrow and curved. Like most of what she'd seen of the Labyrinth, it too was made of wood – varnished, pale, uncomplicated panels. The door she'd come through was in the outer wall of the curve and from this side was more suited to a broom cupboard than a chamber the size of the West Pier Pavilion. It was distinguished only with a small brass handle and a stencilled legend *1A*.

She stood up. The floor was covered in wall-to-wall red carpet, faded and worn but still more comfortable than anything she'd come across so far. The warm yellow light from the electric bulbs that punctuated the ceiling every three metres or so made the sinister dark tumult from which she'd just emerged seem like part of another world. So strong was the sense of discontinuity that before she knew what she was doing she'd opened door 1A and poked her head back inside.

The darkened interior of the inverted pavilion was still there. Shutting the door again she began walking around the curve of the corridor, which was still taking her in the direction she wanted to go, just about. The muffled warmth of this gently curving hallway was having a soothing effect on her state of mind; panic averted. Even the pains in her legs and arms from when she'd just crashed into the wall were beginning to dissipate.

She opened door 1B when she came across it, but that actually did lead to a broom cupboard. Now that she'd lost her hoe she considered arming herself with a mop, but in the end decided to rely on her wits and her fists. They'd got her this far, even if she had lost Nathan. Still it was his own fault for wandering off.

A door came into view on the inner curve, this one larger and stencilled with the word *circle*. Was this a theatre? She pulled the door open and was confronted with a pair of red drapes, thick with dust. Pushing them aside, she stepped through.

Vertigo made the soles of her feet tingle as if effervescing, bolts of alarm shooting up her calves. Her stomach recoiled inwardly. She was standing at the top of a narrow and very steep set of stairs leading down between multiple rows of sharply raked seating. Far below, a desk in front of a blackboard (so, a theatre of the academic variety then) provided the focus for the seats, which were almost all occupied.

Genie emitted an involuntary yelp and the members of the audience sitting nearest her looked around. Mostly men, and mostly in military dress of one kind or another. A US Marine at the end of one of the rows stood up and indicated a free seat halfway along.

The blackboard caught her attention. In a neat but childish hand it bore the legend 'ARMY OF GOD'. She'd found them. Against all odds, she'd stumbled across their latest meeting. *Normal rules…*

'Ma'am?' the Marine whispered. He stepped into the aisle and indicated that she should take a seat.

'Sure, thanks, sorry.' Genie kept her voice low too, squeezing past him and along the aisle before lowering herself into the empty seat between a chubby man in desert fatigues and a Japanese policeman. Had she interrupted anything? It seemed not; they were just waiting, waiting in utter silence. Scattered among the military men was a small handful of women and civilians. Some of them were dressed very oddly indeed.

A door down beside the blackboard opened, admitting another soldier in modern combat uniform; head shaven, bearing confident. The audience rose and Genie had joined them before she knew what she was doing.

'At ease.'

That voice. As she sat down with the rest of them Genie was racking her brain as to why that voice was so familiar, so *horrible.* And then the figure's face angled up, staring directly at her, before splitting in a grin.

Her blood ran cold. She'd never really understood the expression before, putting it down to clumsy metaphor, but now she knew it to be the literal truth. She felt ice in her veins and the unwelcome acceleration of her heart as adrenaline told her to flee.

He was older now, he was stockier, his hair was short and no longer green, but that was him.

'Posh Totty! Glad you could join us.' The sound of his voice and that hated nickname dispelled any last hopes Genie might have entertained about it being a simple case of mistaken identity.

It was Cosmo.

26: Workers Beer

London, summer 1999

It was all very exciting.

As Genie and Tabby climbed out of the back of Tabby's father's car, they could see the crowd of interesting-looking people across there on Clapham Common. People they'd soon be joining.

The driver opened the boot and handed them their brand-new rucksacks and tent. Tabby's father emerged from the passenger seat and looked over the road with an indulgent smile at the grimy horde.

'Now do call me if anything goes wrong, anything at all.' He turned to Tabby. 'Any time of the day or night. Phone fully charged?'

Tabby nodded and held up her pristine pink Ericsson. Genie thought it looked like a giant boiled sweet, but was still jealous. Her father hadn't bought her a mobile phone yet.

Then again, her father didn't do that much for her anyway. He was personable enough and obviously loved her, but if it hadn't been for Tabby and *her* father, they wouldn't be here.

Tabby was obsessed with Fun Lovin' Criminals, and when she discovered that they were playing at the Reading Festival she was determined to go. As luck would have it, her father had

213

been able to provide her with an 'in'. Anthony Twichen MP was a member of the New Labour government and as such he had links with a number of public-sector unions. Apparently, these unions provided teams of bar staff who worked at the festivals under the banner of the Workers Beer Company. In exchange for a little bit of pint-pulling, you could get in free. You might even get a backstage pass and end up hobnobbing with the bands.

'And if you need anything, let Amber know,' Mr Twichen went on. Amber was an intern at Labour HQ who was heavily involved with her union, and it was through her that he'd managed to wangle places for Tabby and a friend.

Even though she wasn't that interested in pop music herself, Genie was happy to have been asked along as Tabby's friend. Tabby had lots of friends and Genie was surprised to have been picked. At school, she'd only been admitted into Tabby's inner circle when one of the other louder girls was otherwise engaged; however, since they'd left sixth form, Tabby had summoned Genie on a number of occasions. All Tabby ever seemed to do was talk at her, but seeing as Genie had always been unpopular – partly due to her height – she wasn't going to question the attentions of one of the more popular girls from House 3. Being talked at was a lot better than being picked on.

Genie thought Tabby was much prettier than her, so it wasn't surprising that she'd already had boyfriends. Genie'd never really had that much of an opportunity to meet any boys, and certainly the ones who'd lived nearby hadn't seemed that interesting. Perhaps she'd meet someone here?

Mr Twichen climbed back into his car, and Tabby struck out for the pelican crossing, leaving Genie to carry the tent. Genie didn't mind, she was happy to help, especially to help someone like Tabby.

Tabby had black shoulder-length hair and pale skin. She was

of average height, but as far as Genie was concerned this was the only average thing about her. Genie wished she had curves like Tabby instead of a figure like a gawky silver birch. Even as they arrived at the outskirts of the crowd, heads were turning to follow Tabby's confident progress, oblivious of the clumsy tree bringing up the rear. Genie didn't mind. Her eyes were on Tabby too.

'Amber?' Tabby strode up to a harassed-looking young woman with red hair in a ponytail. 'We're here. Daddy says hi.'

'Darling.' Amber cracked a half-smile and air-kissed Tabby, clipboard and pen held out to one side. 'And your little friend...?' She cast about for Tabby's plus-one, completely looking through Genie twice.

'Here, silly!' Tabby reached behind her and dragged Genie forward by the sleeve of her coat.

'Hello.' Genie held out a hand, but Amber just glanced at her and made a tick on her clipboard.

'Eugenie Drummond-Calthorpe, yes?'

'Yes,' said Genie, 'Genie. Pleased to meet you.'

Amber wandered off, calling for someone called Stephen.

'She's probably just stressed.' Tabby gave Genie's hand a brief squeeze. 'Don't worry, Daddy says she's quite nice really.'

People were starting to sit down on the grass as the standing around got too much for them. Genie put down the tent and her rucksack and lowered herself to the ground. Tabby remained standing, absently stroking the top of Genie's head as she looked about in excitement.

It was quite interesting, thought Genie, especially what some of the people were wearing. A little way off sat a group of people dressed like the teenagers she used to see in town when she was still at school. A lot of them were wearing khaki and most of them had dreadlocks in various colours.

One of the young men saw her looking and flashed her a

cheeky grin. Genie looked away, but when she looked back he was still staring at her, smiling. She didn't know how to react to this so stared at the ground and started winding a grass stem around one of her fingers. Why was he looking? She remembered her thoughts about possibly meeting someone at this festival and felt herself blushing. Maybe he… liked her? But why? She was sitting next to Tabby.

She glanced up at him out of the corner of her eye. He was still looking and mouthed something.

She supposed he was quite cute. His hair wasn't in locks, it was just messy and dyed bright green. His mischievous smile put her in mind of Loki from Norse mythology. She wouldn't actually go so far as to say she *fancied* him, but there was something about his impudent scrutiny that kept drawing her attention back.

She was flattered.

She felt a tug on her hair and looked up into Tabby's ivory features.

'Come on, daydreamer! That's us!'

It was true. Someone had been shouting '*MSF!*' for the past twenty seconds; that was the group they were part of. She struggled to her feet and hurried after Tabby, who was already walking off in the direction of one of the coaches that had just pulled up alongside the common. She glanced across at Loki who winked at her.

Once they'd stowed their bags, they climbed aboard. Tabby made a beeline for a pair of empty seats four or five rows from the front and sat down by the window. Genie didn't mind sitting in the aisle; at least it would give her room to stretch her legs out a little once they were underway. She'd never travelled by coach before and was surprised at how little legroom there was. From the outside, they always looked so luxurious.

Most of the rest of their MSF comrades had taken up

residence near the rear of the coach; this meant that Genie and Tabby would end up surrounded by people they didn't know. Genie imagined that this might have been why Tabby had chosen to sit here; their vantage point would give them ample opportunity to scrutinise members of the other groups as they boarded.

Genie stared at her feet, clad in the brand-new Doc Martens Tabby had insisted she buy for the trip.

'Hello girls!' Genie looked up. Loki was standing in the aisle right next to them, having just boarded with his group of colourful friends. 'Looking forward to it?'

'Yes, I can't wait to see Fun Lovin' Criminals.' Tabby leaned towards Loki, forcing Genie to sit back a bit. 'Hope we don't have to work when they're on.'

'Not my cup of tea.' Loki pulled a face. 'How about you, darlin'? Anything you're looking forward to?' He touched Genie's shoulder for a second with one grubby hand before letting it fall back to his side.

'Don't know really.' Genie stared at her hands in her lap. Loki smelled odd. Not necessarily unpleasant, but definitely… odd.

'I'm just going for a laugh.' Loki didn't seem to be that bothered by her incoherent response. 'We always send a group along; I've been going for years. Glastonbury, Phoenix, Reading, Tribal Gathering…'

Genie had no idea what he was on about now. She hoped he'd leave them alone soon; even though she was starting to find his possible interest in her a little intoxicating, this was outweighed by the avalanche of embarrassment she was now feeling. What would Tabby say? It was as if she'd somehow blown it before they'd even started.

'Call me Cosmo,' said Loki. He turned and started to walk

back to the seat he'd claimed near the front before pausing and looking over his shoulder.

'Missing you already!' he said and winked.

'What a loser!' Tabby whispered loudly, wrinkling her nose. 'Poor you!' Genie didn't know how to respond. Still it could have been worse; Tabby wasn't actually cross with her.

Seats full, the coach shuddered and pulled out into the slow-moving South London traffic. Tabby handed Genie one of the two pairs of headphones plugged into her Sony MiniDisc player. Genie knew next to nothing about music but had spent just enough time with Tabby over the past couple of days to be able to identify the Fun Lovin' Criminals' first album.

By the time they'd reached the end of track fifteen, the coach was climbing the Westway, finally picking up speed as it pulled free of the London gridlock. Genie felt the acceleration as excitement in the pit of her stomach.

She'd never really been anywhere interesting on her own. She'd been sent away to boarding school, but that had very much been a home away from home. It may well have been on the outskirts of a large town rather than in the middle of nowhere, but for all she'd seen of the town, for all she'd participated in its nightlife, she might as well have been studying on the moon.

That was one of the reasons she'd picked the university she was off to in October. It was in the same town as her school, but she was hoping that the freedom afforded a classics undergraduate at Sussex would be orders of magnitude greater than that available to a shy girl doing her A levels at Roedean. She was looking forward to getting to know Brighton a lot better if she dared.

Some of her school friends had expressed envy at the exotic holiday locations her parents whisked her off to every summer, but despite the length of the beaches, whiteness of the sand and blueness of the oceans, she had never found them that thrilling and usually ended up indoors with a book most of the time. If only they'd taken her to Greece, Jordan or Egypt, places with something to look at, places that appealed to her interest in the classical world.

The Reading Festival wasn't exactly the Parthenon, but at least it promised more activity than Barbados, Tenerife or Lanzarote.

The coach lurched and Genie fell forward, nearly banging her head on the back of the seat in front. Peering into the aisle, she could see through the windscreen that they were joining the back of a long queue of stationary traffic. There were groans from a gang of boys somewhere near the back and someone started swearing.

Loki – or rather Cosmo as she now knew him to be called – poked his head round the edge of his seat before sidling into the aisle and making his way rearwards. As he passed Genie's seat, he winked at her.

'Typical,' Tabby was getting irritated; 'I *knew* we should have met them at the festival. We could have stayed at yours and gone from there. I *told* Daddy. But he wouldn't listen.'

Genie offered her some crisps, but Tabby shook her head, too cross for food.

'Don't mind if I do!' Cosmo was at her shoulder again. He reached into the bag for a handful of crisps and stuffed them all into his mouth at once. Genie didn't know how to react. She'd never come across anyone so bold and unpredictable before.

Cosmo sauntered back to the front of the coach and dropped back into his seat, waking his neighbour who scowled at him. This was an older man with curly grey and black shoulder-length hair and tattoos on his face. Genie thought he looked like her idea of an evil druid. She turned to Tabby to point this out, but Tabby was now studying the central reservation with fury.

Genie closed her eyes. She hadn't slept much the night before, what with the anticipation of today's journey. Before long she dozed. The lurching movement of the coach as it clawed an extra three metres of journey every ten seconds or so began to rock her to sleep, the conversation and giggling from the people all around her morphing into an incoherent babble which her dreaming mind began to interpret in different ways.

She was in a boat, but when she reached the beach she realised that there wasn't any water. It was a desert and she was lost in it. None of the doors seemed to lead anywhere, and now many of them were too small for her to fit through anyway. People started whispering about her, so she started running and the floor splintered and gave way and she was falling, falling...

The dark red of the dream gave way to the intense grey light of the English sky and her plummet became the forward motion of the coach, now free of congestion and accelerating towards its destination. Genie found herself slumped on her seat, leaning towards Tabby. She sat up straight and glanced at her friend.

Tabby was asleep too, and, Genie realised with a delighted horror, snoring quite loudly. She wondered if she'd been snoring as well. She hoped not.

After half an hour of unimpeded progress, the note of the engine changed as they mounted the slip road of Junction 11 and rolled to a standstill at the roundabout. The silence felt refreshing, the sudden absence of the motorway noise reminding Genie of the calmness she always felt after a long, solitary cry.

There was a snorting, spluttering noise.

'Are we there?' Tabby was looking up at Genie, blinking.

'I think so. I saw a sign. Only three miles now.'

Tabby sat up in her seat and began scrutinising the adjacent traffic.

The coach struggled over the mud at the TRADE entrance, lurching from side to side, until finally, they pulled up next to a man in a fluorescent yellow jerkin. The driver wound down his window.

'Workers Beer.'

This magic phrase satisfied the dayglo guardian, who waved them on past a couple of temporary buildings and onto a scruffy patch of brown grass. As the driver turned the engine off, everyone got up at once, chattering, excited. A young man wearing a lanyard stood up at the front of the coach and started shouting what Genie could only assume were instructions. It was impossible to hear him over the din. In the end, he gave up and bent to whisper in the driver's ear. There was a hiss and the door opened.

Genie tried to stand up, but no one pushing past in the aisle stopped to let her out, so in the end she sat back down and waited for the rush to pass. It was just like supper time at school, and just like then, she didn't mind letting the more enthusiastic members of the crowd go first. She looked at Tabby who was squinting at herself in a small circular mirror as she retouched her make-up, seemingly in no hurry either.

Through the window, Genie could see Cosmo and his group laying claim to a patch of grass; Cosmo caught her eye and began showing off, rugby tackling one of his friends and crashing to the ground, rolling over and over and kicking everyone's luggage. Seated cross-legged on the grass, the Evil Druid regarded him with a withering eye.

'Come on G, let's go!' In the foreground Tabby had finished

her make-up job and had decided that Genie was holding up the party. It was true, they were the only ones left on the coach.

As they stepped down, Lanyard Man handed each of them a lanyard of their own marked *The Carling Weekend Reading Festival Friday 27th – Sunday 29th August Bank Holiday Weekend – STAFF (Workers Beer Company)*. Tabby rushed over to Amber, leaving Genie to retrieve their luggage from the coach's under-floor locker.

By the time Genie had joined the little group around Amber, she was already halfway through her instructions, and handed Genie a photocopied sheet of A4 without even looking at her.

'Once you've set up your tent,' she raised her voice so as to be heard over the hubbub of her opposite numbers from other groups issuing almost identical instructions, 'you should go over to the catering tent.' She indicated a grimy white marquee a little way off. 'There's a meeting for everyone there at seven, just before dinner. They'll tell you where everything is, what the shifts are, and fill you in on some of the dos and don'ts.'

Genie had erected the large tent they were sharing under Tabby's supervision and they'd walked over to claim the best seats in the catering tent by ten to seven.

The interior of the marquee smelled of mud and burgers. To be honest, Genie wasn't sure if there were any good places to sit. The plastic chairs were just like some of the cheaper ones from school and were slowly sinking into the grass. All of the long tables were covered with filthy plastic tablecloths.

Still, at least they hadn't had to choose who to sit next to; that was one advantage of having got there a little early. Genie was grateful for being spared that social minefield.

'Is it OK to sit here?' asked a quiet voice. Genie looked up. At first glance, she thought she was looking at a pig-faced ten-year-old boy and wondered what someone that young was doing there. However, the wrinkles at the corners of the creature's eyes plus traces of chipped nail varnish soon disabused her of this notion. There'd been tomboys at school, of course, but none of them quite this boyish.

'Sure,' said Genie. Tabby ignored the scruffy figure and craned her neck towards the entrance, probably to check whether anyone interesting was going to come in.

'I'm Nerys,' the girl said, offering Genie a nicotine-stained hand in greeting. Genie shook it.

'Genie,' she said.

'Where're you from?' asked Nerys, pulling a scruffy packet of tobacco from the pocket of her donkey jacket and starting to fashion a home-made cigarette with hands that Genie could now see were trembling slightly. Nerys didn't look nervous though.

'I don't live that far from here actually...' Genie began, but stopped as Nerys shook her head and waved a hand at her.

'Nah, sorry, I meant who you were working for? What group?' Despite her directness, Nerys was friendly and if anything quite interested in what Genie had to say. This was a new experience for Genie.

'We're with MSF,' said Genie, moving her chair back so as to include Tabby in the conversation. 'This is Tabby.'

'Hiya.' Nerys reached across Genie to offer Tabby the grimy hand of friendship as well, but Tabby just glanced at her and muttered a non-committal greeting back.

'I'm with Hack. Haitch Ay See.' Nerys turned back to her cigarette manufacture, unbothered by Tabby's slight. 'Haringey Anarchist Collective.'

A spasm of panic shot through Genie's guts. Didn't anarchists blow things up? Nerys didn't look violent.

'We provide support for class war prisoners.' Nerys finished making her cigarette and popped it in her mouth. 'Legal aid, reading material. That sort of fing.' She lit her cigarette with a match.

Genie hoped that Nerys wasn't going to ask her about MSF, as she only had a very sketchy idea what it was and wasn't even sure what the initials stood for.

'Smoke?' Nerys offered Genie the tobacco. Genie almost accepted out of politeness before coming to her senses.

'No thank you,' she said, 'but thanks for offering.'

Nerys looked a bit puzzled but smiled before leaning forward on the table with her elbows and resting her head on her left hand as she regarded Genie.

'First time?'

'Yes.' Genie decided against lying to sound cool. She'd only get caught out and that would be mortifying.

'It's a cool gig,' said Nerys, 'even if the bands aren't that much cop. If you're lucky you might get to serve in the VIP bar backstage. It's quite funny some of the shit those rich fuckers get up to...'

'I guess,' said Genie. She wondered if Nerys would think of her as a rich fucker if she knew about her background, so decided against mentioning it. Nerys didn't seem that bad, certainly more friendly than Genie had ever imagined an anarchist might be.

The tent was now full and the distinct odour of sweat had been mixed in to the cocktail of earth, fast food and beer. Over to one side Lanyard Man stood up in front of a noticeboard and shouted for attention. No one took a blind bit of notice of him. He tried again. Nothing. Eventually a stocky woman dressed in denim pushed him aside before roaring at the assembled masses.

'*Shut up!*'

Her spiel was fairly standard stuff, mostly a litany of *don'ts* with a scattering of health and safety. Don't be late for your shift. Don't get drunk before your shift. Don't do drugs before your shift. In fact don't do drugs. Don't go into the VIP area unless you're supposed to. If you nick money from the till you'll get handed over to the police.

She glanced down at Nerys who crossed her eyes and pulled a face. *Don't worry about it*, she seemed to be telling Genie, *they have to say this*.

Tabby was bored and was playing with her bright-pink mobile, which was attracting the attention of some of their nearer neighbours.

Everyone started talking again. They'd get training in serving beer the next morning; now they were free for the rest of the evening.

'Comin' to this club?' asked Nerys. 'There's nothing happenin' on site tonight, but there's a club at the leisure centre down the road. Usually goes on till quite late. They've got a bar.'

'Tabby? What do you think?' Genie was reluctant to commit herself to something Tabby wasn't going to join her for.

'Hmm?' Tabby looked up from her phone.

'There's a club in the leisure centre. Shall we go?'

Tabby appeared to consider this before nodding. She even acknowledged Nerys with a half-smile. The three of them stood up.

'What time does it start?' asked Genie. 'Have we got time to freshen up a bit?'

Before Nerys could answer, Cosmo pushed in front of her to stand before Genie.

'Bet you were wondering how long you could bear to live without me!' he said, doing a little dance on the spot. 'What time does *what* start?'

'The club in the leisure centre. Nerys was telling me about

it. Do you know her?' Genie tried to move so that she could see Nerys again, but it was tricky; she had her legs against the table as it was.

Cosmo didn't even look at Nerys. It was as if she were invisible. If anything, he seemed almost confused by the fact that Genie had referred to her.

'Oh that thing. I might go. It's at nine. Plenty of time to make yourself beautiful! Not that you need it of course.'

'Catch you later, Genie.' Nerys withdrew with a sour look on her face. Genie couldn't understand it. Why wasn't he bothering Tabby? She was much more attractive.

But on some level Genie was glad he wasn't. She enjoyed the attention; had never really experienced anything quite like it before. Despite the gallons of raw embarrassment she was now drowning in at the mere *fact* of someone expressing attraction for her in such a direct way, she had to admit that it was almost intoxicating. To be *liked*. To be liked *like that*. No one had ever liked her *like that* before.

Tabby grabbed Genie's sleeve and began pulling her away in the direction of their tent.

'What a loser!' she reiterated. For a second Genie was unsure whether Tabby was referring to Cosmo or her.

27: Cosmo's plan

Reading, 1999

It was dark, and the dark was exciting. The camping area was oddly lit by the glowing marquee and the floodlights standing some way off behind trees, Portakabins and a formidable metal fence.

Genie and Tabby walked along the perimeter of the metal fence, following Nerys who knew the way. Tabby had persuaded Genie to put on a little make-up, although not nearly as much as she herself was wearing.

Their walk was self-accelerating, the seemingly endless fence encouraging them to stride faster and faster, their lanyards swinging like manic pendulums.

'Whatever you do, don't lose it!' Nerys had warned. 'Those security guards are right bastards. Had a mate lose his at Glastonbury last year and he had to hitch home. They wouldn't let 'im back in. Shitheads.'

Genie was glad of her new DMs, even if the edges were rubbing on her lower calves making sore patches. Walking in anything other than sturdy boots might have resulted in her slipping over or starting to sink into the spongy ground. She'd never been that graceful even at the best of times. Still, at least it wasn't really wet. It wasn't exactly cold either, but even though it was still August, and in theory still summer, there was a bite in the air.

'Through here.' The long metal wall had ended and Nerys was walking towards a gate guarded by one of the shitheads clad in dayglo. She held up her pass without even looking at him as they went past.

'Workers Beer...' he murmured, as if reassuring or reminding himself.

'Thanks.' Genie found it impossible to ignore him as Nerys and Tabby had done. There was no harm in being nice, as Mother always told her.

They were now on the festival site proper, a vast, flat tundra of scrubby grass, compacted mud, cables, vehicles and countless tents, Portakabins and chemical toilets. The cold, bright illumination of the floodlights made it look like a film set, thought Genie as they cut diagonally across the space. At one end the main stage loomed like a deserted temple, and everywhere the dayglo shitheads crawled like ants on a particularly rich seam of peaty garbage.

It was a lot of trouble to go to just to listen to music.

They reached the exit, an array of turnstiles and runs that reminded Genie of the farmer's auction held in one of the villages near home. Past another security guard and then they were out, heading along the track alongside a series of Portakabin ticket booths. Eventually they reached the main road.

Even though she'd only been on site a relatively short time, Genie felt strange being back in the real world. There was traffic, there were street lights and most important of all, there was hard tarmac on which to walk.

'Here we go.' Nerys led them into the car park of a dull, flat building. Other people were crowded around the lit entrance, and looking back Genie could see a steady stream of their comrades in beer making their way along the route they'd already traversed.

Genie had never been to a nightclub before, but this wasn't what she'd been imagining. The building was functional and municipal. No matter how many coloured lights and how much dry ice you used, a basketball court was never going to make a convincing dance floor. Everyone was awkward in such austere surroundings and most of them were crowded into the canteen. Or rather bar.

Maybe this was what nightclubs were like? If so, they weren't as exciting as the ones she'd seen on TV.

They stood around for a minute or so, before Nerys spotted someone she knew and scurried off to greet them. Genie looked at Tabby, who was looking as lost as Genie herself felt.

But not for long. She seemed to reset her poise and with a practised toss of the head set off for the bar.

'Coming, G?'

Before they got there a familiar figure exploded from the congregation as if from nowhere.

'All right, girls? Can I buy you two young ladies a drink?' Cosmo bobbed down in an exaggerated curtsey, a twenty-pound note in his fist indicating the sincerity of his intentions even if he had a funny way of showing them.

'Yes, please!' Tabby seemed to have forgotten her dislike of the man and was suddenly radiating charm. However, this didn't seem to affect Cosmo, who merely nodded and turned to Genie.

'And what about you, darlin'? Fancy a quick one?'

Genie nodded.

'All right, but I think we'd better have a drink first, eh?' Cosmo poked Genie in the midriff before backing off and jigging about for a second like a dislocated deckchair. 'Nah, only kidding, darlin'. You don't hate me now, do you? You wouldn't hate old Cosmo, would you?' He pulled a face like a sad Pierrot. 'Don't go away, I'll be back with your bevvy in the blink of a bastard!'

'Cheeky boy,' said Tabby, laughing. Genie said nothing. She was too busy trying to get her blushing under control. Luckily the lighting in the bar was subdued. She wished she was back in their tent, in her sleeping bag, unconscious.

Or did she? Something inside was telling her to ride out the embarrassment, that perhaps on the other side of it, a larger far more exciting experience lay in wait.

Perhaps this was what life was all about.

'He didn't even ask us what we wanted,' Tabby frowned and peered at the scrum around the bar. 'Perhaps I should go and tell him.' She hopped from one foot to another and then turned to Genie.

'Maybe *you* should go and tell him. I'll have a gin and tonic.'

'OK.' Genie suspected that Tabby was being lazy, but didn't really mind. She took a step towards the bar but stopped when Nerys came skidding towards them through the thickening crowd.

'What do you reckon? Johnny says he can get us some Es. You in?'

Tabby's eyes widened and her mouth opened. She looked excited and glanced up at Genie for support.

Genie was terrified. Never mind the larger more exciting life she'd been promising herself; that wouldn't be any good to her if she ended up dead.

'No, thanks, we're OK.' Tabby came to the rescue, having obviously seen sense. 'After all, don't want to overdo it on the first night.'

'S'cool. Let me know if you change your mind though, eh?' Nerys stood there for a second on the threshold of leaving but then suddenly seemed to notice the absence of glasses in their hands. 'You not drinking either?'

'Oh yes, but that boy's getting them for us.' Tabby glanced in the direction of the bar with an impatient toss of her head.

'Cosmo,' said Genie, trying out the feel of his name in her mouth. Nerys looked heavenwards.

'Oh *him*. He's an arsehole if you ask me. Seen him around at a few of these before. Never seems to be with the same group twice. Watch out for him. Still,' and here she lightened up a bit as if it had only just occurred to her, 'if you can make the fucker buy you drinks all night then why not use him? But be careful.'

Nerys moved off with difficulty. It was really starting to get packed in there now, and Genie wondered if they should retreat to the corridor. She wanted to think about what Nerys had said, but the noise was making it difficult. Was Cosmo really a... a *fucker*? An *arsehole*? He seemed more like a clown.

Perhaps Nerys liked him and was jealous? After all there was the way he'd ignored her earlier on; perhaps they had a history.

'Sorry to keep you waiting, ladies!' As if summoned by her thoughts of him, Cosmo was standing at Genie's elbow, a plastic pint glass full of orange liquid in each hand.

'Thank you!' Tabby reached for one of them, but Cosmo snatched it from her reach, the contents slopping over his fingers as he held it aloft.

'Ah-ah-ah! Ladies first!' He offered the pint glass to Genie who took it and sipped at the watery cider. From Tabby's expression, it looked like she was about to burst into flames of fury. Cosmo poked her in the ribs with his free hand.

'Only kidding with you! Having a laugh!' He handed the remaining pint to her. 'Don't take old Cosmo so seriously.' Again the Pierrot look. 'He means well.'

'Don't you have a drink?' Genie felt bold asking him a direct question, and even risked a look into his eyes.

'Already drank it! 'Sides, I've got me water.' He reached into the pocket of his olive-green anorak and pulled out a half-full bottle of Evian. 'That'll keep me going! Ready for a dance then?' He turned away and started out, confident that they were going to follow him.

Genie downed her pint in one and put it down on the floor before hurrying after him.

'G!' Tabby sounded shocked. 'I had no idea you were such a *lush*!'

'If we're going to have a dance, I don't want to be carrying a drink. It gets in the way. It was only cider, after all. I've had that at home.' On *two* occasions, Genie added privately inside her own head, and both of them with a meal.

'You are full of surprises, G. Next you'll be telling me you're a natural dancer!' Tabby overtook her and walked through the double doors onto the nearest dance floor.

'How hard can it be?' An unexpected boldness had Genie in its grip, but then she saw the interior of the room.

The volume of music and dry ice being poured into it was overwhelming the original sportiness of the space, transforming it into a chamber of depravity. The flashing red-and-green lights and the gyrating bodies were making the whole thing look like Genie's idea of modern ballet based on Dante's Inferno.

Furthermore, despite her casual optimism, dancing proved very difficult indeed. She didn't seem able to get her body to move the way everyone else's was; she was ungainly and awkward. Like a tree again.

The music didn't help. There were no words and no recognisable instruments that she could hear; just an electronic thud and beep that, while it had a certain repetitive charm, wasn't something she could imagine enjoying on its own merits. This had to be techno, that stuff they played at raves. As an inspiration to bop, it was certainly doing the trick for most of the inhabitants of the room.

Tabby was really into it; as soon as they'd entered the room, she'd placed her (still nearly full) glass of cider on one of a row of plastic chairs lined up against the wall and stepped out into the sea of bodies. Almost immediately, she was swaying and jerking with the best of them; she seemed to know the right moment to move the right limb. More importantly she was comfortable in her body and this showed. At least two or three boys had gravitated towards the gyrating Tabby and were now focusing their movements on her presence.

Genie decided that she wasn't any good at this kind of thing, or at least not in the mood. She walked back to the row of chairs and sat down next to Tabby's pint to keep it company.

It was difficult to tell where one song ended and another began, but every couple of tunes Tabby would return for a sip of her cider, offering Genie a wild smile in passing. She was having a good time. Thankfully she didn't want to bully Genie into joining her.

It was getting hot; the room hadn't been designed with this kind of activity in mind. A drop of water landed on the end of Genie's nose. Rain? Indoors? Puzzled she looked upwards just in time for another drop to land in her eye. She stood up, rubbing her eye. Condensation? Condensed sweat. Yuck.

Someone was yelling in her ear. She looked down to see Cosmo's naughty face at her shoulder, another full pint proffered in greeting. Grateful, she took it and took a greedy gulp. It wasn't as cold as she'd have liked, but it would do. She smiled at Cosmo, who indicated with a series of shoulder, thumb and eyebrow gestures that they should perhaps step outside for a moment. This seemed like a very sensible idea.

Out in the corridor it was much cooler, and as the sweat evaporated off her exposed arms Genie felt almost cold enough to shiver. She leaned against the wall, more tired than she'd normally expect to feel at this time. It was all the excitement... so many new experiences in such a short space of time.

Her body decided she'd be better off sitting, and without consciously deciding to do so, she slid down until she was sitting on the floor, skirt tented up in front of her.

Miraculously she hadn't spilled a drop of her pint in the process. She took another sip.

Cosmo slid down the wall to join her at floor level. Now that they were sitting down his eyes were level with hers.

'Having a good time, Posh Totty?' he asked.

'What do you mean *Posh Totty*?' Genie wondered how he knew she was posh. It worried her a little; she had the distinct feeling her background wouldn't go down too well with some of the people around here. Her *rich fucker* background.

'Oh I know who you and your mate are. Old Cosmo knows these things, see? But don't worry, he won't give you away!' He placed a hot hand on her upper arm, his skin like sandpaper.

'So who do you think me and Tabby are then?'

'That was your dad or your mate's dad dropping you off at Clapham, right? MP?'

'Tabby's dad,' Genie was quick to clarify. Cosmo nodded.

'Well, don't worry, Posh Totty, your secret's safe with me. Some people, *some people*, might get pissed off with rich people taking part, but not Old Cosmo. Live and let live, that's what I say. I'm good at keeping secrets.'

Genie felt relieved that he didn't seem to be as judgemental as perhaps Nerys might have been. But why did he keep going on about secrets?

'What secrets?'

'If I told you, they wouldn't be secrets no more, would they?'

He nudged her shoulder and cackled, revealing heavily stained teeth. 'But seeing as it's *you...*'

He leaned close. Genie could feel his warmth; it was like he was burning up. A human radiator, she thought.

'See him?' Cosmo pointed at a figure a little way down the corridor. Genie realised it was the man she'd thought of as the Evil Druid.

'That's one of your friends, isn't it?'

'Yeah, that's right. Jimmy. Old Jimmy. Old Man Jimmy Riddle. Now everyone thinks he's really sound, 'cause like he claims he was at the Battle of the Beanfield.'

'Yes?' Genie hadn't a clue what Cosmo was talking about, but nodded anyway to keep him talking. She wasn't interested in what he had to say, but the sound of someone talking gave her something to concentrate on. She must be getting *drunk*, she thought, sipping her cider.

'Well, I happen to know,' here Cosmo dropped his voice to a whisper and rested his chin on Genie's shoulder, 'I happen to know that he *was* there, but that he was one of the coppers!'

'Really?' This didn't mean anything to Genie, although the idea of that strange-looking man being an ex-policeman was rather odd. The stubble on Cosmo's chin was prickling her.

'Really. I'm not shitting you. PC James Ward of the Wiltshire Constabulary. Probably smashed a fair few heads that day. Now here he is hanging out with everyone and getting stoned.'

'How do you know?' This seemed like a reasonable enough question to Genie.

'Old Cosmo never reveals his sources!' Cosmo sat back and tapped his nose.

'You're not that old,' Genie blurted.

'Aw, you say all the right things, Posh Totty.' Cosmo stood

up and reached down to help her up. As she stood, Genie's head spun.

'Woo...' she murmured and went to take another sip of her cider only to discover she'd finished it. Oh poo. Damn it. She frowned at the empty plastic glass before crushing it in her hand and letting it drop.

'Another one?' Cosmo led her back into the bar, which was a little less crowded now. She supposed everyone was dancing.

'Sit here and I'll bring it over.' Cosmo helped her into a plastic chair. 'Back in a second.'

What a gentleman, thought Genie. She was finding it difficult to focus. Maybe she needed glasses. She'd have to mention it to Father when she got home; he could arrange for her to have an eye test.

There was a fresh pint in her hand and Cosmo was sitting next to her, talking.

That was quick, she thought.

'Old Cosmo doesn't muck about!' he said as if answering her thought. Maybe she'd said it aloud. She took a sip.

They were standing outside the leisure centre; she was walking up and down.

'Yeah, see? All you needed was a bit of fresh air, my girl.' Cosmo was standing a little way off smoking a cigarette. 'If you're getting tired, I can take you back to your tent if you like.'

'That's what I'd like.' Genie's teeth were chattering.

They were crossing the main Festival site. It was deserted, the floodlights flinging their shadows violently to the muddy ground, shadows looming in front of them as they approached the gate that led to their camping area.

They were somewhere different. Loud music was playing, and Genie had the impression of a wild party going on somewhere very close while they stood in darkness. They were still outside.

'Come on,' Cosmo's voice was saying, a serious note creeping into his voice all of a sudden. 'You must have known what to expect...' In the darkness, Cosmo was just a patch of deeper shadow. Genie felt a panic attack starting. Where was she? What was going on? Was this what it was like to be *really* drunk?

They were still standing there, but the music was different. It was that song about everybody needing a bosom for a pillow, and Genie realised she wasn't wearing a skirt any more and there was something small and hot in her hand.

Everybody

'Come on... more...' Cosmo sounded desperate.

Everybody needs

Oh my god, she was holding his penis.

Everybody needs a

A foul, hot little piece of gristle writhing in its own skin, molten blood pumping. She tried to drop it but felt his hand clamped around hers, forcing her to squeeze.

Everybody

And she was holding her hand to her face where it hurt as if she'd been slapped, and her fingers reeked of his sweat.

'—bitch can't even get that right—'

Dancing

His hands on her shoulders pushing her down onto her knees, kneecaps impacting on the grass.

Dancing

His smell. The world upending and the ground flying up and hitting the side of her head.

Dancing

28: Go home

Disconnected sight of the stars as she was carried somewhere. Low voices talking seriously, cold air.

Someone sniffed. Genie was both warm and cold at the same time. Finding she couldn't move her arms, she started panicking but then realised she was in a sleeping bag. The worrying thing was that she couldn't remember getting into it. What was also worrying was that she couldn't open her eyes. She whimpered.

'Easy,' someone said, putting a hand on her brow. They said something else too low to catch and a few seconds later her forehead was being mopped.

Her eyelids finally opened. She was in her tent, Nerys and Tabby sitting either side of her, a vigil in the electric torchlight. Genie pushed herself up on her elbows.

'What happened?' Her own voice sounded strange to her, croaky and slurred.

'I was going to ask you that!' Tabby looked frightened.

'You're all right.' Nerys was more in control. 'Some guys brought you back here a few hours ago. A band. They said you

238

were getting some hassle from a guy round the back of the VIP area.'

'Cosmo!' Genie started to panic at the thought of him. Nerys placed a hand on her shoulder.

'Easy. He's gone. Chased off. The guys took you to the St John's people on duty there; they said you should just sleep it off. You had blood on your mouth but they couldn't find any injury. The St John's kept hassling the band about what you might have taken. They said they didn't know. Don't think you did, either, eh?'

'Blood? I had cider...' Genie wiped her mouth with the back of her hand. She felt a sourceless disgust rising in her throat.

'We cleaned you up,' Tabby said. 'How can it be the cider? I had cider too.'

Nerys leaned forward and peered into Genie's eyes.

'Difficult to tell now, but I reckon he spiked you. Rohypnol, or something like that. Evil cunt. He better not show his face around here again, I'm telling you.'

'I want to go home.' It was too much for Genie to take in. The idea that her own bed at home was at least three more nights away was too much to bear. 'Tabby, can you call my mother? I think she's still there; if not then... someone else can pick me up.' Even in her traumatised state, she was worried about saying too much in front of Nerys, revealing her rich fucker background, the fact that they had servants, a driver.

'I will. Just as soon as it's daytime.' Tabby flourished her phone. 'But we shouldn't call too early, hmm? Don't want to make her panic.'

Genie nodded.

'I reckon you should call the pigs,' Nerys said.

'Oh no,' Genie just wanted it to stop, couldn't bear the thought of spinning it out any longer, 'I don't think he... at

least I don't remember... I don't want to... I just want to...'
Tears started rolling down her cheeks.

'All right, all right.' Nerys was sympathetic. 'He's bound to
sneak back at some point, then we'll get him. More likely to
get what's coming from us than from the pigs anyway.'

'I want to go home.' Genie looked down at her hands. She
wanted to wash them. She wanted a shower.

'You will.' Nerys leaned across and hugged her. After a
moment's hesitation Tabby joined in.

Tabby waited with Genie on the main road by the site
entrance. It was busy, thousands of revellers flowing down the
road like human lava, an atmosphere of excitement totally at
odds with the fear, panic and disgust in Genie's head. Nerys
had offered to wait with them but, worried she'd see the car,
Genie had declined.

At last it appeared, moving down the road in a tentative
manner, driver looking out for his employer's daughter. Tabby
flagged him down, and the large, shiny black car pulled to
a halt, incongruous against the muddy kerbside, hovering,
hazards aflash.

The driver leaped from his seat and took Genie's rucksack
from her, stowing it in the boot.

'Take care,' Genie said, hugging Tabby again. Tabby
nodded silently. She looked as if she half wanted to come home
with Genie, but the lure of Fun Lovin' Criminals was obviously
too much.

'I'll give you a call when I get back, yeah?' she said as Genie
climbed inside and shut the door.

The car pulled away from the roadside and swung round,
heading back the way it had come. Their route through town

took them along the London Road past the Royal Berkshire Hospital.

Genie couldn't breathe. There, limping along the pavement just down from A&E, was Cosmo. She wanted to hide but was frozen. As the car slid past, his eyes locked with hers for a split second. Cold fury. He sneered, making a cut-throat gesture at her before the traffic swept her away out of sight.

29: Vengeance

Underworld, no time

Genie had no idea what Cosmo had been saying for the past ten minutes. Her head was buzzing with the simple horror of having seen him again, something she'd hoped she'd never have to do. Stale adrenaline coursed through her veins; she began to wish she hadn't given her Valium away to Aston. Surreptitiously, she worried open one of the coke wraps in her pocket and helped herself to a couple of dabs. It probably wouldn't help with the panic – if it even worked at all – but it might make her more confident when she confronted him.

She was going to have to confront him.

At least, she kept thinking, *if he's here, he's dead. And I'm still alive. If I ever get out of here, I'm going to find his grave and piss on it.*

He was talking about some kind of military-sounding exercise; his speech full of macho buzzwords and jargon, gobbledegook that most of the rest of the audience were lapping up.

A conclusion must have been reached because everyone stood up as one, some of them saluting. Cosmo disappeared through the door down at the front of the lecture theatre and all around Genie, the dead soldiers started moving.

As they filed out they remained silent; it was eerie. When she reached the aisle Genie tried to go back up to the door through which she'd come into the room, but the sheer pressure of khaki- and blue-clad bodies started carrying her down the steps. If she wasn't going to fall she'd have to go with it.

'Ow! Watch it!' She flung a filthy look at an Asian man dressed in a smart black uniform who'd just trodden on her foot. He glanced at her but didn't say anything. What was up with these people? Apart from being dead.

She reached the lectern, was borne past it and then through the double doors they were all streaming through. She really hoped Cosmo had gone off somewhere but suspected otherwise. He'd clocked her. Of course he'd want to catch up. The universe wouldn't have it any other way.

Of all the billions dead in the entire afterlife, why had she run into him? The same reason she'd run into Wendi, she supposed. Normal rules didn't apply and if hell was indeed other people then it was also very probably other people you knew.

Out here the pressure of the crowd was less intense, and Genie was at last able to stop.

Cosmo was there. Two men dressed in a similar uniform to his were holding the arms of a young Middle Eastern man while Cosmo punched him in the stomach. Again and again. Eventually his two colleagues dropped the victim to the floor at his feet. He absently kicked the young man in the face before turning to face Genie.

'Posh Totty,' he said. 'Nice to see you again.'

The crew cut, desert fatigues and the fact that he'd filled out a bit all conspired to make him look shorter than she remembered. Genie looked down at him with undisguised loathing.

'Fucker,' she growled eventually. He pulled the hurt Pierrot look; it was almost obscene to see it again after all these years.

'What, no kiss?' He stepped forward. 'Bombs and guns may break my buns. I think we've got a lot of catching up to do, eh?'

Genie stood her ground. Inside her head, she was repeating the comforting mantra, *he's dead, he's dead, he's dead*. Then he put a hand on her hip.

She slapped it aside, but he grabbed her wrist and leaned in close.

'I think we've got some unfinished business.' He glanced from side to side and his men stepped closer again. Down on the floor, their previous victim was crawling away, probably hoping not to be noticed.

Genie pulled her wrist from his grip; he just shrugged and smiled.

'That's the good thing about this place. If you wait long enough, you *always* get to finish your business. Settle your scores. Take Tariq down there.' Cosmo jerked a thumb at the crawling man. 'Got into a fire fight with him in the streets of Fallujah. Dirty little cunt shot my head off. Really pissed me off. But I waited. And he turned up down here. So now I get to kick the shit out of him every day.'

Genie spat at him.

'That's uncalled for,' Pierrot face, Pierrot face, 'I think you're going to regret that. Every day from now on. Along with a lot of other things. Lads?'

'Sir?' the two men spoke in unison.

'Hold her.'

Genie tried to struggle, but the two of them were too strong for her. Cosmo walked up and down regarding her with a half-smile.

'Where to start, eh?'

The door banged open and another soldier burst in, dressed in a far more old-fashioned uniform. Almost Edwardian. Cosmo snapped to attention as did her two captors. She took a step backwards.

'Sergeant Milford,' the new arrival said.

'Sah?'

So that was his real name. And this was another of his real personalities by the looks of things; subservient creep. Part of the job, Genie supposed.

'The Boss is here. Get the place cleaned up. We're having a meeting of all the top brass. Figure out our next moves.'

Old habits, thought Genie. As if any of this mattered or would make any difference. What was it with these guys? How were they staying motivated? She took another step backwards and found herself against the wall.

Cosmo and his cronies had forgotten all about her as they dragged a table into the centre of the room and pulled a crazy assortment of chairs around it under the scrutiny of the Edwardian officer. Genie wondered who was going to get the deckchair.

She glanced to one side and saw that Tariq was now standing up next to her and inching his way along the wall towards the door leading back into the lecture theatre. He gave Genie a look, *follow me*. It was probably a good idea. She started edging her way along the wall as well.

Soldiers started filing in though the door by which the Edwardian officer had entered the room. As before, the uniforms on display were as diverse as the chairs now placed around the table. A US Marine. A Napoleonic artillery officer. A Norman. A 1930s gangster. Who could have convinced them to work together like this? Perhaps the relentless centuries of being cooped up in the Labyrinth had finally made them realise that they were all in the same boat. Shame they'd never worked that out when they were still alive, thought Genie, might have saved a lot of bloodshed.

They began to sit down. The deckchair ended up occupied by a giant of a man in skins and sandals. Cosmo and company hovered in the background, eager monkey minions, desperate to curry favour. Genie glanced at Tariq, who grimaced back at her. Five minutes and they'd be at the door.

At the head of the table was a Victorian high-backed Windsor chair. Genie assumed that this was for the Boss. She was now very curious as to who this could possibly be, but not so much that she was going to hang around to find out. Once she reached the exit, she was gone.

A figure entered the room, tall and imposing. Everyone else stood up.

Wild-bearded and sharp-eyed, the Boss surveyed the room. It wasn't bin Laden, was it? The man gestured for his minions to be seated. No, not bin Laden, too young for a start. But there was definitely *something* about him. Something familiar.

Genie felt sick. She'd sussed out who this might be. It would certainly explain everyone's loyalty. And the stigmata were a bit of a giveaway.

But what did that say about the hereafter? If Jesus was just as trapped here as everyone else, that meant he was as human as everyone else, and if that was the case then who was really in charge? Had Aston's musings about an atheist afterlife been correct?

Everyone sat down. Genie glanced at Tariq, who was reaching the edge of the door; but in order to open it they'd have to go past. They were on the hinge side.

Even as Genie watched, the door flew open with a crash, smacking Tariq in the face. A small figure brandishing a curved sword leaped into the room and glared with frightening intensity at the assembled big shots.

Genie forgot both her predicament and the need for silence. This was *insane*.

'Wendi! What the fuck? How did you stop being a tree?'

'Never mind that. Let's get out of here.' Wendi nodded back into the lecture theatre from whence she'd emerged. Genie grabbed the hand of the still-reeling Tariq and pulled him through the door, looking back over her shoulder at the reaction this purple-haired apparition was getting from the cream of history's militia.

Most of them just looked confused. Jesus was wearing a watery smile.

Cosmo, on the other hand, was furious.

'YOU!' he shrieked, deserting his post and heading straight for Wendi with murder in his eyes. Genie staggered back but the simultaneous appearance of two people from completely different areas of her life (not to mention Jesus) was causing her brain to go into meltdown. *It did not compute.*

'Me,' said Wendi, swinging her sword in perfect time to sever Cosmo's head, which flew backwards and hit Jesus squarely in the face before dropping onto the table and then rolling onto the floor.

'After them, you idiots!' Cosmo's head screamed. 'What are you waiting for?' His lackeys leaped forward but got into a tangle with the headless body that was still staggering around by the doorway.

The last thing Genie saw before Wendi slammed the door shut was Jesus slumping forward on the table, unconscious.

30: Escape route

'I'll... explain... later...' Wendi tore past Genie and up the steps of the lecture theatre aisle, towards the door through which Genie had first entered the room. Genie loped after her and, seemingly recovered from his concussion, Tariq overtook both of them and reached the door first, holding it open for them.

There was a crash behind them, and Genie risked a look over her shoulder. Cosmo's goons had charged the door and were now rolling about in a pile of splintered wood on the floor in front of the blackboard.

'Thank you.' Genie was impressed by the fact that Tariq had continued to hold the door open for her as she passed through it and into the curved corridor.

'No, hang on, mate, if you just...' Genie's shout was in vain. Once the door to the lecture theatre was shut behind them, Tariq had sprinted off in the opposite direction to the one in which Genie had been planning to go.

'I think he's got the right idea though, babe!' Wendi was hopping from foot to foot. There were a billion questions Genie wanted to ask her, but for now the most important thing was to get out of sight.

'This way!' Genie ran off down the corridor in the direction of door 1A. If West Pier was still through there then it was a bigger place to hide at least. And if they could climb through the windows, all the better. The darkness through them may have been frightening, but it wasn't as frightening as their pursuers.

Besides, she was no longer alone. It was a start.

As they made their way around the curve of the corridor, Genie slowed; she didn't want to miss her door. She skidded to a halt and inspected the next one carefully. No, that was 1B, the broom cupboard.

'What are you looking for?' Wendi had caught up with her and was regarding her with an amused expression. She was now empty-handed, having abandoned her sword in the lecture theatre.

'It's the next one,' said Genie and grabbed Wendi's hand. Before she could move further, there was a crash from behind them and the thud of military boots.

'Fuck!' Letting go of Genie's hand, Wendi took a few steps back and peered down the corridor before turning and running past her. 'Leg it!'

They legged it, but as soon as door 1A came into view, Wendi skidded to a halt in front of it.

'This one?'

Genie nodded, out of breath.

'Trust me.' Wendi grabbed Genie by the arms and flattened her against the wall opposite their door before spinning round to stand straight in front of her, back pressed against Genie's front, arms held wide and flat against the wall as if trying to shield her from something.

The top of Wendi's hair was tickling Genie's chin. Such a familiar smell: hairspray, shampoo, gel, dye. She remembered that when it was freshly coloured, the shower used to run purple, and Wendi would always joke about having been murdering aristocrats again.

Despite the odds, Genie had another chance. She was not going to blow it this time.

The boot clatter drew closer. Wendi twisted her head to look up at her and winked.

Around the corner came Cosmo's minions, followed by Cosmo himself who now had his head stuffed clumsily under one arm.

'Check them all!' he croaked. 'Every door!'

Genie gasped; that meant they'd be stopping directly in front of them. They were *bound* to be spotted. As if sensing Genie's growing disquiet, Wendi pressed herself backwards, pinning Genie to the wall.

'I said *trust me*,' she hissed.

Cosmo and his men stopped directly in front of them, but even though they were casting about for clues, they looked right through the two women. How could that be? They should have been in plain view.

One of the men opened door 1A.

A cupboard. A cupboard containing nothing more than a primitive-looking vacuum cleaner with brass fittings and some tins of 1930s floor polish. Genie's heart sank. Bang went her escape route. It was just like the door by which she'd entered the Labyrinth all over again. Why couldn't these doors *behave* themselves? Consistency might be dull in people but it was useful in doors.

The soldier slammed 1A shut again and clunked his way off around the corridor with his comrades. Wendi stepped forward and peered after them before turning back to Genie.

'You learn a lot of tricks when you're a tree,' she said and laughed. For a second, the sound of that familiar laugh made

Genie feel as if perhaps everything would be all right after all, but then she remembered the lack of an exit.

'They'll be back in a minute, won't they?' she said. 'And someone's blocked off the way out.' She punched at door 1A in pique and it swung open, silent.

The polish and the antique Hoover were gone. Inside was a red-tinged darkness, the same darkness she'd been all too keen to escape not that long ago, but which now offered the only hope they had of escaping the human monsters that inhabited this Labyrinth.

'I see I'm not the only one who's learned something down here,' said Wendi, climbing inside. 'I wonder what's through here?'

Genie followed her and pulled the closet door closed behind her. When she looked round again, Wendi was disappearing into the gloom ahead.

'Hang on! Wait for me!'

As Wendi turned to face her, a click and hum once more heralded the illumination of the WEST PIER sign almost directly above their heads. Wendi leaned back and gaped at it, laughing again.

'I don't fucking believe it! How cool is that?' She ran forward fifty yards, before turning back to face Genie again.

'How fucking cool is this?' she yelled. Infected by her dead lover's enthusiasm, Genie trotted over to her and took her hands. They were as chilly as ever. That was a good thing.

'Not as cool as that rescue! How the fuck did you swing that? How did you get out of the wood?'

Wendi let go of her hands and walked backwards, animated by a cheeky energy that Genie hadn't seen in her for some time even before she'd died.

'You woke me up, didn't you? I don't know how long I'd been stuck there, but after you'd left I couldn't go back to how I'd been. I was *thinking* again. Then there was your little friend...'

'Nathan?' Genie felt a spasm of guilt. 'I've been looking for him... Did you see what happened to him?'

'He took root, didn't he? While we were talking. The Wood of the Suicides can have a physical effect on some people, and young matey had the right kind of mind for it to get hold of. He might not have belonged there, but when you wandered off, there was a new bush opposite me.' Wendi strolled over to the side of the room and peered through the glass, past their reflections and out into the void.

'So what then?' Genie joined her at the glass.

'We started talking. Tree talk.' Wendi looked up at her, serious now but not morose. 'Most of the buggers in that forest are too wrapped up in themselves to speak much, but like I say, you'd woken me up, and Nathan was a bit freaked 'cause he didn't know why he'd got stuck there.'

'He didn't even know why he was dead,' said Genie.

'He did,' said Wendi, 'but he was too embarrassed to tell you. Do you know how much you meant to him?'

'I've got a pretty good idea. He was obsessive. A nerd. Only a few brain cells short of a stalker.' Genie's guilt was making her aggressive.

'Well, yeah. But he loved you. Still loves you. Whatever. Or thought he did. Or still does. Still thinks he did, I mean. Still thinks he *does*, come to that.' Wendi smacked herself on the forehead with the palm of her hand. 'So we had that in common. Something to talk about.'

Genie said nothing. In life, Wendi had never actually told her she loved her; it seemed that being dead had clarified things in her mind. Genie felt a tightness in her throat. This was very different from her meeting with Wendi's tree-self earlier on.

'So we talked,' Wendi turned around, leaned back on the

glass and stuck her hands in the pockets of her trousers, 'about that, and about all sorts of shit. You're right, he is a bit of a weirdo, but then, hey, so am I! And you like *me*, don't you?' A sly look.

Genie found herself blushing, feeling emotions long buried resurfacing. She nodded.

'Turned out he'd had an accident. He'd gone to see *Chicago* in the West End.' Wendi stuck her tongue out and crossed her eyes for a second. 'He was on his way back to the tube. A bit drunk, but not steaming. Then apparently this fucking nutter, some homeless guy, runs out into the middle of the road. It looked as if he was fighting with invisible monsters.' Wendi took her hands out of her pockets and mimed this for a moment. 'A bendy bus swerved to avoid hitting him and—' She smacked one fist into the palm of the other hand.

'Silly sod,' said Genie. 'You know, I thought it was something daft. But he kept avoiding the issue. He was good at that.'

'Thing is, he didn't belong in Topper's Copse.' Wendi stood up straight and turned to face Genie, excited. 'It was unlucky, but not a suicide. The Wood got it wrong. So that meant he could leave. Or someone else could. If he agreed to take their place.'

'You mean he…?'

'Yup.' Wendi nodded. 'Poor guy was really freaked out by the whole thing; he didn't know what to do. No motivation, you see, no chutzpah. So I asked if he'd look after my tree for a while. He seemed happy enough. So I untreed myself again and pulled him out of his bush.

'I didn't really know what to do next, but as you've probably noticed, abnormal rules tend to apply round here. So I just threw him up into the branches. So what if I shouldn't be able to lift him, let alone thrown him? I've spent the last few years in a fuckin' Prozac tree, so…'

'You mean he's stuck there now?'

'I doubt it.' Wendi appeared to think about it. 'Not for long anyway. He doesn't belong there. This place is a nightmare of a bureaucracy, but sooner or later someone or something's going to notice that he's been filed in the wrong department. In the meantime… Well, he's got his gadgets. And it's not as bad as you might imagine. I was there for over four years.

'The weird thing was that as soon as my tree was occupied, the Wood started fading away and something else faded in. I was in a room. It was like a dressing room in one of those old venues or something, loads of wood panelling. And loads of pictures of *you* on the walls, babe.' Wendi gave Genie's arm a playful slap. 'You *have* been busy since I died. Those *Loaded* and *FHM* sessions looked a bit racy…'

'I didn't want to; Malcolm said…' Genie started to protest before realising how absurd that was. 'Yeah, bit tacky, weren't they?'

'Shame on you!' Wendi grinned. 'Anyway, this was Nathan's afterlife; it's where he should have arrived. In the Labyrinth.'

'A victim of misadventure,' Genie nodded. 'But how did you guess? How did you know it would work?'

'I'm dead,' said Wendi. 'I've got a more natural connection with this place than you. I can feel it, sense how it works. Several years as a tree means you get a feeling for the forest rules. Roots are for more than just drinking. I don't know why Nathan didn't just go straight to the Labyrinth when he died, but I think your presence had a lot to do with it. Given how obsessed with you he was. He was lucky enough to die just as you were on your way in and got sidetracked. I think you might have kicked open some door that'd been shut for… fuck knows how long. Just as well, too. 'Cause now I'm out of my tree!' Wendi stepped back and twirled on the spot for a few seconds.

'There's a bit of a problem though. You may have got out of one trap, but I've been trying to get out of *this* one for a while. And failing.' Genie gestured at the chamber around them. 'This bloody Labyrinth. The doors keep changing. Well, they keep changing for me anyway. You saw what happened out in the corridor – one minute a cupboard, the next... this.'

'I think it's *you*, not this place.' Wendi looked excited now, almost jumping up and down on the spot. 'That's a good thing. You're still *alive*. That's unique – you experience this whole place differently. Your perspective's fresh, not like us deadeyes, and most important, you *don't* belong here. Not *anywhere*, Labyrinth, Wood or anywhere else.'

'How does that help?' Genie was starting to get tired again and fingered the cocaine wraps in her pocket. Had it actually worked at any point while she'd been down here? She wondered if Wendi would like some.

'You *walked* from the Wood to the Labyrinth. I don't think anyone usually *does* that. Somehow you got down here, and *being alive* down here seems to have given you an Access All Areas pass. And I can be your plus-one. We just need to figure out how to use it.' Wendi looked pensive. 'You can go places other people can't even see. Look what happened in the corridor just now.'

'That means this hall isn't really part of the Labyrinth.' Genie placed her hand flat on the cold glass of the nearest window. 'It's a way in or a way out.'

'It's the trade exit,' said Wendi, wandering up and down a little, examining the window frame, 'staff and performers only.'

They walked along the perimeter a little way, but all of the windows had long been painted shut.

'We might have to smash it.' Genie looked around. It was only when she spotted her erstwhile weapon, the hoe, lying on the floor a short distance away that she realised what she'd been looking for. She jogged over and retrieved it. Despite the unreliable behaviour of some of the fixtures, there was at least an underlying logic here. That was a relief.

Now she had Wendi with her, it was possible it might be an easier journey. Or a more difficult one? If the Sphinx had been right she wasn't here for Wendi at all – they'd ended up together again but that had just been an accident. For whatever reason they – whoever *they* were – had Ollie down as her plus-one. How would they react when they found out she was going off script? Against all the odds she'd been given a *third* chance and was *not* going to fuck it up now. She'd have to be *very* careful.

'Nice one!' Wendi took the hoe from Genie and hefted it in her small hands. Without warning, she turned and whacked the centre of the nearest window with the metal end.

With a dull *spangg!* it ricocheted off and skittered over the floor. Wendi dropped to her knees, clutching at her wrist.

'Owww Oww Ow! Fuck! Fuckit.'

'Oh! Are you OK?' Genie kneeled down next to her. Wendi nodded through gritted teeth and took Genie's hand.

'Yeah. Teach me not to think things through. Hang on though, hang on…' She scrambled to her feet and, still holding hands with Genie, walked over to the window she'd attacked.

It was ajar. While the glass had stood up to the impact the ancient paint hadn't and the hinges had given, just a little. There was barely enough room for Wendi to stick a finger through the gap. If they were going to climb through, they'd have to do better than that.

'Great… give us a hand, babe!' Wendi pushed at the bottom

of the frame next to the gap with Genie standing behind her and pushing at the top. The window wobbled and opened a few more millimetres with a crackle and a dusting of rusty paint flakes. They pushed together again. The window relented and gave them another couple of millimetres. Wendi stuck her hand through the gap. They were getting there.

'Once more!'

With a crunching moan the window swung open all the way and Genie fell forward; Wendi ducked out of the way just in time.

'There we go!' Wendi brushed dust and grime from her hands and then inspected them, pulling a face.

Genie stuck her head out of the window. Outside, it was warm. Warm and dry. The hairdryer wind that she remembered from much earlier on was still blowing, and if it hadn't changed – and if she hadn't got her directions wrong – it was blowing from the direction in which they should be heading.

But where should they be heading?

'Wendi?'

'Yes, babe?'

'What are we doing?'

'Getting out of here, I suppose. Don't sweat it. You worry too much. I mean if you think about it, it's odd how *we* ran into each other. I think it's to do with you. Being still alive. The fact you're here means it's all lit up from a certain point of view, and we'll only notice the bits to do with you. So if you're meant to rescue someone, you will. And why shouldn't that someone be me, eh?'

'I don't know. Suppose… whoever brought me here has other ideas about who I'm supposed to be pulling out of here?'

'Fuck 'em.' Wendi shrugged. 'When have we ever followed the rules?'

'This isn't like putting one over on some stuck-up security men.' Genie was starting to feel really tired again, and she just didn't share Wendi's certainty. She couldn't let this third chance slip through her fingers, but what if this was all just steering her to a reunion with a man she didn't even love? She'd just have to take that chance. She had to try. 'I just want to go home. But first...' She pulled one of the wraps out of her dressing gown pocket. 'Fancy a top-up?'

'You beauty!' Wendi's eyes lit up, her mouth dropped open and Genie could have sworn she was about to start salivating.

Once they'd had a couple of dabs each, they climbed out of the window and into the inexplicable void. They stood there. Genie took hold of Wendi's hand again and pointed into the wind.

'This way.'

Underfoot, the ground felt to be made of smooth varnished wood, ancient material weathered to a fine finish by the ceaseless wind. It was the roof of the Labyrinth, and Genie imagined all the drama still going on beneath their feet, the soldiers, Aston, a billion other misadventurers.

'Remember what you said to me? Back in the forest?' Apparently something was bothering Wendi. 'Do you still *want* to bring me back?'

Genie stopped and turned to face Wendi. Something stirred in her. It was very rare that Wendi had ever let Genie – or anyone – see her this vulnerable. Fuck it. Despite her reservations about what would or wouldn't be allowed, she was going to *do it*. That was one thing she was certain of. 'Of course! You're coming with *me*.' The confidence she'd always pretended to possess during her career was now real. What was more, she finally felt on an equal footing with Wendi, no longer Wendi's toy but Wendi's lover. She wrapped her arms around the smaller woman and held tight for a few seconds before releasing her. 'But we'd better get a move on, eh?'

Hand in hand, they walked across the strange surface. Genie looked back over her shoulder, the West Pier's windows now a tiny row of lights in the distance, winking out even as she looked at them. What little light they'd been throwing on the scene vanished, and total darkness fell on them like a giant duvet dropped from the sky.

'Jeez...' Genie stopped walking and swayed. The hot wind was still blowing which meant that if they kept walking directly into it, they wouldn't lose their way – but, yes, suppose it *did* change direction? It wasn't an exact science.

'Just keep going, babe.' Wendi's voice was odd in the darkness, as if the absence of a visual reference had robbed her of a location. It was as if she was starting to exist only as a voice in Genie's head. Genie squeezed her hand for reassurance and Wendi squeezed back. They continued to walk.

'This is freaking me out,' said Genie after an indeterminate amount of time had passed. She was starting to get the impression that the smooth wooden floor was sliding backwards and that she herself was motionless.

'Maybe if we talk?' Wendi's voice now lacked any kind of resonance, existing free from a physical space as a pure pattern of sound, a waveform. Even the sensation of her hand in Genie's was starting to seem false, replicated, a mere stimulation of Genie's nervous system to give the impression of a small hand in hers.

Maybe she'd overdone the cocaine?

'Maybe.' Genie couldn't tell how long she'd taken to answer Wendi's question. 'And if nothing else, at least we lost them.'

'Fuckers,' agreed Wendi.

'I mean, this is freaky, but I'm glad we got out of there.' Genie hoped she was speaking aloud rather than just thinking.

'Escaped.'

Wendi's voice was starting to become indistinguishable from Genie's thoughts. This was alarming. Genie couldn't tell if she was holding anyone's hand any more and furthermore could no longer feel the ground beneath her feet. She started to get the sensation of slowly falling forward through a warm fog rather than walking.

She panicked, scrabbled in her pocket for her iPhone and switched it on. Only 10% of the battery left, but even the glow of the screen was enough to pull her mind back down to the here and now.

'What are you doing?' Wendi's face emerged out of the darkness, a diminutive purple-topped shape. 'What's that?'

'My phone. Sorry. I was starting to lose it just then.' Genie slipped the phone back into her dressing gown pocket.

'Maybe I should do the talking, eh?' Wendi gripped her hand in the renewed darkness. 'It doesn't bother me as much. 'Cause I'm dead.'

'Maybe.' Things were improving; Genie could feel the ground beneath her feet again, the warmth and smoothness of the primordial varnish.

'I started looking for you,' Wendi went on, 'after I found myself in Nathan's little hidey-hole. Had no idea where you'd be, but I could feel it in my roots that you were around somewhere. Somewhere nearby. Found that sword in an old umbrella stand, seemed like a good idea to take it with me. I hadn't met anyone yet, but felt like I was going to any second. Kept hearing footsteps just on the other side of doors and walls. Thudding away.

'Then I found a hatch in the floor. My stomach was tingling, I knew you were beneath it, even if not directly. Once I got it open, I found that it looked down on that lecture theatre – way too far to jump but there were ropes and stuff all over the ceiling. Took a while to climb down, but I did it. Kicked open the door and there you were.'

'Hmm.' Genie was much calmer now, Wendi's voice comfortable and familiar. She was starting to believe that despite everything they'd make it in the end.

'Wasn't expecting to see *that* fucker again,' Wendi went on, 'but he had it coming. He got away far too lightly the first time.'

'Hmm,' said Genie, and then, 'What? What? How did you know him?' The mere mention of Cosmo awoke her panic, which uncurled from its slumber in the pit of her stomach and stretched its limbs. She still hadn't told Wendi about him.

'Just some cunt I met at Reading Festival once. Before I met you. It was the first night and me and the band were having a drink when we heard something going on behind one of the chemical toilets. Peter went to have a look and we heard him shout. That ugly fucker was trying to force a young girl to give him a blow job. She was off her head, poor lass. Bet he'd drugged her. Anyway Peter and Nigel pulled him off her and I lost it. Kicked him over and over again, until the bouncers pulled us apart and chucked him out. I went to lie down. The boys were looking after the girl; I hope she was all right.'

Genie cried silent tears in the darkness.

'Are you all right, babe?'

'I think,' said Genie, 'I am now. You saved me twice.'

31: Horizon

They talked as they walked, although Wendi did most of the talking. This suited Genie fine; that way around, it helped her maintain her grip on herself. Stopped her succumbing to sensory deprivation. In this level of darkness, it was difficult *not* to hallucinate, trying to make sense of a complete lack of visual stimulus. The warm wind and the smooth wooden ground were her only constants, and their homogeneity wasn't helping.

'You remember those guys who supported us on the tour just after you and Claudia joined the band? Payload or whatever they were called? What a bunch of creeps.'

'Oh yeah...' Genie remembered the sub-Oasis three-piece of loud-mouthed lads from Devon. In their heads, they'd obviously been fantasising that they were going to pair off with the three women in Beam – Wendi, Genie and Claudia – but had made the mistake of trying to make it reality and as a result had been booted off the tour.

'They didn't ever make it big, did they? Hate to think of them on *Top of the Pops*.'

'*Top of the Pops* isn't on any more,' Genie turned to face the sector of blackness that probably contained Wendi, 'but I don't think they did, I don't remember seeing them again. Maybe they're still doing the rounds.'

'No *Top of the Pops?*' Wendi sounded shocked. 'Fuck. End of an era. I remember dancing in front of the TV when I was five. Space Oddity.'

Genie blinked. Was it another hallucination? Maybe not. There were the usual floating pineapple rings and neon amoebas she always started seeing in the dark, the hypnagogic fauna, but beneath the sliding false images there was something solid. A background. Something that moved independently of her own heartbeat. Genie stopped walking.

'Babe? You OK?' The shape moved as Wendi spoke.

'Yes!' Genie was waving her hand in front of her face now. 'I can see. There's *light*.'

It was true, but only just. A negligible red glow in the non-sky ahead, against which a sharp black horizon was now visible, the silhouettes of both Wendi and her own hand extrusions of this distant line.

'Fuck, you're right!' The Wendi-shape bobbed and weaved for a second. 'And it's straight ahead as well.'

They continued walking towards the false dawn. After a while the maroon glow started to illuminate the intolerable sky-ceiling; still the huge forms moved overhead, faint obsidian continents in a sluggish jostle for position. Best not to look at them.

Wendi was now visible as more than just as a profile against the glow, her pale face reflecting the light, eyes glinting occasionally.

There was the distinct impression that they'd passed a high point and were now heading downhill. The horizon was lower, urgency tugging at their forward movement.

The roof of the Labyrinth was no longer as smooth as before. Protrusions had started to invade the flat wooden world; here a shed, there a chimney, there an upturned boat. Once or twice, they had to stray from their forward path, but now they were no longer reliant on just the wind, this didn't matter as much.

'Fucking cool!' Wendi ran on ahead and started circling a large vertical form. When Genie caught up, she could see it was a totem pole. At its apex was the carved shape of an eagle, wings spread, facing the light. It was difficult to tell and could have been an illusion, but she got the distinct impression it was better lit than the lower half of the pole. Might there be something just over the horizon illuminating it?

Wendi was ahead of her there. The pole was set at a slant and without stopping to look for the best way up, she started climbing it, using the grotesque features of the lower creatures as hand- and footholds.

'Be careful!' Genie didn't suffer from vertigo herself, but always worried on other people's behalf. Still, Wendi probably knew what she was doing and besides, she was already dead. What else could possibly happen to her?

She reached the eagle, put her arms round its neck and stared ahead. Her mouth opened, but no sound emerged.

'What is it?' Genie hopped from foot to foot.

'Come and see!' Wendi managed.

'I'm not sure it'll take both our weight,' Genie said. 'Can't you just tell me?'

'It's a… it's like… fuck no, I can't. Hang on.'

Genie choked back a scream as Wendi leaped from the top of the totem pole and landed in a heap at her feet. This didn't seem to affect her enthusiasm for what she'd seen though; she leaped up straight away and, grabbing Genie's hand, started towing her in the direction of the light.

'We'll be there in a minute – it's easier to show you. I never thought I'd see… I'd kind of felt but…'

Wendi wasn't making any sense, but her incoherence was

piquing Genie's curiosity. What was it just over the horizon? A way out? The real sky? Perhaps another escalator. That would be useful.

Like a square sunrise, the source of Wendi's excitement came into view over the horizon as they ran forward. At first Genie interpreted it as the top of a skyscraper and her immediate thought was the World Trade Center – had that ended up down here just like the West Pier?

Then it became clear that it was much larger than that. The structure looked artificial but it couldn't possibly have existed in the real world. No civilisation ever had those resources.

It was a vast, crenulated cube illuminated from within by a billion red-lit windows. Each face they could see was divided into nine smaller squares, each of which seemed to be a miniature copy of the larger face right down to the subdivisions.

Every subdivision in turn appeared to be an exact replica of its parent and so on and so on... until Genie's eyes ached trying to make out the smaller details and she stopped. This self-similarity made it impossible to tell just how big the structure was. Was that particular window a tiny pane letting light into a closet space or a vast acreage of glass the size of a football field?

It didn't help that from here they couldn't see its base. The dark curve of the Labyrinth's top obscured the miraculous building's lower half; it *felt* like it was square but for all they knew it could have been the top of a much more elongated structure and without anything on the ground to compare it to, it could have been anything from one to a hundred miles high.

'Come on!' Wendi started running down the gradual incline towards this edifice, and Genie wasted no time hurrying after her. There was something about it that was exercising an almost magnetic attraction on her thought processes; *this is it,* she thought, *my destination, the answer to all the questions I've ever had*. The shape of the thing spoke to the brain on a level deeper than language, and it was as if the solution to all the problems ever faced by sentience lay just inside the front door.

If they could only reach it.

The surface of the Labyrinth roof continued to fall away, becoming ever more complex; caravans, train carriages and gazebos protruded from the surface as they made their inexorable way from the horizontal to forty-five degrees. Yet all the time the Great Cube seemed to remain at the same distance, moving ahead of them in the same casual way that the full moon receded from a speeding tour bus heading towards it down the motorway.

They rested in the lea of an outhouse. For a minute or so they just sat there, getting their breath back, flinging excited looks at each other.

'Are you getting it?' Genie asked.

Wendi nodded. 'Yep. There's definitely something about that thing that just feels… *right*. I can't put my finger on it. It's like the first time I ever kissed. I felt *yeah, this is what I've been missing all along*. This building thing is just like that. Only not. Know what I mean? Like when you have a really brilliant idea in a dream but can't remember what it is when you wake up. You know it was fantastic but all you're left with is the feeling rather than the idea itself.'

'I do know what you mean,' Genie stood up and looked ahead at what she was sure was their destination, 'but I wonder if it's a liar? We've both seen the way things work round here. What if it's like, oh I don't know, a bug zapper? We'll do anything to get there but when we do it'll kill us?'

Wendi joined her and added the weight of her own gaze

to the scrutiny. 'Maybe. But it would be worth it, wouldn't it, babe? Just to find out…'

'Find out *what* though?' Genie looked down at her friend. 'It's like… well it's difficult to say but I feel like I want to *fuck* that thing or die trying! That's not right, is it? It's messing with me. With *us*. With our urges. I mean *of course* we should go there, investigate the thing – it could be our ticket out of here – but we should do it on our own terms.'

'How about we walk backwards then?'

Wendi's suggestion turned out to be a very sensible one. As the Labyrinth roof grew ever more precipitous by the minute, their journey changed from walking down a steep hill into climbing down a cliff face, albeit a wooden one. The jumble of elements was starting to become familiar to Genie; it was exactly the kind of layout she'd encountered on the other side of the Labyrinth when seeking shelter from the desert blizzard. Door handles and window sills were the two women's hand- and footholds as their climb became vertical, and then without any ceremony, they discovered they'd reached the bottom.

A nondescript boardwalk disappeared into coarse yellow sand; another desert.

This was a desert with a difference though. The Great Cube loomed on the horizon, but it was now obvious that it wasn't a cube at all but a taller structure, one at least twice as tall as it was wide. A cuboid. The orange glow emanating from its roof – more windows? bonfires? – illuminated the sky-ceiling directly above it, making the maddening cloud deck resemble something far more prosaic – a patch of light-polluted London night. Somehow this uplighting contrived to make the finer details of the sky-ceiling harder to see; less motion, less mass. More sanity.

It was still unclear how distant the Great Cuboid was. Its base could still have been over the horizon, and certainly there was

nothing visible beyond it, but how far away was that exactly
– what was the curvature of the afterlife? Did it curve at all?
To either side of them, the Labyrinth's wall disappeared into
the gloom. It was apparently straight, but there was something
about it that made Genie think of it as an *inner* wall, just as
the one she'd first encountered on the other side during the
blizzard had seemed outer.

The Labyrinth was a circle, she was sure of it. Just one far
too big to see.

'It's not as bad now, is it?' Wendi walked up and hugged her
from behind, looking around her at the distant Great Cuboid.
'Not so *come to me my pretties*. I mean, we're gonna go there
anyway, but right now I'm not bothered that we have to walk.'

'Well it depends what's in the way.' Genie screwed up her
eyes in an attempt to wring more information from the ruddy
landscape, but the light was at just the wrong level for her eyes.
Like twilight or the darkness just before dawn, the details were
deceptive.

The horizon was no longer flat. Quite apart from the
looming cuboid, other geometrical silhouettes along the
skyline indicated that this desert wasn't nearly as empty as the
one from which Genie had entered the Labyrinth.

'Shall we go?' Genie started walking and Wendi fell into
step. 'At least we're not going to lose our way.' The warm wind
had died away but the air itself remained parched, and smelled
of museums. It was prickly too, as if it had electricity dissolved
in it.

'I was going to ask you if you had any more coke,' said
Wendi, 'but that was just a habit. I don't need it. Don't think it
even affected me. It didn't work. It's going to be a long walk,
but I'm not going to be getting tired any time soon.'

'Speak for yourself.' Genie's calves had started aching again,
her head was still sore, and she wanted nothing more than to

soak her poor abused feet in a bowl of warm water. For about a week.

32: Halfway house

Off to the right, one of the shapes was starting to appear larger. The women exchanged glances and wordlessly decided to go and investigate, even if it did mean a slight detour.

On closer inspection, it turned out to be a long, low building fashioned entirely of marble. It appeared red, but in this light everything did.

'Shall we have a look inside?' Genie turned to Wendi.

'Why are you whispering?'

'I don't know. Come on, let's have a look.'

The building was like a mausoleum and was set on a slab of the same marble that made up the rest of its material so that a smooth, flat surface about three metres wide surrounded the whole thing. A marble moat, Genie thought, as she stepped onto it, the marble as cool and pleasant as water would have been.

'Where's the way in though?' Wendi wandered along one side. There were no doors, no windows, which contributed to the mausoleum aura the thing was radiating. But that didn't really make sense. This was the afterlife. What use would the dead have for tombs? Wendi disappeared around the corner and Genie scurried to catch up.

'Aha!' came Wendi's voice. Genie skidded around the corner.

This was the end of the building that faced the Great Cuboid on the horizon, and as a result was better lit than the rest. It also had what looked like a door, a huge square sheet of hammered bronze set into a recess over two metres high. Above this lettering was carved into the marble:

NEVER MET A WISE MAN

'What does that mean?' Genie couldn't recall any classical allusions or mistranslations that this might represent. It had to be some sort of clue though.

'Nirvana,' said Wendi, 'Territorial Pissings.'

'Eh? What do you think *that* means?'

'Dunno,' Wendi shrugged, 'Kurt's lyrics were difficult to suss out sometimes. If I'd found him in the Wood, I could have asked him. But the trees didn't talk to each other much…'

'No, I mean… why is it here? What does it mean?'

'Let's find out, shall we?' Wendi walked straight towards the brass door. Before she reached it, it slid down into a slot in the floor. Cold air rolled over the two of them, as refreshing as spring water.

'Ahh…' Genie closed her eyes and followed Wendi inside. Genie was reminded of the respite that air-conditioned shops had offered in Los Angeles, when she'd been there during the summer that time, just after meeting Ollie.

Opening her eyes again, she could see that the light was different in here too. Gone was the angry red gloom; this long, low chamber was suffused with a gentle blue-white radiance, medicinal and calming. She couldn't see where the light sources were; the ceiling did appear to be glowing, but it was more as if something in the cool air itself was supplying their vision, some subtle element from an archaic belief system.

Like the rest of the room, the floor was formed of pale blue marble slabs, and it must have been from here that the chamber's temperature was controlled. It was *cold* to the touch. For the moment, this was still refreshing, but Genie could foresee a time in the not too distant future when she'd be willing to sell her soul for a warm pair of slippers.

'Yo!' Wendi shouted. Her voice reverberated without a distinct echo; from the sound of it this hall was deceptively large. A wide aisle led off into the distance towards a far wall hidden more by a perceptual haze than by mere perspective. Either side of the central aisle a row of square marble pillars marched off en route to the vanishing point, and behind these off to each side in semi-darkness lay a series of large marble boxes. Sarcophagi.

But sarcophagi containing *what*? Who could possibly be interred down here?

Genie wandered over to the nearest, the first on the left, and stepped in between its guardian pillars. The darkened alcove lit up, the light still gentle and blue but with an unmistakable impression of activation, of attention.

Wendi joined her and took her hand as they watched the blue marble coffin flicker, streaks of tiny electrical sparks scintillating briefly into existence just below the surface of the stone and burrowing out of reality. The wall above the coffin lit up, a screen displaying blue noise accompanied by the faint but distinct sound of a crowd of people screaming in terror. Wendi stepped back, pulling Genie with her, and the alcove returned to shadow.

'Fucking freaky.' She let go of Genie's hand and started wandering up the aisle. 'I wonder if they're all like that?'

'I'm not sure I want to know.' At first this place had exuded an atmosphere of relaxation and respite, but there was something about the blue stone sarcophagus's inexplicable reaction to their presence that had made the hairs on the back of Genie's neck stand up and goose pimples bloom across her arms and legs.

'You cold, babe? Here, put this on.' Wendi shrugged off her leather jacket and reached up to place it over Genie's shoulders. 'You know me. Cold blooded.'

Genie was grateful for this gesture. The jacket didn't make that much of a difference, but it was good to know that there was someone looking out for her, even if only a dead woman. And it was true, the pale skin on Wendi's thin arms showed no sign of the cold conditions as she continued her exploration of the building.

She didn't seem to have a plan of action but just ducked into an alcove at random; this one on the right and about ten down. By the time Genie had caught up with her, it had already lit up. This one was different.

The screen on the wall showed rows of numbers and graphs that had a medical look about them. Pulse. Respiration. No sooner had she thought this than the confirming sounds reached Genie's ears, the alarming bleeps of the equipment in an intensive care ward. Did they have *hospitals* down here?

The coffin itself was now glowing periodically in time with the high-pitched pulse, and on top of it, at every moment of greatest brightness, Genie could see a very definite indication of a body, a body in a hospital gown, a body hooked up to invisible equipment.

The body sat up and Genie leaped back with a shriek. Still only visible at the height of the pulse and even then semi-transparently, it looked around, more confused and tired than alarmed. A voice like a badly tuned radio asked indistinct questions, a wizened face hectoring them both as they stared.

Investigation of some of the other alcoves further down the room turned up similar equally alarming apparitions. Judging by their mode of dress and surrounding ambient noise most of the transparent figures had to be in hospitals of one kind or another. They were of all ages, genders, races, with no common factor other than their apparent location.

They also weren't really aware of Genie and Wendi. Even though they responded to their visitors' presence, it was in a perfunctory manner and, when comprehensible, the litany of gripes had an involuntary feel about it, as if they'd been complaining about the same things for a very long time and couldn't stop. It was obvious that they weren't really conscious of their surroundings.

They were barely sentient.

'What is it with these guys?' Wendi wandered further up the aisle, turning slowly to face Genie and continuing her walk backwards.

'It's like they don't know they're dead,' Genie said. 'Something about them…'

'Nah, I don't buy that *Sixth Sense* shit.' Wendi stopped her retro-ambulation and held up her hands. 'We're all dead down here, and don't we know it. Well, apart from you, babe, that is. This is different. This is…'

'What?' Genie watched as Wendi wandered into the next alcove. It lit up as expected but showed no other sign of animation. Genie shivered; as predicted her feet really were starting to get cold now and her legs were following suit. She joined the pensive Wendi at this latest coffin.

Still nothing. Apart from the light, their presence had made no difference whatsoever to conditions in here; the coffin remained inert and the wall above showed no sign of any medical information or blurred film footage of a life interrupted.

Genie put one hand on the coffin and, upon discovering that it wasn't nearly as cold as the floor, climbed up and sat cross-legged on the edge, looking down at Wendi.

'They don't know they're dead 'cause they're not.' Wendi looked straight up at Genie and snapped her fingers. 'They're still alive! This is a halfway house.'

'What makes you think that?' Despite the coke she and Wendi had taken earlier, Genie was feeling tired again. She was sure now that it hadn't had any effect on her other than placebo. She twisted round and stretched out on her front, elbows on the coffin lid, chin resting on her arms. Up here, the marble was almost warm. That was unexpected.

'It's a hunch. You get a feel for this place. For the people in it. And these people aren't even *in it*. They're in an antechamber, they might not even die. People in comas. People in accidents. You know I reckon that if we went far enough in that direction,' Wendi's eyes shone as she pointed down the hall into the unexplored infinity, 'we'd find people who were just asleep. Little slices of death as old Edgar said.'

'Wish I was asleep.' Genie rested a cheek on her forearm and continued to peer down at Wendi though half-closed eyes. 'I'm knackered. I could do with a slice.'

'Maybe even people having sex.' Wendi flashed a wicked grin up at Genie. 'The French call an orgasm *la petite mort*. Imagine that. Open your eyes when you're coming and you see us staring at you from the other side. That'd kill the mood.'

'Hmm...' Genie's eyelids closed. Even though she'd wondered earlier on about falling asleep down here, now she didn't really think that was possible. She was just resting her eyes and deserved a break after such an onerous journey. It was nice to just lie here and listen to Wendi's flight of fancy. Comforting.

'...so sometimes people must be here for a while and then

go back to life. Not surprising they don't seem to really know where they are...'

Genie frowned. It was good having a little lie down like this, but her head was starting to ache again. That was unfair. Now that she thought about it, if the coke hadn't affected her after all, then in theory she *should* have been immune to other bodily symptoms like neuralgia.

'...I mean, it's hardly a tunnel of light with your gran waiting at the end of it, is it, babe? I see no grandmothers...'

In fact, thought Genie, not only should she be headache free, but she should be immune to fatigue as well. Down here normal rules didn't apply. Was she just imagining that they did? Should she leap up from the bed and start doing press-ups? Although it wasn't a bed, was it? It was a coffin.

'...babe, are you listening...'

The frisson of horror passed; coffin it might be, but it was a very comfortable one. It didn't even feel like marble any more. Genie moved her forearm and rested her cheek directly on the surface. It was more like fitted carpet and smelled of mothballs. It reminded her of something. The inside of the fitted wardrobe back at her Soho flat.

Her head really was beginning to ache now. In the distance she could hear tinny music and police sirens.

There was a sudden sharp pain in her shins, and she opened her eyes to find herself lying almost on top of Wendi between the two pillars separating the empty alcove from the central aisle in the Halfway House.

'Jeez, babe, don't *do* that to me! You'd started to *go*.' Wendi's eyes were wide with fright. 'You were turning into one of those dumb ghosts. Fade-out. *Fuck!*'

'How...?' Genie rolled off her and sat up. The chill of the floor was dispelling any lingering after-effects that the coffin might have had on her.

'I had to pull you off there.' Wendi kneeled up and massaged her own shoulders. 'I'd have lost you. You're not dead either; this place could tell. It was trying to suck you into the machinery.'

Genie was conflicted. If this was true then Wendi had ruined the best chance she'd had so far of getting out of here, mission or no mission. But no. She'd found who she really wanted. She wasn't going to leave Wendi behind. She'd been given another chance and she wasn't going to mess it up this time. They were going to have to finish this the long way round.

'Wonder if this means I'm in a coma back home?' Genie stood and held out a hand to help Wendi up. 'A *stupor*, maybe...'

'Dead to the world,' said Wendi, 'and alive to the underworld. It's this place. It's bureaucratic. It was trying to file you in the right drawer. Lucky I got you down from there 'cause *this* way we can get out of here.'

'Let's make a move then. Nothing more to see here, eh?' Genie decided not to mention that she suspected she'd been about to wake up. From the defensive tone of Wendi's voice, she could tell that she knew that too, even if only subconsciously, and was making excuses to herself. Genie gestured towards the exit, and together they walked towards it.

Just before they reached the square aperture, something caught Genie's eye. A flicker in the alcove to their left – the one to the right of the door they hadn't looked at on the way in. That was odd. Previously they'd had to actually step into an alcove before anything had happened. This was new then.

'I know that voice.' Wendi stopped and took a couple of steps towards the alcove. Inside, it remained dark, but the coffin itself was throbbing with faint luminescence and yes, Wendi was right, Genie could hear a voice now. A voice on a telephone. A mobile with a bad signal.

'*...yeah, sure, but just let me check with the office first, right? No problem sweetheart... OK. See you then. Ciao...*'

It was a familiar voice. The wall above the coffin lit up with what looked like CCTV footage of central London streets at night, flickering in and out of existence in time with the voice.

'*...let you know. Yeah, pointless now, we're exercising our get-out option. No, watertight, won't have a leg to stand on. Monika's drawing up the papers...*'

'Malcolm?' The women spoke simultaneously and then stared at each other. Was it really their erstwhile manager? And if so, did this mean that he was in a coma or worse?

The London scene switched cameras. It was Shaftesbury Avenue.

'Malcolm? Can you hear me?' Genie stepped into the alcove. It didn't light up, but the impression of a man's head and shoulders now hovered above the coffin, fading in and out with the rest of the son et lumière performance. Malcolm's glasses flashed as the head and shoulders rotated, as if filmed by a tiny camera orbiting his head. He was still on the phone.

'*...on my way to Storm now, meeting one of our prospects there...*'

'I don't think he can, you know.' Wendi had joined Genie and was staring up at the rotating head. 'He never really *listened* to me when I was actually there... and I don't think he knows we're eavesdropping now.'

The CCTV scene switched again. There was a man walking along Shaftesbury Avenue speaking on his mobile. It was in sync with Malcolm's head and shoulders.

'*...and if all goes well we could get her in to sign a contract within a week. No, just backing tracks...*'

Screen switch. Long shot of Shaftesbury Avenue, the figure

of Malcolm now an inch high in the middle distance. Slow-moving traffic crawling past him.

'*...think you'll like her... got a bit of an Amy Winehouse vibe, but more mainstream... should be able to keep her more under control... yeah, just like Genie... I know, it's a shame, she could have worked out... well true, but if you look at the projections... punters aren't interested in tragedy any more, and that shit's going to stick... they want superficial, they want silly... that kind of zeitgeist is going to hang about – but luckily the new girl's got it in spades... once we've dropped Genie, we'll be able to transfer all the resources she's tying up to the new girl... play our cards right and we'll be able to transfer half the audience too...*'

'What? You filthy shit!' Genie had been able to follow enough of what ghost Malcolm had been saying to know that she was about to get royally screwed in the outside world. She leaped forward. 'Listen to me, you cunt!'

'Good for you, babe!' Wendi was shocked and delighted, eyes wide and vital.

'*...I'm sure there's a market for it somewhere... well celebrity biogs are big these days... if she knows what's good for her that's the angle she'll go for, might be able to wring a bit more cash out of it, but it's not our problem any more...*'

'Hey! Listen to me!' Genie thumped her fist on the surface of the coffin. Maybe this thing wasn't broadcasting live? The rotating Malcolm vanished.

Up on the screen, everything happened in rapid-fire slow motion; CCTV footage edited together by an idiot monkey on crack.

Malcolm walking down the street on his phone. Some homeless guy, all dirty wool and beard, running out of a side street yelling. Another familiar figure walking the other way, oh god, it was Nathan. Homeless Guy – and *he* was familiar now too – running out into the road with wild gesticulation. The traffic starting to move faster. Homeless Guy running into the path of a bendy bus which swerved and struck Malcolm a glancing blow, flinging him back into a travel agent's window before crushing Nathan against a lamp post.

'Knock yourself out,' whispered Genie.

33: Through a glass, Genie

Underworld, no time

Genie looked back. The Halfway House had vanished against the dark maroon bulk of the Labyrinth's inner wall. How far had they come? And would it ever be far enough?

'Babe. Take a rest, hmm?' Jogging alongside, Wendi looked up at her. Genie shook her head.

'Come on, it's not your fault!'

But wasn't it? Inadvertently she'd killed Nathan and very possibly Malcolm. How could she live with herself after that? Ollie's death had re-opened old wounds; but Wendi's death had made them in the first place. Four years of buried grief and pain and the charade her life had become since then meant that they'd never really begun to heal. Ollie's death had brought it all to a head and broken her. Despite the accident, she had been there for him, but she hadn't been there for Wendi. Which was what it had always really been about, hadn't it? To try and make up for it she'd played at *being* Wendi, trying to be crazy and unpredictable – and because of that there were now two more lives on her conscience. Despite Malcolm's view of her as a commodity to be traded and Nathan's view of her as a series of jpegs on a marble pedestal, they didn't deserve to die, did they?

'How do you work that out?' Genie stared straight ahead at the Great Cuboid on the horizon, not looking down at Wendi. 'I did it. I started it.'

'That's a bollock and a half, and you know it!' Wendi leaped in front of her and grabbed her arms. 'It's coincidence. The universe is taking the piss. *You* didn't do anything. You were pretty damned generous giving Old Beardy all that locoweed. Better than 10p for a cup of tea. Not *your* fault he couldn't handle it.'

'But,' Genie closed her eyes, 'it just seems too much. How come Nathan and Malcolm just happened to be there?'

'Coincidence.' Wendi reached up and took Genie's chin between thumb and forefinger, forcing her to look her in the eyes. 'Or not even that. Just your way of looking at things.'

'But…'

'Let's take a breather.' Wendi sat down cross-legged in the sand and after a few seconds, Genie joined her.

'It's like this place,' Wendi went on, starting to draw circles and lines in the sand. At first Genie wondered if they had any significance to what she was saying, but then realised her friend was just doodling. 'This place – how many people down here have you met that you know? More than you should, given the billions of deadeyes that must be down here.'

'Hmm.'

'It's to do with your way of looking at it, right? Like we said. *Through a glass, Genie.* You only see the things and the people that make sense to you. That mean something to you.'

'But why?' Genie asked, although she could feel that Wendi was talking some kind of twisted sense.

''Cause you're alive,' Wendi smiled. 'Like I said before. You're the light illuminating this underlife, and so the only people visible to you are those who are looking at you anyway. Your light slides past everyone else.'

'OK, fair enough.' Genie realised that they were going off-topic. 'But what about what we were actually talking about?'

'Don't you see, it's *like that...*' Wendi's eyes widened. 'As below, so above – you might think it's all a conspiracy and plotting against you, but it's just life. Sure, there are loads of threads you can pull on to link it all to you, but imagine it from the perspective of everyone else involved. Bet the bus driver has a different story to tell, and I bet it's just as full of coincidence and fate playing silly fuckers with *him*. Old Beardy too – some rich woman he's never seen before gives him a load of drugs outside an off-licence? What are the chances of that?'

'I love you.' Genie reached over and took Wendi's hand. 'And I know you're not just saying this to make me feel better, although it's doing the trick. It all makes sense as well. When did you get so wise?'

'Oi, watch it!' Wendi swiped at the tip of Genie's nose. 'I'm not as thick as I might look. I know I always used to come across as impulsive, but a lot of that was an act. It's what people expected. It's what people wanted. Besides, you get a lot of time to think when you're a tree.'

'I guess you do. Poor old Nathan. Even if it's not my fault, he's still stuck down here now. As a tree, until they find out you swapped with him.'

'Yeah. But he's *dead*. This is where he *should* be. And it's not half as bad as it could have been. He could have been in some kind of Hell. Or even worse he could have been *nowhere* – after all some people just don't believe in any of this bollocks.' Wendi swept a hand around, indicating their surroundings. 'Peter was always like that – confirmed atheist. He never stopped going on about it, trying to get me to see sense. But I've seen too much weird shit in my time to buy into it. Didn't stop him trying though. The record company told him not to make a big deal of it, 'cause it might have alienated potential punters. Turned out he was wrong.'

'I don't think he was.' Genie unfolded her legs and stood up. 'Not necessarily. Have you seen God? Any god, anywhere down here? Seems to me like this place is as rudderless as the world back home; no one in charge of the whole thing.'

'I guess so. Weird shit and gods don't necessarily go together; maybe you can have one without the other. I've always believed in weird shit though.' Wendi stood up as well and stared at the Great Cuboid. 'I suppose we're going to find out though, eh, babe? If there's anyone in charge, that's where they'll be.'

'Please don't let it be a committee,' muttered Genie under her breath as they resumed their journey.

34: Death drive

Now the desert itself was starting to angle downwards, and at last the base of the Great Cuboid was visible far below, way beyond the distant foot of the slope. Scattered on the plane around it were a number of smaller buildings that looked like scale models next to the Cuboid. For all Genie knew perhaps they were. There was nothing to compare them to, no human yardstick, and the dry air was so clear it was impossible to tell how far they still had to travel.

It was getting warmer. Genie had returned Wendi's jacket to her some miles back and Wendi had now tied it around her waist. Whenever there was a pause in the sultry breeze wafting in her face, Genie could feel raw heat radiating off the Cuboid itself.

She still couldn't make out the finest details of its structure, the fractal self-similarity still disappearing into a lower infinity too small to see.

'Hang on, what was that?' Up until this point, the only noise Genie'd heard for miles had been that of her own breathing, footsteps and heartbeat, but now there was something else. A crack and rumble. It was faint but there was something about its timbre that spoke of great power and enormous forces held in check.

'Thunder! Look up there at the top!' Wendi pointed at the Great Cuboid's summit. At the limit of Genie's perception, she could see tiny sparks and arcs of electricity leaping between crenulations and from the Cuboid's roof up towards the sky-ceiling. The flashes weren't synchronised with the noises at all; upon spotting a particularly bright one, Genie started counting but reached one hundred before giving up; no corresponding crack had made itself known to her ears in that time. It was just as well, she decided – knowledge of how far they still had to go might prove disheartening at this point.

Besides, she could never remember the formula for calculating the distance of lightning.

The sand now started to give way to expanses of flat rock, like lava flows softened by millennia at the bottom of an ocean. However, if these rocks had ever been underwater there was no sign of that now; they were as dry as Genie's throat felt.

'I'm imagining it,' Genie muttered, 'I'm not thirsty.'

'Do what, babe?'

'Sorry,' said Genie. 'Trying a bit of mind over matter. I keep thinking I'm thirsty but I don't think I can be, can I?'

'No. Don't think our bodies work in the same way down here. Well, mine doesn't anyway. That coke we had – nice idea and all and at first I was imagining it was working, but I don't think so now.'

'I had my doubts,' Genie nodded. 'Shame we couldn't have carried on *thinking* it was working; that'd be a lot healthier in the long run, wouldn't it?'

'Homeopathic coke, like it!' said Wendi. 'But no, I don't think you're thirsty. Wouldn't mind a drink myself though. Vodka and orange would go down a treat right now.'

'I should have needed a pee by now as well,' said Genie, 'but my bladder's behaving itself.'

They came upon another building much sooner than Genie had been expecting. They still had a long way to travel to reach the ones visible on the flat wasteland at the foot of the escarpment, but this building had been camouflaged against the coarse boulders and rocks of the mountainside as they approached. It was tiny, little more than a rough stone hut of the kind Genie imagined might be found halfway up a Welsh hill. She didn't want to look inside, not after what had happened the last time.

'I'll just have a quick look.' Wendi bounced over to the empty door-socket and peered in. 'You never know, might find something useful.' She disappeared inside and there was the sound of scraping. She emerged holding a rusty bicycle chain at arm's length.

'Planning on getting into a fight with some Hells Angels?' Genie asked. Wendi appeared to consider this.

'Nah.' She dropped the chain and wiped her hands on her trousers before stepping away from the hut. As she did so, there was a creaking noise and the entire structure collapsed.

'Fuck,' Wendi looked worried, 'was that all that was holding it together? Better be more careful next time.'

As they walked onwards and downwards, they started passing more and more of these stone huts of varying sizes. Wendi refrained from investigating any more of them. Some were larger than before, and one or two were almost habitable.

Eventually they approached one that was more of a cottage than a shed and came with two storeys, a barn attached and a yard surrounded by a drystone wall. The main doorways of all the buildings were pointing at the Great Cuboid. At Wendi's insistence they walked all the way around it before doing anything else.

'Let's just go.' Genie was impatient to continue. The Great Cuboid didn't look any closer and she was keen to make some kind of progress.

'Nah, what's the rush?' Wendi wandered over to the wall and started worrying one of the stones loose. 'It's not like we've got an appointment or anything. Is that big box starting to exercise its mojo on you again?' The stone came free and Wendi tossed it in one hand a few times.

'What are you doing?' Genie sat down on the wall with her back to the cottage, facing the Great Cuboid. There was something in what Wendi had said; she was starting to feel the strange attraction to it again that they'd first experienced while still on the roof of the Labyrinth. But was it an instinct that would benefit them both or a suicidal lemming urge?

'Watch this.' Wendi hurled the stone at the cottage and struck the roof a glancing blow. 'Fuckit, try again.' She kicked down a small section of the wall and selected a larger stone from the rubble. This time she scored a direct hit on one of the darkened windows, the unmistakable sound of breaking glass providing a welcome contrast to the now almost constant rumble of thunder from the Cuboid's distant summit.

'Can I ask one thing?' Genie said. 'Why?'

'Just testing.' Wendi looked pleased with herself. 'Wanted to make sure it wasn't going to collapse as well. Want to take a look inside?'

'No.' Genie would have been happy just to sit there for a while. 'What for?'

'You never know.' Wendi turned and jogged towards the front door. Genie followed more slowly. Inside the wall, there was a layer of gravel over the lava flow. Wendi disappeared through the door, and a few seconds later was looking out of the window she'd smashed.

'Well?' Genie put her hands on her hips. 'Anything?'

'People!' Wendi pointed towards the Cuboid.

'People?' Genie wasn't sure whether this was a good thing, given the behaviour of the last people she'd encountered.

'Yes, come up here and look!'

The interior of the cottage had been stripped bare; aside from the glass of the remaining windows and the wood of the door- and window frames, everything was bare dark stone. The ceilings were low, but even so Genie felt a twinge of unease at having to climb a staircase with no banister.

'Ow!' Upstairs the ceiling was even lower. Genie rubbed at her skull and stopped as she walked over to Wendi.

Something about the extra elevation made their view of the Great Cuboid and its environs clearer. The structures scattered around it no longer looked quite as much like models – and was that movement around their bases? Wendi was right, it could only be people milling about. From this distance, they were at the very periphery of vision, each one barely a dot. It was little more than the view of an ant heap from the top of a house, but there was definitely something there.

It meant the buildings around the base of the Great Cuboid must be on the scale of cathedrals. It meant the cube itself… defied definition – no metropolis had ever been that large, vertical or self-contained; this was something altogether new.

'Must be *miles* still to go.' Genie placed her arm along the top of the window frame and rested her forehead against it.

'I wonder…' Wendi glanced around the room. 'Hang on a second.' She disappeared down the stairs and moments later appeared on the gravel outside.

'What are you doing *now*?'

'I had an idea!' Wendi pointed in the direction of the barn. 'Just let me check in there.' The crunch of her footsteps measured her walk to the barn doors, but by the time she reached them she was out of sight of the windows.

Genie made her own way back downstairs. She heard a wooden shudder and bang as Wendi forced the doors open. Stepping outside, there was nothing of Wendi to be seen, but a clattering thud from inside the barn indicated she was still busy.

'Find anything?' Genie called. There was a huge grinding response, a cough and bark from something very large and very unwell. 'Wendi? Are you OK?'

The beast coughed again and began to growl. As it continued, Genie realised that the sound was far from organic. She reached the barn and peered inside.

Wendi sat behind the wheel of a large brown car; it was unclear where the paintwork ended and the rust began. Somehow she'd got it running; clouds of thick black smoke belched from the exhaust, filling the barn. Wendi released the handbrake, and the car moved forward in unpredictable lurches. As it emerged into the open, Genie could see it no longer had any doors, that the tyres were all flat and the windscreen lacked glass. Wendi eased it to a standstill right next to Genie and looked up at her.

'Hop in then.' She jerked a thumb at the empty passenger seat. Genie walked round in front of the car. The large circular headlamps gave it a startled look, the broad metallic grille a mouth wide with panic. Battered chrome lettering spelled out F O R D across the bonnet and a filthy badge in the centre of the dented front end revealed that it was a Cortina. Genie had never heard of it.

She lowered herself into the brown leatherette seat. The interior of the car smelled of copper coins and oil. Automatically she reached for the seat belt. There was nothing there. She looked over her shoulder at the back seat; it was covered with dried-up old paint pots and rusty farm implements.

'I didn't know you could drive.' She turned to Wendi, who

was looking dwarfed by the large round steering wheel. When they'd known each other in the past, there'd always been someone else doing the driving.

'I can't.' Wendi gave her a manic look. 'Well, I never had lessons. But how hard can it be? Used to watch the drivers on tour when I was bored. Something to do with clutches, isn't it? Doubt there are any speed cameras down here anyway. Or police.'

From the inside, the unpredictable bounces felt as if the car was on the brink of tearing itself apart. After a few false starts, Wendi found the right combination of controls, and they started rolling forwards more smoothly, crunching across the gravel and through the gap in the wall that led back onto the lava flows.

As the car picked up speed, the combination of a lack of a door and absence of a seat belt began to make Genie very nervous. Never mind normal rules not applying, if she fell out here, she could probably hurt herself very badly. Look what had happened to Cosmo. She reached down and grabbed the sides of the seat's frame with both hands.

She shrieked as it slid backwards unexpectedly. She'd grabbed a control lever.

'You all right, babe?' Wendi glanced across at her, hair fluttering back in the stream of hot air pouring through the windscreen, deranged excitement all over her face. 'This is great, isn't it?'

'Not exactly... Oww...!' The car leaped over a ridge in the lava and Genie's head bumped against the roof. 'Not exactly my idea of... my idea of FUN!'

'It'll get us there in no time, though, look!' Wendi took one hand off the wheel for a second to point at the looming cathedrals ahead. The car chose this moment to hit another bump and swing around sideways. Genie grabbed onto the windscreen frame to stop herself being flung out.

'Sorry!' Wendi once more had both hands on the wheel and was almost standing up in her seat trying to keep the car under control. 'That was close!'

'Can't you... can't you slow down?' The hot wind was really buffeting the car's interior now.

'Not really,' Wendi bellowed. 'The brake isn't working!' To demonstrate she pumped at the loose pedal a couple of times with one booted foot.

'Terrific.' Genie looked over her shoulder again and out of the rear window. A huge plume of black smoke was rising from the car's rear end, a comet's tail of pollution. Bang went any hope of a subtle arrival; they must have been visible from the base of the Great Cuboid already, like some meteor entering the earth's atmosphere or a fighter plane that had been shot down.

Genie hoped they weren't going to end up in a crater.

Mind you, with no seat belt, no airbags and no brakes, there was no guarantee they were even going to end up in one piece. Gripping the seat frame more carefully this time, Genie braced herself by pushing her legs against the bottom of the footwell in front of her. This was a mistake; the rusty floor crumbled away beneath her feet like stale pastry. She shrieked and pulled her legs up onto the seat.

The glove compartment chose this moment to flip open; its contents poured out and straight through the new orifice in the car's floor. A handful of change, a pair of old leather gloves and what looked like a revolver tumbled past Genie's knees, as a cloud of red dust and grit began blooming upwards into her face through the same opening.

Bugger it. She was getting grit in her eyes now but didn't dare let go of the seat frame. She risked a glimpse sideways at

Wendi, who was now kneeling up on the seat, gripping the wheel with both hands and seemingly having a great time. She even appeared to be singing, but what with the sound of the engine and the relentless grind of flying shingle against every available surface, it was impossible to hear the words, let alone the tune.

There was a sharp bang followed by a deafening absence – the engine had stopped. Genie hoped that this was good news; out of the back window, she could see that their filthy contrail was thinning out, the black smoke being replaced by the dust flung up by their passage. The ground was levelling out too. Was it possible that they were going to be able to coast to a stop unharmed?

Perhaps not. Now freed from the cacophony of the engine, the myriad complaining noises of the rest of the car's superstructure could be heard in all their glory. There was a repetitive, feverish flapping which, combined with the piercing shrieks from deep in the remains of the suspension, gave the unnerving impression of a nest of pterodactyls somewhere in the engine housing. Some of the rattles were so severe that Genie was surprised not to be able to see more evidence of their source with her eyes; as if in response to this thought, the bonnet chose this moment to spring open, obscuring their view of the obstacles ahead.

'Fuck it!' Wendi yelled, keeping hold of the wheel with one hand and grabbing the windscreen frame with the other, craning out to peer around the flapping square of sheet metal.

They slowed still further, and Genie closed her eyes. There was little point in praying, she decided, but if they got out of this OK she determined to lodge a serious complaint with whoever was in charge. They probably had an office somewhere in the Great Cuboid ahead.

Genie opened her eyes again. In the brief moments of

visibility afforded her by the bonnet's flapping, Genie could see that now the Cuboid was taking up nearly half the sky ahead of them. It was still seemingly receding as they approached the outskirts of the conglomeration of smaller structures around its base. It was like they were entering a city, albeit one that was deserted. Where were the people they'd spotted from the cottage back there?

It was difficult to see clearly out of the side of the car, but on closer inspection, Genie thought she'd spotted movement down one or two of the side streets they were passing.

'Whoa! Hold onto your ball sacks, people!' Wendi plonked herself back into the driver's seat and performed a complex dance on the accelerator and clutch while hauling the steering wheel round like the handle of a bank vault. This time, the spin forced Genie into the car interior, banging against Wendi, who was struggling to prevent herself being flung out by inertia. Genie spotted one of their wheels flying free and bouncing off into the distance, before the interior of the car filled with thick red dust to the accompaniment of a grinding noise that seemed to go on forever.

35: Shanty City

Genie's ears were ringing, but at least the car was no longer moving. It sat at a slight angle, creaking occasionally as it settled. The bonnet fell shut in front of her, but there was still little visible through the cloud their arrival had thrown up.

It was difficult to persuade her hands to unclasp themselves from the seat frame, but eventually Genie managed it and climbed out to stand on the hot earth outside. On the other side, Wendi had already disembarked and was leaning one forearm on the car roof, resting her chin on it.

'I always like to make an entrance,' she remarked, digging around in the pocket of her leather jacket with a free hand and producing her sunglasses.

Genie followed suit, and not just because of the protection her Ray-Bans would afford against the grit still in the air. As the dust of their arrival settled, she could see that there was something hyperluminous about the dead Shanty City in which they'd arrived.

The light was all wrong.

They stood in the shadow of a building into the front of which they'd nearly crashed, a shadow cast by the red light pouring off the Great Cuboid behind it. The mental effect of such a large quantity of illumination shining not from a point source but from a large flat area above and to one side was peculiar; it was like a sunset gone wrong or as if the horizon had tilted through ninety degrees. Just thinking about it made Genie feel dizzy.

Turning her back on the Cuboid didn't do much good either. Now that the dust had cleared, the nearby buildings were visible, brightly illuminated, as was the rising ground in front of which they stood. The evidence of their passage down the slope was a fresh scar in the landscape disappearing upwards. The buildings and these nearer slopes contrasted sharply with the darkness of the heights beyond and the inky blackness of the sky-ceiling under which they'd crossed the roof of the Labyrinth.

There was nobody about. If whatever they'd seen from the cottage had been people, they were all indoors now. Genie walked around the car to examine the building in front of which they'd ended their journey.

It was a vast cathedral fringed with Gothic spines and sculptures, topped off by a bell-shaped dome. It was difficult to see much detail, silhouetted as the building was against the Cuboid's radiance. Genie mounted the stone steps at the bottom of which they'd arrived and peered through the doors set in a larger panel of wood, itself set in an enormous stone archway.

Inside, the smell was ecclesiastical and the air cool. This was a welcome change from the hot grit and oil of the last leg of their journey. Genie limped over to the nearest pew and lowered herself into it. No matter how much she kept telling herself that none of this was actually real in any physical sense, she felt like she'd been dragged through ten hedges both backwards and forwards *and* a wringer just for good measure. Her bloodstream was reporting the aftermath of a massive fight-or-flight event.

Her adrenal glands were exhausted.

Wendi dropped down into the pew next to her, zips on her leather jacket jingling faintly. The pew rocked in a slightly alarming fashion but remained upright.

'It's like being on holiday, isn't it?' Wendi leaned in close to whisper in Genie's ear. 'Heat, dust and cathedrals. Shame there's no one outside selling ice cream.'

Genie wobbled her head in a non-committal gesture. She couldn't recall ever having visited a cathedral quite like this one. The interior space matched the exterior shell, resulting in an enormous tall circular chamber, the vast majority of which was filled with long rows of pews just like the one in which they were sitting. Far ahead was an altar of sorts, squat and square, below two tall, thin multi-paned windows. The multifaceted glass in them wasn't stained, but it didn't need to be. The windows faced the wall of the Great Cuboid itself; red, orange and yellow shafts of cubelight coruscated against the glass like a Titan's kaleidoscope, filling the cathedral's interior with an ambience that was more hellish than heavenly.

Still, at least it was cool. Statues of classical-looking figures lurked in alcoves set around the walls, frozen in attitudes of mock surprise.

Someone started playing the organ.

Genie sat up straight and looked around her, but couldn't see where the organ actually was. Wendi had already stood up and was walking down the aisle in the direction of the altar. The music was formless, more like modern jazz arranged for church organ than classical music. However, it was in a minor key and carried an unmistakable undercurrent of menace.

'Whee... I'm getting vertigo just looking up there!' Wendi was spinning round, staring straight up into the dome far above. Genie was more concerned with the altar up ahead. It was difficult to tell, what with the flickering of the cubelight, but she could swear that there were now two or three robed figures kneeling in front of it. She stood up and started making her way forward.

'Quiet!' she hissed in Wendi's ear, placing one hand on her shoulder as she caught up with her. 'Were they here all along?' She pointed at the altar with her free hand. The music had started getting louder and more complex, but then cut off suddenly, continuing with only a few bass chords and a few high-register tinkles.

The three figures stood up. Their robes were long, dragging on the floor, and hoods hid their heads. Turning simultaneously, they began walking down the aisle towards the two women.

The music took on a plodding regularity that reminded Genie of the theme from *Mastermind*. As one they reached up and removed their hoods. The tops of their heads gleamed unexpectedly in the cubelight.

They were skeletons.

Genie moaned and began backing away from them. Her irrational fear of skeletons went further than the spine of that book Grandfather had given her. She'd been unable to watch *He-Man and the Masters of the Universe* as a child. There was even a recurring childhood nightmare she used to have that was still scheduled at least once a year throughout her adult life so far. Whether her osteophobia was inspired by or had itself inspired the nightmare she had no idea, but it was terrifying nonetheless.

It always started the same way; she was outdoors in the countryside and had turned her back on her picnicking parents for just two minutes only for them to disappear. The light would then start leaching out of the sky in a manner far too swift to be natural. She'd start walking along the exposed ridge in the growing dusk. Her eyes would start playing tricks on her, and she'd catch a glimpse of something white moving through a grove of trees in the valley below. She would remember she was wearing Grandfather's binoculars on a strap around her neck and would hold these to her eyes to get a closer look at the movement. For a second, she'd be unable to locate it, but then a flash of white would pass through her field of view, and her hands would follow it, fingers turning the control to bring the half-light into focus.

It was always a skeleton. For a second, she'd be observing it in secret, but then it would somehow notice her scrutiny and look straight up at her through the binocular barrels, its jawbone opening in a rictus of surprise and pleasure. It would alter its course and start jogging towards her, sometimes offering her a wave of acknowledgement, as if to say, *I'll be with you in a minute.*

She would always turn and run, but the most terrifying thing of all was not the way that her legs would get tangled in briars or the fact that she kept getting stuck in the undergrowth through which she was trying to escape. The worst thing was the knowledge that the skeleton was behind her, would never give up, and that no matter how far she ran, it would always catch up with her in the end.

It was a fairly straightforward intimation of mortality made all the more impressive by the fact that it was her four-year-old mind that had thought it up.

These skeletons weren't jogging, and as she was in theory already on a package tour of the undiscovered country, albeit unconventionally, they shouldn't have scared her as much. However, this reasoning did her no good. In fact, as they continued their slow sacerdotal march towards her, this made it all the more terrifying. Whimpering, she started actually running backwards, not wanting to turn her back on them for a second. Wendi didn't seem to have moved, and Genie wanted to scream at her to get out of there, but her throat refused to emit anything other than a low wail.

Her backward-questing fingertips touched the edge of the wooden door, and she dashed back right through it, ran down the steps and hid behind their car.

It was far from comforting outside, what with the bizarre lighting, and the silence broken only by the distant sound of organ music, and the crackling of electrical discharge up at the Cuboid's summit. The suspense was getting too much – she half expected to hear Wendi's scream, for the doors to burst open and for skeletal monks running down the steps to *get* her.

The door moved and Wendi slipped out, unharmed. In one hand she held a skull she was tossing up and down like a tennis ball. She trotted down the steps, looking pleased with herself.

'That was weird.' She reached the car and placed the skull atop it, facing Genie. 'They totally ignored me. Even when I nicked one of their heads. You OK, babe?'

'I *hate* skeletons. They freak me out.' Genie unfolded herself from behind the car and looked with distaste at the bone orb sitting on the car's roof.

'Shit. That must have been a bit nasty for you then.' Wendi seemed a bit blasé, as if she couldn't imagine what it was like to have an irrational fear. 'Still. There were only three of them. Two and three quarters now.' She picked up the skull, turned and punted it back through the half-open door. There was a faint clatter from inside, and Genie realised that the organ music had stopped.

Before either of them could speak, a single bell somewhere up in the cathedral's dome rang out. Loud and pure, it blotted out the thunder from the Cuboid's summit and shook Genie's body right down to the atomic level. It rang again. And then a third time.

Something changed. A creaking, skittering sound erupted

from everywhere; faint but obviously multitudinous. In the side streets around them figures appeared from doors and archways and started to move, the original people they'd spotted from afar.

All of them skeletons.

Genie looked about, too frightened now even to moan. Somewhere inside her, a voice was telling her it was an irrational phobia, but right now she was more interested in identifying the least bony direction in which to run.

'Take it slowly, babe.' Might the voice of Wendi from outside succeed where her inner dialogue had not? 'They don't seem in any hurry. 'Sides, what could the fuckers do to us? They're not exactly tough. One tap and they fall apart.'

Genie nodded. She was fairly sure that there were fewer of them towards the right of the cathedral, making that direction seem the least unattractive. Without speaking, she indicated with her eyes and head to Wendi that she was about to head off in that direction. Wendi put a hand on her arm.

'OK, let's go. But walk, don't run. For your sake, not theirs. Running will freak you out and make it worse.'

They stepped away from the shell of the car and started making their way hand in hand around the cathedral. The only sound Genie could hear aside from her own breathing was the click of bone on bone as the skeletal population went about their business – completely disinterested in Wendi and her, thankfully. They didn't seem to have a particular purpose at all; they were just wandering at random, a drunkard's walk that added up to precisely nothing. Bonian motion.

'I'm just going to try something, babe, OK?' Wendi dropped her hand and jogged over to the nearest specimen. It ignored her. She waved a hand in front of its empty eye sockets. Nothing. Even when she sat down cross-legged in the dust directly in its path, all that happened when it bumped into her was a pause in its progress and a turn through a rough right angle before it shuffled off.

'They're not all there, are they?' Wendi returned to Genie's side. 'Like dumb machines. Nothing to worry about, eh, babe?'

The ground ahead lay in direct cubelight, striped with the occasional shambling shadow of the Shanty City's aimless inhabitants. The two of them paused before stepping into the direct radiance.

36: The Great Cuboid

Underworld, no time

Genie had been expecting an increase in heat, but hadn't been prepared for the full reality of it. This close to the Great Cuboid, she could feel the surface of her eyeballs drying out. It was like standing next to a ten-mile-high three-bar electric fire. And yet she could cope. After she got over the initial shock, it was bearable.

The cathedral was at the cubeward edge of Shanty City; beyond it, there were no more buildings and only a couple of the bony citizens stumbling across the space that led out into the final stretch of desert between here and the wall of the Great Cuboid itself.

'Come on.' Now that they'd passed the bulk of the source of her phobia, Genie was keen to strike out for the Cuboid itself, and quickened her pace. Wendi shrugged and joined her.

The wall of the Cuboid still appeared exactly the same, its self-similarity holding sway even this close. Panels within panels. It was making it difficult to judge distance; surely they only had a few hundred metres to go? The increasing heat was the only real indicator of progress.

Genie looked over her shoulder. The cluster of buildings that made up Shanty City were shrinking against the slope beyond;

the darkness of the Labyrinth wall and the distant sky-ceiling hung like a thunderhead over the brighter country they'd more recently crossed.

The Great Cuboid's height began to lose its power. From a distance it had been staggering, mind-defying, but foreshortened as it now was by their proximity it appeared merely very tall. Genie recalled a similar sense of anticlimax when she'd looked up at the Empire State Building on a weekend she'd spent in New York City with Ollie shortly before his death.

Its width was another matter. It filled half her field of view, giving her the unnerving impression that she was about to crash into it at any second.

She probably *was* about to crash into it at any second. A glance at the ground in front of her revealed only four or five metres of clearance before the translucent red glasslike structure of the Cuboid began.

Genie walked over and touched it. It was hot, but not too hot to touch. It was smooth, her fingertips sliding over the surface. There was something about this combination that gave the impression that the Cuboid was made of ice. Dry, hot ice.

Even from close quarters the self-similarity of the detail didn't let up. Genie pressed her face close to the surface; the repeating pattern of squares within squares continued to dwindle beyond her ability to see.

It was as if she might cut herself if she looked too closely.

One of these squares had to be the door. Or at least *a* door. Surely a structure as large as this would have numerous entrances? There was certainly no shortage of quadrilateral panels, any of which could conceivably open inwards or slide aside. None of them she could see were the windows she'd imagined when looking at the Cuboid from afar.

'Do you think you should announce yourself?' Wendi was

walking up and down, hands in pockets. 'I mean, *I'm* not supposed to be here, am I, but you're a girl with a mission, woman with a plan. Even if you don't know what that plan is.'

It was true. There was no point in procrastination. Genie rapped sharply on the surface of the Cuboid with the knuckles of one hand. Given the absence of a visible entrance it was as good a place as any to start.

Her knock sounded flat and was swallowed up by the substance of the Cuboid before it had a chance to resonate. Genie wondered if there was a doorbell anywhere. She flattened her hands against the surface, feeling for... for... something. A doorbell, a handhold. A difference that might tell her that she was on the right track.

'Holy shit...!' Genie yelped in alarm as the Cuboid started tipping towards her. At this range she'd be squashed to atoms. She squeezed her eyes shut.

She could feel the pressure on her hands, on her body, but the very fact that she could still feel was encouraging. Something was wrong. Or rather something was *right*. She opened one eye. The surface was still in front of her face. But... but...

It wasn't on top of her. She was lying on top of it. She sat up. The flat surface of the Cuboid stretched away to the horizon, distant arcs of lightning writhing at a summit that was no longer above her. She stood up.

'Nice one! How the fuck are you doing that, babe?'

Genie turned and jumped back in alarm. Just two metres away, a rough earth wall rose in front of her, disappearing off upwards. And Wendi was standing on it, her body seeming to hover in the air above the Cuboid with no support.

'Oh bugger...' Genie realised that Wendi hadn't moved and that it was in fact her who was doing the impossible, standing on the vertical face of the Cuboid. 'How did that happen?' She walked towards the now vertical ground and put one foot up on it as an experiment, half expecting her sense of gravity to revert to normal.

No. She could no more step back onto the ground than she'd have been able to take a stroll up the side of a building back home.

'Can't you come up here?' She looked over at Wendi's sideways face; Wendi shrugged and put one boot up on the Cuboid's surface and promptly fell over backwards. Well, at least they were the same way up now.

'Doesn't seem to work,' said the now vertical but prone Wendi. 'I'm lying on the floor. You're poking out like a diving board! Hang on though, gives me an idea...' Wendi got up and beckoned Genie over. 'Stand with your back to the floor.'

Genie stood flat against the dirt wall. Ahead the shining surface of the Cuboid looked enticing. Could this be it? Was the Way Out across there somewhere?

'Oof!' Genie grunted as without warning Wendi sat down across her midriff.

It felt like she was wearing a very tight corset or that someone was pushing her against the wall, but she could see the logic here. She could probably carry Wendi if she had to. So what if her weight was pointing in a different direction from normal?

'We might as well give it a try, babe.' Wendi put one arm out to the wall by Genie's ear and lowered herself until she was lying sideways on top of her. She snaked one arm behind Genie's neck. 'Go for it.'

'Absolutely.' Genie nodded and put her arms round her friend. They could do this. She took a step forward and straight away was pushed back against the wall. Wendi's altered gravity made it feel as if she was walking into a hurricane. Bracing herself, Genie tried again and, now that she knew what to expect, started to make progress. She leaned forward as she walked.

It could be worse, she thought. At least it's not raining.

She'd only been going for thirty seconds or so when the imaginary wind began to drop and she was able to straighten up.

'Whoa... I feel weird.' In her arms, Wendi groaned. It was true, her friend's weight had shifted and Genie was now just carrying her normally.

'I think we did it.' She lowered Wendi to the surface of the Cuboid.

'Good job it wasn't the other way round, eh?' Wendi looked about her with interest and turned pale. 'Er... babe. Don't look back whatever you do.'

Up until this point it hadn't even occurred to Genie to do so, but now she did so without thinking.

The desert. The Shanty City. The whole of the rest of the Underland hung over them like a rock tsunami poised to crash down and destroy. If Genie had thought that the Cuboid had seemed impressive when viewed from the desert, that was nothing compared to the other way round.

'You're right.' Genie spun round and looked at the Cuboid's upper horizon far ahead. 'Let's pretend it isn't there.' She began a resolute march forwards and upwards, forgetting any imaginary protestations of fatigue or any other physical failures her body was dreaming up.

The surface of the Cuboid wasn't as smooth as it had first appeared. It was uniform, true, the repetition of the square pattern almost sickening in its relentlessness, but there was a subtle variation in the third dimension. Some of the larger square panels were recessed, others protruding. This was never by more than about ten centimetres or so, but it made a difference and once or twice both Wendi and Genie stumbled, taken unawares by an unexpected change in elevation.

'Are we getting lower?' Genie stopped. The last few steps they'd taken had all been downwards. Looking about her (careful not to look behind) she could see that it was true. They were just inside the lip of a vast, low recess. Ahead of them the depression of the panels wasn't uniform in any way that she could see but the lowest point was more or less at the centre.

They continued forwards. Every step down seemed a little higher than it really had a right to be and just before they reached the centre Genie stopped. To enter the lowest point, they'd have to sit on the edge and drop down into a large square as deep as a medium-sized swimming pool. It wouldn't be impossible to get out the other side, but why bother? Easier just to walk around the edge.

Too late. Wendi had already leaped down into it.

'We could have walked around!' Genie called to her.

'Nah!' Wendi shook her head. 'Much quicker this way, babe!'

Genie sighed, sat down on the edge, and jumped down into the pool's interior. She could still see over the edge – it came up to her collarbone, but getting out again wasn't going to be as easy as Wendi obviously thought it was. She followed Wendi towards the far side. It really did feel like a swimming pool; Genie even imagined she could detect a faint whiff of chlorine. But that was ridiculous.

They were heading towards the deep end. Genie stopped when she spotted that the sides were now higher than the top of her head. She reached out an arm to grab the oblivious Wendi by the sleeve of her jacket.

'Stop! We can't get out that side. It's too high.'

'Ah, fuck it, you're right.' Wendi frowned. 'Shit, what a waste of time.'

The two women turned round and headed back the way they'd come, but the side of the pool continued getting higher. Genie looked about. The floor was parallel to the edge all the way around. They hadn't been walking into a deep end, the pool itself had been getting deeper. The edge was now at least three metres from the floor all the way around.

37: In at the deep end

Underworld, no time

'Fuck everything!' Genie wailed and sat down on the ground. It just didn't seem fair. After all she'd been through, to end up sitting in a dry pool for the rest of eternity wasn't the reward she'd been expecting. She was close to tears. She felt Wendi kneel down close behind and put her arms round her.

'Never say diet,' Wendi whispered in her ear. It had been one of their little jokes. She started to feel a little better and curled her fingers through the bars of the metal drain she was half sitting on top of. She could have sworn it hadn't been there a few seconds ago.

She spun round and peered at it on her hands and knees.

'Bit small for a way out,' Wendi remarked.

This was true. The drain was circular and about thirty centimetres wide. Even if she'd been able to remove the grille, she wouldn't have been able to squeeze through. But the mere presence of something new meant that their surroundings were still in flux. Who could tell what else was going to appear?

She stood up. They were positioned at the exact centre of the pool, which was now deeper than it was wide. As the space became more enclosed, Genie could see that the glassy red walls were glowing, the only source of illumination. The heat she'd felt earlier was no longer quite so extreme. Either she'd got used to it or it had actually started cooling down.

'Over there!' Wendi was pointing at one of the walls. Up until now, they'd been indistinguishable and Genie could no longer remember over which one they'd entered. For the first time in her journey she'd lost her sense of direction. She supposed it no longer mattered.

What mattered was the shape becoming visible on the wall that Wendi was now walking towards. It was only a variation in the intensity of the red glow, but there was definitely a darker square coming into view as the walls continued their relentless upward movement.

The square started elongating, until it was twice as tall as it was wide, the same proportions as the Cuboid itself.

The proportions of a door. Genie walked over to it; up close, it was clear that it was over three metres high. Far above, the lip of the pool had stopped receding for the moment. She turned to Wendi who was hanging back.

'Shall I?'

'Sure,' Wendi said in a quiet voice. 'I'll stay out of sight. Don't want to draw attention to myself. I'm good at that now. Remember the Labyrinth? You can't see the trees for the wood.'

'OK, but I'm not leaving without you now.' Genie stepped back and gave Wendi's hand a tight squeeze, before turning to face the darkened portal. As she brushed her fingertips across its surface, she could hear a series of sonorous tones deep in the glassy interior, like the bastard offspring of a set of wind chimes and a doorbell.

A hatch opened near the top of the door and a large red face looked down at her.

'And you are?' The voice was like James Earl Jones in an echo chamber and was somewhat at odds with the fastidious expression and pince-nez the face was wearing, although it went rather well with the horns.

Genie gulped. She felt small, and was reminded of her first day at boarding school, when she'd been eleven and had yet to experience the growth spurt that had branded her as a beanpole for the remainder of her schooldays.

'Eugenie Drummond-Calthorpe, sir.' Her full name slipped out before she had time to think. She had to fight the urge to glance back at Wendi for support, remembering the latter's wish to remain out of sight at this point.

'Ah, so you finally made it.' The demon sighed and slid the hatch shut with a petulant snap.

A moment's silence was broken by the sound of a large number of bolts and chains being unfastened, before the door opened inward. The demon looked down at her through the crack.

'You're late, you know,' he said before stepping aside to allow her to pass. 'Mr Fox will be wondering where you are.' Genie felt the suggestion of Wendi sneaking behind her and slipping inside, but dared not look down to confirm it.

38: Red tape

Underworld, no time

It was certainly dark and crowded enough, thought Genie as her eyes adjusted to the gloom, for Wendi to be able to conceal herself with ease. There was far too much furniture, most of which was constructed of cast iron and fossilised wood, ill lit by dozens of guttering candle stubs all seconds from extinction.

The demon himself was over half again as tall as Genie and dressed in an uncomfortable-looking Victorian three-piece suit, complete with pocket watch and tailcoat, his large red hooves concealed by grubby spats. He was leafing through a bundle of papers bulldog-clipped to an A3-sized wooden board, his forked tongue protruding from one corner of his mouth as he concentrated.

'Here it is,' he sighed, placing the clipboard down on the nearest horizontal surface and rummaging around inside his jacket. He extracted a large pen that looked to be constructed from the wing of a pterosaur and, dipping it in a demijohn of what Genie hoped was only ink, scrawled something next to one of the finely printed paragraphs, then made a cross a little bit further down. He picked up the clipboard and handed both it and the pterosaur pen to Genie. 'Sign here.'

Genie had to push the bottom of the oversized clipboard into her belly and hold it in place with her left hand to provide a surface on which she could write. She hesitated, pen hovering over the space for her signature. He was a demon. Probably best to read the small print.

'Er... what am I signing?' she asked when she realised that the combination of the smallness of the print and dimness of the light made reading impossible.

'Standard Heath and Safety waiver,' snapped the demon. 'Can't have you slipping over then making a big deal about it. You enter at your own risk. Our insurance doesn't cover the living.'

Genie hadn't signed anything apart from autographs for a while and had to stop herself from adding kisses after her name. She handed the clipboard back to the demon and wrinkled her nose. His aftershave had a distinct hint of frying sewage about it.

The demon tore off the lower half of the page and, using a machine that looked more like it belonged in an ironmonger's than an office, punched holes in it before wrestling it into an overstuffed lever arch file. He took a speaking tube from a hook on the wall and wiped the brass attachment on the end with a filthy lace handkerchief, before blowing into it and holding it to his ear.

'Yes, she's here.' The demon went cross-eyed when speaking into the tube. 'Orpheus Procedure, yes... I know... Several hours... All right.'

He hung the tube back on its mount, handed Genie a begrimed raffle ticket numbered 729 and pointed at a narrow doorway between two of the desks. 'If you could just wait through there, one of my colleagues will see you as soon as they can.'

'Thanks.' Genie was quite keen to get away from the demon's smell and hurried over to the cramped space between the desks. As she pushed the door open, she felt something brush against her legs. She looked down; Wendi was crawling through ahead of her.

The demon hadn't noticed and was now wedged into an armchair reading a three-year-old copy of *Take a Break*.

Genie squeezed through the doorway. There was barely enough room for *her* to pass, let alone a demon the size of the one she'd just left. She stepped down into the room and realised that she'd just stepped out of a grey metal locker, one of a row of ten.

There was a very different ambience in here. A range of strip lights bathed the room in their sickly luminance. Perhaps one or two of them weren't flickering. The walls were white with a hint of nicotine, the paint flaking off where it was visible between the desultory posters that appeared to have been put there by someone who'd had the process of 'brightening the place up' described to them but hadn't a clue what it actually meant.

In the middle of the wall opposite the lockers was a large door, to either side of which was a row of plastic chairs. At the centre of the sticky linoleum floor, a low coffee table with a few ragged copies of *Hello* and *Heat* completed the picture.

Wendi picked up one of the magazines and leafed through it before flinging it back down onto the table.

'I've seen that one before,' she said and sat down on one of the chairs. Genie meanwhile was wandering up and down looking at the posters. An ancient torn copy of *Tennis Girl Scratching Her Bum. Muscle Man And Baby.* Others were more obscure; there were one or two movie posters she could have sworn were for films she'd only imagined existed or had dreamed about once. Others yet looked at first like the kind of thing you'd see in a hospital waiting room, but upon closer inspection made no sense whatsoever:

Enhance your Civilising Influence by following the five–step Vexillum checklist.

'Sit down, babe.' Wendi patted the seat next to her. 'We're probably going to be in here for a while.'

HYSTERIA: It only takes seven bites.

Genie acquiesced. She closed her eyes and watched as the organic floaters pulsed and drifted against the dark orange shutters of her eyelids. Her mind wandered. She started getting the unmistakable impression that something was missing. She wished she could have hopped into the shower, or preferably submerged herself in a long bath. Surely after such a long journey they at least deserved a chance to freshen up with a complementary makeover?

No, her inner voice told her, *that's the Wizard of Oz.*

'Don't fall asleep on me now!' Wendi said, pulling her back to more coherent thought. Hang on though, *that* was odd. Even though she had her eyes shut, she could sort of see Wendi out of the corner of her peripheral vision. Opening them, Wendi remained in place.

'Do you think you can keep it up?' Genie asked her. 'This hiding, I mean. Surely we should come clean at some point, yeah? Tell them it's you I want to bring back with me?'

'Dunno.' Wendi looked a little alarmed at the idea. 'Somehow I don't think it'll be allowed. I've been down here too long. I think you should just ask for yer man and I'll sneak out with you. I get the impression they like doing things by the book in here.'

'Yeah, but come on! I think I've done pretty well, all things considering. I might be the first person to do this kind of thing since Orpheus, and I bet he didn't really exist.' Genie stood up again, filled with a sense of her own importance and achievement. 'They'd better damned well listen to me. I've had enough of being pushed around! Bringing me down here against my will…'

Wendi reached up and pulled her back down into a sitting position.

'Yeah, OK, very good, but be careful, yeah, babe? Keep your voice down and don't just jump in with both feet. Scope it out. Sure you did well getting me out of the wood, don't think anyone's ever done that before, but don't spoil it by getting arsey with them. They don't owe you anything. Rub them up the wrong way and you could end up stuck down here too.'

'You're probably right,' Genie put her arm over Wendi's shoulders and gave her a squeeze, 'but I'm not going to be told what to do any more. When I see the opportunity I'm going for it.'

She leaned forward and plucked a magazine from the wilting pile. It turned out to be a copy of *Heat* from October 2006 and was primarily concerned with how much weight Mariah Carey had put on in recent months. After a few minutes' listless leafing, she tossed the magazine back onto the table, where it slid across the cover of one of its siblings and slithered onto the floor. As far as Genie could see, there'd been nothing of *any* note in it whatsoever, and yet she clearly remembered the excitement she'd felt, shortly after they'd come back from America and been papped outside The Ivy, when Malcolm told her that she and Ollie had made the cover story. It was around then she'd realised that she'd really made it.

But at what price? She resolved to do everything very differently if – or rather *when*, she mentally corrected herself – she got back home.

Wendi was nosing around in the lockers opposite. From one she pulled out a beige Dunlop bowling bag full of rusty film cans, an old German army helmet with a spike on top, and what looked like a fossilised pork pie. The next one refused to open and the one after that unleashed an avalanche of bent coat hangers on top of her.

'I thought you were trying to keep your head down?'

'Shit!' Wendi scrambled to return all the objects to their original hiding places and forced the locker doors shut before returning to the seat next to Genie. 'I was…'

They both jumped as a loudspeaker above the large door crackled into life.

'*NUMBER SEVEN TWO NINE.*'

'Guess that's me.' Genie stood up and held her raffle ticket between thumb and forefinger. She was nervous again. For all her bravado a few minutes before, she was now going up against the bureaucrats of Hades.

'I'll be right behind you,' whispered Wendi, 'hiding.'

Genie took hold of the door handle. As she turned it she realised that her palms were sweating. She opened the door and stepped through.

39: The Orpheus Procedure

The decor in this third chamber was different again. The floor was covered with a thick charcoal-grey carpet, which was a pleasant change from the tacky lino. The room itself was semicircular in shape, the door by which Genie had entered one of several studding the surface of the flat white wall which formed the diameter. The circumference was a long sweep of glass; a panoramic picture window offering a superb view of infinite nothingness that reminded Genie of the Underland's sky-ceiling in that she preferred not to look at it. Instead her eyes were drawn to the large desk that dominated the centre of the room.

Its support consisted of a maze of intricate wrought ironwork, a maddeningly complex snarl of fractal patterns supporting a large granite slab the size of a large family dining table. Behind it was suspended a banner bearing an intricate red logo incorporating a broken heart icon that Genie could have sworn she'd seen before. But it was the desk's owner that had really caught her eye.

It was another demon. As it rose from its seat Genie could see that it was notionally female, and this wasn't the only difference between it and the door-demon she'd already encountered.

This demon was classy, dressed in an immaculate black business suit that contrasted sharply with her bright-red skin, a complex sigil hanging on a thin silver chain around her neck. Her horns looked as if they'd been polished. She walked around the desk and held out a large manicured hand in greeting. Genie shook it, noticing how much larger the demon's fingers were than her own. The demon was wearing a powerful floral perfume which didn't quite mask the odour of frying sewage, which Genie now decided must be the natural scent of the species, rather than something the door-demon had splashed on when stepping out of the shower that morning.

'Genie. Delighted to meet you at last. Call me Jezebeth. Do take a seat.'

Genie sat down in a human-sized chair facing the desk. The presence of the demon was making her feel fragile. It wasn't so much the scale – after all, the elephant house at London Zoo had never given her any similar qualms – but more the fact that this enormous being was humanoid and more importantly *sentient*, regarding her with deep-red eyeballs the size of apples. And the voice...

Jezebeth walked back around the desk and sank down in her own demon-scale chair, an upmarket swivel job all smoked chrome and white leather.

'Can I get you anything before we start?'

The voice made Genie shiver. Like the door-demon's, it had far more echo than would be natural in a space such as this, but unlike his it was a warm contralto, the sort of voice you'd tell all your secrets to before you could stop yourself.

'No... no thanks.' Genie's own voice sounded feeble in comparison. She wondered where Wendi had got to. There were a few other items of furniture scattered around, each of which could serve as a temporary hiding place. Remembering her strange experience out in the waiting room, she closed her eyes and swivelled her head a couple of times. And *there* Wendi was, quite clear, over to one side, probably right next to the window. Opening her eyes, Genie identified the coat stand behind which she must be crouched, a coat stand from which an enormous fur coat hung. Wendi was taking care to keep it directly between herself and the demon; Genie could just make out a reflection in the window, although it looked more like a small sapling than a small rock star.

'Sorry, is it bothering you?' Jezebeth leaned forward on the desk and smiled, clasping her hands.

'What?' Genie panicked. Had she given Wendi away? She then worried she was overcompensating by trying to maintain eye contact with Jezebeth.

'The windows.' Jezebeth waved a hand at the expanse of glass and the blackness beyond. 'I tend to leave it blank as it helps me concentrate, but I can change it if it's bothering you.'

'Oh. OK. Thank you.' Genie looked down at the surface of the desk. This eye contact stuff was hard going; she was getting the impression that, if she so wished, Jezebeth could have just pulled her thoughts straight out through the eyes and picked them apart at leisure.

The demon swiped and tapped at an area of the desk with her fingertips and the flavour of the room changed; the windows now looked out onto a soft white cloudscape stretching to infinity under a bright-blue sky.

'I prefer this one,' said Jezebeth. 'The beach always makes me want to go to the toilet, and I don't think you'd appreciate some of the others. Anyway, if you're sure you don't want anything to drink, we might as well get down to business.'

Jezebeth leaned back, pulled a slim dossier out of a desk drawer and slapped it down with a resounding crack on the granite surface, bare apart from a large glass of water and what looked like a tombstone mounted on an anglepoise stand. Opening the dossier, she began leafing through it, treating the pages with care.

'The Orpheus Procedure,' she said. 'Different every time, but when it comes down to it, the same old story which is, after all, what we're here for.'

Genie could see some of the dossier's contents. Among other things, it contained a couple of her signed Walkerprints as well as that copy of *Heat* with her and Ollie on the cover.

Jezebeth paused in her perusal of the Genie file and looked up.

'People these days are far more polite than they used to be.' She leaned her chin on one hand and regarded Genie with a powerful gaze. 'You wouldn't believe the fuss they used to make hundreds of years ago. Came storming in here, all threats and ultimatums. We had to put some of them in their place, I can tell you.'

Genie gulped. Was this a veiled threat? Was she being told to behave herself? Not that it was necessary; she felt exactly as if she'd been hauled up before the headmistress for some minor indiscretion, although while at school she'd been far too well behaved for this to have been necessary very often.

'But the last century or so? Everyone's been very well mannered. I think it's because they didn't really believe in it. Did you?'

'Well,' Genie swallowed, 'probably not, but it's difficult to say.'

Jezebeth straightened up in her seat and smiled. 'Of course. Your Ollie was quite the agnostic too, never really even thought about it. Which is good; the human mind is so much easier to influence when it's... a bit of a blank slate, let's say.'

'Influence?'

'I'm going to take you into my confidence here.' Jezebeth leaned forward again and lowered her voice. 'We can't have Proserpine or any of her department finding out about this. Do I have your word?'

'Well, sure, I guess.' Genie felt confused. She'd thought Jezebeth was the boss, had everything under control. Perhaps that wasn't the case?

'Good. As I say, people used to be a lot ruder in the old days. Orpheus was one of the worst, and it was thanks to him that I was asked to set up Doo-dah to administer the Orpheus Procedure.'

'Doo-dah?' Genie muttered under her breath, frowning. The confusion must have showed on her face because Jezebeth smiled.

'Sorry, that's the Department of Unfair Deceasement Appeals. D-U-D-A. Once it got out that Orpheus had tried to cheat the system and get his girlfriend back, we had no end of chancers showing up down here, seeing if they could do better than he had. Most of them did as well – the reason for his failure was made public, and it wasn't exactly the hardest lesson to learn. Not much of a moral to *that* story. It got so bad we might as well have installed a revolving door. We had to block up the earthly entrance in Avernus to stop it getting unmanageable.

'Even so, still they came, but after a while the rate started to drop to a more acceptable level.' Jezebeth picked up Genie's dossier, stood up and walked over to a filing cabinet the size of a wardrobe.

'Then quite suddenly there was a sharp decline in numbers.' She pulled open the top drawer of the cabinet and riffled through the contents with long red fingers until she found the space in which to drop the dossier. 'Couldn't work it out at first. In the end, we had to pull someone living in to find out why. The dead were no good for questioning. For a start, they always seemed to think they were getting whatever they'd expected, but more important we've always been strongly discouraged from fraternising with the guests. *Very* strongly. Sackable offence, in fact. And one thing you don't want to do down here is lose your job.'

'What happens if you lose your job?' Genie was starting to feel a resurgence of the comfort the sound of Jezebeth's voice had initially given her. *Demonly wiles*, she thought.

'You get incarnated as a human and sent *up there*.' Jezebeth shuddered as she slid the top drawer shut with a bump of her shoulder. Bending, she opened one lower down and pulled out a leather-bound folder full of handwritten parchment. She leafed through it with a smile on her face.

'So we pulled this Italian guy in. Dante Alighieri. It was a lot of work getting the information out of him, but we managed to find out in the end. Turned out a lot of our feeder population had started believing in something else, some infallible god that they weren't allowed to question. So if their lover died prematurely, they'd wait until they died themselves to be reunited in the afterlife. They were told it was romantic.

'We sent Dante packing in the hope that news of his experience might turn people back to the old way of thinking, but can you believe what the little bastard did? Turned his experiences here into some kind of morality tale, twisting them into what he already believed. He was no better than a dead person in that respect. And he had the nerve to call it a comedy. When he actually did die, I was all for hauling him back in here and giving him a right dressing down. I'd have shown him *comedy*. Unfortunately Proserpine said no.'

Jezebeth closed the Dante file with a snap and dropped it back into the filing cabinet before kicking the drawer shut with one leather-clad hoof. She walked back to the desk and sat down again, leaning forwards with enthusiasm. Genie felt the full force of her demonic glare like an almost physical blow.

'What's more, Proserpine started talking about economising. Making cuts. Closing down some of the less busy departments. We'd already had to transfer some of the dead between enclosures, so we could close down some of the less populous ones, and best projections showed that we could expect a population explosion within a few hundred years. We had to rationalise.

'So I had a problem. No more intrepid lovers turning up down here to rescue their dead lovers meant no more DUDA, and no more DUDA meant I'd lose my job. I wasn't going to let that happen. I didn't want to become *human*. Especially not in the Middle Ages. Can you imagine how gross that would have been?

'I was fortunate to have some quite clever staff on the payroll. I held a closed meeting with them to discuss what could be done and one of them, Bifrons, came up with the answer. He pointed out that although it was impossible to fake the results, there was no reason we couldn't go behind the scenes and *make* it happen. Covert operations. So we did.

'It was far easier than I'd expected. We just had to organise things behind the scenes, tweaking reality here and there to set up the right coincidences and synchronicities at the right times. All you really need to get into the underworld is to abandon all hope, throw yourself into a hole of despair so deep it goes all the way down to... well, here. You just have to... half believe you're here already. The odd cloak-and-dagger trip to earth for a couple of operatives just to plant a few prompts, maybe nudge someone's fortune a little, and one spiral of self-destruction later, you have a coma victim Orpheus arriving on the shores of the Styx, caught in a state between life and death.

'It's not even as if we had to *kill* one half of the couple as long as we arranged matters to set up the right relationships to begin with. Matchmaking. It was quite sweet really. All we had to do was bring someone primed to self-destruct together with someone sufficiently stupid that sooner or later they'd manage to get themselves killed, tipping our Orpheus candidate right over the edge.'

Genie frowned. Jezebeth was starting to sound like Malcolm. Furthermore, Genie was getting the feeling that she'd been used by her. *Exactly* like Malcolm. The memory of the betrayal she'd overheard in the Halfway House was still fresh in her mind, and she felt a swell of distressed fury rising in her gut. At times during her career, she'd been made to feel like a queen, but she was beginning to think she'd just been a chess piece. Was she cursed to be used forever by others in their games?

'Humanity being what it is, there are always a *huge* number of star-crossed lovers being rent asunder by Eurynome's amateur blunderings – so what with that and our own efforts, all we had to do was cherry-pick the very best.' Jezebeth reached across the desk and placed one hand on Genie's shoulder for a second. 'And believe me, you certainly were one of the best we've had for a very long time.'

The demon was far more frightening than Malcolm could have ever hoped to be. Genie held her tongue, hating the tiny part of herself that was pleased at the demon's praise. *For now*, she told herself, *let's see where this leads*.

'You're a smart girl,' Jezebeth sat back and smiled, 'and well worth it, even if it did take us six months. Any longer and we'd have given up. Rules, you see. An Unfair Deceasement Appeal has to be lodged within nine months of the death or it becomes void.'

Genie closed her eyes and directed her attention over to

the coat stand. She could see Wendi shifting, adjusting her pose as if ready to bolt. She'd been right; it would be best not to mention her. She opened her eyes again and looked up at Jezebeth. The demon pulled a sympathetic face that was almost frightening in its sincerity. Genie could almost have believed that Jezebeth cared more about her plight than she herself did.

'I know. It's a bit of a shock. Coming on the heels of losing your lover and the trials of the journey, you're probably feeling angry, upset. Well, don't worry. Everything is going to be OK. You've helped us out and in return you won't find us ungrateful.' Jezebeth swivelled the anglepoise tombstone, so Genie could see that it was in fact a monitor displaying overhead footage of some men playing poker.

'For a start, we arranged for Oliver to end up in the Heroes enclosure rather than in the Labyrinth where he would have done otherwise.' She tapped the screen with the nail of her forefinger and Genie leaned in for a closer look. It *was*. It was Ollie. He looked well.

'He's been well looked after; we gave him access to the VIP section.' Jezebeth looked pleased with herself. 'It's the least we could do. Besides… there aren't that many heroes to go around these days, so we've had to relax the entry requirements a bit. If anyone was hero worshipped by a significant number of the living – and furthermore venerated after they died – they're pretty much a shoo-in.'

Genie peered closer. Ollie's poker buddies were George Best, John Peel and Yasser Arafat.

'Are they drinking?' Genie had spotted an array of half-empty pint glasses on the table between the cards and chips.

'Ah, yes. It's one of the only places down here where food and drink are allowed. Historical precedent. It used to be called Valhalla, before that Elysium. They can eat and drink all they want – doesn't really affect them, as they're not alive. We don't have to provide toilet facilities for the inmates. All the advantages with none of the disadvantages.'

Genie continued to stare at the image of Ollie as he laughed, apparently sharing a joke with George Best. She was deflated. It was as if she was going to get him back whether she liked it or not.

It had been a foregone conclusion.

At least Ollie had been enjoying himself in the meantime.

'Aww... Young love...' Clearly Jezebeth wasn't as good as interpreting human behaviour as she thought she was. 'I bet you just can't wait to see him again, hmm? There are just a couple of pieces of admin to attend to and you can be on your way. As I said, I'm really grateful for your help, but must insist that you don't mention this to anyone else. *This is very important.* I'll need you to sign a non-disclosure agreement.'

Jezebeth pulled a sheet of paper from a drawer and slid it across the desk. As Genie reached for it, the demon took her hand in a gentle but firm grip, twisted it so the wrist was facing upwards and stabbed a large silver quill into a vein. Genie yelped.

'I'm sorry.' Jezebeth released her and handed her the quill. 'It has to be in blood, and I know some people can be squeamish about that sort of thing.'

Genie stared at the wound on her wrist, looked down at the paper, at the quill in her hand, and then back up at Jezebeth's face.

'I know,' Jezebeth said. 'People never seem to want to sign agreements with us these days! All Dante's fault. Him and his type, anyway. Don't worry, I'm not going to trick you out of your soul. Whether you sign or not, you're going to end up down here one day; all the contract says is that you agree not to mention anything to anyone. In return, you get Ollie back as well as favourable treatment by Tyche for the next ten years.'

'Tyche?'

'One of us. She's in charge of fortune. Luck. You'll have a good time when you get home, I promise.'

Genie dipped the nib of the quill into the drop of blood blooming at her wrist, and paused. If she was going to ask about substituting Wendi for Ollie, this would be the time. But… bureaucracy. Wendi had been right. Suppose they said no? It all seemed to be about the rules, and there was that nine-month time limit for a start. Wendi had been dead for years.

Genie shrugged and signed, sliding the paper and quill back across to Jezebeth when she'd finished. She didn't imagine she'd get out of here without it. They'd just have to do this clandestinely. She sucked at her wrist. The bleeding had stopped.

'Thank you!' Jezebeth picked up the contract and blew on it to dry the signature. 'I'm sure I don't need to tell you this, but I have to – it's part of the procedure. *Don't look back on your way out*, otherwise you void the contract and Ollie stays with us. Just a formality. Apart from Orpheus himself, no one's ever been that dumb.'

Jezebeth placed the contract back on her desk and stood up, indicating that Genie did likewise.

'So, you did it! Well done.' She walked around the desk. Genie was expecting another handshake, but instead the demon ruffled her hair. 'I expect you can't wait to get home. You start your journey just through there.'

She pointed at the back wall of the office, at the door closest to the left-hand edge of the wall, right next to the beginning of the window's arc. Not that far from the coat stand as it happened. Genie walked across the carpet and pulled at the door. It was a little stiff.

'Give it a yank! It's a devil to open sometimes!'

Genie looked back over her shoulder at Jezebeth, who was

back behind her desk. She gave Genie a wave without looking up from the granite slab where she was swiping at invisible controls on its surface. The stubborn door lurched open just as the view from the windows reverted to the infinite blackness it had displayed when Genie had arrived. On the other side of the door was a wooden panelled elevator with brass fittings, collapsible scissor-gate standing open. Something dashed past her, and then Wendi was standing inside at the back, wide-eyed and sweaty.

The outer door swung shut, bumping against Genie's buttocks as she stepped inside. She turned and pulled the scissor-gate shut. Instantly, the lift began its shuddering ascent, the interior of the heavy door sinking out of sight to be replaced by the rough red rock of the shaft rolling ever downwards.

This way out, thought Genie.

40: This way out

Underworld, no time

'Do you...?' Genie started. Wendi hissed at her to remain silent, finger held to her lips. Genie shrugged. They'd been safe enough in the waiting room to Jezebeth's office; surely they could talk now that they were rising so far above it? Wendi beckoned with a forefinger and Genie bent her head.

'Don't want that horny bitch to catch us,' Wendi whispered, ''specially as we've nearly done it. Can't believe we got away without her suspecting anything.'

The shaft beyond the scissor-gate changed from rough red rock to slabs of pre-poured concrete and then grimy wooden panels. The elevator shuddered and slowed in its ascent. Genie gulped. It seemed unlikely over the noise of the machinery, but had they been overheard? Was Jezebeth calling them back down to face the music?

No. As they slowed even further, the sill of an outer door came into view and sank down, stopping at floor level with a heavy clunk. The mechanism sighed and fell silent. The outer door was similar to the one in Jezebeth's office. Genie felt goose pimples rising on the back of her neck as she became aware of a familiar sound from beyond the door.

Clunk-clunk-clunk-clunk... Squeeeeeeeeeeeeee...

'What's that noise?' Wendi joined her as she struggled with the latch of the scissor-gate. With a click and a shriek, the gate gave way, and Genie pushed at the outer door, which after initial resistance flew open.

Genie stumbled out into the chamber. The lift opened into one end of a poorly lit hallway decorated with grimy purple-and-cream ceramic tiles, a smell of urine and burning dust hanging in the air. And at the other end of the hallway...

Clunk-clunk-clunk-clunk... Squeeeeeeeeeeeeee...

A single wooden escalator, leading upwards.

'Brilliant!' Wendi ran forward and brushed her hand against the rubber handrail as it curved round and began its long journey upwards. 'At least we're not going to have to walk!'

'It might take a while though.' Genie walked over and peered upwards. Unlike the one by which she'd arrived, this escalator shaft was lit by an irregular succession of ancient glass light bulbs strung up along a frayed cloth-covered cable. Pools of darkness punctuated the passage. Genie took Wendi's hand and stepped onto the bottom step. After the briefest of horizontal movements, they were swept along upwards.

Clunk-clunk-clunk-clunk... Squeeeeeeeeeeeeee...

'I suspect this is where the not-looking-back comes in,' Genie remarked once the *clunk-squees* had faded. 'I was wondering how that applied when we were in the lift.'

'Guess so. Still, you did it, babe! I'm proud of you.' Wendi squeezed her hand.

'Did I though?' Genie was still deflated and despite having apparently got away with it felt a sense of foreboding about the immediate future. 'You heard what the demon said. *She* did it. I was just the thing that she did it with. No different from when Malcolm was pulling my strings.'

'Nah, but we cheated the system, didn't we?' Wendi offered

her a lopsided grin. 'I'm not supposed to be here. Two for the price of one, eh?'

'That's another thing. What am I going to do with Ollie when we arrive? Whatever the demons might think, I don't think it was ever him I was really down here for. I don't think I knew *what* I wanted until I found you again.'

'Dump the fucker.'

'That's what I was originally going to do anyway. Before he died. Well I thought about it. But I'm not sure it's going to be that simple. *They* planned this. *They* did this.' Genie felt the foreboding increase as the escalator carried them though a particularly long dark zone. 'And I signed, didn't I? In blood. I don't know what's going to happen when they find out, but I'm sure it's not going to be good. And they *will* find out. They'll find Nathan in your spot in the Wood, then no one in his spot in the Labyrinth.'

'Can't link it to you though, can they?' Despite her relentless optimism, Wendi sounded uncertain. Genie was reminded of that time at school when one of the other girls had convinced Genie to accompany her on a shoplifting spree. As she'd walked out of the shopping centre, she'd been expecting to feel a heavy hand on her shoulder any second; even when she'd got back to school without incident, she'd been so sick with fear that she'd thrown the damned headscarf in the bin.

'Who knows what they can do?' Genie looked down at Wendi as they passed into another lit section of stairwell. 'I don't think I should have signed it, but then we wouldn't have got out of there, would we?'

Wendi looked pensive, and then a massive grin started spreading over her face. She looked up at Genie with eyes sparkling.

'Void!' she shrieked.

'I beg your pardon?' In life, Genie had become used to

Wendi's odd non sequiturs, but since their escape from the Labyrinth she'd seemed a bit more together.

'Void! VOID!' Wendi grabbed Genie's hand and jumped up and down on the spot.

'What about a void?'

'Looking back voids the contract!' Wendi was almost laughing with excitement. 'Old Horny said so herself! You wouldn't owe them anything, but I'd still be able to get out with you – I wasn't *in* the contract.'

'Should we?' Genie felt the foreboding metamorphosing into exhilaration as the idea took hold. 'Dare we?'

'Fuck yeah!' Wendi jumped up onto the next step and turned to look Genie straight in the eyes before grabbing her head and pulling her forward into a forceful kiss. 'Just try and stop us!'

'I suppose Ollie *did* seem to be having a good time down there.' Genie realised that she wasn't really taking much persuasion and she was doing most of it herself. 'And it *was* his own stupid fault that he was dead. Thanks to me, he's having a party in Valhalla rather than being stuck in some corner of the Labyrinth. He'd *probably* prefer to stay.'

'Too right! So *do it!*'

Genie turned and looked back down the elevator shaft, feeling Wendi's arms go around her neck.

41: Null and void

Underworld, no time

There was a figure down there, just coming into view as the escalator carried him further into the purview of one of the light bulbs. A tall, attractive man dressed in an Armani suit. He looked up at her and surprise flickered across his features.

'Gene?' he called. Genie had forgotten just how much she hated being called that.

The escalator started shuddering as a wave of chaos rushed up towards them from the depths, accompanied by the sound of a million voices groaning in disappointment then roaring in rage. Genie could see that the wave consisted of the escalator flying apart and spinning off into the chasm left in its wake. An instant later, it reached Ollie and the step he was standing on exploded up from under his feet. He tumbled backwards and up, turning over and over into the void, shrinking, becoming indistinguishable from the rest of the cascade of debris that was still rushing upwards towards the two women.

'Oh fuck...' Genie heard Wendi murmur into her ear. Then it was upon them.

Please be all right, please be all right, please be all right... Genie could hear herself repeating over and over in her head. She was still standing on one of the steps, but it was no longer attached to its neighbours and was soon swept away by the force of the hot hurricane in which they were now embroiled. As they were caught up in a surge of energy, the rubber handrails and chain of light bulbs whipping about in the maelstrom, she felt Wendi's arms tighten about her neck. She crossed her arms over her chest, grabbing Wendi's hands and curling into the foetal position. But she should be protecting her lover, not wearing her like a parachute! She struggled to untangle herself, to take a firmer hold of Wendi by wrapping her arms around her. Unfortunately this sent them into a spin, and Wendi flew upwards. Genie glanced up. They were still holding hands like skydivers. OK. Good. It was important not to let go, she decided.

One of the rubber handrails had other plans for them. A loop of it swept between them, whacking Genie's knuckles and causing her to lose her grip.

'Fuck!' Wendi plummeted into the void, turning over and over. Genie had no time to respond before spotting a wooden escalator step headed straight for her head at a frightening velocity.

This is going to hurt, she thought. It stuck her hard across the forehead. Everything went blank.

42: Hangover from Hell

London, late 2007

Genie opened her eyes and found herself staring at some thick red carpet from a distance of about two inches. There was a twenty-pence piece just at the edge of her peripheral vision. OK. That was a bit odd.

The shade of the carpet was familiar. She was lying face down in her walk-in wardrobe. She winced. Her head was killing her, and she felt as if she was about to be sick. She sat up, noticing that in her collapse the night before she'd knocked the contents of two clothes rails onto the floor. She fell over backwards and just lay there, staring at the ceiling until even that became too much of an effort and she closed her eyes. This was the worst hangover she'd ever had.

What the fuck had she been up to last night?

She'd been angry and she'd been drinking. She remembered that much. She'd been absolutely *fucked*. Then something else had happened... had she gone out? Couldn't have. Ah, fuck it. It'd come back to her in a minute. She started to feel nauseous again, so rolled back over onto her front and began crawling out of the walk-in wardrobe.

Ouch. It was morning and a very bright one at that. Intense yellow sunlight threw the disarray of the penthouse lounge into sharp relief. An empty vodka bottle lay on its side, flinging abstract reflections across the ceiling, and a wrap of coke was open on the coffee table next to the TV remote. Shit. Anyone in the building opposite with a pair of binoculars would have been able to tell exactly what she'd been up to. On the TV, the newsreaders whispered something about a bright comet that had been visible the night before.

She managed to drag herself up onto her knees as she passed the coffee table, scrabbling for the remote and switching the TV off before dropping it. Perhaps the remains of that coke might make her feel better? *No*, she decided. Never again. Well, not until next week anyway.

Besides, she was going to throw up, and throwing up while on coke was extremely unpleasant. You could feel every nuance, every centilitre of bile.

Still walking on her knees, she shuffled into the bathroom and leaned over the toilet bowl. The smell of bleach cleared her head a little and she started at the dark blob of her reflection in the blue water. She'd forgotten something very important, hadn't she? She could feel it lurking there, just beyond the meniscus of recall.

She probably wasn't going to be sick at this stage, she decided, but if she didn't take something for her headache, she was liable to start smashing her forehead against the porcelain to take her mind off it. There was some Demerol in the cabinet, she remembered. Making sure she had a firm grip on each new handhold before letting go of the last one, she hauled her way upright and opened the cabinet door.

There was something about opening the cabinet that was familiar. She was beginning to remember. The Demerol was in the bottle next to the Valium tablets. But the Valium tablets were missing. That was significant. She tipped a couple of Demerol out into her palm and swallowed them dry. The knuckles of both her hands were bruised; what had she been doing? She slammed the bathroom cabinet shut and caught sight of her face.

She screamed and spun round to look at herself in the full-length mirror. There was an angry purple bruise on her forehead that bore the unmistakable imprint of the ridges of an escalator step. Her face was filthy, her hands and arms smeared with grime. Her dressing gown was a write-off.

She staggered as huge chunks of memory slid into place in her head like icebergs reverse parking. If that journey, that quest, had all been a drug-induced nightmare, how had she managed to get in such an insanitary state? Looking down, she could see that her feet and legs were equally as grimy, with nasty bruises across each shin. Where Wendi had dragged her off the coffin in the Halfway House...

'Wendi...' she whimpered. Starting to shake, she reached into the dressing gown pocket for her iPhone and switched it on.

Oh Jesus. The photos were all there. OK, so they were blurred and would never prove anything in a court of law, but *that* was the skull of Cerberus, *that* was the Sphinx and *that* was the interior of the inverted West Pier pavilion. As she stared at these images from beyond reality, the phone itself shut down, battery finally exhausted. She wished she could do the same. It hadn't worked after all. She started running a bath, tears dropping off the end of her nose and mixing with the water and bath foam.

Someone coughed.

Genie peered around the bathroom door frame into the lounge. There was no one there. She knew that Mallard had a set of keys, but surely they'd have rung first? Then she could have told them to go fuck themselves.

Someone coughed again. This time she could tell that it

came from the inside of the walk-in wardrobe. Whether it was the Demerol kicking in already or the shock, she had no idea, but she was unexpectedly clear-headed. She tiptoed back to the wardrobe and looked inside.

The pile of clothes she'd knocked over was *moving*.

That annoying silver dress slid aside, and a bright-purple mop of hair emerged, followed by a delicate head and shoulders with pallid skin. Wendi looked up at Genie with eyes wide and mouth open, for once lost for words.

Genie was equally astonished and sat down heavily on the floor as her legs concertinaed under her. It had *worked*. This changed everything. OK, so the attention and all the baggage that went with Being Genie DC, she now realised, hadn't been what she wanted after all. But there was no denying that the reappearance of a famous rock star some four years after her apparent suicide was going to attract some *serious* column inches. Together they wouldn't need the favours of Tyche to make the next ten years fantastic. And they wouldn't need Mallard Music.

The little hellion was *alive*.

The two women regarded each other for what felt like hours, but in reality was probably only thirty seconds.

'I think your bath's overflowing,' said Wendi.

Unbound is the world's first crowdfunding publisher, established in 2011.

We believe that wonderful things can happen when you clear a path for people who share a passion. That's why we've built a platform that brings together readers and authors to crowdfund books they believe in – and give fresh ideas that don't fit the traditional mould the chance they deserve.

This book is in your hands because readers made it possible. Everyone who pledged their support is listed at the front of the book and below. Join them by visiting unbound.com and supporting a book today.

Andrew Adam
Marcus Agar
Anya
Ali Baker
Katie Bancroft
Zena Barrie
Kirstie Battrick
Sibilla Becchetti
Miki Berenyi
Rhian Bowley

Gabriella Cinquemani
Sue Clark
Ian Clarkson
Kat Cole
Roben Das Gupta
Stephen Davies
Mary Davies
Sharon Dickson
Eugenie Drummond-Calthorpe
Tomye Durkin

Michelle Flower
Alison Goodier
David Guest
Louise Halvardsson
Kat Humble
Simon Ibison
Gemma James
Janh1 Janh1
Finn Jordan
Min Kay
Laura Kerr
Dan Kieran
Alejandra Kim
Shona Kinsella
Daphne Learmonth
Michael Legge
Dawn Lintern
Alison Lodge
Lucy Martin
Sean Tobias May
Steve May
Peter McGladdery
Dan Mersh
Alex Meyers
Wednesday Meyers
Cami Miceli

John Mitchinson
Ali Murray
Rhel ná DecVandé
Carlo Navato
Dave Owen
Michael Paulini
Justin Pollard
Lucy Porter
Carmen Prieto Lopez
Ronald Probst
Jamie Pullman
c r
Mike Scott Thomson
Rebecca Seibel
Kim Sheader
Paul Silver
S Simonon
Tim Standish
Katherine Stephen
Judy Thomson
Mattie Tucker
Laura Tyler
Amy Walker
Sig Waller
Peter Wiltshire
Matt Zandstra